Tyrell Caracticus grimaced. It was not as if his students were simpletons, but sometimes they gave answers that just boggled the mind.

"No, no, no," he said. "The founder of the Dome, or rather of the Grand Edifice of the Arcane Wizards Council, to use its proper name, was not the High Mage Weldwyn. How could it be? He died in the very war that founded our realm."

"Was it King Loran?" offered Ekthyn Ramark.

"He provided the funds, of course, but would you honestly expect a king to know how to construct a building like this? Think, people. Use those brains that nature has blessed you with."

He looked around at the students but saw nothing except blank expressions staring back at him. Then the door opened, revealing a senior apprentice.

"Arcanus," the man said. "The magic circle has activated."

"Oh? How interesting. Are we expecting anybody?"

"No, sir."

It took only a moment for Tyrell to realize the implications. "It must be one of the Mercerian mages, coming for a visit. I'd best get down there before they appear."

"And your students, Arcanus?"

The mage turned to see their looks of wonder. "It appears we're all going down to welcome a foreign mage. Come along, students, and you'll see a true master of magic at work."

He led them outside the chamber and then up a flight of stairs to the casting circle. Ekthyn ran ahead, opening the door just in time to witness a cylinder of light flare up, blinding the vision of all who peered within.

The light dimmed, leaving a solitary figure standing unsteadily at its centre. Tyrell recognized Aegryth Malthunen, but she collapsed to the floor before he could get a word in.

"Aegryth?" he cried out in alarm as he rushed forward to investigate, only to spot fresh blood streaming from her eyes and ears. "My goodness, what's happened?"

Also by Paul J Bennett

WAR OF THE CROWN

Heir to the Crown: Book Nine

PAUL J BENNETT

First Edition: July 2021

ePub ISBN: 978-1-990073-00-7
Mobi ISBN: 978-1-990073-01-4
Smashwords ISBN: 978-1-990073-02-1
Print ISBN: 978-1-990073-03-8

Dedication

To inspiring authors everywhere.
May your dreams become a reality.

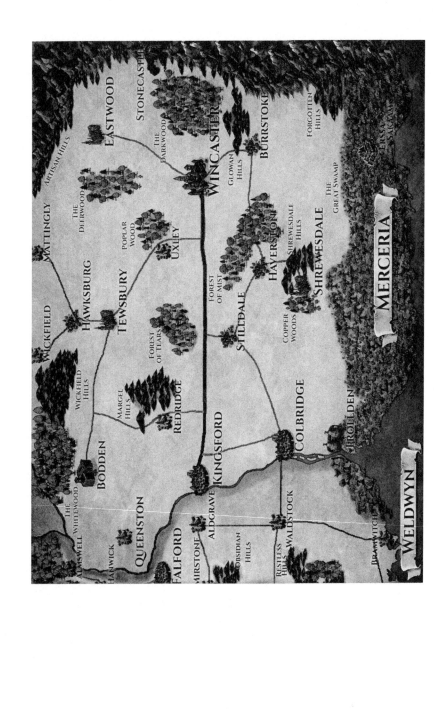

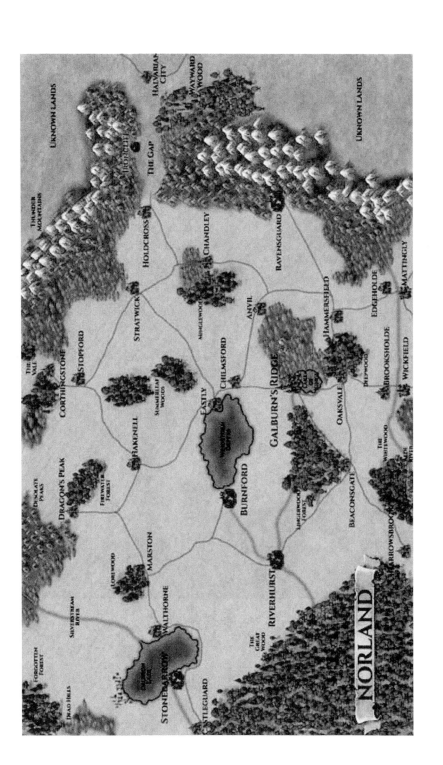

NORLAND

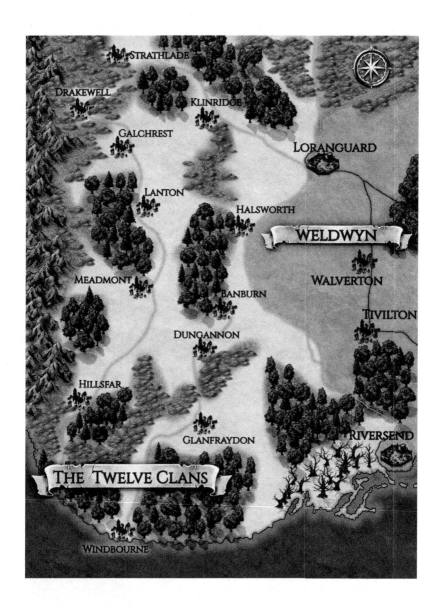

ONE

The Return

SUMMER 965 MC* (MECERIAN CALENDAR)

Tyrell Caracticus grimaced. It was not as if his students were simpletons, but sometimes they gave answers that just boggled the mind.

"No, no, no," he said. "The founder of the Dome, or rather of the Grand Edifice of the Arcane Wizards Council, to use its proper name, was not the High Mage Weldwyn. How could it be? He died in the very war that founded our realm."

"Was it King Loran?" offered Ekthyn Ramark.

"He provided the funds, of course, but would you honestly expect a king to know how to construct a building like this? Think, people. Use those brains that nature has blessed you with."

He looked around at the students but saw nothing except blank expressions staring back at him. Then the door opened, revealing a senior apprentice.

"Arcanus," the man said. "The magic circle has activated."

"Oh? How interesting. Are we expecting anybody?"

"No, sir."

It took only a moment for Tyrell to realize the implications. "It must be one of the Mercerian mages, coming for a visit. I'd best get down there before they appear."

"And your students, Arcanus?"

The mage turned to see their looks of wonder. "It appears we're all going down to welcome a foreign mage. Come along, students, and you'll see a true master of magic at work."

He led them outside the chamber and then up a flight of stairs to the casting circle. Ekthyn ran ahead, opening the door just in time to witness a cylinder of light flare up, blinding the vision of all who peered within. The light dimmed, leaving a solitary figure standing unsteadily at its centre. Tyrell recognized Aegryth Malthunen, but she collapsed to the floor before he could get a word in.

"Aegryth?" he cried out in alarm as he rushed forward to investigate, only to spot fresh blood streaming from her eyes and ears. "My goodness, what's happened?"

"Shall I fetch a healer?" asked Ekthyn.

"We have no Life Mage. Arcanus Roxanne is with King Leofric." He looked down at his injured comrade, a thought coming to him. "You were with the king," he said.

A low moan escaped her lips. Bending over, he tried to make out her words to no avail. Then, suddenly, the runes began glowing again, signifying that yet another mage was attempting to use it.

"Come," he called out. "We must move her." He directed his students to assist, lifting Aegryth and carrying her outside the circle. They had just crossed the outer ring when another cylinder of light shot up to the ceiling, forcing everyone to avert their gaze.

It soon dissipated, and Tyrell allowed his eyes to re-adjust to the ambient light. Another person lay in the middle of the circle, this time face down. He ran across the room, hoping against all hope it wasn't what he feared, but when he saw blood pooling on the floor, he knew it was too late. Grasping the figure's shoulder, he turned the body over, revealing the blood-soaked countenance of Roxanne Fortuna, Weldwyn's only Life Mage.

He stared at her, not quite believing his eyes. Then, slowly, he became aware of someone beside him, and when he looked up, Ekthyn was staring down at him.

"What happened?" she asked, her face pale.

"She's dead," he replied. "Killed by the very power that brought her here."

"I don't understand."

"Perhaps you'd have a better understanding if you actually read your books," he snapped. Tears came to the young woman's eyes, and he immediately felt ashamed at his outburst. "Sorry," he added. "This is not an easy thing to witness." He stood facing the other students. "Arcanus Roxanne was an experienced mage, but even she had her limits. As you know, magic is powered by the energy found within each of us. When that energy is consumed, magic can eat away at our very flesh. Such was the fate of Mistress Roxanne." He gazed back at the body. "She must have been in a far, distant place. Either that or her energy had already been spent."

"And Lady Aegryth?" asked Ekthyn.

"Likely came from the same location." He failed to mention they'd been with the king, for now was not the time to foment unease amongst his students.

"Fetch Osbourne Megantis," he ordered, "and Gretchen Harwell, if she is about. Tell them to meet me in the library."

"What of Mistress Aegryth?"

"Take her to her quarters, and send a message to Queen Igraine—" He caught himself. "Never mind, I'll do it myself. Now, hurry. There's much to be done, and I can't waste any more time with you lot." They scurried off, leaving Tyrell with his thoughts.

The mages of Weldwyn prided themselves on their mastery of the arcane arts, yet one of their number was dead, and another's recovery in doubt. This was a loss of monumental proportions. Their deaths signified more than a lost comrade, for each was the sole master of their school of magic. Without Roxanne, there could be no further training of Life Mages, and Aegryth's knowledge of the magic of the earth was singular.

He briefly thought of their counterparts in Merceria. Would they help rebuild the mages of Weldwyn by taking over the education of their students? Somehow he doubted they would have the time.

The door opened, admitting Osbourne Megantis. The Fire Mage was in a typically foul mood, ready for an argument at any moment, but the sight of two prone mages evidently caused him to set such behaviour aside.

"Tyrell, what is going on here?"

"They both recalled to our circle."

Osbourne examined the Earth Mage, carefully prying open her eyelid. "Aegryth lives, but I fear she'll need time to recover." He glanced at the still form of the Life Mage. "Roxanne?"

Tyrell shook his head. "I'm sorry, she didn't make it."

"By the Gods," said Osbourne. "Do you know what this means?"

"I'm fully aware of the implications. There's no way in the Four Kingdoms that either of these mages would abandon their king. I'm afraid it can only lead to one conclusion—Leofric is dead."

Queen Igraine of Weldwyn waited as the Grand Mage made his entrance. He walked right up to her but then halted, his shuffling feet revealing his nervousness.

"If you have something to say, Arcanus, I suggest you say it."

"It pains me to be the bearer of sad tidings, Majesty," said Tyrell Caracticus. "It appears King Leofric is dead."

The queen paled. "What do you mean 'appears'?"

"I just came from the Dome, where only a short time ago, Aegryth Malthunen, our Earth Mage, recalled from gods know where. She was immediately followed by Roxanne Fortuna, but I'm sorry to inform you that the Life Mage is dead, consumed by the effort."

Incapable of responding, Igraine stared back, her mind, as yet, unable to articulate her feelings.

"Where is Aegryth?" she said at last. "I need confirmation of the king's death."

"She is resting at present, my queen, but due to the injuries sustained during the casting, she is incapable of speaking."

"Then we must find her a healer."

"We have none, Majesty. Lady Roxanne was the last master of such magic."

"Then find someone who deals in more... traditional medicine. We need to know what happened to Aegryth. The fate of the kingdom depends on it."

"You may rest assured we will do all we can."

"I shall count on it. Send word immediately if there's any improvement in Arcanus Aegryth."

"Yes, Majesty." Tyrell Caracticus bowed solemnly, then backed from the room.

Igraine turned to one of her ladies-in-waiting. "Inform my son, Alstan, he is needed here this instant."

The woman curtsied. "Yes, Your Majesty."

The queen looked around, but everyone avoided her gaze. She suddenly felt incredibly alone—a coldness gripping her heart. Could Leofric truly be dead? She mentally shook herself, for it was no easy task for someone to make such a claim in her presence. Such a thing would not have been done without a careful examination of the facts. The truth of the matter was the mages Aegryth and Roxanne had both accompanied the Royal Army when it set off to help the Mercerians in their Norland campaign. It was difficult to imagine a scenario where either might return without him, let alone both.

The door opened, admitting Prince Alstan. He was the spitting image of Leofric, and the sight of him only served to deepen the sense of loss felt by the queen.

"Is something wrong, Mother?"

"It is your father. I fear he has met an untimely end."

Alstan's eyes widened. "Are you sure?"

"As sure as we can be. The two mages who accompanied the army have returned. One is dead and the other too weak to speak at present." She watched as the full import of the words dawned on her son.

"The army…"

"Is likely destroyed. Why else would the mages abandon it?"

"But surely their duty would be to bring back his body?"

"Indeed," said the queen, "but, as of yet, we have no idea of what transpired. It may well be that such an act was deemed impossible, for whatever reason."

"If that's true, the entire Norland campaign would be in jeopardy. We must get word to our allies."

"I considered that, but until we know for certain, such a message might only sow confusion. My hope is Aegryth recovers, and then we can learn the truth of what has occurred."

"We should at least send riders to Merceria."

"No," insisted Igraine. "Until we have confirmation, we shall wait. I shouldn't like to spread false rumours."

"But they could be in danger!"

"Do you not think I know that?" she snapped. "Your father would want us to think dispassionately, and losing those men makes us vulnerable. If word gets back to the Clans, they'll be across the border in a thrice."

"I hardly expect they're in any position to do so," said Alstan. "We gave them a good thrashing the last time they attempted an invasion, and we still have their High King rotting in our dungeons."

"Do not underestimate the Clans," she warned. "They are a treacherous people, ready to seize any opportunity to destroy us."

"What of the Crown?"

"I shall rule in your father's stead until we have confirmation of his death. In the meantime, we must make arrangements for your own coronation, should it prove necessary."

"And the army?"

"You must raise the militia with all haste. Only by projecting the image of strength can we keep our enemies at bay."

"Surely," said Alstan, "they knew Father had gone north?"

"Yes, but any thoughts of invasion would have been tempered by the belief he could return at any moment at the head of a massive army. With that hope now dashed, they'll see it as a golden opportunity to finish what they started four years ago."

"I still say we owe it to Merceria to tell them what has happened."

"And we shall," said the queen, "but sending word now would only cause havoc. Once we learn the true story of what transpired, we'll send Gretchen Harwell. She is quite capable of using her magic to travel to Wincaster. A day or two's delay won't make much of a difference to our allies, but it will, hopefully, provide us with information that could prove invaluable to them."

"And what of Alric?"

"What of him? He's in Wincaster, is he not?"

"No, Mother, he is with the Mercerian army in Norland."

The queen's countenance turned frosty. "Why wasn't I informed?"

"It's not my place to be my brother's keeper. He is prince consort to a queen. You can hardly expect him to do your bidding."

"Is that what you assume? That I try to control him?"

"These are trying times, and I know you only want what's best for Alric, but you must give him the freedom to make his own choices."

"I worry about him," said the queen. "And now that your father is no longer amongst us, I feel lost."

"I'm still here, Mother."

She reached out to take his hand. "I know you are, Alstan. I know. Where are your sisters?"

"Edwina is at her lessons."

"And Althea?"

"In the stables, I would expect. We can't seem to pry her out of that place of late."

The queen chuckled. "She shares her father's fascination with horses."

"She's quite an accomplished rider," added Alstan. "I recall you were no slouch in that area yourself."

"That was long ago before your sisters were born."

They sat in silence awhile, the rest of the court continuing to keep a respectful distance. Alstan reached out, placing his hand on that of the queen.

"We will get through this, Mother. I promise you."

Tyrell Caracticus looked at Ekthyn. "Are you sure you can do this?"

"Yes," the young woman replied. "That is to say, I believe I can. I've never actually cast the spell before."

The Grand Mage managed to avoid a grimace. New students were notoriously shy when it came to casting spells, and now he was asking Ekthyn to cast one she had never before attempted. No wonder she was nervous.

"Take your time," he soothed, "and remember to breathe." She glanced down at the book and commenced reading the words of power.

"Remember," he continued, "you must use your mind to imagine what it is that you're healing."

"But nothing's happening!"

"Concentrate, and put everything else out of your mind. Some mages find it beneficial to wave their hands around. It acts to keep their minds focused."

She tried again, and this time Tyrell felt the buzz of magical energy as if a swarm of bees had entered the room.

"Good, good," he said. "Now, keep it going."

The power began to build, and then the student's hands lit up with a pale white light. Her eyes went wild as she witnessed the transformation.

"Now, put your hands onto Mistress Aegryth before the spell dissipates."

As she placed her hands onto the unconscious Earth Mage, the light flowed into the woman's body. Aegryth's eyes opened.

"Where am I?" she croaked out.

"You're back in Summersgate," said Tyrell, "at the Dome."

The Earth Mage sat up but was obviously still weak. "The Dome? Oh yes, I remember now."

"What happened, Aegryth? You appeared unexpectedly."

"Roxanne!" the Earth Mage called out.

"She arrived shortly after you, but, unfortunately, the spell of recall proved too much for her, and she perished."

"We were attacked by an army of ghosts. The king is dead. We tried to save him, but there were just too many of them. Our only hope of escape was to use recall, but we had to cast in a hurry."

"Why did you each cast recall?" asked Tyrell. "Could you and Roxanne not have travelled using the same spell?"

"We were separated during the battle. It was terrible, so much death and destruction."

"Who led this army?"

"I don't know. We saw robed figures amongst their ranks, but from where I stood, I could see little of their leader."

"Was there no defence against them?"

"We inflicted casualties," said Aegryth, "but for every spirit that fell, two more were ready to take their place. They overwhelmed us."

"Overwhelmed? That was the largest army Weldwyn has ever assembled? How could it possibly be overwhelmed?"

"You don't understand," she pleaded. "They're creatures of the spirit world. They never tire, and each Weldwyn warrior that falls adds to their numbers."

Tyrell paled. "How do we fight such creatures?"

"If there's a way to do it, it's beyond me."

"And you are sure the king is dead?"

"I saw him fall with my own eyes," she sobbed out. "He led a group of horsemen directly into the enemy ranks before he was cut down, along with every single one of his companions."

Tyrell sat in silence, contemplating what he had learned. He had no doubt Aegryth's recollection was sound, but it promised far worse to come, for the men of Weldwyn would now be added to the ranks of this army of ghosts. How do you fight an army that never tires? That absorbs the dead as new warriors? The prospect was frightening, and even the thought of it terrified him.

He'd spent a lifetime dedicated to the study of magic, but that study had, admittedly, led to a soft life behind the hallowed walls of the Dome. Some said he was the most powerful spellcaster in the kingdom, but now he struggled to see how his skills might be used to help defend that which he held so dear.

"We must get word to the Mercerians," said Aegryth. "I can use the spell of recall; I've been to Wincaster before."

"No. You are still recovering from your encounter. Mistress Harwell has made the trip before, so I shall send her in your stead. Can you tell us where you met this foe?"

"We were far to the north, near a place called Hakenell."

"The name means nothing to me, but I will pass it along. Now, you need to rest. Your body requires time to recover."

"I cannot, Tyrell. The danger to our kingdom is too great."

"Precisely why you SHOULD. At the moment, you couldn't resist the efforts of a flea, let alone an army of spirits. The time for fighting will come, but until then, you must recover your strength." He left her, stepping outside to find Gretchen Harwell waiting for him.

"You were looking for me, Tyrell?"

"I was," he replied. "Doubtless, you've heard what occurred?"

"I have."

"We need you to get word to our allies in Wincaster."

"And if the Queen of Merceria is not in the capital?"

"Then take whatever steps necessary to find her. Travel into Norland if you must, but take care. The enemy is powerful, and we can't afford to lose another mage. We have few enough as it is."

"When do I leave?" she asked.

"Soon, but first I must report to the queen, and she may wish for you to carry a message. I shall seek you out when I return. Until then, you should rest and conserve your strength."

"Anything else?"

"Yes. If you feel so inclined, pray to Malin for wisdom. It may be the only thing that can save us."

TWO

The Clans

SUMMER 965 MC

L ochlan gazed around the room. The chieftains of the Twelve Clans sat at the table, all except for his father, Dathen. Instead, his seat was occupied by Brida, the next in line according to Clan tradition.

Dathen had been proclaimed High King over five years ago, but with him rotting away in a Weldwyn dungeon, the Clans had slipped back into their constant state of bickering. Lochlan wondered if the Clans could ever be truly united. It had been a dream, of course, and for generations, tales were told about how one ruler would bring them all together. Everyone thought Dathen was the one to lead them, but then disaster had struck, and with his defeat came imprisonment.

In the wake of that defeat, Weldwyn had dictated the terms: never again would an army of the Clans assemble within one hundred miles of the border. And so they fell amongst themselves, eager to advance their own causes at the expense of their fellow Clansmen.

It had always been thus, and Lochlan, despite his seventeen years of age, knew nothing could change that. The Clans were, quite literally, their own worst enemy.

The conversations died down as Brida stood. "It's been four years since we were defeated at the hands of Weldwyn." Everybody grumbled, but Lochlan detected no true passion.

"In that time," his sister continued, "we have fallen to fighting amongst ourselves once more. As High Queen, I cannot let this continue."

"What gives you the right to call yourself High Queen?" called out Warnoch. "Your father was given that title, not you."

"And I sit in his name, or did you forget he still lives?"

"Does he?" yelled Rurik. "We have no proof of that. For all we know, he died in the dungeons of Summersgate."

"He speaks the truth," added Warnoch. "The Clan chiefs cannot sit around pining for the days of glory. Instead, we must get on with our lives."

"By warring amongst ourselves?" Brida's voice was high now, a sure sign she was frustrated. "We need to learn to live together in peace."

"Fine by me," said Warnoch. "Just tell Rurik and his people to stay off our lands."

"Those are not your lands," warned Rurik. "They've belonged to us for generations!"

The room erupted into arguments, and Lochlan closed his eyes, trying to will it away. He wished his father were here, for he knew how to control the Clan chiefs. Brida, on the other hand, had no such skill. Her relatively young age also added to the problem, for the Clan chiefs were, by and large, an aged group.

He decided he'd had enough. Being only an observer, no one would likely note his absence, so he left the room, letting the raised voices fall into the background as he made his way out of the great hall.

The fresh air brought a welcome respite from the cloying interior of the building. Lochlan looked around, seeing villagers at work, oblivious to the arguments that raged only a few dozen paces away. Part of him wished he were a commoner, for, in his mind, the simple life of a farmer had a certain appeal.

So entranced was he by his musings that he almost missed the arrival of a stranger. Whoever it was was tall and lithe, wearing a hooded cloak that hid their features, but there was no denying the bearing with which they carried themselves. This person was clearly born to a noble house.

"Greetings," said Lochlan, "and welcome to Dungannon."

The stranger bowed, answering in a husky voice, "Thank you. I come seeking Brida of the Twelve Clans. Is she here?"

"My sister? Yes, she is within the hall, but I'm afraid she's occupied. Is there something I can help you with?"

"Sister, you say? How curious. I would deem it a great honour if you would introduce me. My name is Lysandil, and I travelled a long distance to speak with her."

"As I said, she's rather busy at the moment. The Clan chiefs have gathered."

"All the more reason to hasten my introduction."

"Where did you say you were from?"

"I didn't, but it matters little. They will all want to hear what I have to say."

Lochlan shook his head. "I'll take you in, but I warn you, they're just as likely to tear your head off as listen to you."

"I am more than willing to take that chance."

"Fine. Follow me, Lord Lysandil, and I'll announce you to the gathering."

Lochlan re-entered the great hall, his guest in tow, pushing his way past the onlookers. The Clan chiefs sat arrayed around a great 'U' shaped table, and he led the visitor into the middle of this arrangement, halting before the head of the gathering.

The room slowly quieted as, one by one, the chiefs took notice of their new visitor. For his part, the newcomer waited until all eyes were on him before speaking.

"Greetings, noble lords," he said. "My name is Lysandil, and I bring salutations from Queen Kythelia." He threw back his hood, revealing the pointed ears of an Elf.

Everyone stared back, dumbstruck. They'd all heard of Elves before, but the presence of one here, in Dungannon, was unfathomable. The silence stretched out for what felt like an eternity until Brida broke the spell.

"Greetings, Lord Lysandil. You say you represent Queen Kythelia, yet that name is not known to us. What land does she rule?"

"A kingdom of Elves," he replied. "One that lies far beyond your borders. We Elves call it Estlaneth, but in your tongue, the closest translation would be the Kingdom of Moonlight."

"You honour us with your visit, Lord, but if your land is as far away as you say, why would you grace us with your presence?"

Lysandil smiled. "Let's just say we share a mutual interest."

"Which is?" pressed Brida.

"The destruction of Weldwyn."

"Where was your queen when we marched on the walls of Summersgate four years ago?"

"I regret we were unable to assist in your endeavours at that time."

"And what makes you believe we'll accept your help now?"

"Because this time," Lysandil said, "I bring allies more powerful than you can imagine."

"Allies?" sneered Warnoch. "What kind of allies? Not more of those useless Kurathian mercenaries, I hope?"

"Mercenaries? No, I offer you the army of Prince Tarak himself, possibly the most powerful of all the Kurathians."

"What nonsense is this?" said Rurik. "The islands are months away at best. Why, it would be years before such an army could be assembled."

"I'm afraid you misunderstand my meaning," said Lysandil. "Prince

Tarak and his army are already on the way. I'm giving you the chance to join him in subjugating your old nemesis."

"How would this be any different from last time?" asked Brida.

Lysandil looked around the room, a smile creeping into place. "Did you not hear the news? Leofric is dead, and with him, a large portion of the Weldwyn army."

"We heard nothing."

"The army of my queen defeated him some weeks ago. There are no survivors."

"An easy thing to claim," said Warnoch. "Have you any proof? This could be some sort of trick to lure us to the slaughter."

The Elf reached into his tunic, pulling forth a ring, which he tossed onto the table. Brida immediately snatched it up, examining it closely while all eyes were on her.

"It's the Royal Seal of Weldwyn!" she proclaimed.

"Then it's true," said Rurik. "Leofric is dead. This calls for a celebration!"

"This is not the moment for such frivolity," said Lysandil. "Rather, it is the time for action."

"What would you have us do?"

"Invade Weldwyn, alongside the army of Prince Tarak."

"What's in it for you?" asked Lochlan.

"My queen seeks only peace with the Twelve Clans after the war. Is that so much to ask?"

Brida wasn't exactly convinced. "How do we know this isn't some sort of elaborate ruse?"

"Come with me to Windbourne and see the fleet for yourself. It should be here by the end of the month."

"And if it isn't?"

"Then you did nothing save waste a little time, unless, of course, you have more pressing issues to deal with?" He looked around at each chieftain in turn, but none would meet his gaze, save for Brida.

"What say you?" he pressed.

"I will go to Windbourne," she declared, "but if I find you lied to us, it will mean your head."

He bowed. "So be it. I accept your declaration. In the meantime, I take my leave of you, such that you may discuss the matter amongst yourselves."

Lysandil turned, leaving the great hall without further word. Everybody quietly watched him go, then exploded into excited chatter. Lochlan made his way out, once more seeking peace and quiet.

. . .

He didn't see Brida again until that evening when she entered the house with little fanfare and sat by the hearth, taking a cup of mead from one of the servants.

"Well?" said Lochlan. "What did everyone decide?"

"They're going to hold off on making a decision until I've been to Windbourne. Upon my return, if I confirm the existence of this fleet he spoke of, the other chieftains will join in the attack."

"And if not?"

"Then the Elf dies, and that puts an end to it, but I doubt it'll come to that."

"What makes you so sure?"

She took a sip of her drink. "Why come all this way if it were a ruse?" she said. "Clearly, this Kurathian prince is on his way, but we need a better idea of his numbers."

"Could he be planning to invade us?"

"I thought of that already," said Brida, "but I believe it unlikely. Our lands are considerably poorer than theirs. Why go to such lengths to trick us when the fertile fields of Weldwyn are so tantalizingly close?"

"But didn't the Kurathians try to take Riversend a few years ago?"

"They did, but the attack was ill-conceived. It's said the Mercerians helped defeat it."

"Mercerians?"

"Yes, the kingdom that lies to the east of Weldwyn."

"Oh yes," said Lochlan. "Their princess managed to manoeuvre Prince Alric into a marriage, didn't she?" He watched his sister scowl. "Wasn't that the prince who YOU were supposed to marry?"

"And I would have if that Mercerian hadn't come between us."

"I suppose it just goes to prove not everything goes your way, Sister."

Brida wheeled on him. "Don't talk to me of things you don't understand!"

Lochlan knew his sister's temper well, but this time there was something else. "You still love him, don't you?"

"Don't be ridiculous. That was purely a political move, and we needed the marriage to cement an alliance."

"I think it's more than that. I see the way you look at the men of the Clans, Brida. It's clear you want more. There's nothing wrong with that."

"Then why are you lecturing me?"

"Because I fear your lust for power will steer you down a dark path."

"What's that supposed to mean?"

"Your ambition makes you blind, Sister. We know nothing of this visitor,

Lysandil, other than what he's told us. Have you stopped to consider his motives?"

"He comes at the bequest of his queen."

"A queen we have never heard of. He talks of this land called Estlaneth, but we have only his word it even exists or his queen, for that matter."

"We'll know the truth of that when we get to Windbourne."

"Will we though?" he asked. "I have my doubts."

"We've always been open with each other, Lochlan. Speak your mind and share your fears."

He paused, gathering his thoughts. "I don't doubt a fleet will arrive at Windbourne, and I believe this Lysandil when he says he wants us to conquer Weldwyn."

"Then what is it you distrust?"

"It's what comes next that worries me. It'll take most of our resources to garrison the cities of Weldwyn, leaving our own towns undefended. Who's to say the Elves of Estlaneth won't turn around and take over both our lands?"

"They would need a powerful army to do so."

"What about the army of a Kurathian prince? That's the other thing that bothers me. The Kurathian Isles are thousands of miles away; why would one of them be interested in Weldwyn?"

"We cannot begin to understand the mind of a foreigner," said Brida.

"You say that only because you wish Lysandil's offer to be genuine."

"And what if I do? Don't you want to see Father released from his imprisonment?"

"Of course, but I won't sell the soul of our people to do it."

"You are young and inexperienced in the ways of the world," said Brida. "So I'll forgive you for your lack of trust, but opportunities like this only happen once in a lifetime."

"I agree with you in principle, but whose opportunity is it? Ours or the Elves? I can't help but feel someone else is pulling the threads that control our lives."

Brida frowned. "You're overthinking things. You should trust more in your fellow man."

"Ah, but you forget, Lysandil is no man—he's an Elf."

"Close enough."

"Is it?" he said. "What do we know of the woodland race? Very little, if the truth be told. There are none of them on Clan lands, and the few stories we do have are little more than bedtime tales."

"The same could be said of Dwarves or Orcs, for that matter."

"Not quite," said Lochlan. "We drove the Orcs deep into the mountains less than two generations ago, and as for Dwarves, well, we still see traders from time to time, peddling their wares."

"Ah, I concede your point, but how would we go about learning more of the woodland race?"

"There's a scholar in Glanfraydon who might be able to help us, a man by the name of Camrath."

Brida shook her head. "You and your books. Sometimes I think all you do is pore over old manuscripts. There's a whole world out there, Lochlan. You should get away from those musty tomes and experience life."

"Still, if it helps us, it's worth investigating. In the end, it's on the way to Windbourne."

"I can't afford the delay."

"True," he said, "but I can."

"What are you proposing, Brother?"

"Drop me off in Glanfraydon. I'll find Camrath and learn all I can."

"That could take weeks. In the meantime, I must deal with Lysandil and this Kurathian prince—what was his name?"

"Prince Tarak," replied Lochlan, "but you needn't worry quite yet. Our interests are aligned, at least for the moment. It's the long-term goals that are of more concern to us."

"Easy to say. You're not the one going to welcome a large fleet of warships."

"Windbourne is hardly the place to launch an invasion. The coast is rocky and treacherous."

Brida laughed. "The same can be said for most of our lands. No wonder the Weldwyners never invaded us! Very well, you go to Glanfraydon, and I'll continue on to Windbourne. If you find anything that might support your fears, make sure to send word."

"I will," he promised.

"I expect I'll be there for some time, but I'll arrange for another boat to pick you up. No sense in wasting coins on hiring someone."

"Should I seek permission from Erlach?"

"I doubt the Clan Chief of Glanfraydon has any interest in your scholarly pursuits."

"Still, it might be seen as an insult."

"I believe we can safely take that chance. In any event, I suspect Erlach will be coming with me down to the coast, as will the other chieftains. They all want to see this Kurathian prince for themselves."

Lochlan thought it over. The Clan holdings were mostly wilderness and certainly didn't lend themselves to a quick conquest. Roads were virtually non-existent, with the only real means of safe travel being by boat, but there was no way a deep draught ship was going to be able to navigate the waterways. How did this Kurathian prince plan on helping in the conquest of Weldwyn? Would this be the start of a sea-borne invasion? They'd tried that before, at Riversend, but most likely the Elves had another strategy in mind.

"What is the strength of our fleet?" he asked.

"Our fleet? You mean from all the Clans?"

"I was thinking of our deepwater fleet at Windbourne."

"That belongs to Calindre, not us," said Brida. "She holds dominion over the coast."

"Yes, but how many ships does she possess?"

"I haven't any idea. Why?"

"I believe this Kurathian prince means to land on the southern coast of Weldwyn. How else would he get a large army ashore without taking a city?"

"What if he is?" she asked.

"Wouldn't it make sense for us to send our own vessels to assist? That way, we could keep an eye on things."

"You really don't trust them, do you?"

"Do YOU?" he asked. "We used Kurathians in our last attempt to take Weldwyn, and look what it got us."

"Does your mind ever stop working? We haven't even met this prince yet, and you already see conspiracies at work. Sometimes things are exactly as they appear."

"I suppose you're right, but I'm having a hard time wrapping my head around the whole idea. You must admit, it's a bit strange? An Elf shows up at the precise moment we're holding a meeting of all the Clan chiefs, and he just happens to have an army available for us to use? It's a little too... what's the word I'm looking for?"

"Serendipitous?" said Brida. "I'll admit the timing is fortuitous, but why argue when it's in our favour? For generations, we struggled against the might of Weldwyn. Why not take advantage of this offer?"

"And the coincidence doesn't bother you?"

"It could be a gift from the Gods."

"I wish I had your outlook on life, but the pragmatic side of me won't allow it. You keep your faith, Sister, and I'll stick to my scholarly ways."

"All right," she agreed, "but you won't find a bride skulking in the catacombs looking through old scrolls."

Lochlan blushed. "Who said I'm looking for a bride?"

"You're the son of a chieftain. You must wed, eventually."

"Having said that, here's you, my older sister, still unmarried? How can that be? Isn't there some son amongst the chieftains who would have your hand? Or is it something a little more foreign you desire? Perhaps this Kurathian prince will be to your taste?"

Now it was Brida's turn to blush. "Stop that. It's unbecoming in one born to a High King."

"Then let's leave this topic and call a truce, shall we? I have no desire to be rehashing an old argument."

Brida drained her cup, setting it down with a firm hand. "I shall mention it no further. You go to Glanfraydon; I'll go to Windbourne, and we'll argue no more until we've both done our duty, agreed?"

"Agreed."

THREE

Ravensguard

SUMMER 965 MC

C rows circled overhead as Gerald Matheson looked across the battlefield, taking in the bodies that stank in the heat of the day. Men made their way amongst the carnage, seeking those who still lived to carry to the healers' tents.

As the Marshal of the Mercerian Army, he'd seen his fair share of battles, but even after all these years, the death and destruction that followed such things still sickened him.

"Our casualties were light," said Urgon. The Orc chieftain had come to stand at his side, his eyes, like those of his comrade, sweeping the field.

Gerald looked at him, noting for the first time the grey that speckled the Orc's hair. "We fared better than the Norlanders, but I fear another victory like this could well end our chances of carrying this war to its conclusion." He paused for a moment. "I'm sorry. I didn't mean to sound so glum. Your tribe did well today. Without their aid, the city wouldn't have fallen."

"And if you hadn't been able to hold the Norlanders in check, we would have been slaughtered. It appears we both did our duty this day."

"I suppose that's true, now that you mention it."

"And is the war going how you thought it would?"

"Not precisely," said Gerald. "I hoped most of the fighting would be done by now. Instead, the Norland capital still remains in enemy hands, while an earl runs around with another army."

"Yes, but Hollis is dead, Thurlowe captured, and Rutherford has no army left. I would say, on principle, the campaign has gone well so far."

"I didn't know you had such an interest in strategy."

"I have always had an inquisitive mind," said Urgon, "and you are a fine example to learn from."

"Careful now, or my head might begin to swell." Gerald's eyes returned to the field. "I wish we could have avoided all this bloodshed."

"War is something best avoided, but there comes a time where there's no other option. You brought war to this country in retaliation for their invasion of Merceria. What else could you do?"

"I suppose that's true, but I don't need to like it."

The sound of horses drew their attention, and they both turned to see the approach of the queen.

"Your Majesty," said Urgon. "You honour us with your presence."

"Come now," said Anna. "I'm a person, just like you and Gerald here. Let's not worry about such formality. After all, this isn't the court of Wincaster."

"How are the Saurians?" asked Gerald.

"Ecstatic that they were able to assist. That reminds me, Ghodrug, the Chieftain of the Black Ravens, is coming to visit this evening. I'd like you both there if it isn't too much of an inconvenience."

"I would be delighted," said Urgon.

"As would I," offered Gerald. "Though I'm not sure what I can add to the conversation."

"You're my marshal," said Anna. "I'll need your military assessment of the campaign. We might have defeated Hollis's army, but there's still a long way to go before this war is over."

"Yes," added Urgon, "and there is still the matter of the spirit army. Have we any idea where it might be found?"

"Not yet," replied the queen, "but we're keeping our wits about us. Now, I must be off. I'll be expecting you two at sundown, so don't be late." She rode off, leaving them with their thoughts.

Aubrey flopped to the ground. "I'm exhausted," she declared. "I don't think I've got another ounce of energy left after all that healing."

"That bad?" replied Beverly. "I thought our losses were light?"

"They were, but the Norlanders took a terrible toll. It's a good thing the Orc shamans are here, or I'd be completely overwhelmed."

"You'd best rest while you can, then. We must march shortly."

"So soon?" the Life Mage said.

"We can't rest on our laurels. There's still another army out there, and the last thing we want is for it to threaten our supply lines." Beverly noted the approach of a familiar face. "Don't look now, Cousin, but I believe your rest is about to be disturbed."

"Sophie?" called out Aubrey. "Is everything all right?"

The maid wore a worried expression. "It's the queen. She's feeling a little under the weather."

"Really?" said Beverly. "I just saw her talking to Gerald, and she looked fine to me."

"This morning she was quite ill, and I was wondering if you might be able to take a look at her?"

"I can," replied the mage, "but I'm afraid I've no energy left for casting."

"Still, you can examine her, can't you?"

"I suppose so. Let me drag my sorry arse off the ground here, and I'll come and check on her."

"I'll join you," said Beverly, "if only for moral support." She held out her hand, helping Aubrey to her feet. "Lead on, Sophie."

They made their way through camp. With the city of Ravensguard now in their hands, many commanders would have billeted their warriors in town, but Gerald insisted on maintaining discipline. For this reason, the army of Merceria remained camped outside its walls, all except for the rangers who were helping the Orcs of the Black Raven in their occupation of the city.

The queen's tent was guarded by a pair of soldiers who, upon recognizing the visitors, allowed them entry inside where Anna was discussing matters with the High Ranger, Hayley Chambers.

"Still no sign of Lanaka?" the queen was saying.

Hayley shook her head. "He was seen fighting the enemy cavalry, but so far, we've been unable to locate his body."

"Could he have gone after enemy horsemen?"

"By himself? I suppose it's possible, although I would imagine that unlikely. It's more reasonable to assume he's amongst the dead and wounded."

"Keep an eye out for him," declared the queen. "He's a valuable ally."

"Yes, Majesty." Hayley noted the entry of Aubrey, Beverly, and Sophie. "With your permission, I'll get back to the search."

"Of course," said Anna. Her eyes swivelled to the new arrivals. "What's this, now? Even more visitors?"

"I brought them," said Sophie. "You haven't been yourself of late."

"Nonsense. I feel fine."

"Even so, this morning, you could barely get out of bed," the maid scolded, "not to mention how little you've eaten these past few days."

"I've been exceedingly busy overseeing a war."

"That's still no excuse to avoid seeing a healer. You're a queen, Majesty. You can't ignore your health."

Anna's face fell. "I suppose you're right."

"So, you've been tired?" asked Aubrey.

"Yes, but I've had troubling dreams recently. I thought that's only natural, considering we're in the middle of a war, but it's starting to wear me out."

"And why aren't you eating?"

"I'm too busy."

Aubrey put her hands on her hips. "What's the real reason? Come now, Your Majesty. You can't fool me with your flippant answers."

"My stomach has been testy of late, and I've had a hard time keeping anything down."

Aubrey smiled. "Well, that seems to make sense, all things considered."

"What does?" said Beverly.

"Well, unless I miss my guess, I'd say our Royal Sovereign is carrying a child."

"Are you sure?" said Anna.

"Give me time to regain some of my strength, and I'll cast a spell if you like, but I already know what it's going to say."

"Wait," said Beverly. "There's a spell to tell if someone's expecting?"

Aubrey laughed. "Not exactly. The spell is called detect life, and it has a number of uses, but it can also tell when there's a child inside someone. So yes, I suppose you could say it reveals if someone is expecting."

"This is glorious news," said Sophie.

"This couldn't have come at a worse time," countered the queen. "We're in the middle of a war."

"You're still in the early stages at the moment," soothed Aubrey. "I see no reason to worry."

"Should I be riding a horse?"

"I don't see why not. My mother rode until very late in her pregnancy, right before I was born, in fact, or so I'm told."

Beverly laughed. "That explains your gift for riding."

"Gift?" said the mage. "You had to teach me how to ride. How can you call that a gift?"

"You must admit you picked it up extremely quickly, and look at you now, you're a natural in the saddle, Cousin."

Sophie cleared her throat. "Is there anything you can do to help her keep down food?"

"I'm afraid this isn't my area of expertise," said Aubrey, "but I'll consult with Kraloch. I'm certain he's seen a birth or two."

"Of Orcs," said Sophie. "Have you no one with Human experience?"

"Well, I suppose I could ask Revi."

"No, you can't," said Beverly. "He's off with Sir Heward, remember?"

"Oh yes, I'd forgotten. Well then, I guess that answers your question. I'll talk to Kraloch. I'm sure Orc births are not so different from Humans."

"You're not exactly filling me with confidence," said the queen, "but thank you for your candour."

"The Orcs make a kind of porridge," suggested Beverly. "Maybe you'd be able to keep that down?"

"At this point, I'd be willing to try anything."

"How are you feeling at the moment?" asked Aubrey.

"Not too bad, but the mere thought of food is upsetting."

"I'll inform the others the meeting this evening will be AFTER dinner," said Beverly.

"Thank you," said Anna.

Kraloch examined the hunter. "How is it you came to be wounded so?"

Gorath grimaced. "Lord Thurlowe took exception to me jumping on the back of his horse and stabbed me with his dagger."

"Well, you are lucky. The injury is not serious. Now, hold still while I cast my spell."

The shaman dug deep, calling on the power within him to invoke his magic. When his hands glowed with a white light, he placed them on Gorath's leg, and the light faded into the wound, knitting flesh, then slowly dissipating.

"There," he announced. "All is as it should be."

"Thank you, Master Kraloch."

"Master, is it now? We have known each other for many years, Gorath. I think you can dispense with the formalities."

"But you are an elder now," insisted the ranger.

Kraloch stared back in surprise. "Am I? I never stopped to consider it, but I suppose I am. Strange how quickly time passes when one is kept busy."

"When was the last time you were back home, in Ord-Dugath?"

"Not since we joined the Mercerian cause. You?"

"Like you," said Gorath. "I've been far too busy."

"Does something worry you?"

"I have spent a good portion of my life away from the village of my birth. How do I return to such a simple life and settle down?"

"Who says you have to?" said the shaman. "Your life is yours to tread, my friend. Let no one tell you otherwise."

"And what of you? Do you miss it?"

"I see Hawksburg as my home now, as do many of my tribemates, but for me, it is different."

"How so?"

"I am still in communication with Kurghal, and she keeps me abreast of events at home."

"With your spirit magic?"

Kraloch nodded. "I talk to her at least once a ten-day. Why? Is there some message you wish passed along?"

"No," said Gorath. "I have no one left there now, not since the death of my foster mother, Arshug."

"Still, you have made friends amongst the rangers, have you not?"

"Yes, and I shall cherish those for my remaining years."

"Then you should regret nothing," said Kraloch. "You must accept the choices you made, for they have forged you into the Orc who stands before me this day... or maybe I should say ranger?"

Gorath grinned. "These Humans are an interesting race. On the one hand, they value the ability to fight, and on the other, they wish to avoid it whenever possible. Why do you think that is?"

"They are ruled by their hearts, as we must be, and like us, know fighting is something to be avoided on occasion."

"Do other Humans feel the same?"

"Not at all," said the shaman. "Our brethren to the east often find themselves beset by violent kingdoms of men. We are fortunate that the Mercerians are so well trained for battle that they know the full cost of fighting."

"I am not sure I comprehend."

"Let me put it more plainly, then. The Mercerians will fight if it should prove necessary, but realize that in any war, there is death; thus, they do their utmost to avoid it if they can. It is a lesson they have taken to heart, especially their queen."

"She is, indeed, a remarkable woman."

"She is," agreed Kraloch, "but it is more than just her. She has surrounded herself with like-minded people."

"Much as our chieftain, Urgon, has."

"You are merely trying to flatter me. Now, there are other patients to attend to, so unless there is something else you require, I must be off."

"Thank you for healing me, Master—"

"What did I tell you about calling me master?"

"Sorry. Thank you, Kraloch."

"That is much better. Now get back to your duties as the High Ranger's aide."

. . .

Gerald entered the tent only to notice the rest of the party already there. "Sorry I'm late," he muttered.

"*No need to apologize*," said Anna, in the Orcish tongue. "*Now come, sit over here to my right. There is much to discuss.*" She turned to Ghodrug. "*You may continue.*"

The Orc stood. "*You returned our ancestral lands to us, and we shall honour your wish to treat the Humans there the same as the Orcs. In return, we want to help you in your quest to rid the land of the oppressors you call the earls.*"

"*Might I ask what help you mean?*"

"*I offer you hunters, many of them highly skilled with the bow.*"

"*Can I suggest an alternative?*" said Urgon. "*The marshal has shown us how to fight in formation with long spears as did our ancient ancestors. You might consider having your hunters do the same.*"

"*And how long would that take?*" asked Ghodrug.

"*A few weeks at most. My hunters are already used to such things and can assist where needed.*"

"*Have we enough spears?*"

"*There are a lot of extra weapons from Ravensguard,*" said Gerald. "*I'm sure something can be arranged.*"

"*Then I will accept your proposal.*"

"*Might I ask how many hunters you would be providing?*"

"*Three hundred,*" replied Ghodrug. "*The rest must remain to keep the peace in Ravensguard.*"

"*Understood,*" said the queen. "*I'd like Chief Urgon to oversee that, if it's all right with you?*"

"*Of course, the Ravens would be honoured.*"

Anna turned her attention to Gerald, reverting to the Human tongue. "Now that we've taken the city, what's next?"

"That's a good question," he replied. "I've given it some thought, but there are a lot of unknowns. For sure, we'll need to capture Galburn's Ridge, but the fact of the matter is that's likely to take some time."

"Is it even possible?"

"Herdwin assures me it is, but I have my doubts. When we were there last year, it impressed me as a difficult place to attack."

"And what of the last holdouts, Lords Calder and Waverly?"

"Waverly's lands lie far to the northwest. If anything, it'll be King Leofric who has to deal with him. Calder, on the other hand, is much closer."

"He's the Earl of Greendale," said Anna, "and his lands lie to the north of our present position, correct?"

"As far as we know. Of course, there are no reliable maps to be found, so at this point, we have no sense what the road situation is like, and since our loss of cavalry, I haven't had the horsemen to spare in order to find out."

"So we march north?" said Urgon. "Has Sir Heward not already been advancing in that direction?"

"He has," said Gerald, "but his orders were to only go as far as a town named Anvil. Any farther, and he risks being outflanked, at least until we can catch up with him."

"And General Fitzwilliam?"

"His main force is holding at the crossroads at Oaksvale. Herdwin has advanced to Galburn's Ridge, as has the rebel brigade under Princess Bronwyn."

"And will that be enough to take their capital?"

"Fitz would like to move his men up to assist once the siege commences, but with this spirit army out there somewhere, he's loathe to give up a strategic location."

"I believe it's safe to assume it's not behind us," said Anna. "Send word for him to advance on the capital and assist Herdwin. The sooner we can take it, the better."

"Sieges often take months," warned Gerald, "and in the meantime, I've been considering another strategy."

"Go on."

"I'd like to march this group north, hugging the western side of the mountain range."

"You expect to find Lord Calder?"

"I'm hoping as our approach gets noticed, it'll draw him out."

"Anything else?" asked the queen.

"Yes, do you remember hearing about a place called Ironcliff?"

"Yes, Bronwyn told us it was a Dwarven stronghold in an area known as the Gap. What about it?"

"I thought I might send a small detachment there to make contact. Let's hope they can be persuaded to lend us aid."

"You feel they might fight for us?"

"If we're lucky," he said, "but at the very least, we might be able to convince them to remain neutral."

"Who would you send? Beverly?"

"No, I can't spare her, and in any case, we'd need someone who knows the Dwarven language."

"Well, Herdwin's at Galburn's Ridge," said Anna, "and you're certainly not going. You're needed here."

"I was thinking of sending Revi. He has the spell of tongues, so he could speak with them."

"Yes, but we can't send him all by himself. What if he was attacked along the way?"

"Naturally, we'd send an escort. I thought Lord Armin might appreciate the offer."

"That works," said the queen, "but if an enemy army is in the area, we need to make sure they're well protected."

"I'll scrape together a hundred horsemen. That'll give them enough men to fight if needed and enough speed to avoid contact if possible."

"I shall draft a letter for the Dwarven king. Have we any idea of his name?"

"Unfortunately not," said Gerald, "nor do I even know if they have one. Maybe their ruler is a queen? I'm led to believe it's not unheard of amongst the Dwarves."

Anna chuckled. "Very well, I shall give them two letters, in case it's as you suggest. When would you like this flying column to depart?"

"Flying column? Is that a term you learned from your books?"

"It is, as a matter of fact. The term is attributed to an ancient kingdom of the Continent. They don't, in truth, fly, of course, but they were mounted warriors, said to move so fast it was as if they were born upon wings. It sounds impressive, doesn't it?"

"It does," agreed Gerald. "I'm sure Arnim will like the reference."

"And Revi?"

"You know what he's like. All he truly cares about is his research."

"That being the case, how are you going to convince him to go?"

"By telling him that it'll shorten the war and allow him to get back to his magic."

"That's my Gerald," said the queen. "Always on the lookout for new ways to inspire. Any idea when the rest of this army will be set to move?"

"Not for some time yet. We still have wounded to look after, and these Norland prisoners are a handful. Ideally, I'd also like to see Ghodrug's Orcs ready to march before we move."

"I see. Shall we say the end of the month? That gives you ten days."

"Ah," said Urgon. "A ten-day. How fitting."

"Will that be enough time to train the Orcs?" asked Gerald.

"They will learn the basics. The rest can be taught as we march."

FOUR

Forgotten Souls

SUMMER 965 MC

Marik lay on the ground, staring up at the sky. As ready as he was to pass between the veil that separated the living from the dead, something still held him back. He'd been the champion of Lord Hollis until the traitor, Jendrick, used Necromancy to sap the very life from him. Now, instead of a strong warrior, Marik was little more than an old man, lacking the strength to wield a weapon or the vision with which to fend for himself.

Hunger gnawed at his belly, for it had been two days since his last meal, but he had resigned himself to death, so he remained where he was, waiting for the Afterlife to claim him.

As birds chirped off in the distance, his mind drifted to his youth. Back then, he was a simple farmer with no thoughts other than settling down with the local seamstress, then the drought had come, and his Harriet had died. Crestfallen, he had left the village to join the army of Lord Hollis. Years of raiding Merceria forged him into a seasoned warrior, so much so he earned the notice of the earl himself. Years later, he became Hollis's champion and, he had thought, achieved the pinnacle of his career. All that remained was to settle into a life of luxury and peaceful aging, but then Jendrick came along.

From the beginning, it was clear the sorcerer had his own agenda, but the earl wouldn't listen. Marik had finally called the interloper out, but it hadn't gone as expected. Lured to a remote location with the promise of a duel, he became a victim of a powerful Necromantic spell, forever depriving him of a graceful descent into old age.

A snort drew his attention, then the jangle of horse tack. Had it been the growl of a mountain cat, he would have accepted his fate, but a horse was a whole different story. He raised his head, seeking the source of the sound, only to spot a lone rider approaching.

Whoever it was sat low in the saddle, and it wasn't until they were within hailing distance that he noted the rider was actually slumped forward. The horse drew nearer, then halted. Marik watched the stranger lean to one side before falling to the ground.

Marik stood, consumed by the need to see who this person might be. He closed the distance, moving slowly lest he startle the beast. The man before him was covered in dirt and blood, his leg twisted out at an unnatural angle. At first, Marik took him for dead, but as he knelt to feel for a pulse, he noted breath bubbling from the man's blood-encrusted lips.

"Can you hear me?" Marik asked.

The injured man struggled to open his eyes, then shut them again, letting out naught but a groan.

The Norlander tried again. "Can you hear me? My name is Marik. Who are you?"

It was no use. The poor sod was incapable of speech. Marik's eyes automatically went to the horse, examining the tack. Clearly, the rider was no Norlander, or Mercerian, for that matter, for their southerly neighbours used the same kind of saddle. He thought about what he knew of the mercenaries who helped Merceria and decided this was the most logical conclusion.

"Are you Kurathian?" he asked. The man nodded but still uttered not a word.

Mere moments before, Marik was waiting for death, but now, seeing this man in such horrible shape, he felt the need to help the poor fellow. The wounds looked dreadful, particularly the leg, and his body was battered and bruised, likely as a result of being dragged along by a horse. How had he managed to get back into the saddle? Marik could think of no explanation but decided it mattered little, for the man obviously needed help. Soldiers will seldom hesitate to kill their foes on the battlefield but put a wounded man into their care, and they'll go to extremes trying to save them.

"I can't leave you here," he said. "You'd be fodder for a mountain cat." He cast his gaze around, seeking anything that might help, his eyes finally alighting on a rocky outcropping. "That would give you some shade from this heat," he mused, "though I doubt you'll live much past sundown. Still, we must do what we can."

He moved to the man's head, the intention being to lift him by his shoulders and drag him, but as he tried this, his own strength gave out. He cursed Jendrick as he sat on the ground thinking things over. It appeared he was going to see little progress if he relied on his own waning strength, so he considered the horse—the beast had already carried his master some distance, so hopefully, it could be convinced to do so for a little longer. Of course, Marik lacked the strength to put the man back into the saddle. How, then, should he proceed?

The surrounding area was mostly open plains, while to the east sat the edge of the mountains. Sporadic bushes popped up here and there, leading him to wonder if they might be of use. He considered chopping up the branches with his axe, but even lifting the damn thing was a chore. It was then his eyes noticed a knife tucked into his patient's belt. Marik reached forth to take it, but the stranger's hand gripped his arm, and he mumbled something.

"I'm not going to kill you," Marik soothed, "but I need the knife to help." The man's grip relented, and the Norlander took the knife, pulling it from the finely wrought scabbard to examine the blade. It was unusual as far as knives went, for the blade was curved, unlike those found amongst the men of Norland, or Merceria, for that matter. Instead of being wooden, the handle was made of some type of bone, with intricate patterns carved into it—definitely the work of a skilled artisan. The person who carried such a weapon was clearly no ordinary fellow.

"I don't know if you can understand me," continued Marik, "but I'll be back shortly. Unfortunately, I'm much too weak to pull you, but if I can lay you on something, I believe I can convince your horse to do the work for me."

There was no sign of acknowledgement from the man, but Marik hadn't expected any. He walked to the bushes and started hacking away at their bases. The knife proved more than equal to the task, and soon, he had two of them cut down. Now began the process of cutting away some of the branches in order to flatten it.

The day dragged on, and Marik found himself cursing his earlier stubbornness, for if he had accepted his new fate, he would be in better shape. Instead, he had been filled with self-loathing and consigned himself to death and, as a result, was even weaker than he should have been. Focusing his anger on the Elf, Jendrick, gave him the strength to carry on.

He dragged both bushes back to where the rider lay, although it took two trips to do so. Once he removed the man's sword belt, he used it to secure the bushes to each other, before taking stock of the horse's trappings. The foreign tack had ample straps, so he cut some away, using them to form a makeshift rope. One end he tied to the base of the bushes, the other to the saddle. Now, all that remained was to roll the poor wretch onto this contraption and drag him to shelter.

The horse seemed agreeable to his ministrations, so he led the animal around until the sickbed lay beside his rider. Now came the challenging task of rolling the man onto it. Marik heaved, but once again, his muscles proved inadequate to the task.

"You must roll onto this," he said, "else I can't get you to safety."

The patient nodded before Marik heaved once more, and then onto the bushes rolled the injured man. The Norlander breathed a sigh of relief, resting for a moment before leading the horse to the outcropping he'd noticed earlier. The sun was sinking in the west by now, but Marik's work wasn't done yet. He dug through the man's armour, finding a small bag containing what looked like dried meat. He sniffed it before taking a bite, noting the taste of exotic spices. His stomach protested, but at least he had sustenance. He tried giving some to the foreigner, but the man had fallen unconscious.

Daybreak came far too early for Marik's liking. He opened his eyes to see an overcast sky and thought of the army. By now, Hollis was most likely celebrating a great victory, but Jendrick had threatened him with death should he try to return. How could he survive? His gaze drifted to the foreigner.

"Where is your army?" he asked.

The man looked around, noting the shadows before finally pointing south.

"Impossible," said Marik. "The army of Lord Hollis lies there, and we would not be welcome amongst its ranks."

The rider shook his head. "The army is crushed," he managed to say.

"Are you sure?"

The man only nodded.

"Then I shall take you there, and perhaps amongst your own people, you can find some solace before your life abandons you."

The rider's hand gripped that of Marik's. "Life Magic," he said.

The Norlander sat back on his heels, the words running through his mind. He thought back to Galburn's Ridge. There he'd met the Mercerian delegation, and they claimed to possess such magic in the form of a young woman. Could that be the answer to Marik's problem? If a Necromancer had cursed him, it only stood to reason that a Life Mage could restore his vitality? Hope surged through him, and he felt a renewed sense of determination. He would see this stranger returned to his people and hope that there he might find the answers he sought.

· · ·

Captain Caluman turned his Kurathian horsemen east, heading towards the mountains. There was no sign of the enemy this day, clear evidence that whatever survivors might have gotten away had long since fled. His patrol had been up since before dawn, riding out under cover of darkness, lest enemy scouts spot them, but the precaution proved unnecessary. Now, with the afternoon wearing on, he was eager to return to the army and get out of the heat.

A shout to his left drew his attention, and he noticed one of his men pointing north. Caluman slowed his mount as he noted a distant rider coming towards them.

"What do you make of it?" asked Ragar.

"It's a curious thing," replied Caluman, "but hardly a threat. Still, we should leave no stone unturned." He ordered the men to wheel left, and they altered their course to intercept the distant figure.

As they drew closer, it soon became apparent the horseman was dragging something. Caluman bore left to get a better view of the horse's trappings.

"That's a Kurathian horse," he declared. The unknown rider halted, waiting as the mercenaries surrounded him.

"I found this man," the person declared. "He was badly wounded from a recent battle. I did all I can for him, but I fear he won't last much longer."

Caluman dismounted, running to the figure being dragged behind the horse. "Lanaka!" he called out.

Ragar moved closer, seizing the reins from the stranger and keeping a close watch while others dismounted, making their way to their fallen commander.

Lanaka wasn't moving, so Caluman lifted his eyelids to peer beneath, noting movement. "He's alive! We must get him back to camp." He looked up to his men. "Ragar, you are the fastest rider. Return to the army; seek out the healer, Lady Aubrey, and bring her here, and be quick about it."

"What of this prisoner?"

"He may have saved Lanaka's life. He is free to go, should he wish it. Now ride while there's still life in the commander."

"I would go with you once this man is healed," said the Norlander.

"Who are you?"

"My name is Marik. I was once champion to Lord Hollis."

Caluman's hand went instinctively to his sword. "Lord Hollis?"

Marik raised his hands. "I was betrayed and serve him no longer. Take me to your queen, and I will tell her all I can of the darkness that infects the army of Lord Hollis."

"Lord Hollis is dead, killed in battle at Ravensguard, as were most of his men."

"Was there an Elf amongst the dead?"

"Not that I'm aware of."

"Then the real danger is not yet passed," warned Marik.

Beverly arched her back.

"Getting old?" said Aubrey.

"I was helping move the wounded," the knight replied.

"And for that assistance, I am greatly indebted to you."

"How ARE the wounded, anyway?"

"They're all on the mend now, although it was touch and go for a few of them."

"I thought magic could heal all wounds?"

"Only if we get to them in time. Part of treating the wounded is assessing who needs healing first, but I'm afraid we healers are only Human. Well, Human and Orc, anyway. Internal wounds are the hardest to recognize; we do what we can, but there's always a few who slip by us." She looked at Beverly, intending to say more, but the red-headed knight was staring north. "What is it?"

"A rider," said Beverly, "coming south as fast as he can. Something's got him in a panic." Even as she spoke, the horseman turned to head directly towards them. "It's a Kurathian," said the knight.

They both watched as the rider drew closer. "We found Lanaka," he called out, "but he's badly injured. We need Lady Aubrey."

"Come on," said Beverly, turning to her cousin. "We'll take Lightning. He's already saddled."

"He is?"

"Yes. I intended to take him out for a ride, and he's more than capable of carrying the both of us. You wait here. I'll be right back."

She ran off, leaving Aubrey to greet the rider.

"Ragar, isn't it?" the Life Mage said.

The rider halted his horse and bowed. "You flatter me, Mistress Brandon."

"You say you found Commander Lanaka?"

"We did. He was being carried south by an old man on horseback."

"What was his condition?"

"Near death, my lady. We must hurry if we are to save him."

Aubrey looked around to spot Beverly approaching atop her massive

Mercerian Charger. Lightning halted while Beverly held out her hand, and Aubrey grasped it, hauling herself up behind her cousin.

"Lead on, Ragar."

Sometime later, they came upon Caluman's group. Aubrey hopped off Lightning, making her way over to Lanaka to assess his injuries. They must have been dire, indeed, for no sooner had she knelt than words of power issued from her mouth, and her hands began to glow. Beverly watched as the flesh knit back together, then the Kurathian coughed.

"His injuries are severe," said Aubrey. "He'll need to spend about a week recovering, but he should be fine." The Life Mage turned to the old man. "You saved his life. Thank you."

"It was my pleasure."

Beverly stared at the man, for something about him looked familiar. "Have we met before?" she asked.

"We have indeed, Dame Beverly."

"Who are you?"

"You knew my younger self. I am Marik, once champion to Lord Hollis."

"That's impossible! Marik is only slightly older than me. You, on the other hand, appear to be even older than my father."

"It's the work of dark magic."

Aubrey had returned her attention to her patient, but his words made her look up. "Dark magic?"

"A Necromancer is amongst the earl's advisors," said Marik, "although they never knew it. He went by the name Jendrick, but I fear that was all a ruse."

"Tell me more," said Aubrey.

"He claimed to be a sorcerer, but our people have little knowledge of such things. Jendrick wormed his way into the earl's confidence. I never trusted him and had it out with him, but he tricked me, using his vile magic to steal my youth."

Aubrey moved closer. "Are you saying Death Magic did this to you?"

He nodded. "We were to duel, he and I, but as my back was turned, he cast his spell, and I grew feeble as an infant. Now I am as you see me, weak of limb and short of sight. You're a Life Mage, is there any way to reverse this aging?"

"Not that I'm aware of, although I might be able to help you with your eyes. I suspect a spell of regeneration would do the trick."

Beverly was suspicious. "How did you come to be here?"

"After my altercation with Jendrick, he forced me to leave."

"Why didn't he just kill you?"

"He wanted me to suffer. There's something else—he's not human."

"Then what exactly is he?" the red-headed knight asked.

"An Elf."

Everybody fell silent. Marik looked around at the group. "Why does that not surprise you?"

"An Elf infiltrated the court at Wincaster," said Aubrey. "We knew her as Lady Penelope but later discovered she was actually an Elf and a Necromancer."

"Did you kill her?"

"No, she escaped, but not before leaving chaos in her wake. She very nearly brought about the downfall of Merceria."

"I rather suspect they intended the same for Norland," said Marik. "Did you find out who she worked for?"

"We have our suspicions," replied Aubrey. "We recently found references to something called the Shadow War. It appears a group of mages worked diligently to suppress the practice of Necromancy."

"Shadow War?"

"Yes, it wasn't fought on the battlefield, but rather in the back alleys and estates of the kingdom, all hidden from the common man."

"As well as the Crown," added Beverly.

"And these mages," said Marik, "do they know more?"

"I'm afraid they're no longer amongst us," said Aubrey. "And whatever group they organized to watch for their return is also gone."

"But you have mages. You yourself are a healer."

"I am, but I knew nothing of this until quite recently."

"Might Jendrick be one of these Necromancers?"

"That would be my suspicion, along with Penelope. The writings speak of the Dark Council, but they claimed to have defeated it decades ago."

"Elves are immortal," said Beverly. "They likely laid low for years, decades even, plotting their return."

"We should bring this to the queen," said Aubrey. "It may tie into our problems with the spirit army."

"Spirit army?" said Marik.

"Yes, we suspect Necromancers bound the spirits of the dead to form an army."

"What would make you say that?"

"The Orc shamans."

Marik grunted. "The Orcs are a savage race and can't be trusted."

"I find them to be quite the reverse," said Aubrey. "They are a people to be admired. Their shaman even taught me the ways of spirit magic."

Beverly eyed the Norlander. "You'd best change your opinion of them if you intend to stay with us. They make up a large portion of our army."

"I did hear of how you enslaved them," said Marik.

"Enslaved?" said Aubrey. "Is that what you think? They are our allies, Marik, here of their own free will. I'm insulted you would even presume we might take slaves."

Beverly looked at her cousin. It was clear Marik had hit a sore spot with the young mage, for her face was flushed.

"Come," the knight said, reaching out her hand. "We can discuss this at length once we return. Is Lanaka fit to ride?"

Aubrey nodded, then took Beverly's hand and allowed herself to be pulled up onto Lightning once more.

"Caluman," said the knight, "Lanaka will ride with you. Marik is not under arrest, but have your men keep an eye on him. He may have information that could be of value."

The Kurathian bowed his head. "As you wish, Commander."

FIVE

Ord-Dugath

SUMMER 965 MC

(In the tongue of the Orcs)

K urghal made her way through the village, sparsely populated these days, what with the bulk of the hunters gone to help the Mercerians. She paused by the great firepit, gazing at the chieftain's hut. It had been built to house the entire village, with one end sectioned off for the tribal chieftain, but Urgon refused to use it as such, instead remaining in the hut of the master of wolves.

She smiled at the thought. Her half-brother was an excellent chieftain even if he did have some peculiar ideas from time to time. She continued on to the wolf pen, only to be surprised to see Zhura feeding the pack. She gazed at the strange-looking Orc whose pale skin appeared as if all the colour had been washed from it, while her face was framed by a mantle of hair the colour of moonlight. Yet behind her odd appearance, Kurghal knew a sharp intelligence resided.

"Greetings, Zhura," she called out. "How fare the wolves today?"

"The new litter is starting to howl," the ghostwalker replied. "It is quite endearing."

"I am surprised to see you outside."

"The Ancestors no longer echo in my head."

"It is concerning that very subject I came seeking your wisdom," said Kurghal.

"Then come inside, and we shall talk," replied Zhura. She tossed the rest of the meat to the ground before she went inside the hut. Moments later, she appeared at the outer door, pushing aside the skins to allow Kurghal to enter. She guided her guest to the fire, then sat, pulling forth a small gourd and pouring some refreshment into a cup.

"Would you like some sweetberry juice?"

Kurghal took the cup. "Thank you."

Zhura poured herself a drink before setting the gourd down. "Now, what is it you wish to speak of?"

"As you know, the Ancestors no longer answer our call. I consulted with Kraloch, and he informs me he had the same experience. The situation was first reported by Andurak, shaman to our brothers and sisters in the Netherwood. He travelled east seeking Albreda, the Witch of the Whitewood."

"You tell me that which I already know," said Zhura.

"What I do not understand is why he would seek a Human?"

"I have heard much of this Albreda. She is a powerful Earth Mage, what we would call a master of earth, maybe even the most powerful one who has ever trod these lands."

"Even so," said Kurghal, "what use would she be against an army of spirits?"

"I do not believe it is her power he sought, but her knowledge of things arcane."

"I do not follow."

"Albreda is connected with the living world in a way we cannot be."

"But you are a ghostwalker," said Kurghal. "You tread the twilight zone between the living and the dead. Surely, if anyone was to know how to defeat such an enemy, it would be you?"

"What do you know of Necromancy?"

"It is the magic of death. What else is there to know?"

"Did you know the magic of life and death are intertwined?"

"Meaning?"

"They are two sides of the same spear. You yourself are a shaman or, in Human terms, a Life Mage. Yet, had you been raised differently, you could have just as easily become a practitioner of Death Magic, although admittedly, there would be no one here to teach you."

"It is that common?"

"It is," said Zhura, "and yet the Ancestors tell us it takes much longer to master the magic of death. Orcs, being amongst the shorter-lived peoples, seldom delve into such matters, with one exception."

"Who might that be?"

"A shaman by the name of Khurlig, who lived far to the east. It is said she had power over death itself, but in the end, she succumbed to it as we all must."

"Kraloch believes the Elves are behind the disappearing spirits."

"I suspect he is correct," said Zhura, "but there is more to this than appears."

"Meaning?" asked Kurghal.

"Even Necromancers have limitations on what they can do. Summoning an army of spirits is one thing, but such an army would be impossible to control. It would require much more power than any single caster could ever manage."

"What are you suggesting?"

"There is something else at work here, something far more sinister than an Elf."

"What could be worse than a Necromancer?"

"A Volgath," said Zhura.

"And what might that be?"

"A Volgath is a creature much like me: a denizen of the twilight world, but whereas I am of the mortal realm that borders on the spirit, a Volgath is a spirit that borders on the mortal."

"But spirits are not born, are they? How could such a creature come to be?"

"As you know, each living creature possesses a spirit. Upon death, this spirit travels to what we call the spirit world, there to dwell briefly until fading away to who knows where. Those who are strong of spirit do not fade. Instead, they continue to exist as phantoms, allowing us to contact them through our magic."

"You speak of the Ancestors," said Kurghal.

"I do, but also others."

"Others?"

"There are many dangers that lurk on the fringes of the spirit realm, although we know little about them. It is thought that particularly strong-willed spirits can be corrupted by Necromancers."

"Can any spirit be enslaved?"

"Yes, in theory," said Zhura, "but most become mindless minions, serving at the will of their master. Volgaths, on the other hand, retain their powers of reasoning and intellect, making them particularly dangerous."

"And how are these things created?"

"A Necromancer must be willing to give up a part of themselves, ultimately surrendering some of their power."

"Much as we shamans do," said Kurghal, "when empowering something with magic."

"Very similar, but it is also a ritual involving Blood Magic, requiring the sacrifice of one who is skilled in such Necromancy. In essence, they must sacrifice one of their own to draw the Volgath to the land of the living."

"Then why do it? Surely they would be better off to have more spell-casters?"

"Not so," said Zhura, "for it allows for the massing of large armies. The caster controls the Volgath who, in turn, controls the army." She saw the look of confusion on her companion's face. "Think of the wolves that serve our tribe. We control the pack leader who, in turn, looks after the rest of the pack, freeing us up to do other things."

Kurghal shivered. "It makes my skin crawl to even think of such a thing. I have known many strong-willed individuals in my time—to think of them twisted so is most distasteful."

"Fear not, for if they are pure of heart, they are immune to such temptations."

"Pure of heart?"

"Spirits, like their living counterparts, have a desire to exist. Many value their freedom, and therefore make poor servants."

"Like my brother, Urgon."

Zhura smiled. "Yes, my bondmate has a good heart and would make a poor choice for a Volgath. The Humans, however, are said to be more corruptible, as are the Elves."

"Who, then, would be a candidate to be treated like this?"

"A great warrior or, better yet, a leader of men. It is said that the realms of Humans have provided plenty of fodder for such practices."

"You have given me much to think on," said Kurghal.

"As you have me," Zhura replied, "but I believe the time for such thoughts is coming to an end. Instead, we must now concentrate our efforts on taking steps to defeat this Volgath and release the spirits of our Ancestors."

"And how would we go about this?"

"The first step would be to join Urgon. There shall find the Mercerian queen."

"And how will she help? She is no mage."

"True, but she commands much respect. With her help, we can convince others of the true danger, hopefully even find a solution to our dilemma."

"I shall leave at once," said Kurghal.

"You misunderstand me," said Zhura. "I mean to accompany you."

"But you are a ghostwalker? You cannot set foot outside the walls of this mud hut!"

"Under normal circumstances, that would be true, but mud huts are meant to protect me from the voices of the spirits, voices that no longer walk this land."

"And if we defeat this Volgath?"

"Then the spirits will be released."

"There will be no mud hut to protect you in the north. Would their presence not drive you mad?"

"Most likely, but it is a risk I am willing to take if it saves our people."

Kurghal stared back at the pale Orc. "It is a great risk," she said, "but I will honour your wishes. I shall assemble a group of hunters to escort us. When would you like to leave?"

"At first light tomorrow. You should contact Kraloch and inform him of our intentions."

"I shall, but I must take my leave of you now. I have much to see to. Thank you, Zhura. You have given me clarity."

"As have you. Let us hope we are not too late."

When they met the following morning, Kurghal had gathered half a dozen hunters, three of which had only recently completed their ordeal to become full-fledged members of the tribe.

They had assembled in front of the hut, waiting until Zhura emerged. Trailing her were three wolves, and Bagrat, the youngest Orc there, jumped back in alarm.

"Do not be afraid," said Zhura. "The wolves will warn us of any danger that might threaten along the way."

"I was not afraid," replied Bagrat, "merely startled."

"What of the other wolves?" said Kurghal.

"Ragash shall see to them. She has been helping since Urgon left."

The shaman shook her head. "Sometimes I do not understand my half-brother. He is chieftain of this tribe, yet still, he keeps the mantle of master of wolves. Is he so controlling that he refuses to relinquish the responsibility?"

"You have him wrong," replied Zhura. "He cares for the wolves, not for himself but for me. They provide me with companionship and help keep the spirits at bay."

"They do?"

"Indeed. It was not apparent at first, but I have come to realize the truth of it."

"You give me food for thought," said Kurghal. "Could the wolves be the secret to taming the Volgath?"

"I do not see how. By and large, the spirits avoid them, true, but some do not mind their presence at all."

"I wonder if this might be the secret held by Mistress Albreda?"

"This is something to be considered," said Zhura. "Now, shall we begin our journey?"

"Of course."

Kurghal, the elder of the two, led them out of the village heading west, the intent being to get out of the Artisan Hills and down to the plains where they could make better time. Once there, they would begin the trek north. They cleared the village and began the long descent.

"We shall only go a short distance for the first few days," said Kurghal. "I am getting old, and you are not used to such strenuous activity."

"A reasonable precaution," Zhura replied, "and one with which I heartily agree. Have you any idea how long it will take us to reach the camp of the queen?"

"More than a ten-day if my calculations are correct, possibly as much as two. It all depends on where the army is by the time we arrive."

"Twenty days? I find it hard to conceive of such a distance."

"We shall make little progress until our limbs are used to such exercise, but I am hopeful our range will increase once we are more accustomed to it."

The wolves ran ahead, but there seemed little to endanger them.

"It is a nice day," mused Zhura, "though perhaps a little too warm."

"You should keep your head covered," suggested Kurghal. "Your pale skin will attract the sun."

"A good idea." Zhura lifted the hood of her robe, placing it over her head.

"There, you look like a shaman now."

"I shall take that as a compliment. Tell me, do you not find it odd Kraloch is considered the senior shaman? After all, you are several years his elder."

"I relinquished that position when I realized his power. He learned the skills of a shaman remarkably fast and has grown in power significantly since that time. It would be foolish of me to stand in his way."

"And how do you account for his growth?"

"He was always a quick study," said Kurghal, "but since his association with the Humans, he has learned much more."

"He has a desire to feel needed."

"As do we all, but Kraloch's loyalty will always overcome any simple desire to be liked. He and Urgon are like brothers."

Zhura laughed. "Yes, it is hard to imagine one without the other."

"I could say the same for you and Urgon. Your bonding was controversial, but there is no denying the connection you share. Few bondmates would be willing to undertake a journey like ours."

"I would be lying if I said my heart did not yearn to see Urgon, but there is more at stake here than a simple bonding."

"Simple? Is that how you see it? By the Ancestors, Zhura, Urgon risked everything, even banishment, to have you as his bondmate."

"And I would not have it any other way. Do not mistake my meaning, Kurghal. I would give my last breath for my beloved, but if we do not find a solution to the problem before us, we may never speak with the Ancestors again."

"Would that be so bad? Other races took that route."

"True, but as we are a short-lived people, who would pass down the wisdom of our kin? And you of all people should know better; you are a shaman, the very connection to our Ancestors."

"Still, it would be nice to be in charge of our own future for once."

"But we are," said Zhura. "The Ancestors can advise all they like, but when it comes down to it, they are mere spirits. Amongst the living, the only effects they can have is the strength of their words."

"Strange to think it is you, not I, who defends them."

"You forget, I have been surrounded by them all my life."

"Until now," corrected Kurghal. "Part of you must wish they would never return?"

"I would be lying if I said otherwise, but I know how important they are to our way of life."

"Maybe there is a way to keep their voices at bay? Something we have yet to discover?"

"Perhaps," said Zhura.

"Then you would become just another Orc."

"I would like that, but it is not something I have given much thought to. What of you? Without the Ancestors to call on, what would you do?"

Kurghal smiled. "A shaman is more than merely a connection to the spirit realm. We are arbitrators in disputes and, of course, healers."

"And you can remove a chieftain who is troublesome."

"Not quite. We can definitely bring the tribe together to decide a chieftain's fate, but it is their voice that determines the result, not mine."

"True, but you are not without influence."

"In such things, a shaman must strive to be impartial."

Again, Zhura laughed. "Impartial? I think not. You are Urgon's sister after all."

. . .

As the morning wore on, they came to the plains, making much more progress than they had expected. The walk was not too tiring, and the companionship amenable, so the day passed even as their legs carried them westward.

It wasn't until nightfall that they discovered their problem. As the hunters built up the fire, Kurghal and Zhura sat.

"My legs are sore," announced Zhura.

"As are mine," agreed the shaman. "We would have been wiser to cover less distance."

"We will need to keep that in mind for tomorrow."

They sat, watching, as Bagrat put some meat on a stick before placing it into the fire.

"I should contact Kraloch," said Kurghal. "He will be eager for news."

Zhura watched as the three wolves padded over to her, settling at her feet. She reached out, stroking their fur, and one of them rolled over on its back.

Bagrat laughed. "Your wolf acts like a pup. Does he not realize he is full grown?"

Zhura gave him a steely gaze. "SHE simply likes to have her belly scratched. Tell me, Bagrat, can you not tell the difference between a male wolf and a female one? If not, maybe Kurghal would agree to explain it to you?"

The younger Orc closed his mouth and refocused his attention on spearing another chunk of meat.

"Do not be harsh with him," said Kurghal. "He is still young."

"He is a full-grown hunter and should know better."

"Agreed, but with so many of the older hunters away, there are few examples for him to learn from. Will it always be this way, do you think?"

"I hope not," said Zhura. "I should like to believe that eventually, the land will be at peace, and we will no longer need fear death in battle for our hunters."

"It is strange to think on my youth. When I was younger, I wanted nothing more than to follow in my mother's footsteps. As I grew older, however, I began to see how set in her ways she was. It took Urgon's boldness to convince me things could change for the better."

"And have they? Changed for the better, I mean?"

"Most assuredly," said Kurghal. "The tribe has flourished under my brother's guidance, and since we allied with the Mercerians, the increase in trade has benefited all."

"Despite that, I detect a sadness amongst our people," said Zhura.

"While it is true the tribe has grown, it also shows signs of discontent. Many of our hunters found a new home in one of the Human towns, Hawksburg. Before long, they will wish to establish their own tribe."

"Would that be so bad? It is our way to expand and grow. Better that than wither and die. We are merely getting old, you and I. Such things are for the young to consider."

Kurghal sighed. "And what will future generations think of us?"

"That we gave them a future of hope and prosperity. What more could anyone ask of us?"

"And if Urgon asks you to go to Hawksburg?"

"Then I shall go, of course," replied Zhura. "It would be interesting to see these Humans for myself. I understand their houses are very different from ours."

"As is their leadership," added Kurghal. "Kraloch tried to explain it to me once, but I found the concept confusing."

"In what way?"

"They have a queen; that much is easy to understand, but beneath this woman, there are what they call nobles. It is a concept that is most baffling, and they think rulers inherit their right to rule from their parents."

"I believe you are teasing me."

"No," said Kurghal. "It is true, I swear by the Ancestors."

"But their queen is said to be wise, if I am not mistaken."

"She is. Wise enough to see us as allies, although in that regard, she appears to be the exception rather than the rule."

"How well do you know these humans?" asked Zhura.

"Kraloch tells me much of a Human named Aubrey, although I have yet to speak with her."

"How would you converse?"

"She is fluent in our language and has learned to use spirit talk."

"Kraloch taught her the spell?"

"Yes," said Kurghal, "but only on the condition she not teach it to others."

"Can she be trusted to follow through on that promise?"

"He believes she can. She has, in essence, become a protégé of his, although he has also learned much from her. It appears she is a gifted... what is the term?"

"Mage?"

"Yes, Life Mage. It is her family who rules over Hawksburg."

"I should like to meet this Aubrey."

"You shall have your chance," said Kurghal, "for she is with the army."

SIX

Arnim and Revi

SUMMER 965 MC

A rnim halted the column. He and Revi had ridden north with one hundred Kurathian horsemen, the plan being to locate Ironcliff. It lay somewhere past a region known as 'the Gap', but so far, they had seen nothing that might indicate the location of such a place.

He looked over at Revi Bloom, but the Royal Life Mage's eyes were closed as he reached out to his familiar, Shellbreaker. It was odd to watch, for the mage kept moving his head around as if searching the countryside, occasionally peering downward and focusing on some distant object.

"Well?" said Arnim, his patience wearing thin.

"There's a town close by," replied Revi.

"How close?"

"Half a morning's ride, maybe a little more. It might be worth investigating."

"I doubt they'd welcome Mercerian horsemen."

Revi opened his eyes, taking a moment to reacquaint himself with his surroundings. "No, I don't suppose they would. Perhaps it would be best if I go alone?"

"The last time you went off alone, it didn't go well."

"You can't blame me for that. I was looking for a way to harness the power of the magical flames."

"Still, I have specific orders to keep an eye on you, and I don't intend to ignore them."

"Orders from who?"

"Hayley, if you must know."

"She's the same rank as you."

"Yes," said Arnim, "but she's your fiancée now. You can't honestly blame her for being concerned about your well-being."

Revi smiled. "I concede the point, but I DO believe a visit to this place would prove fruitful."

"In what way?"

"For one thing, we could find out what the place is called, not to mention learn of the area. We have no maps of Norland, if you recall, so we're riding about in the dark, so to speak. A little more information about the area could prove useful, don't you think?"

"All right, you made your point." Arnim turned to his cavalry commander. "Captain Ruzak, hold your men here. Revi and I are going to visit that town and see what we can discover."

"As you wish, Commander."

Revi led the way, heading northwest. There was little to see from here, but the mage insisted they were going in the right direction.

"This is a pretty desolate place," said Arnim. "I wonder why anyone would live here?"

"Likely because they have no choice. They came to this land after fleeing Merceria."

"I know they fled Merceria after a failed rebellion, but that's not what I'm talking about."

"Then what DO you mean?"

"Why this particular area? Doubtlessly there are greener pastures to the west?"

"I haven't a clue," replied the mage. "Not that it really matters, though; it's not like the success of our mission hinges on such things."

"Still, it would be nice to know."

Revi smiled. "It's the children."

"What is?"

"The reason you're so intent on learning things all of a sudden."

"It's not 'all of a sudden'. I've always been interested in learning."

"You could have fooled me," said the mage.

"What's that supposed to mean?"

"Only that fatherhood suits you, but if the topic annoys you, maybe we should move on to something else?"

"Such as?"

"The Dwarves?" offered Revi. "You know, I've been learning their language."

"You have?"

"Yes, but unfortunately, I haven't had much time to devote to it, so I'll still be relying on my spell of tongues. It's similar to Orc."

"What is? Your spell?"

Revi laughed. "No, the Dwarven language."

"No surprise there," said Arnim.

The mage looked at him in astonishment. "Are you an expert in languages, now?"

"No, but I heard that thousands of years ago, the elder races spoke a common tongue of their own. Of course, these days, each has developed its own dialect."

"Do my ears deceive me, or have you become a bit of a scholar?"

Arnim grinned. "I can't be a warrior forever. Age has a way of creeping up on all of us."

"Then I shall delight in the company of a fellow academic."

"Are you saying you didn't like my company previously?"

Revi blushed. "Well... that is, I..."

"Relax. I'm only pulling your leg."

They topped a rise, and the town came into view.

"Looks like a decent enough place," said Arnim. "Any sign of an army?"

"None Shellbreaker could see, nor any sign of fortifications, for that matter."

"Who are we?"

"Well, I don't know about you, but I'm Revi Bloom, the Royal Life Mage."

"Don't be ridiculous, my friend. We can't very well go into a Norland town as ourselves. We need to adopt personas."

"Yes, I suppose you're right. We could always claim to be from Galburn's Ridge?"

"Or Anvil," suggested Arnim. "That way, we won't be asked any questions about the capital."

"Anvil it is, then."

They continued on their way, passing by some tilled land. Workers were out, presumably clearing the weeds from between their crops, but no one took any notice of them. As they got closer to the town, the sounds of life drifted towards them.

"Ah," said Revi. "Civilization."

Arnim scowled but kept his thoughts to himself. A wagon approached, loaded up with workers. The Norlanders said nothing, merely nodding their heads as they drew alongside.

"Excuse me," called out Revi, catching their attention. "Might I enquire as to the name of this town?"

"Chandley," came the reply.

"And who rules here?"

"The Earl of Greendale."

"Ah," grumbled Arnim. "That would be Lord Calder."

The wagon continued on its way, its occupants returning their conversations to more mundane matters.

"Well," said Revi, "they didn't appear to detect anything out of the ordinary about our accents."

"We all speak the same language."

"Yes, but regional dialects often crop up between peoples separated by long distances."

"You think too much," said Arnim.

"And you, too little. Now, where would you like to start our enquiries?"

Arnim thought for a moment. "I suppose a tavern might be a good place, but we have no Norland coins."

"Speak for yourself," said Revi. "I came prepared. Care to choose a tavern?"

Arnim pointed. "That one looks as good as any."

They brought their horses to a halt and dismounted. If the arrival of two strangers raised any alarms, it certainly wasn't obvious, for the townsfolk continued on with their affairs.

Revi tied up his horse, then waited as his companion did likewise. They stepped inside the tavern to find a large common room, much like any other tavern in the land. They took a seat, scanning the small crowd to see if anyone stuck out.

"No sign of soldiers," said Arnim, keeping his voice low.

"Strange, isn't it? I would have thought they'd at least have a local garrison."

A woman appeared at their table. "What can I get you?"

"Two ales," said the mage, "if you would be so kind." He dropped some coins onto the table, and the server scooped them up, then hustled off.

"Not exactly a fountain of helpful knowledge," said Revi.

"What did you expect? We're strangers after all."

"True, but a nice 'hello' or 'how are you' would have been appreciated."

Arnim shook his head. "You expect too much, Revi. These are simple folk, used to simple ways."

The woman reappeared, two tankards in hand.

"Here you go," she said.

"Excuse me," said Revi before she could disappear once more. "Do you have a local garrison here?"

"Usually," she replied, "but the earl marched them all north."

"You mean south."

"Why would they go south?"

"To fight the invasion?"

"The invasion? Haven't you heard? That's all been taken care of."

"It has?" said Revi, his surprise on display for all to see.

"Yes, Lord Hollis defeated a large invasion force at Ravensguard."

The mage was about to argue the point, but Arnim stepped in. "This is good news indeed. What, exactly, have you heard?"

"Apparently, he trapped the enemy between the city and his own army. It was quite a slaughter, or so I'm told."

"Did you hear that, Revi? Lord Hollis saved the realm!"

"Good for him."

Arnim turned his attention once more to their server. "You say Lord Calder took the garrison north?"

"Yes, to Holdcross, more than likely."

"Why would he do that?"

"Well, it's obvious, isn't it? It guards the crossroads."

"The crossroads to where?"

The woman scowled at him.

"I'm sorry," he said, "but we're not from this area." The scowl increased. "We came from the west," Arnim hastily added.

The words appeared to mollify her. "Have you not heard of the Gap?"

"Can't say that I have."

"It's a flat area of land between two mountain ranges. We've had trouble there for years if rumours are to be believed."

"What kind of trouble?"

She shrugged. "No idea. All I know is the earl's men marched there to take care of the situation. Anything else I can get you?"

"No, thank you." He waited until she was out of sight, then looked at Revi. "You don't suppose it's the spirit army, do you?"

"I certainly hope not. We were sent to make contact with the Dwarves. If the spirit army is in the Gap, then it's likely Ironcliff has fallen."

"Let's not jump to conclusions. Perhaps he's only fighting another earl?"

"Either way, it's our duty to find out."

"Yes," agreed Arnim, "but let's at least finish our ale first, shall we? I shouldn't like to draw undue attention to ourselves."

They returned to Captain Ruzak and continued the ride north. The progress here was much faster, owing to the presence of a road to guide them. Not that the road itself was used much, consisting primarily of wagon tracks that had churned up the mud, but it offered a telltale promise of civilization.

The road led into some hills, and they spent the night under a deluge of rain. Arnim slept little, but Revi was able to block out the torrent and get a full night's sleep despite being drenched. Morning promised even more rain, and they set off again with dark clouds looming overhead.

"I hope this trip isn't all for nothing," said Arnim.

"I'm confident the Dwarves will help," replied Revi.

"What makes you so sure?"

"The Dwarves are a pragmatic people. Norland is losing this war, and those on the winning side will benefit the most."

"Yes, but everyone around here believes Hollis crushed our army. How do you know the Dwarves don't have the same opinion?"

"You offer a valid argument. I may need to revisit my optimism." Revi rode on in silence for a while, then returned to the subject. "What do you make of the Dwarves?"

"I'm not sure I understand what you mean."

"I'm referring to their military prowess," said Revi.

"I'd prefer them by my side over the Orcs."

"You would?"

"Yes. For one thing, they're heavily armoured, not to mention those arbalests of theirs. Those things can punch through metal plates at short range."

"Yes," agreed the mage, "but they're slow to reload. The Orcs have those warbows though."

"Only a few of them," countered Arnim. "Although, admittedly, they are extremely effective."

"And the Orcs can move faster than the Dwarves."

"I'll give you that, but the Dwarves are very sturdy troops."

"And, by sturdy," said Revi, "do you mean stubborn?"

"I prefer the term steadfast. You won't catch a Dwarf running from battle."

"That's because they can't—their legs are too short. And in any event, the Orcs don't run from battle either. I'm afraid your argument is flawed."

"You're the one who asked ME what I thought of them. I'm only giving you my opinion."

"I suppose," mused Revi, "that it comes down to armour versus mobility. The Orcs are far more manoeuvrable but lack the heavy armour of the Dwarves."

"Of course, we only know those who come from Stonecastle. Maybe the Dwarves of Ironcliff are different?"

"We shall just have to wait and see."

. . .

After following the road for two days, Arnim began to wonder if it truly led anywhere. The tracks had washed away multiple times, and they had to spend a considerable amount of time sending riders out to find where the road continued.

It eventually took them northeast, where the mountains finally came into sight. Late that afternoon, as they watered their horses, Revi sent out Shellbreaker, watching through the coaster's eyes as it flew eastward.

"I see a city," said the mage, "with roads heading north and south."

"And to the east?"

"A plain that stretches on as far as the eye can see, bordered by mountains."

"That must be the Gap they spoke of. Any sign of an army?"

"There are warriors massed outside the city."

"Are they attacking?"

"No," replied Revi. "They appear to be camped there."

"Likely the earl's army. Can you get an idea of their numbers?"

"At a quick guess, I'd say at least a thousand. I see lots of footmen, and there are archers practicing, but surprisingly few horses."

"That's unusual," said Arnim. "The Norlanders do seem to favour their cavalry. Could they be out on patrol somewhere else?"

"Possibly, but if they are, I see no evidence of it."

"And still no sign of this elusive enemy the serving woman spoke of?"

"None whatsoever," said the mage, ending his spell. "I'm beginning to wonder if there's anything out there at all."

"Could Lord Calder be massing his army to move south?"

"Then why bring them all the way to Holdcross?"

"An excellent question," said Arnim. "I wish I knew. How do you think we should proceed?"

"We should definitely head eastward if only to find out what these Norlanders are afraid of. After all, the enemy of my enemy is my ally—isn't that what they say?"

"Close enough. If we are to move past Holdcross, though, we'll need to take care not to be spotted. I would suggest we head south, well out of sight of the city, then move out onto the plains."

Revi nodded. "Very well. I'll try and get a more accurate accounting of the enemy's forces. In the meantime, we should send some riders ahead to see if they can find a secluded place to camp. We don't want to give our presence away." He closed his eyes, re-cast his spell, and soon his head was bobbing again.

Arnim shook his head. He had known the mage for many years now, yet the man was still largely a mystery to him. He knew, of course, of Revi's relationship with the High Ranger, but that was common knowledge, and, if truth be told, Hayley had been the one to let everybody know about it.

Perhaps, he thought, mages didn't think like mere mortals? He quickly dismissed the thought. Lady Aubrey was a mage, and she was one of the most personable people he'd ever met. Then again, Albreda wasn't the most approachable, so maybe Aubrey was the exception rather than the rule? He would have continued down that line of thought if he hadn't been interrupted by his companion.

"Interesting," said the mage.

Arnim waited for further details, but none were forthcoming. "What's interesting?" he asked, his voice revealing his frustration.

The mage, oblivious to Arnim's manner, simply answered the question. "The bulk of this army appears to be footmen."

"And when you say bulk…?"

"I would say a good six hundred."

"And the others?" pressed Arnim.

"Roughly two hundred bowmen, but only one hundred horse unless I miss my guess."

"And you're still convinced they haven't ridden out somewhere?"

"It's always a possibility," said Revi, "but Shellbreaker has exceptional eyesight. I would expect to see hoofprints if that were so."

"Could they have taken losses?"

"I didn't consider that, but if that were the case, I think the camp would have set up more precautions. I'm not an expert in military things, but they appear unconcerned about posting guards and such."

"So whoever their enemy is, they're not in the vicinity."

"So it would seem," said Revi.

"I suppose their lack of horsemen could have something to do with the terrain. It's not exactly horse-friendly."

"Oh, I don't know about that. The land is fairly flat as you go eastward."

"Yes, but unless I miss my guess, there are rocks strewn all about the plains."

Revi turned, seeing through the eyes of his familiar. "Saxnor's beard, you're right! How did you know?"

"It was merely a deduction. Horses are few in number here. It only makes sense there's a reason for that."

"What if they were sent south to help repel our invasion?"

"Do you honestly believe a Norland earl would willingly lend warriors to one of his rivals?"

"No," said Revi, "I suppose not."

"Besides, I think I know who the earl fears."

"Oh yes? Do tell."

"The Dwarves," said Arnim.

"What makes you say that?"

"Even regular footmen could outpace the Dwarves, and, frankly, horsemen are expensive to maintain. This army composition would be just the thing to deal with them, don't you think?"

"I'll concede your idea has some merit," said the mage, "but the only way to find out for sure is to continue travelling to the east."

"Then what are we waiting for?"

The next day they kept to the edge of the mountains, careful to keep the noise to a minimum lest the enemy discover them. Shellbreaker flew overhead, keeping a vigilant eye, but it proved unnecessary for no troops rode out from Holdcross.

By noon, they had found the remains of a village, abandoned some years ago by the look of it. A small path led in the direction of Holdcross, but they ignored it, heading eastward into the Gap. As Arnim had suggested, the terrain was littered with rocks as if the very ground had spat them out. The horses were forced to proceed slowly to avoid hurting themselves, significantly slowing their progress.

By nightfall, they were still within range of Holdcross, so much so that the light of the town lit up the distant sky. As a result, they camped without fires to prevent detection.

A chilly wind blew in that evening, causing no end of grief. As he sat shivering, Arnim hoped this was not a portent of things to come. It wasn't that he was a superstitious man, rather the opposite, in fact. He considered himself a reasonable sort, yet he couldn't quite shake the feeling that something terrible waited for them to the east.

Revi soon joined him, wrapped in a saddle blanket. "I wish we had a Fire Mage," he said.

"What good would that do? There'd still be a fire, and that would give away our presence."

"Ah, but there's more to Fire Magic than simply setting things aflame."

"Like what?"

"Well, for one thing, they could cast a spell of warmth."

"Oh yes?" said Arnim. "And what does that do?"

"It lets a person maintain a constant body temperature."

"So it keeps people warm in the winter?"

"Yes," replied Revi, "but it can also keep one cool in the summer."

"With fire?"

"As I said, there's more to a Fire Mage than flames. They work with heat, both its production and its suppression."

"So they can put out fires as well?"

"Well, I suppose that's true, although it's an oversimplification."

"You're a Life Mage, Revi. How do you know so much about Fire Magic?"

"I make it my business to know. I am THE Royal Life Mage."

"Yes," agreed Arnim, "but you're also an Enchanter now."

The mage paused as he was about to speak, suddenly finding himself at a loss for words. Arnim smiled, pleased with the result, but it wasn't to last.

"Ah well," said Revi. "I suppose now I'll need to call myself the Royal Enchanter as well."

SEVEN

Treachery

SUMMER 965 MC

Richard Fitzwilliam, Baron of Bodden, stared at the monstrosity that sat before him. "You say this thing can hit the walls from this distance?"

"So my experts tell me," said Herdwin. "It's called a trebuchet. In a sense, it's only a giant catapult, but it uses a counterweight—"

"I know what a trebuchet is," said the baron, "but I don't see how it will reach the height of that fortress. It's up a very steep hill."

"Ah well, we Dwarves have made a few modifications to the design."

"How many will you have?"

"This one here's almost complete, and two more are under construction."

"And how long before we're ready to begin the siege?"

"I would say a week at the most. I have my Dwarves stockpiling stone, but we can just as easily bombard the place with burning pitch if it would suit your purposes."

"I'm confident you can bring down a wall with this thing," said Fitz, "but we still need to get warriors inside."

"Maybe not," offered Herdwin. "The castle is well fortified, it's true, but there's a glaring weakness."

The baron turned his gaze towards the distant fortification. The Royal Fortress, as it was known, was situated atop an imposing cliff. So steep was its approach that the road leading to it had to run back and forth to navigate the incline. Above this sat an impressive-looking wall, complete with murder holes to pour down boiling oil or pitch on those who approached. Try as he might, Fitz could spot no weaknesses.

"All right," he finally said, "I give up. What's the weakness?"

Herdwin smiled, crossing his arms to appear more knowledgeable. "That wall sits atop a cliff."

"What of it? You could send rocks against that wall for weeks and make little or no difference."

"Ah, but that's the problem, you see? You're looking in the wrong place."

"I'm afraid I don't understand."

"We don't target the wall. We target the cliff."

A smile crept over the baron's face. "I see now. If the cliff collapses so, too, will the wall atop it."

"Precisely."

"But how difficult would that be to do?"

"With an army of Dwarves? Not at all. Our experts learned how to read rock long ago. We understand how it sits and where its strengths and weaknesses are. It might take us a few days to find the right spot, but when we do, that wall will come crumbling down like fresh-baked stonecakes."

"You make cakes out of stones?"

Herdwin blushed. "Never mind the reference. The implication is clear."

"How do we then get warriors inside?"

"By scaling what remains of the cliff. Of course, with the wall down, they might see the error of their ways and surrender."

"I imagine that would be a tough climb."

"Not for us Dwarves. Having spent time amongst the mountains of Stonecastle, I've yet to see a Dwarf who couldn't climb."

"I thought you were from Wincaster."

"I am, but I didn't spend my entire life there, only the last sixty years or so."

"Wouldn't your warriors be open targets while they climbed?"

"We would cover their ascent with our arbalesters. You'd be surprised what kind of range we can get on those things. There's also the matter of the wall being in ruins, making it difficult for the defenders to counterattack. The Norlanders use crossbows, don't they?"

"We saw them in use recently, but they're not used with any regularity. Why?"

"That's good news. It means their archers will need to crawl out of their cover to rain arrows down on the attack. That makes easier targets for my arbalesters."

"Clearly you have things well in hand here," said Fitz.

"How goes the rest of the campaign?"

"The marshal reports a victory at Ravensguard. I expect he'll begin moving his army north sometime in the next week."

"And yours?" asked the Dwarf.

"I'll move the bulk of my men here to Galburn's Ridge. With the defeat of the Norlanders to our east, we no longer need to fear them getting in behind us. You can expect us by the end of the week."

"Hopefully, by the time you arrive, the other trebuchets will be up and running."

The baron smiled. "I look forward to it."

Bronwyn climbed into her saddle. Beside her, sitting atop a Mercerian Charger, Sir Greyson stared at the Dwarven camp.

"Are we ready?" she asked.

Her words caused him to turn his head, displaying a grim determination. "Ready when you are, Your Highness. Are you sure this is what you want?"

"Do you question my resolve?"

"No, my lady. I would willingly give my life for you. I ask only to make sure there's no misunderstanding. Once this attack commences, there'll be no turning back."

Her gaze swivelled to the Dwarves, then to the great fortress beyond. Inside those walls, she would find all that she desired: power, glory, and the throne of Norland! She felt a sense of euphoria as if her entire life had led up to this moment.

She looked once more to her knight. "You may commence the attack at your leisure, General."

Sir Greyson bowed his head, pleased with the compliment. "You honour me, Highness." He called out to his aide, "Sound the advance."

Captain Carlson heard the call and turned to his sergeant. "What nonsense is this?"

Sergeant Gardner stared back. "I have no idea, sir. I thought we formed up for the princess to inspect us."

The Norland rebels beside their company drew steel, causing the sergeant to call out in disbelief. "Saxnor's balls, they mean to attack!" he shouted.

"Attack who? There's no enemy in sight."

"Could it simply be a practice?"

"Without informing us?" said the captain. "I hardly think so."

The rest of the rebel army moved forward, but Carlson kept the

Wincaster Light Horse in place. His men, seasoned and disciplined, followed his example, remaining still, all eyes on their captain.

Carlson watched as the rebel horsemen trotted forward, then the footmen began to follow. The rebel princess, Bronwyn, had close to five hundred men under her command, the vast majority of which were natives of Norland. Only the Wincaster Light Horse was Mercerian, a situation the captain now found to be immensely unsettling.

He heard shouts as the rebel archers began loosing their arrows. A Dwarf atop the closest siege engine took a hit to the shoulder and fell to his death. Then the rebel horsemen were in amongst them, cutting left and right, slaying those who, until only a moment ago, had been their trusted allies.

"This is madness," yelled the captain. "Order the advance."

"Sir?"

"We must attack."

"The Dwarves are our allies, sir?" said the sergeant.

"Not the Dwarves, man, the rebels!"

Gardner gave the order. The light horsemen began to trot, weapons drawn, breaking into a gallop after about a dozen paces.

The captain held his sword out, pointing it forward, signalling the advance. He glanced to check on his men, but he needn't have bothered, for they kept to their formation.

The rebel footmen were in amongst the Dwarves now, but the mountain folk did not stand idly by. A large group gathered around the base of one of the trebuchets and were forming into a rough line. The rebel horse rushed past them, the siege engine being too much of an obstacle for them, but the footmen were another matter.

~

Herdwin heard the distant horns but thought little of it, as it was not uncommon for the rebels to practice their manoeuvres. After all, they were trying to impress the Mercerians. He concentrated on the task before him, examining the cliff that supported the fortress of Galburn's Ridge. The wall of stone was almost vertical in places, but there were signs that rock had sheared away over the years, revealing weaknesses that could be exploited.

The clash of steel echoed behind him, and he turned around in irritation, expecting to see someone practicing their swordplay. Instead, hordes of men rushed towards him, weapons in hand. It took only a moment to realize the danger, and then he was running as fast as his legs could carry him. Many of his Dwarven comrades were formed up near one of the trebuchets. He dashed towards them, eager to be free of the melee, but before he could get there, something smashed into his back, pitching him forward. He tumbled as he fell, then came back up on his feet just in time to see a horse rushing past. A sword swung at his head, and he ducked, feeling the edge scrape along his hair.

"By Gundar!" he shouted. "What in the name of the Gods is going on here?"

Another horse appeared on his left, rearing up. Any other time he would have been carrying his axe and could have struck back, but who would have thought he'd need it in the middle of his own warriors? He cursed his bad luck as he continued running for the safety of the trebuchet, but a hoof struck him square between the shoulder blades, throwing him back to the ground. The rider struck down with his sword but lacked the reach to hit the now prone Dwarf.

Herdwin rolled left a moment before another hoof struck where he had just been, sending dirt flying into his face. He heard a dull thud, then looked up to see the rider falling backwards with a quarrel through the neck. All around the Dwarf were horses, and he struggled to get his bearings, then he saw it—the extended arm of the trebuchet. He crawled forward, and rough hands hauled him to his feet, dragging him through a makeshift line of Dwarves.

A rough-looking sort, with a yellow beard, handed him an axe. "*They've gone mad,*" he said, using the language of the mountain folk.

"*Aye,*" agreed Herdwin as he gripped the axe, feeling the reassuring weight of it.

The rebel horsemen rode past them, deeper into the siege lines where the fighting continued. Behind them, however, came the footmen, screaming their lungs out as they tried to build up their courage.

"*They're fools,*" declared his benefactor. "*They have the drop on us, but they can't possibly hope to outfight us.*"

"*They outnumber us two to one,*" said Herdwin. "*They might not beat us, but they're going to play havoc with our work.*" Even as he spoke, he noticed smoke drifting up from one of the other trebuchets. He felt it like a punch to the gut. It had taken weeks to assemble the mighty siege engines, and now all was in danger of being lost.

A flurry of arrows descended on the group, and the Dwarf in front of Herdwin went down. He moved in to take the spot, lifting the shield from the corpse and bracing for impact right as the enemy struck. A Dwarf was, on average, about five feet tall, putting them at a height disadvantage in a fight such as this. However, they more than made up for that with their muscular build, allowing them to plant themselves with their powerful legs and become well-nigh immovable.

The Norland rebels hit the line like a wave crashing against rocks. Swords stabbed out, drawing blood, but they were no match for the Dwarven steel that struck back in response. Axe blades cleaved through armour like a scythe through wheat, blood flying everywhere.

The Humans started to falter, and then shouts of anger turned to those of fear as horsemen cut into their rear ranks. Herdwin struggled to understand what was happening as the rebel footmen broke, streaming eastward towards the distant fortress of Galburn's Ridge. The horsemen drew closer, and then Herdwin recognized the face of the Mercerian captain.

"Captain Carlson, your arrival has proven most timely."

The veteran looked down at the Dwarf's bloodied countenance. "Are you injured, Commander?"

"No," said Herdwin, "but do you know what's happened here?"

"We've been betrayed," replied the Human, "by our so-called ally."

"We must save the siege engines," said the Dwarf.

"I'm afraid it's too late for that."

"Tell me what you can see from the top of that horse of yours."

"The rebels are streaming up the hill towards the fortress. They flowed around your troops like waves around the rocks. My men will hold here and secure this trebuchet, but the other two are in flames. Had I more manpower, I'd pursue, but the numbers are against us."

"Let them go. We're better off without them."

"And the siege engines?" asked the captain.

"There's no way we can save them now. Let them burn. We'll pull everyone back here and regroup. I'll need your men to watch the perimeter and give warning should they return. In the meantime, I'll have my Dwarves armour up."

"We'll need to get word to General Fitzwilliam."

"He's already on the way," said Herdwin, "but I suppose a dispatch rider wouldn't hurt. Hopefully, he can send Preston's cavalry force. They ought to be able to keep that lot at bay." He cast his eyes at the distant enemy stronghold. "I should have seen this coming."

"There was no way you could have expected such treachery," said Captain Carlson.

"This never would have taken place if Dame Beverly still commanded the rebels."

"You don't know that."

"Yes, I do," declared Herdwin. "She would never allow such foolishness."

"If the rebels were predisposed to turn against us, it was inevitable. Had they not attacked us now, they would have risen in rebellion against their commander at some point."

"I find that hard to believe. No, I think we both know who's responsible for this calamity—Bronwyn. I won't deign to call her a princess."

They gathered the wounded Dwarves, making them as comfortable as they could. Seventeen had died in the initial assault, with another twenty-three suffering grievous wounds. Many, like Herdwin, had gotten away with only light injuries, but even so, the effect on morale was devastating. Adding to that was the lack of healers, resulting in wounds that would go untreated.

Herdwin's force was significant, although small in number. There were five companies in total, numbering roughly fifty Dwarves each. Two of those were the arbalesters, while the others were equipped with the axes so beloved by the mountain folk. Protecting them all was Dwarven chainmail, the construction of which was a closely guarded secret. Of course, such armour can only prove useful when it's worn, a fact not lost on Herdwin, who berated himself yet again for his lack of preparedness. His poor foresight had cost them dearly. He swore he wouldn't be fooled like that again.

~

Bronwyn rode through the camp, struggling to keep pace with Sir Greyson while her rebels struck out, leaving mayhem in their wake. Her eyes focused on the distant fortress, praying they would honour their agreement and grant them entry.

Flames licked at a nearby trebuchet, and she briefly glanced to see her men swarming over it, torches in hand. To her sides rode the cavalry, HER cavalry, and she took pride in the thought. Mere months ago, she had believed her role relegated to that of a political prisoner, held in check by the powerful lords of Norland, but now? Now, she was a fierce warrior, a respected leader, and a future queen!

They began the ascent, following the winding road as it climbed up the heights. The road was steep, and more than once, she needed to avert her gaze to prevent feeling dizzy. Bronwyn concentrated on Sir Greyson instead, her eyes boring into his back to avoid the view below.

Shouts came from above, and she glanced up to see faces from the distant battlements peering down at them. The road curved back on itself again, and she turned her mount, wishing this nightmare were over. She thought of the comfort of being in the castle, of sleeping in an actual bed by a hearth, but all that came crashing down in an instant as a rock struck the road just in front of her.

She looked up again, only to witness more rocks hurtling their way, one smashing into the rider directly behind her, careening off the poor fool's helmet and breaking his neck. The man slumped forward, then rolled to the side, his mount now unnerved. Then another stone struck nearby, and the horse reared up, but when its hoof missed the edge of the road as it landed, it plunged to its death, letting out a forlorn scream as it fell.

Bronwyn's horse started to panic. She could almost smell the creature's fear as it, too, reared up. Then the reins slipped from her grip, and she threw her arms out, trying to maintain her balance. Suddenly Sir Greyson was there, his arm wrapping around her waist, pulling her to him, and placing her across the saddle. He then turned his mount around, forcing his way back down the path.

Her men looked about in alarm. The footmen, far to the rear, easily retreated, but the horses were another matter. Within the strict confines of the narrow path, even turning around was a complicated procedure, and the hail of stones and rocks only made things worse.

The Princess of Norland could only look on in horror as all her hopes and dreams came crashing down around her. She had betrayed the Mercerians, and now the army of Norland had turned their back on her, trapping her between two enemies.

She closed her eyes, trying to shut out the chaos surrounding her. All she wanted to do was scream, but even that was impossible, so paralyzed was she by fear.

Time seemed to drag on for an eternity, and then Sir Greyson was staring at her, his mouth saying something she couldn't quite hear above all the screaming. He took her by the shoulders and shook her, forcing her to acknowledge his presence.

"We must leave this place!" he was yelling.

She only nodded, too afraid to give voice to her fears.

"You know this country better than I," he shouted. "Where do we go?"

Bronwyn's mind snapped into sharp focus. She closed her eyes again, trying to imagine the great map back in the king's hall. They needed somewhere to regroup, somewhere she'd be welcomed with open arms.

"North," she said, "to Chilmsford."

The princess glanced westward, fearful the Dwarves might prevent their departure, but the mountain folk had pulled back, using the remaining trebuchet as a rallying point. She looked behind Sir Greyson to see the rebel warriors streaming along in her wake. They'd taken a pounding, but it looked like most had survived. With luck, she could recruit again and yet take the Crown for herself, but she must look to the survival of her army in the meantime.

She gathered her courage. "Find me a horse," she ordered, "and make haste before the Mercerians decide to pursue."

"With who?" said the knight. "Dwarves? I think you overestimate their speed."

"No, you fool, the Wincaster Light Horse. They're more than capable of catching up to us. Our own troops are disheartened and would be easy fodder." She saw how the rebuke had stung and so softened her approach. "I'm sorry, Sir Greyson. You have done all I asked of you, but it appears the Gods were against us this day."

A grim smile of determination creased the knight's lips. "We shall recover from this, Highness, I promise you. I shall see you sit in your rightful place on the throne of Norland."

EIGHT

A New Plan

SUMMER 965 MC

U rgon reached out to open the tent flap, but Kraloch's voice interrupted him.

"A word, my friend?"

The chieftain turned, noticing the troubled look on his comrade's face. "Is something wrong?"

"I received word from Kurghal. She is coming here to join us."

"My half-sister? Why? I left her to watch over Ord-Dugath in my absence."

"She is not coming alone. She is bringing Zhura."

Urgon's heart skipped a beat. "Zhura? Here?"

"You do not appear pleased."

"I fear for her health, for the trip is long and arduous. Could she not have sent word by Kurghal's magic?"

"She was most insistent that she come. She has information she believes can help us defeat the army of spirits."

"And she could not tell of this through a message?"

Kraloch smiled. "In this, I fear, she is much like you—stubborn."

"You would speak like this to your chieftain?"

"No, but I would speak thus to my oldest friend."

Urgon nodded. "And you are right to do so. Forgive me. I am pleased by the thought that she will once more be close to me, but at the same time, I am fearful for what it might portend. These armies of men are nothing compared to the real danger that threatens us. When is she to arrive?"

"Not for some time yet. They only just left the village."

"Then we must make preparations for her eventual arrival."

Kraloch's eyes went to the tent. "And what of the queen? Will we tell her of Zhura's suspicions?"

"I believe it is the time for such things. Would you not agree?"

"I would."

"Then let us go and see what can be done." He entered, with Kraloch following.

Inside, gathered many of the queen's advisors—Gerald, of course, as well as Beverly and Aubrey. Rounding out the group were Dame Hayley, the Earth Mage Aldus Hearn, and the massive presence of the troll, Tog.

"I hope we have not delayed you," said Urgon.

"Not at all," replied the queen. "We were just discussing some new information. I don't know if you heard, but Commander Lanaka's been found."

"Alive, I hope?"

"Indeed, although he will need some time yet to recover from his ordeal. Of particular significance is that he was found by an old man named Marik."

"Marik?" said Kraloch. "Was he not the champion who fought Dame Beverly?"

"He was," added Beverly, "but now he is old and frail—the victim of dark magic."

"I assume that means there are Death Mages within the Norland ranks?"

"There are," said the queen, "or at least there were. According to Marik, the earl was unaware this fellow, Jendrick, was anything other than a typical sorcerer."

Kraloch stared back. "That is a term I am not familiar with. What precisely is a sorcerer?"

"A wielder of magic," offered Aldus Hearn. "The term is an old one, dating back long ago to when we Mercerians knew little about magic. These days, we classify users of the arcane arts based on the type of spells they utilize, but it appears old habits die hard with the Norlanders."

"And how sure are we that this Jendrick is a Necromancer?"

"I'm afraid there can be little doubt," said the queen. "He used a spell to drain the youth from Marik. I can imagine no other explanation of his condition. Can you, Aubrey?"

The Life Mage thought for a moment. "Our information on such things is somewhat limited. Revi might know more, but he's off with Arnim, chasing down potential allies. Whatever he is, he managed to elude capture by using Blood Magic."

"Ah, yes," said Beverly. "The strange corpse and the smell of rotting flesh. We saw that near Oaksvale too."

"We did," said Aubrey, "but I think we have a bigger problem at the moment. I heard from Andurak today. It appears Bronwyn has turned against us."

"This is news," said Gerald. "Why didn't you tell me sooner?"

"I only just found out myself, and the queen thought it best to wait until everyone was gathered."

"How bad was it?"

"They attacked the Dwarves. Luckily, Herdwin's forces didn't take too many casualties, but their siege work was set back considerably."

"Did all of her soldiers take part?"

"Everyone except the Wincaster Light Horse. I'm afraid we have a new enemy out there—one of our own making."

"Saxnor's balls," said Gerald. "I knew we shouldn't have trusted that upstart princess."

"Careful, now," said Anna. "I was once an upstart princess myself."

"That's different, and you know it."

"There is more," said Urgon. All eyes turned to him.

"Go on," urged the queen.

"Zhura is coming here to join us."

"Isn't Zhura your bondmate?" said Gerald.

"She is," the chieftain admitted, "but she is also a ghostwalker—one who treads the thin line between life and death."

"Might I ask the significance of that?" said the queen.

"A ghostwalker is rare," explained Kraloch, "and is highly prized by our people. They are in constant communication with the spirit world and, as such, are much more connected to the events that affect it."

"Is she coming here because of the spirit army?"

"She is. Normally, she would not be able to leave her hut, but the absence of the Ancestors has given her a unique opportunity."

"I'm sorry," said Hayley. "Did you say she can't usually leave her hut?"

"That is correct. Her presence in both worlds means she hears what transpires in both. To her, the mere act of walking outside floods her with the words of the dead and the living. Every living person holds a spirit within them, a spirit that often lingers in the Afterlife before fading into nothingness. Zhura can see those spirits, making each person look like two."

"Like the spell of spirit talk," said Aubrey. "When I cast that in the presence of Kraloch, I can see both his physical form and his spirit. It's almost as if two people are occupying the same space."

"That sounds very disturbing," said Beverly.

"I must admit it does take some getting used to."

Hayley jumped back into the conversation. "And this is what Zhura experiences?"

"It is," said Urgon. "We built a special hut for her to live in, one encased in mud."

"Yes," said Kraloch, "but not just any mud. It must be from the Rugar Plains."

"The Rugar Plains?" said Hearn.

"Yes," said Urgon. "Our name for the area slightly south of Eastwood. Kraloch believes there is something mixed in with the mud that allows it to dampen the spirits' noise, but he has yet to determine what that might be."

"To get back to the main matter," interjected the queen. "You said she's coming here. Any indication of why?"

"No," said Kraloch, "but it must be important to bring her all this way."

"We should send an escort."

"She is accompanied by a large party. She will be safe enough."

Gerald grimaced. "Why do I get the feeling this isn't good news? Not that I'm complaining about meeting your wife, Urgon, but this doesn't bode well for the rest of us."

"Something in which I think we all can agree," replied the chieftain. "I wish it were a better omen."

"Maybe it is," said the queen. "What if Zhura is the one with the answers we need to defeat this threat?"

Gerald didn't look happy. "Even if she is, we don't know where this army is, AND there's still a Norland earl or two out there marching around with an army, not to mention Bronwyn and her rogue warriors."

"So what do we do?" pressed Anna. Everyone cast their gaze around the room, but no one appeared eager to put forth a suggestion. In desperation, she turned to her oldest friend. "Gerald?"

He paused only an instant, sorting out his thoughts before continuing. "Arnim and Revi are already well on their way, so there's no calling them back now. The immediate concern to us is the presence of Bronwyn and the rebels. We should divert our resources to tracking them down and crushing them before they gain more followers. Where's Fitz?"

"On his way to Galburn's Ridge," said Aubrey. "Do you want him to pursue Bronwyn?"

"No, he's better off concentrating on taking the capital."

"Sir Heward is still out there, chasing down remnants of the earl's army. Do we recall him?"

"What was his last reported position?" asked the marshal.

"Just outside Anvil."

"Let me take the Kurathians," said Beverly. "I can be in Anvil by week's end."

"No," said Gerald. "I'm taking the bulk of the army there directly, but I'll give you a screening force. Your job, once we begin, will be to guard us against incursions from the north. The last thing we want is one of those earls turning our flank while we're trying to deal with Bronwyn."

"How do you want to split the army?" asked the queen.

"The rangers will go with Beverly, along with two companies of bowmen and Tog's Trolls. Urgon, I wonder if you might speak with Ghodrug? Do you think she'd be willing to lend us some of her hunters as a screening force?"

"I'll need horsemen," said Beverly.

"Take a company of Kurathians and what's left of the Guard Cavalry."

"They were already folded into the heavy horse."

Gerald swore under his breath. Clearly, the pressure was getting to him. The queen placed a gentle hand on his shoulder. "Take your time, Gerald. Another day or two won't make much of a difference."

"Yes, it will," he said. "Split the heavy horse, Beverly—take half and leave the rest."

"That would leave you with next to nothing."

"It gives me the same number as you," he retorted. "I'd love to have more, but we must work with what we've got." He turned to the queen. "Remind me when this is all over that we need more cavalry."

Anna nodded. "Very well. What of our mages?"

"Kraloch will stay here with us. Aubrey, you go with Beverly; that way we'll be able to stay in touch. If you locate either of the remaining earls, make sure to tell us right away."

"And Bronwyn's army?" asked the queen.

"You commanded them, Beverly. How many men did they have?"

"No more than five hundred," replied the red-headed knight, "and they would have taken casualties fighting the Dwarves."

"That's not all," said Aubrey. "I would suspect many of those rebels will desert now that they're stuck in the middle."

"The middle of what?" asked Kraloch.

"They already fought against the renegade earls, and now they're at war with us. That puts them in a terrible position."

"Yes," agreed Anna, "but they're still a threat."

"The queen makes a good point," said Gerald. "Small they may be, but they can still make our lives difficult. It's imperative to bring them to battle as soon as possible."

"But why?" asked Aldus Hearn. "If we just left them alone, they'd probably disband, wouldn't they? In the end, Bronwyn doesn't have the supply lines to feed her army, let alone smiths to keep their weapons and armour in good shape."

"The marshal is right," said Urgon. "Left to themselves, they would have little option but to raid to support their army. Once that starts, it would require many warriors to hold them at bay. In a sense, they would be even more effective at tying down our own soldiers."

Anna turned to Beverly. "You've worked with Sir Greyson. How do you rate him as a commander?"

"That's a difficult question," replied the knight. "He's an experienced Knight of the Sword, having fought against us during the civil war, but you gave him amnesty afterwards, as were all of that order."

"He served Shrewesdale, didn't he?"

"He did, although only for a few years, but that was long after I was there."

The queen frowned. "We know so little of him."

"Actually," said Gerald, "we know more. He's been a knight of the order for some years yet has never held command. Until now, that is. If you recall, you made the Knights of the Hound the senior order after the war, relegating the Swords to more mundane responsibilities. Sir Greyson and Sir Hector were both given the job of guarding Bronwyn."

"Why is that?" asked Aubrey. "Weren't the Palace Guards good enough for her?"

"She saw them as beneath her station. Baron Fitzwilliam suggested using the Knights of the Sword."

"And what of Sir Hector?"

"He's with the baron," said Gerald. "Bronwyn never trusted him, so we can guess where his loyalties lie."

"Perhaps Sir Hector could give us a better idea of Greyson's abilities?" suggested Aubrey. "It would be nice to know what we're dealing with."

"A good idea," said Kraloch. "Andurak is still with the baron's army. Shall I contact him and make enquiries?"

"Yes," said Gerald, "and find out if Fitz knows anything that could help. The more we know, the better prepared we'll be."

"Don't forget," said Anna, "we also have the Saurians. Where shall we use them?"

"I'll take them with me. I've had enough of splitting up our army. It's time we massed. If that spirit army is out there, we're going to need every last soldier we can get."

"I wish I could be of more assistance," said Anna, "but I need to get back to Wincaster. The kingdom won't rule itself."

"How will you return?" asked Gerald.

"I thought to use one of our mages, but I realize now that you need Aubrey and Kraloch for relaying messages."

"I can take you," said Hearn. "It's not as if I'm doing much here."

"My biggest concern is there's no way of receiving updates on our progress here in the north."

"There may be a solution to that," said Urgon. "My half-sister, Kurghal, is an accomplished shaman. Once she arrives with Zhura, I shall see if she is willing to travel to Wincaster with you. That way, she can use her spell of spirit talk to keep you up to date."

"That could be some time yet," said Beverly.

"Nonsense. She will likely be here in the next ten-day."

"Yes," said Kraloch, "and then Master Hearn could teach her the spell of recall."

"I'd be delighted," said Hearn. "Does she speak the common tongue?"

"I thought you knew our language?"

"I've a passing familiarity with it, but I'm afraid not sufficiently so to explain the intricacies of learning a spell."

"Then you must take someone to translate."

"Such as?"

"Well," said Hayley. "You could take Gorath. He's fluent in both our languages."

Hearn smiled. "An excellent solution." He turned to the queen. "When would you like to leave, Your Majesty?"

"I want to wait until Zhura arrives, however long that will take. In the meantime, I believe we're done for now, unless there's anything else you would like to discuss?"

They remained silent.

"Good," she said. "Then you know what you must do, people. Let's be about our tasks."

They all filed out, save for Gerald, who hung back, waiting until it was only he and Anna.

"Well?"

"I hear congratulations are in order."

Anna smiled. "Who told you?"

"Aubrey."

"I suppose I should have expected that. You are family after all."

"You should have her accompany you back to Wincaster. You may need her magic."

"I only just discovered I'm carrying this child. I doubt there's much I need a Life Mage for at this point in time. Women have been having children without a healer for centuries."

"Sorry, I can't help but worry. Childbirth can still be an ordeal, and I'd feel better knowing there was someone there to keep an eye on you."

"I've got Sophie," said Anna, "and the Palace staff are more than capable of looking after me."

"Does Alric know yet?"

"No, I thought I might pay him a visit before I return."

"How would that work?"

"I'll have Master Hearn take us directly to Wickfield. From there, we can travel north until we find Baron Fitzwilliam and the rest of his army."

"You could just send word. Kraloch could get a message there in mere moments."

"And miss the look in his eyes when I tell him the news? I'm not willing to give that up."

"Then at least let me send word to Fitz. He can have a small honour guard meet you on the road."

Anna smiled. "That would be acceptable."

"And once you tell him, you'll return to Wincaster?"

"I promise."

"Good," said Gerald. "It's getting dangerous around here, what with all the Death Mages lurking about."

"Aldus Hearn will be with me. He's no slouch in the area of magic."

"True, but we know so little of Necromancers, I'd prefer not to take the chance. You're too valuable to us, Anna." His voice choked up. "If you were to die…"

She moved closer, giving him a hug. "I won't take any chances, I promise, and you should do the same. I want this child to see his grandfather."

He held her at arm's length, seeing the same look of determination she'd always possessed, even as a child. It was what made her a good queen, and he knew in his heart she would be true to her word.

"I wish I could promise you that," he said, "but we face an unknown foe, and I'm not talking about Bronwyn."

"Have you given thought to how we might combat an army of spirits?"

"Plenty, but I am yet to come up with any ideas."

"Perhaps Zhura will provide the answers we need," Anna suggested.

"We must hope so. There is precious little to go on at the moment, and our lack of horsemen is putting us at a severe disadvantage. Don't get me wrong, we have lots of captured horses, but we lack the manpower to train riders. As it is now, we're relying more and more on our allies."

"Couldn't we train Orcs to be used as cavalry?"

"Eventually, but such things take time."

Anna smiled. "Ah, but you're forgetting one thing."

"Which is?"

"Ghodrug and the Orcs of the Black Raven have a master of earth."

"Yes, Kharzug," said Gerald, "but how does that help us?"

"If he's anything like Albreda, he could communicate with the horses, couldn't he?"

"Albreda has a unique connection to nature. I'm sure Aldus Hearn does too, but the Orcs? I'm not so sure."

"Well, it definitely bears investigating, wouldn't you say?"

He smiled. "I'll give it some thought, although I'm hesitant to ask. The Ravens only just joined us."

"Ah, but that's where you're wrong. They've always been our allies. You forget, when Urgon promised to ally with us, he did so on behalf of all the Orcs."

"It still feels wrong. They already account for more than half of the troops under my direct command."

"They're part of Merceria now," soothed Anna. "Urgon knows this, as does Ghodrug."

"And yet sentiment against them grows within the kingdom."

"Likely fomented by those seeking to advance their own causes. We'll get to the bottom of that in time, but until then, we must stay the course. Of course, if we fail to defeat this new threat, it could be the end of all of us."

"It would be nice to have some good news every once in a while, instead of all this shite that only keeps piling up."

"Don't you consider the royal baby to be good news?"

He let out a breath and smiled. "Yes, of course. I suppose I've been dreading this threat ever since the moment we first learned of those Death Mages."

"Then try to focus on the good for a little while. At least it'll let you get some sleep."

NINE

Prince Tarak

SUMMER 965 MC

B rida stood on the walls of Windbourne, gazing out over all the ships that lay in the harbour.

"It's an impressive sight," she said.

"As I promised," replied Lysandil. "His Highness, the Prince of Kouras, is a wealthy man, and with wealth comes a large army. There's more down along the coast."

"Truly? How many ships does he have?"

"Hundreds. He's brought his personal army with him along with every mercenary company he could lay his hands on."

"And exactly how many men does he command?"

Lysandil shrugged. "I don't know the precise number, but I'd hazard a guess it's in the range of three thousand."

"That many?"

"Yes, he's determined to destroy Weldwyn, then move on to Merceria."

"Why? He's thousands of miles from his home, isn't he? How could he ever hope to rule such a land?"

"You need to understand the Kurathian Isles. Their land is ruled by dozens of princes, each with only a few small islands to call home. Land is more valuable to them than lives. I think he would gladly abandon the home of his birth if he could conquer a kingdom."

"Is that what he intends to do to us? Conquer?"

Lysandil chuckled. "If he wanted to do that, he wouldn't have sent me to warn of his arrival. No, he needs your help. He'll help you conquer Weldwyn, and then, in return, you can give him Merceria. It's an arrangement that would benefit both of you."

"And this Prince Tarak, have you met him?"

"Yes. I spent almost a year at his court and found him to be a most generous man."

"Generous in what way?" Brida asked.

"He rewards those who see fit to support him."

"And those who don't?"

"Well," said the Elf, "let's just say they don't stick around long."

"We worked with Kurathians before," said Brida, "but I must admit to some trepidation where their quality is concerned."

"How so?"

"We found them to be lacking in armour and ill-trained in battle tactics."

"That's because you were dealing with mercenaries, not household troops. They make good light troops if used properly, but Tarak's men are in a whole different category. They're heavily armoured and well-trained, maybe the best troops in the world."

Brida frowned. "Everybody says their men are the best. How do I know that's true?"

In answer, Lysandil merely smiled. "I think once you see them, you will understand."

"Why? Are they giants?"

He chuckled. "No, merely men. I understand you've seen the Kurathian Mastiffs before?"

"We have, yet they failed to live up to their reputation when they fought for us. They ended up doing little damage, and I have heard they're now in service to the Mercerians."

"A regrettable outcome, but I can assure you it will not happen a second time. Prince Tarak's army is far more formidable than a few companies of mercenaries."

"I have only your word for that."

"Does this fleet alone not inspire confidence?" The Elf let his gaze wander over the anchored ships. "I suppose it matters little. Once you meet His Highness, I'm sure you'll see there can be little doubt as to who will win this war. Speaking of which, are preparations in place for his arrival?"

"Calindre assures me they are."

"Good. Then I shall row out there and invite him to come and meet with you."

"Don't you mean us? I'm sure the other Clan chiefs will want to be included."

"You are the daughter of the High King, Brida. It is you, and you alone, he wishes to talk with."

"The others won't like that."

"Then they will need to put aside their disappointment. They need the prince far more than the prince needs them."

"Then why reach out to us at all?"

Lysandil smiled. "You have a destiny, Brida. One that has already been delayed by the interference of the Mercerians. The time has come to right that wrong and place you on the throne of Weldwyn."

"But Prince Alric is married to the Mercerian queen. And, in any case, he has an older brother to inherit the throne."

"My dear, it is not through marriage you will be made queen, but by force of arms."

"And if I wish a Weldwyn prince as my husband?"

"Then we shall do whatever it takes to make one available to you. If that happens to involve making one a widower, then so be it."

"You promise much. How do I know you can deliver on your commitments?"

In answer, he waved his hand at the ships. "Is this not sufficient proof?"

Lochlan stood before the old house, noting the sad state of the thatched roof. Camrath was said to be the greatest scholar of the ages, yet this humble abode did little to inspire confidence.

"Well?" came an old man's voice. "Are you going to stand around out there all day or come in?"

Lochlan pushed open the door, peering inside at a small space consisting of a single room with a fireplace at one end and a bed nearby. However, what made it stand out were the piles of books and scrolls that littered the place.

"Are you Camrath?" he asked.

The old man stepped from behind a tower of books. "I am, and who might you be?"

"Lochlan, son of High King Dathen."

"Well, you'll pardon me if I don't sound suitably impressed. The very notion of a High King is mere political expediency."

"I beg your pardon?"

"My apologies. I didn't mean to offend." He moved towards the fire and a small table that sat nearby. "You must excuse my manners. May I offer you something to drink?"

"No, thank you."

Camrath shrugged, then helped himself, pouring a tankard of golden wine. "What brings you to Glanfraydon?" the old man asked.

"I'm here to see you, actually."

"Me? I'm honoured, of course, but what garners the attention of the High King's son?"

"I need to learn what you know of Elves."

"Elves, is it?" said Camrath. "How curious. They are such a rare race these days."

"We had one visit our court."

"Did you, now? I should have liked to have seen that. What did they want?"

"To broker an alliance with a Kurathian prince," said Lochlan.

"Fascinating. Tell me more."

"He goes by the name of Lysandil. Are you familiar with him?"

"Can't say that I am."

"He claims to represent someone named Queen Kythelia."

The scholar's eyes widened. "Are you sure?"

"Quite. Why? Does the name mean something to you?"

Camrath didn't answer. Instead, he searched through his books, pulling them out, seemingly at random. He flipped through some pages, then quickly tossed it aside, selecting another.

Lochlan watched, afraid to break the scholar's concentration.

"Ah, here it is," the man finally said. "It's said Queen Kythelia ruled over an Elven realm well before the arrival of Humans."

"How do you know that?"

"Simple—it's mentioned in this book."

"And that writing is accurate?"

"Of course, why wouldn't it be? People don't make things up and then write them down."

"So this queen has the same name?"

"I doubt that," said Camrath. "No, it's far more likely the two are one and the same."

"But that would make her thousands of years old!"

"Ah, you must put aside any concepts of age when dealing with Elves. They lived in this world long before we came along and will likely linger in the dark forests long after we're all dead and buried."

"Are you implying she's immortal?" asked an astonished Lochlan.

"That's what they say. Mind you, I have a hard time believing that. I prefer to think they're merely naturally long-lived."

"What else can you tell me about this Queen Kythelia?"

"Not much, I'm afraid. There's a reference to a Great War, but I can't say who they fought."

"Could it be Humans?"

"No," said the old man. "This was long before we were here. It has to be someone else."

"Then who?"

"My guess would be the Orcs; we know they lived in these parts."

"What about the Dwarves?"

Camrath shook his head. "No, I don't believe so. Elves prefer to live in the forested regions, while the Dwarves... well, they don't call them the mountain folk for nothing."

"Anything else you can relate?" asked Lochlan.

"Not much, unless you want to talk about their armies. They favour the Elven bow, a unique weapon that's said to be more powerful than a crossbow."

"Do they use cavalry?"

The scholar looked down at the book, skimming over some pages. "There are some vague references to riders, but nothing substantial." He looked up at Lochlan. "Tell me, my young friend, what specifically are you looking for?"

"Something that might let me know whether or not they're trustworthy."

"You mean individually or as a race?"

"Either?"

"I'm afraid there's little of that in here"—he held up the book—"though I suppose we could infer things."

"How?"

"According to what we know, this war proceeded without any assistance from allies."

"Might I ask how you know this?"

"It's right here," the old man said, pointing at the book in his hands.

"Yes, yes," said Lochlan, "but where did this book come from? Is it Elvish in origin?"

"Not at all. It's written in the common language of Humans. These accounts were passed down by word of mouth from the Dwarves, if the book is to be believed. It says so right in the front."

"And is that book the only information you have about Elves?"

"No, of course not, but you asked specifically about Queen Kythelia." He rummaged through some more tomes. "I have one here, but it speaks more of their customs and beliefs."

"Beliefs? They don't worship the Gods?"

"No," said Camrath. "They venerate those who came before."

"Meaning?"

"That they worship the dead, I suppose. There's no mention of gods in this book, and trust me, I know, I've read it multiple times."

"Is there any mention of a place called Estlaneth?"

"That's a name I've not read of before. Might I ask where you heard of it?"

"From Lysandil," said Lochlan. "He claims it's a realm of Elves. It translates to Kingdom of Moonlight."

"I still don't recognize it. Could it be a mistranslation? We know there's a place in Weldwyn called the Draenor Wood. They say Elves live there."

"He spoke of it as a kingdom, not a wood."

"Then I suppose it must be farther afield."

"I know only of our own land and the borders of Weldwyn. What exists outside of that?"

"Well, let's see—you mentioned Merceria. That land lies beyond Weldwyn to the east. There are rumours of a kingdom to its north, but I have nothing that confirms such speculation."

"And north of Weldwyn?"

"Only the Great Wood, said to be inhabited by all sorts of vile creatures. I suppose that might be where the Elves are, now that I think of it, unless…"

Lochlan waited for the man to continue, but he just stood still, staring at the walls as if they provided some form of inspiration.

"Unless what?" the young man finally asked.

"Could this fellow, Lysandil, be lying?"

"To what end?"

"That, I couldn't possibly fathom, but who truly understands the thoughts of such creatures? Perhaps he wants us to believe he represents a queen so we'll take him seriously?"

"He told us a Kurathian prince was coming to help us. Why do that if he's making everything up?"

"You make a compelling case. I think we must therefore assume his intentions are as he has stated. What did he ask for?"

"That we support another invasion of Weldwyn. He claims King Leofric is dead, and with him, a sizable portion of his army."

"Then it would seem an opportune time for an invasion, yet I sense some unease."

"I can't bring myself to trust him."

"Might I ask why?"

"His actions don't make sense to me," explained Lochlan. "Why arrange for a Kurathian prince to arrive without consulting us beforehand? Wouldn't it make more sense to arrange things months in advance?"

"I can't argue with your logic. Do you fear treachery?"

"I do, although not at this precise time."

"I'm afraid you'll need to explain that one to me."

Lochlan took a breath, letting it out slowly. "I don't doubt his desire for us to invade Weldwyn is genuine, but I'm afraid he's going to let us take the brunt of the fighting, then clean up afterwards."

"That would be a clever strategy," said Camrath, "but surely there are ways to mitigate the risk?"

"Such as?"

"Well, for one thing, you could insist this prince does his fair share of the fighting? You could also ask the Elves to show proof of their actual army."

"How would we do that?"

"Have them send some archers to your holdings. They were willing to send someone all the way to the Kurathian Isles. Couldn't they at least spare a company of Elves armed with their famous bows?"

"That's an astute observation," said Lochlan. "I shall pass those nuggets of wisdom on to my sister."

The scholar looked at the young man for a moment, deep in thought. "Might I ask a boon?"

"Ask away. I'm no ruler, but if it be within my power, I'll do what I can for you."

"When this war is over, and we sit in the Weldwyn capital, I should like a proper building to house all this…" He swept the room with his hand.

"I'll do my best, but let's see about winning the war first, shall we?"

"Of course," said Camrath.

Brida watched, along with the other Clan chieftains, as the Royal Barge rowed His Highness, Prince Tarak, across the bay. Manned by fifty oarsmen, it was an impressive sight, especially with the sun glinting off its ornate, gold-encrusted stern. The prince was an imposing figure himself, bedecked in white-and-gold silk, accompanied by a dozen fearsome-looking warriors in heavy armour.

The boat drew closer, and then the vessel made a turn and raised the oars, allowing it to glide gracefully up to the dock. Two men leaped onto the deck and tied it off, then the guards placed a boarding plank to allow His Highness to disembark. The prince let his men lead the way, then made his way ashore, saying nothing.

Brida stepped forward, unsure of what was required in the way of a greeting. She finally decided on a simple nod of her head. "Welcome to Windbourne, Your Highness."

"Thank you," the foreigner replied, his mastery of the common Human tongue clear for all to hear. He gave a slight nod of his own. "Are you Princess Brida?"

"We do not use that title here," offered Calindre. "She is a Clan chief's daughter, nothing more."

The prince levelled a withering glare at the interloper. "She is the daughter of High King Dathen, is she not? What else would that make her if not a princess?" He returned his attention to Brida. "Come, let us dispense with formalities and go somewhere more private, where we might discuss strategy." He turned his attention to the rest of the Clan delegation. "Your princess can inform you of her decisions when we finish talking. Unless, of course, you disagree with this course of action? If so, I would be more than willing to lend her the assistance of my vast armada and its warriors?" Everyone looked away, intimidated by his steely gaze.

"I thought not," he continued. "If you'll lead on, Your Highness, there is much to discuss."

Brida's attention was on his guards, who were encased in so much metal they looked like iron statues. "What armour is that?" she asked.

The prince gave his men only a cursory glance. "It is called plate armour and is all quite the rage right now back on the Continent."

"Surely such armour must cost a fortune?"

"It does, but I'm a man who doesn't believe in cutting corners when it comes to ensuring victory."

Brida tore her eyes away from the warriors, smiling at their guest. "If you'll come this way, Highness, we'll offer you some refreshment before we start the formal discussions."

He bowed his head ever so slightly. "You honour me, Princess. I'm looking forward to it."

She led him into one of the grander houses set aside for this occasion. Servants scurried to retrieve wine as the two of them took their seats, then more entered bearing trays of food. Prince Tarak ate sparingly, spending much of his time taking in his surroundings.

"I imagine this place pales in comparison to your court," said Brida.

"It has its charms," he replied. "Not every kingdom has the advantage of living under the rule of a Kurathian prince."

"Might I ask how many islands there are?"

"Far too many to count, if the truth be known. I rule one of the larger ones, a place called Kouras."

"And are there many princes like you?"

"There are many, but only a dozen who rule islands of any consequence. It is they who are the dragon masters."

"Dragon masters?"

"Yes," said the prince. "Our people have bred dragons for generations.

Those magnificent creatures are the reason we settled the islands all those centuries ago."

"Exactly how many dragons do you have?"

"They vary in size greatly, but you may rest assured I only brought those I could easily transport."

Brida couldn't believe her ears. "You brought dragons here to Clan territory?"

"Do not fear. They are safely tucked away on ships. They are the penultimate weapon, Highness. In our hands, they will guarantee domination over your enemies."

"How does one counter a dragon?"

He laughed. "You can't, not unless you have a dragon of your own, that is. They are the perfect weapons, don't you see?"

"Lysandil tells me you desire land. Is that true?"

"It's true; I'll not deny it. Kouras is overgrown with people to such an extent that there's no longer any room to expand."

"But why come here? There must be easier places to conquer?"

"Ah, but that's where you're wrong. This land of yours has many wide-open spaces, and your armies are weak."

"How do you know all this?"

"A group of mercenaries returned to Kouras intending to purchase breeding stock from our mastiff handlers. They told of this land, of how the entire area wore outdated armour as if trapped in the past."

"For this reason, you thought it an easy conquest?"

"Easier than any of the Petty Kingdoms."

"I don't know what those are."

"No," said the prince, "I don't suppose you do. You are isolated here, Princess, but all that can change with Kurathian ships to ply the seas on your behalf."

"How do I know you won't turn around and conquer us?"

"I have no need. The Kingdom of Merceria is more than suitable for our purposes. This land of yours offers uncounted riches, riches that it would take generations to exploit. Ally with us, Brida, and my smiths will teach you how to craft that armour you so admire."

"You said it was expensive. How, then, are we to afford it?"

He smiled. "The riches of Weldwyn will soon be yours for the taking. Do not worry about such things. Let us work together, and we will build a better future, one your descendants will appreciate for generations."

Brida smiled, feeling hope return once more.

TEN

Zhura

SUMMER 965 MC

(In the tongue of the Orcs)

Kurghal topped the rise to view an army camped in the distance. "We are almost there," she announced.

Zhura climbed up to take a look while the three wolves circled at her feet. Tents lined the field with warriors going about their daily chores. Off to her right, she spotted a black banner bearing the image of two arrows. "It appears fortune has smiled on us today."

Bagrat ran up to them. "Shall I go and announce your arrival?"

"By all means," said Zhura. "And make haste; I would see my bondmate."

The young hunter ran off, eager to be about his business.

"He is passionate," said Kurghal. "Would that we could have the energy of youth once more."

"I am content with my life as it is," replied Zhura. "Lamenting that which was lost will accomplish nothing. Let us instead celebrate what we have."

The elder shaman turned to look at her. "And what do we have? We are at war, the very thing my half-brother wanted to avoid."

Zhura nodded. "It is a fair observation, yet these last few winters have seen a significant shift in the fortunes of our people. We are no longer a tribe who stands alone."

"And you trust these Humans?"

"I do."

"I might remind you Urgon's predecessor trusted the Earl of Eastwood, and that almost led to our destruction."

"True, but the earl had no sense of honour. These Humans, however, fight for the same things we believe in."

"How can you possibly know such things?" asked Kurghal.

"I trust the instincts of Urgon and Kraloch."

The shaman pointed. "Horsemen approach," she said.

Sure enough, a trio of riders rode towards them at a slow trot. They paused about thirty paces short of the group as one of them dismounted, a Human woman.

"Greetings," she called out, using the Orcish tongue. "My name is Lady Aubrey Brandon. I'm here to welcome you."

"Greetings," said Kurghal.

"Kraloch told us to expect you. We had people searching the area, but I am the one lucky enough to finally locate you."

"An auspicious development," said Zhura, "for I understand you have a good understanding of the spirit realm, maybe even the greatest amongst your people. Indeed, your aura is particularly strong."

Aubrey smiled. "You can see my aura?"

"In a sense. I see your spirit form within you, and that is, in truth, your aura. I understand you travelled to the spirit realm yourself. Surely you are familiar with such things?"

"I am. It's just... unexpected to meet someone who can see it here in the realm of the living."

The Orc peered around her host to look at the two men behind her. "And these other riders?"

"Merely an escort, for we are still at war. You must be tired after your journey, and I imagine you're eager to see Urgon. If you follow me, I'll take you to him."

"That would be most appreciated," said Zhura. "Thank you."

Aubrey led the group down into the field but chose to remain afoot, the better to talk to her new guests.

"I myself have been working on a spell to view auras," she said.

"Why?" asked Kurghal.

"I discovered that a person's aura reveals their aptitude for magic."

"I have noticed no such thing."

"Neither has Kraloch," said Aubrey. "It appears Orcs do not see colours quite the same way as Humans. Then again, you have the gift of night sight, and we don't, so I suppose that evens everything out."

"Evens?"

"I'm sorry, it's a Human expression."

"I assume," said Zhura, "that you could use this colour to pick future mages?"

"Yes, that's correct. Our race has difficulty when it comes to determining those with the capacity to use magic. We waste years on people who prove to have no aptitude for such things."

"It is the same way with Orcs," said Kurghal. "Life would be so much easier if we could locate those who carried the gift."

Aubrey smiled. "I should be delighted to share what I've learned. Hopefully, together, we could find a way of putting such doubts to rest."

"I would welcome such a sharing, but it is Zhura who would likely be of more use. She is the one who can see these auras you speak of."

"I shall assist in whatever way I can," offered Zhura.

They drew closer to the army, and then Zhura's face lit up. Urgon stood waiting, Kraloch by his side, but as his bondmate approached, the chieftain stepped forward to embrace her.

"Welcome," called out Kraloch. "It has been some time since I have seen you, Kurghal."

"And yet we speak regularly," replied the shamaness.

"*And there she is*," said Kraloch, temporarily switching to the Human tongue. "*The same old Kurghal.*"

"What did you say?"

"I was merely expressing my delight at your arrival for our Human friends' benefit."

Aubrey struggled to keep a straight face. "I'll let you settle in."

At that precise moment, a trio of wolves padded up to her, sniffing the hem of her dress. She looked down in fascination. "What have we here?"

Zhura turned but kept ahold of Urgon's hand. "Those three came with me. I am surprised you are not alarmed. Wolves are considered dangerous creatures amongst Humans, are they not?"

Aubrey knelt, petting the animals. "I spent some time in Albreda's domain, so I'm well used to them."

"Albreda? The Witch of the Whitewood?"

"You've heard of her?"

"I have. Kraloch tells me our distant cousin, Andurak, came seeking her. I believe I might know why."

The Life Mage looked up in surprise. "You do?"

"Yes, but perhaps that is a topic best left until we meet with your queen."

"I shall tell her you're ready. In the meantime, I'm sure Kraloch can fill you in on everything you need to know." Aubrey halted, then blushed. "I'm sorry, I imagine he's already kept you up to date. It's so strange, getting used to all this spirit talking."

"You may tell Her Majesty we are available to talk at her earliest convenience."

Kraloch led Urgon and Zhura to the Royal Pavilion, where the guards, posted on either side of the entrance, appeared unfazed by the sight of the ghostwalker.

The shaman halted before entering. "If it is too much for you to bear, Zhura, you must be sure to let us know. The queen is aware of your sensitivity to spirits and will not be upset if you feel the need to leave us."

"I understand," she replied, "but there is little to fear at present—the voices have been stilled."

"You may proceed," said Urgon.

Kraloch pulled the tent flap aside, allowing them access. Urgon stepped through, his bondmate's hand held tightly in his. Zhura pulled up short as soon as her eyes beheld the queen.

"Is something wrong?" said Urgon.

She squinted. "The queen's aura is unnaturally bright as if lit by a hundred torches."

Those gathered stared back but said nothing.

"My pardon, Majesty," said Zhura. "I had not expected your aura to be so intense."

Anna looked at Aubrey, but the young woman only shrugged. "I told you."

"Welcome, Zhura," said the queen in Orcish. "We are honoured by your presence."

"*It is I who am honoured,*" replied the ghostwalker, using the common tongue of Humans, before switching back to her native Orcish. "Tell me if you would, do all your people speak our language?"

In answer, the young queen turned to the oldest man present. "Gerald?"

"We thought it wise to adopt your language within our army, at least for any written communication. In this manner, any intercepted dispatches would be unreadable to our enemies."

Zhura eyed him. "And you are?"

"He is Gerald Matheson," said Urgon, "Marshal of the Royal Army and a good and loyal friend. It was he who came to Ord-Dugath along with Redblade and the queen, although, of course, she was only a princess at the time."

"Your village welcomed us warmly," said Gerald, "and your people have proven to be valued allies."

A large dog pushed its way past the queen, moving towards Zhura. In return, she reached out, letting him sniff her hand.

"And who is this?" she asked.

"Tempus," said the queen. "He's a Kurathian Mastiff, a type of dog bred for war, but he's my friend."

Zhura smiled. "I, too, have friends of this nature. Urgon is the master of wolves as well as the chieftain of our people, so I am constantly surrounded by wolves."

"She even brought a trio with her," added Urgon, "but we thought it best to leave them in the camp, along with her escort."

"And Kurghal?" said Anna.

"Resting. She is several years our senior and is feeling the effects of her age."

"I can sympathize with that," said Gerald.

"While this talk is pleasant enough," began Zhura, "there are more pressing matters that need our attention. With your permission, Majesty, I should like to talk of what I discovered."

"Of course," said the queen. "You may proceed at your own leisure."

"As a ghostwalker, I dwell in the twilight world that exists between the living and the dead. As such, I see and hear what transpires in both. It also permits me to communicate with those who came before us in a way that a mere spell could not. This has allowed me, over the years, to develop a good understanding of those creatures that make up the spirit realm."

She took a breath, then continued. "You have, I am told, become aware an army of spirits marches across the land. Our shamans are unable to contact the Ancestors as they once did, and I can now affirm that they have, in fact, vanished. The real question, however, is why?"

"We've been pondering the very same question," said Aubrey. "What are your thoughts on the matter?"

"A creature of the spirit world has manifested in the land of the living, likely brought about by the application of dark magic."

The queen was enthralled. "By what name is this creature known?"

"A Volgath," said Zhura. "A being much like me, living its life on the border between living and dead. The big difference between us is that I was born a living creature, whereas the Volgath was created using the spirit of someone who passed to the realm of the dead."

"Volgath," said Urgon. "That sounds ominous."

"And it is," she agreed. "Such creatures were, in life, those with strong wills. In death, they linger in the spirit world until summoned by one with access to dark magic."

"Like a Necromancer?" said the queen. "We know there were at least two operating within the Norland court."

"Two?" said Gerald. "I thought there was only one, and he went by the name of Jendrick?"

"You forget what we discovered near Oaksvale," said Aubrey. "Beverly and I found evidence of the use of Blood Magic."

"What makes these Volgaths so dangerous?" asked Gerald.

"In life, they were strong individuals," explained Zhura, "with a will to accomplish great things. In death, they linger, the very thing that served them in life acting to prolong their spirit. Their minds, you see, are still strong, their memories intact, making them extremely valuable to those who would enslave them. A Death Mage can control spirits, that is true, but each spirit so enslaved becomes a drain on the Necromancer's power. A Volgath, however, is capable of a great deal more control over such minions."

"So you believe a Volgath controls this spirit army?"

Zhura nodded. "And they would retain whatever knowledge they had in life, making them that much more powerful."

"How would a Necromancer control such a creature?" asked Aubrey.

"The Death Mage who summoned such a Volgath would control the Volgath's spirit, essentially anchoring it. It is a clever tactic, for if the creature turned on whoever summoned it, the link would be broken, and the Volgath returned to the spirit realm."

"How do we stop such a creature?"

"It cannot be stopped, only returned to its old haunt—the realm of spirits."

"And how do we do that?"

"As I said earlier, the creature is bound to the physical world through a spirit anchor, held by the summoner. Kill that Necromancer, and the link will be broken."

"Not an easy task," said the queen. "We suspect Lady Penelope is behind all of this, and she hasn't been seen for years."

"Would she be accompanying this army of spirits?" asked Gerald.

"I doubt it," said Zhura. "For to do so would expose her to great danger. Instead, she will likely be miles away."

"This is not the greatest of news," said Gerald. "Are you sure there is no other way to destroy this thing?"

"There is one, but it involves getting close to the Volgath."

"How close?"

"Close enough to engage it in combat."

"Can normal weapons even damage it?"

"It does have a mortal presence," explained Zhura. "Destroy that, and its link to the material world will vanish."

"But couldn't the Necromancer simply re-summon it?" asked Aubrey.

"Only if they were present to do so."

"Let me get this straight," said Gerald. "If we destroy this body, it would be sent back to where it came from?"

"The body must be completely destroyed, but yes, you are correct."

"How does one completely destroy a body?"

"Fire?" suggested Aubrey.

"How about a magical weapon?" came Beverly's voice. They all turned to see the red-headed knight. "Sorry I'm late. I've been getting my new command organized for the march."

"Redblade," said Zhura. "Your fame precedes you."

Beverly bowed. "Pleased to meet you. Did someone say something about destroying a body?"

"Yes," said Aubrey. "Zhura here believes the spirit army is controlled by something called a Volgath. If we can destroy its host body, it'll be forced back to the spirit world."

"You mentioned something about a magic weapon?" said Zhura.

The knight produced her hammer. "This is called Nature's Fury. Albreda empowered it with the force of nature."

"I have heard of this Albreda. I believe she may be the key to our problem."

"That is what Andurak said," noted Kraloch, "yet we still do not know how."

Zhura looked at Tempus. "Creatures such as this possess a spirit, one that serves to calm the dead that are close by."

Gerald wore a puzzled look. "I'm afraid you lost me there."

"As I mentioned earlier, I see spirits all around me, or at least I did before they vanished. Over the years, I came to discover wolves have a calming effect on the Ancestors. Likely Tempus would have a similar effect."

She looked around, but few could follow the logic. Her gaze fell on Gerald. "You, of all people, should understand."

"Me? Why me?"

"The grey wolf resides inside you."

The marshal paled. "Who told you about the grey wolf?"

"No one. I can see it for myself."

"Remember the mastiffs?" said Anna. "They're always calm when you're around."

"I just have a way with dogs," said Gerald, "that's all."

"No," said Zhura, "it is more than that. Your spirit is entwined with that of a wolf. Andurak's tribe believes such a bond is a special gift, a spiritual link if you will."

"I still don't see the significance here."

"Kraloch, you mastered the spell that conjures forth spirit warriors, correct?"

"I have," replied the shaman.

"The link you share with those conjured warriors is not unlike that of the grey wolf. In many ways, it emulates that between the Volgath and its victims. The only real difference is the Volgath's link is not voluntary, but forced."

"You talked earlier of a calming influence," said Kraloch. "Could this behaviour be used against a Volgath?"

"Not directly," said Zhura, "but it might serve to limit the control over its minions."

"In what way?"

"Such control requires concentration. Imagine you are trying to skin a deer, but people keep interrupting you. You can likely still complete the task, but more time and effort would be required."

"So we'd be forcing him to concentrate more on his control," said Gerald, "and less on his tactics?"

"So I believe."

"Great," said Gerald. "So all we must do is fight our way through an army of spirits, find this Volgath, and have Beverly destroy it with Nature's Fury. And here I thought it would be something difficult!"

"Now, now," soothed the queen. "No one said it was going to be easy."

"There's a big difference between difficult and impossible. We don't even know where this army is, AND we still need to deal with Bronwyn, as well as the last of the Norland earls." He calmed himself. "It's not your fault, Zhura. I'm sorry I lost my temper."

"Your frustration is understandable," the ghostwalker replied, "but it at least offers hope, even if it is somewhat small. As to the army, it draws nearer."

The queen moved closer. "How can you possibly know that?"

"I, too, am a creature of the spirit world, and I can feel its call."

"Tell me," said Gerald, "can a Necromancer summon the spirits of the recently deceased?"

"Of course."

"And in order to do so, would they need to be close to the location of that person's death?"

"They would. When someone dies, their link to the spirit realm, their anchor, if you will, is the body they held in life. This vanishes in time, allowing the spirit to become free to wander."

"How much time?" asked Gerald.

"A season at the very least. Why do you ask?"

"One of the problems we face is that any defeat will create a supply of spirits for our enemies to entrap. If we were to hold the field of battle, however, they would be unable to summon them, wouldn't they?"

Zhura smiled. "I can see no fault in your logic."

"And just to make sure I'm not making the biggest mistake of my life, a spirit warrior can be destroyed, correct?"

"Destroyed is perhaps a poor choice of words. Destroying what exists in the material world will send the spirit back to its native domain. In effect, you are banishing it, but the result is the same."

"Could such a spirit be summoned once more?"

"Yes, but it would require a ritual, hardly the type of thing one could do under battlefield conditions."

Anna looked at her marshal. "What are you thinking, Gerald?"

"It seems to me the key to defeating this army is remaining in control of the battlefield. If we can do that, we can deny them reinforcements, at least in the short term. The only real problem will be getting close to this Volgath."

"The bigger problem," said Aubrey, "is how we convince the living to fight the spirits of the dead? Most people would be far too terrified to do such a thing."

"The men will stand," insisted Gerald, "because they know there's no other choice. If they flee, the entire army will disintegrate, and with it, any hope of Merceria surviving."

"My Orcs do not fear the spirits," added Urgon. "They will stand and fight, I assure you."

"Good," said the queen, "because it sounds like it won't be long before we're forced to make a stand."

ELEVEN

Ironcliff

SUMMER 965 MC

"I see crops," said Revi. "We must be getting close to Ironcliff."

Before them, the rock-strewn terrain gave way to greener pastures and, off in the distance, were the first signs of cultivated fields. Standing in amongst them at regular intervals were stone towers, jutting out of the land, giving the place an odd appearance.

"What in the name of Saxnor are those things for?" asked Arnim. "They certainly don't seem very imposing."

"Let's find out, shall we?" Revi closed his eyes, beginning the incantation that would connect him to his familiar. Moments later, he was soaring through the sky, his mind seeing through Shellbreaker's eyes.

"There are people in those towers," he said. "Dwarves, by all appearances."

"So they must be on the lookout for something. Are they defensive in nature?"

"Not that I can tell. Maybe it's only a watchtower?"

"Made of stone?" said Arnim. "Why would anyone go to that extreme when a simple wooden construction would suffice? It must have taken months to build those things. How tall are they?"

"No more than twenty feet, and they're fairly narrow."

"How narrow?"

"I would say scarcely ten feet across at the base."

They were soon spotted as they continued their approach. Field workers ran towards the mountain that rose to the north, and then horns sounded from the towers.

"It appears it's a warning system," said the mage.

"You don't need to point out the obvious, Revi. I can hear that for myself."

"Perhaps we should stop?"

In answer, Arnim turned to his riders. "Captain Ruzak, halt the column."

The men halted their advance, and then he wheeled back to his companion. "Well? What do you suggest we do now?"

"Wait," said Revi. "We'll let them make the first move. I shouldn't like to alarm them."

They sat in silence as the sun grew higher. By all rights, it should have been quite warm, but the wind brought a chill from the mountains, and Arnim pulled his cloak tighter.

"How long do you reckon this is going to take?" he asked.

"Not long, now," said the mage, his head dipping and swaying as he peered through his familiar's eyes. "There's a group of them heading towards us. Just be patient."

Arnim stared to the east, finally spotting their hosts, armoured in chainmail and armed with an assortment of axes and hammers, their shields emblazoned with a lightning bolt.

"There looks to be about a hundred of them," said Revi.

"So I see. The real question is whether or not they're hostile."

The Dwarves marched in a tight formation, most likely leery of the presence of the horsemen. They were an impressive sight, reminding Arnim of those from Stonecastle, who had proven so effective in battle. They moved up beside one of the small towers, then halted.

The Mercerians waited, but no one came forth to welcome them. Arnim was about to suggest they ride forward in an attempt to engage the group, but then Revi interrupted him.

"There's more coming," said the mage, "and this new group looks... unusual."

"Unusual? Can you be more specific?"

"They're covered in armour."

"So are the ones to our front."

"No," said Revi. "I mean, they're completely encased in metal. I've never seen anything like it."

"Our knights wear plates of steel over their chainmail."

"Yes, but this is different—the steel is fully articulated. I wonder what our smiths would make of it?"

Arnim chuckled. "I daresay Aldwin would like to get his hands on some."

"Or Herdwin, for that matter. Say, do you suppose the Dwarves of Stonecastle have such armour?"

"If they do," said Arnim, "they certainly didn't share it with us. How many of these extra warriors are there?"

"About fifty," replied Revi, "and it looks like someone important is with them."

"How can you tell?"

"Whoever it is, appears to be wearing gold armour."

"That's rather impractical, isn't it?"

"I'm sure it's not made entirely of gold."

"Still," insisted Arnim, "it's got to be an expensive proposition, don't you think? How are these newcomers armed?"

"With axes mounted on long handles."

"How long?"

"Like a spear?"

"So, poleaxes, then."

Revi broke his concentration, opening his eyes to stare at his companion. "How do you know about poleaxes?"

"It's an axe on a pole—what else would you call it?"

They watched as the new group took up a position to the right of the first batch.

"Should we approach them?" said Revi.

"I'm game if you are."

"Any suggestions on how to proceed?"

"Yes, I would suggest we dismount. Dwarves might not take kindly to us looking down on them from on horseback."

They both dismounted, moving towards the line of warriors.

"Shouldn't you cast your spell of tongues?" said Arnim. "We WILL need to understand what they're saying for this to work."

"I'm not about to start casting a spell with that lot looking on. They might take it as an attack."

"I suppose that's a reasonable assumption."

They approached to within thirty paces, then halted.

"*We come in peace,*" called out Arnim in the Dwarven tongue.

Revi looked at him in surprise. "I didn't know you spoke their language."

"That's because you spend so much time hiding away behind your books."

In answer, the gold-plated warrior stepped out from amongst the defenders' ranks. In typical Dwarven fashion, a helmet hid any features, save for the flowing brown beard that hung in braids from beneath the chin. The warrior approached, halting only five paces away.

"Go back to your home," said the Dwarf, using the common tongue, "and tell Lord Calder his intrusions will no longer be tolerated."

"We are not servants of Lord Calder," said Revi, "but rather Queen Anna of Merceria."

The warrior stood stock still, although what was on the Dwarf's mind was impossible to fathom. "Merceria?"

"Yes, we claim friendship with the Dwarves of Stonecastle. Do you know them?"

"We know OF them," came the reply, "but Stonecastle lies far to the south. Why are you here?"

"We seek an audience with your king."

"Oh, you do, do you? And why would you wish to see our king?"

"We are at war with Norland," said Revi, "and would seek the friendship of your people."

"You waste your time," said the Dwarf. "King Thalgrun has no reason to trust the word of Humans."

"Then let him say that to our faces."

"What are you proposing?"

"Take us to your king, and leave it for him to decide. To prove our intentions are honourable, we shall leave our weapons here."

"We will?" said Arnim.

Revi gave him a dirty look, then returned his attention to the Dwarf. "I assure you we wish only to speak."

The Dwarf stepped forward, and Arnim was surprised to see the face of a female as she removed her helmet. For a moment, he wondered if he had imagined the beard, then he saw it dangling from the bottom of the helmet and understood.

"I am Kasri Ironheart," said the Dwarf. "Let me take you to my father, King Thalgrun Stormhammer."

"Greetings. I am Revi Bloom, Royal Life Mage and Enchanter of the Court of Wincaster. This is Arnim Caster, Viscount Haverston."

"I'm surprised your queen would allow her mage to travel so far. Are mages that common in Merceria?"

"We have a number of them. Why, have you none of your own?"

"Oh, we have a mage," said Kasri. "A master of rock and stone, to be precise. He goes by the name Agramath. Have you heard tell of him?"

"I'm afraid we know little of the Dwarven lands," said Revi, "but I should very much like to meet him."

The Dwarf chuckled. "And unless I miss my guess, he'll feel the same way. Now come, let us be away from here, and I will show you the hospitality of Ironcliff."

. . .

Captain Ruzak and the Kurathian horsemen remained in the fields while Kasri led Arnim and Revi past the gathered warriors.

"Tell me," said Arnim, "how does that armour of yours work?"

"I'm not sure what you're asking. It's much like any other armour—you wear it, and it protects you from harm."

"No, I mean, how do the joints allow you to move? The metal isn't flexible, is it?"

"Are you a smith?" she asked.

"No."

"Then I doubt you'd understand the intricacies of plate armour. Suffice it to say, it distributes the weight perfectly well while allowing a high degree of mobility."

"How long have you had such armour?"

"Close to a century, now. Do you not have something similar back in Merceria?"

"No," said Arnim. "We only recently began placing plates of steel over our chainmail."

"You'd best learn quickly, then. The entire Continent has the knowledge of it these days."

"The Continent?"

"Yes," she said. "Haven't you heard of it?"

"Of course I have, but it's far across the sea."

She halted, pointing eastward. "The Continent is right there, beyond the mouth of this valley."

Arnim looked as though someone had slapped him. "Truly?"

The Dwarf mistook his reply. "Are you calling me a liar?"

"No, not at all. You must excuse my ignorance, but Merceria is cut off from the east by the mountains. We know little of the world beyond our shores."

"Despite that, you said you'd heard of it."

"Naturally, our ancestors came from there by ship."

"Ah," said Kasri. "That explains a lot."

They were getting closer to the mountain now, revealing an immensely long set of stairs that led up to a massive iron gate.

"This," said the Dwarf, "is the main entrance to Ironcliff. There are more hidden entrances, of course, but we only let visitors use this one." She looked at them with an apologetic look. "Not that we get many, you understand."

"You said your father is the king," said Revi. "What can you tell us about him?"

"He's ruled for nigh on a hundred years," said Kasri. "We have always been a wealthy folk when it comes to the riches of the mountains, but he brought us even greater wealth through trade. Until Lord Calder came along, that is."

"How long ago did the earl start becoming a problem?"

"Ten years, give or take a few months. He succeeded to the earldom after the death of his father. Unfortunately, the son was not nearly as forward-thinking as his predecessor. Instead, he looked to our wealth with greed, trying to extract payment from us in return for his warriors leaving us alone."

"I don't imagine that went over well."

"It did not. Of course, there wasn't much he could do about it. We halted all trade with his people, but then he started sending horsemen to raid our fields. We ended up building those warning towers as part of our defences."

"So you're not afraid he'll attack you directly?"

"These are Dwarven walls," said Kasri, "moulded from the very rock itself. There's no Human alive who could breach them." She paused as she reached the bottom of the stairs. "We'll head inside now, shall we?"

Arnim looked up at the long stairway, suddenly feeling his age. They began their ascent, but it turned out he needn't have worried. Built for Dwarves, the steps were fairly shallow, although there were an inordinate number of them. Consequently, the climb wasn't nearly as exhausting as he would have thought. At the top, they found several guards, but seeing Kasri was with them, they paid little attention to the unknown visitors.

"Notice the walls?" said Revi.

"How could I not?" countered Arnim.

"No, I mean the construction. There's no sign of individual blocks."

"How is that even possible?"

"Earth Magic," offered Kasri. "Of course, over the years, they added some artistry to make it look nice. I'm particularly fond of the false arches on the outside. They hide the murder holes quite effectively, don't you think?"

Through the doors they went, entering a massive hall with columns on either side, rising high into the darkness above, leaving Revi guessing how high the ceiling truly was. They were within the very rock of the mountain now, with sconces attached to the pillars illuminating the way, casting flickering light off the floor, which appeared to be made of highly polished rock.

"I imagine it must have taken generations to make this," said Revi.

"The great hall of Ironcliff dates back more than three thousand years. Back then, we weren't nearly as prosperous as we are today, but they could still work wonders with stone."

"Was this done with magic?"

"No, by skilled artisans," said Kasri. "Don't get me wrong, our mages are more than capable of manipulating stone, but it takes an artist to do this kind of work. The skill of stone cutting is highly prized amongst our people."

They passed by at least a dozen pillars before an ornately carved set of double doors came into view, guarded by two warriors wearing golden armour, much like Kasri's, although slightly less decorative.

"These Humans are here to see the king," she announced.

The guards nodded, then one stood aside while the other leaned upon one of the doors. Revi marvelled at the construction as it swung open at the slightest touch. In Wincaster, the wooden doors would often become stuck, necessitating a shoulder push, but these works of art had no such problem.

King Thalgrun's throne room was enormous, easily three times that of Merceria. The pillars here supported a raised balcony upon which resided a few well-dressed Dwarves, presumably members of the elite. At the far end of the room, the king sat upon a throne carved from blue marble. His luxurious robes were of the finest material, but even more impressive was his long, grey beard, twisted into two braids interlaced with silver wire that fell across his lap to cover his knees. Partially hidden by this growth was an ancient face, with bushy eyebrows atop eyes the colour of coal peering out at them.

Kasri halted. "Father," she said, "I bring you visitors. May I present Revi Bloom, Royal Mage of Merceria, and Lord Arnim Caster, Viscount of Haverston."

The king leaned forward on his throne, motioning for them all to advance. They stepped closer until they were only three paces from him.

"What brings you to Ironcliff?" he asked.

"We come bearing greetings from Queen Anna of Merceria," said Revi.

"Of course you do, but let's get straight to the point, shall we? Why are you really here?"

"To seek your assistance," replied the mage.

"Ah, now we have the truth of it."

"These men are at war with Norland," said Kasri.

The king arched his eyebrows. "Are they, now? That's a most interesting development, and one I hadn't expected. Tell me, if you will, Mage, what started this war?"

"Norland invaded our realm last year," replied Revi. "We managed to push them back to their border and then marched into Norland to put an end to their raiding, once and for all."

"So they raided you as well? I suppose I should have expected that from them."

"I'm led to understand they've been raiding your farms hereabouts?"

"They have, indeed, but without cavalry, we're unable to bring them to battle."

"These people have horsemen," added Kasri.

The king's gaze grew even more intense. "How many horsemen?"

"One hundred Kurathians," offered Arnim. "Have you heard of them before?"

"I have, indeed, for who has not? Their prowess on the battlefield is legendary."

"We could work together to defeat Lord Calder and his army if you're willing?"

"That's an interesting thought." King Thalgrun turned to a group of Dwarves, who stood nearby, surely advisors if their clothes were any indication. "Fetch Agramath. I would value his opinion of these Mercerians."

The command was relayed down the great hall, and then the king returned his attention to his visitors. "I will consider your proposal, but know this, there will be a price. A shadow grows in the east, one which threatens our very existence. I have no doubt a day will come when we shall be hard pressed to defend these hallowed halls. I need a guarantee you would come to our aid should my prophecy prove true."

"Begging your pardon, Your Majesty," said Arnim, "but how do you know you can trust us?"

"I've heard of your dealings with our cousins in Stonecastle. This queen of yours is not completely unknown to us."

"And this eastern threat, any idea when it might attack?"

"Not for some time yet," replied King Thalgrun. "Their eyes are diverted away from us for the moment, but mark my words, one day we will have their undivided attention."

"You called for me, Majesty?"

The Dwarf who entered the hall carried a large staff topped by a green emerald pulsing with light. He was much younger than the king, so much so there was only a touch of grey to his hair, which was otherwise red.

"Ah," said Thalgrun. "Allow me to introduce you to Agramath, our master of rock and stone."

"How may I be of service?" said the mage.

"These humans came all the way from Merceria seeking our help. I should like you to get to know them and see if you judge them trustworthy."

"And they are?"

"Revi Bloom," said the Life Mage, "and this is my comrade, Arnim Caster."

"Then follow me," said Agramath, "and we shall find someplace more comfortable to talk."

He led them from the hall, taking a side entrance that led into the heart of the mountain.

"I hope you don't mind," the Dwarf said. "The court is no place for informal discussions, and my study will allow us to escape the eyes of the guild masters."

"Guild masters?" said Arnim.

"Oh yes, don't you know? Dwarven society is controlled by the guilds. They poke their noses in everywhere."

They passed by an open doorway guarded by two Dwarves in gold armour. Inside, Revi saw someone cleaning what looked like a magic circle.

"Is that what I think it is?" he asked.

"If you mean a circle of earth, then yes, that's precisely what it is."

"We have circles similar to that in Merceria."

"You have more than one?" said the Dwarf. "That surprises me. I didn't know you Humans had such mastery of magic."

"They're a recent addition. Albreda introduced them to us."

"The Witch of the Whitewood?"

"Yes. You know her?"

"Not personally, but her reputation is well known amongst my people. She is said to be most powerful. Are you saying you count her as a friend?"

"Indeed," said Revi. "She's been a great help these last few years."

"Who are these guards?" asked Arnim, eager to change the subject. "They wear armour like Kasri."

"Of course they do," said Agramath. "She commands them. What you see here is the Hearth Guard, made up of our most experienced veterans—"

"Tell me," interrupted the Life Mage, "are you familiar with the spell of recall?"

"It's not a spell I've mastered and would be of little use to me in any event, seeing as how we only have the one circle. Why?"

"We regularly use it to move between cities. We even have the ability to travel to the capital of our ally, Weldwyn."

"Never heard of it," said Agramath, "though your talk of recall intrigues me. I assume you're a mage?"

"Yes, a Life Mage, to be exact."

"Then come, let us continue to my study. There is much to discuss."

"Oh great," grumbled Arnim. "Just what I needed—another long, boring discussion about magic."

TWELVE

Bronwyn

The troops moved forward in a line, but the flanks lagged, sending the whole formation into disarray.

"I don't like it," said Sir Greyson. "The men are slow to respond."

"Maybe it's their training?" mused Bronwyn.

The knight looked at her with some annoyance but quickly hid it. "It takes time to train men in the art of war."

"Dame Beverly managed it well enough. Could it be your methods that are lacking?"

"I might remind you we no longer have Mercerian troops to set an example."

"Are you saying you're not up to the task?"

He bristled. "I can assure you I'll make these men into the best warriors in Norland, Princess. I merely need more time."

"Time is a luxury we don't have. General Fitzwilliam will be keen to punish us after our betrayal. Don't think for one moment he'll let us stay here for long."

"Then we'll train them on the march. In truth, it might be a better alternative anyway."

"What makes you say that?"

"They were pressed into service, Highness. Taking them away from their homes will allow them to concentrate on their training instead of being distracted by their families."

"But won't that increase the chance of desertions?"

"Perhaps," said the knight, "but making examples of one or two will quickly dissuade them from trying."

"Examples?"

"Yes. The punishment for desertion is death."

"So you would execute the very people who will be my subjects?"

"What choice have we? We require an army, Your Highness, and we need it quickly before the Mercerians catch us. If I had it my way, we'd take even more."

"We can hardly train the men we have," countered the princess.

"These villagers are, at best, a peasant levy, and as such, we must rely on numbers. I say we arm them with whatever is at hand and take them all."

"And how do we feed them?"

"We live off the land, as did our ancestors. The farms in these parts have enough grain to feed an army."

"But you would be taking food from the families of the very men you're pressing into service."

"Such is the burden of war, Highness. I know this will be hard on those left behind, but surely their sacrifice is worth it to place you on the throne?"

"How many men have we at present?" asked Bronwyn.

"The debacle at Galburn's Ridge cost us dearly."

"How many?" she demanded.

"Not including these new recruits, our army now stands at less than three hundred."

"And if you press the entire village into service?"

"I could easily add another hundred and fifty."

"Then do so. Have we the wherewithal to equip them?"

"There's no armour," said Sir Greyson, "but I've had the local smiths working on spears since we arrived. Give me a few more days, and they'll be ready to march, although I wouldn't expect them to be ready for battle for another week or so."

"I can't guarantee they won't be needed sooner. The Mercerians will be eager for revenge, but there is another option," said Bronwyn. "What if we marched north?"

"That's the domain of Lord Calder."

"True, but the north is open country, and Calder will soon be busy dealing with the Mercerians."

"Say we do go north, what then?"

"We recruit," said the princess. "We can tell everyone we're raising troops on Calder's behalf."

"The idea has merit were it not for one simple problem."

"Which is?"

"As soon as the men mingle with our current troops, they'll realize they were lied to."

"Then tell our men Calder is our ally."

"But he's not!"

The Norland princess persisted. "They don't need to know that."

"They'll find out soon enough if we meet him in battle."

"And should that time come, we'll tell them the earl has betrayed his country. Tell me, Sir Greyson, do any of the people hereabouts even know the names of the earls?"

"They would know their own liege lord, certainly, but I doubt any of them give any thought to the others. They are a simple folk, Highness, more concerned with their crops than the intrigues of court."

"Then we shall take advantage of that. Gather the men. We march to Eastly."

"And then?"

"Then I will decide whether to march northeast or northwest. I'm hoping we'll receive further news regarding the war by the time we arrive."

"And if not?"

"Then we march into the heart of the north, to Hakenell. That gives us the least chance of running into any Mercerians."

"I had no idea you were such a strategist, Your Highness."

"I may not be trained in the art of war, but I grew up surrounded by my grandfather's maps. I know this country, Sir Greyson, and the Mercerians lack any knowledge of the area. That will enable us to gain the upper hand over them."

The knight looked at the practice field. "And these new recruits?"

"We'll take them with us." She turned to face Greyson. "It's all up to you now, General. Prove to me you're worthy of my trust."

"I shall do all I can, Highness. I promise you."

A week later, they were on the road, with what remained of their cavalry leading the way, followed by the footmen. The archers, more accustomed to operating on their own, brought up the rear.

Sir Greyson had pushed the new recruits as much as he dared. It was a tricky balancing act, for treating them too harshly would lead to desertions, while leniency would do little to prepare them for the grim realities of war.

He watched the men as they marched past. The smiths of Chilmsford had done their best, but a lack of iron meant most of their new soldiers were armed with little more than pitchforks or flails. His hope was Eastly would be better equipped to handle such requests, but he would just have to wait and see.

Bronwyn rode up beside him. "They appear to be in good spirits."

"Yes, surprising, really. Many of these men rose in rebellion to fight against oppression. Now they're the very men they fought so hard to oppose."

"I assume you had no trouble securing the food?"

"That was the least of my problems. I simply had the men from down south collect the food. They have no family in town, so there was little sympathy for the locals. It's really amazing when you think about it. Starve a man for a few days, and he'll do almost anything to eat."

"And how long will the supplies last?"

"They'll get us to Eastly, but I wouldn't count on them lasting more than a week."

"I expected longer."

"I'm afraid the earl already extracted his tribute, and the crops aren't due in for some time yet." He gazed back at the distant town of Chilmsford. "I shouldn't like to go back there anytime soon. They'll be starving by month's end."

"Sacrifices must be made if we are to be victorious, and the best way to reward that sacrifice is by defeating the enemy. We can't do that without food. Are you having second thoughts about this?"

"No," said Sir Greyson. "They are nothing but peasants. It's their lot in life to suffer."

"Good. Now, turn your attention to Eastly."

"Has it a garrison?"

"Only a militia," said Bronwyn, "and that's likely been sent off to help the earl. I expect we'll be able to march into the town with little in the way of opposition, particularly once I make my presence known."

A yell from the front of the column drew their gaze to a small group of horsemen who approached from the north, doubtless the return of a scouting group. They soon drew close enough to make out faces, and Sir Greyson relaxed, recognizing the warriors.

Halting before the princess, one of them spoke up, "Your Highness, General, we must report troops along the road."

"What types of troops?" asked the knight.

"Unknown, my lord. They carried no flag that I could recognize."

"And how many were there?"

"Several hundred, at least, including cavalry."

"Could the Mercerians have gotten ahead of us?" asked Bronwyn.

"Unlikely," said Sir Greyson. "This is the only road in the area."

"Maybe Lord Calder, then?"

"Anything is possible, I suppose. With your permission, Highness, I'll ride out under a flag of truce, and hopefully, we'll get to the bottom of this."

"By all means," said the princess, "but be on the alert for any sign of treachery. We were already double-crossed at Galburn's Ridge. I'm not eager to repeat that ordeal."

Sir Greyson turned his attention to his men. "Lead on," he ordered, "and let's see this army you speak of."

The road topped a gentle hill, and then the knight halted, for off in the distance, he saw the threat, and he had to admit the sight was an imposing one. Footmen lined up along the road, with archers on either side, while behind them waited a mass of horsemen. Granted, not the most original of formations, but it was pretty typical of Norland forces. He was about to conclude Lord Calder had arrived, but then the wind caught one of the banners, allowing it to stream to the side and reveal its colours. Icy fear gripped his heart as he recognized the Royal Banner of Weldwyn.

"Saxnor's beard," he said. "The Westlanders must have marched clear round the Windstorm Depths."

A stench drifted to his nostrils, and he wrinkled his nose. "What is that smell?"

"It's coming from those troops, sir."

Even as they watched, the men of the west began to advance.

"We must return to the column," said the knight. "It's time to put our men to the test."

The army waited. Sir Greyson, having ridden up and down in front of the warriors, returned to Bronwyn's side.

"Are you sure they'll hold?" she asked.

"They have little choice, Highness. The enemy cavalry would tear them apart if they ran."

Off in the distance, they could barely make out the enemy, marching down the road with their cavalry now on either flank. Sir Greyson glanced back at his own thin line anchored on either side by some trees. He had deployed his horses on the right, hoping to counter the enemy threat, but as they drew nearer, his hopes started to fade. He turned to the princess.

"Your Highness, we are badly outnumbered. Given the circumstances, I would suggest you flee. I'll dispatch some riders to escort you, but you must leave now."

"Can we not beat them?"

"We are outnumbered more than two to one," said Sir Greyson.

"Nevertheless, I shall stand with my warriors."

The sun disappeared behind some clouds, and the enemy warriors appeared to glow with a ghostly sheen.

"What in the Gods' name?" he cursed out.

"Those horses," said the princess, pointing, "there's something not quite right about them."

He stared at the Westland horse, who trotted along slowly, keeping pace with the footmen, but the movement looked unnatural. "They're in perfect step," he said. "How can that even be possible?"

As they drew closer, and he beheld their ghostly visage, he turned pale, struggling to come to grips with what he saw before him. Just then, a stench so foul permeated the air, and many of the Norland rebels vomited while the remainder stared north at the spectral army.

Bronwyn gasped, and then the unholy army surged forward, making directly for them. The rebel forces, unable to bear the thought of such terror, broke and ran. Some streamed down the road, back towards Chilmsford, while others headed due east, frantic to escape the clutches of the army of spirits.

A few stalwart souls grouped around their princess in a desperate bid to keep her safe, withdrawing to the southeast while maintaining their order. Sir Greyson, meanwhile, rode off to join his horsemen, desperate to rally them and keep some semblance of order.

Bronwyn watched in horror as the ghosts overwhelmed her army. Men threw down their weapons, trying to avoid slaughter, but the enemy was relentless. She saw ghostly horses trample down an entire company of militia. A few brave souls tried to fight back but were quickly overwhelmed. Blood flowed like a river, and she felt the bile rise in her throat. Even worse were the screams, not only of her own men but those of the enemy—a high, keening wail that shook her to her very bones.

Men ran as quickly as they could, but the army of the dead was faster. Unencumbered by the limitations of flesh and bone, they easily outpaced the rebels, slaying all before them.

A group of spirit horsemen struck Bronwyn's guard, and she heard the clattering of steel on steel as her men fought back. That was when she realized these spirits had a mortal form. The men around her were the pick of her forces, yet even so, they paled in comparison to the fury of their enemy.

A spirit horseman broke through their line, coming close enough to threaten Bronwyn herself. She recoiled in terror, and then Sir Greyson was there, leading a countercharge by some of the rebel horse. She saw spirits dissipate, their physical forms destroyed by the ferocity of the attack, yet even more approached from the north.

Glancing to the west, she hoped to see her army making a stand, but all that remained was a horde of ghosts surrounding those who were left, slaughtering them.

Her horse, wild with fear, reared up, throwing her from the saddle. A group of mortal horsemen rode past, crashing into the enemy, and then her own guards grabbed her by the arms, dragging her off. She heard screaming and then the agonizing death wails of dozens of men as the ghosts descended upon them.

Bronwyn broke free and ran as fast as her legs could carry her. There was no more throne, no more kingdom to save, only the instinct to survive against impossible odds.

She crashed through the trees, felt branches cut her face in her haste to escape. Behind her, the sounds dimmed, although the high-pitched keening continued unabated.

Her group finally emerged from the trees, and she looked around, trying to get her bearings. Less than two dozen men were nearby, many of them wounded, and she tried to make sense of what she had seen. It defied all logic, yet there could be no mistaking what her own eyes had witnessed. The dead had come to reclaim the land of the living, and there was precious little she could do about it. In a few brief moments, her warriors had been reduced from four hundred and fifty men to barely two dozen.

The sound of horses caused her heart to freeze, and then Sir Greyson rode into sight, accompanied by what was left of their horsemen. They trotted along, conserving their strength, although their horses were lathered. He halted by the princess, dismounting to bow solemnly.

"Our army is destroyed, Highness."

"Does the enemy pursue?"

"No. They appear to have stopped their advance, content to hold the field for the time being."

"To what end?"

"I haven't a clue, but they've given us a breather, Highness. Best we use it to our advantage." They waited as a few more stragglers made it out of the woods.

"How many died this day?" asked Bronwyn.

"Hundreds, Highness, but there was little we could do about it. Had we stayed, I have no doubt we would have faced the same fate."

"Gather what few remain," she ordered, "and we shall head farther east."

"What lies in that direction?"

"The Minglewood, and south of that, the city of Anvil. Let's hope, there, we can find safety."

"I fear there's no longer any place that can truly be called safe, Highness. That army of spirits will tear through all who stand against them."

"Nevertheless, we must warn the Mercerians."

"The Mercerians? You betrayed them, my lady. They will execute you for treason."

"What choice have we?" she replied. "Like it or not, the Mercerians are the only ones who stand between that... that army and complete chaos gripping the land."

"And if the Mercerians can't stop them?"

"Then we are all doomed."

Sir Greyson surrendered his horse to Bronwyn, then they resumed their flight, trekking eastward for the rest of the day until the sun began to sink in the west. Here they halted to rest, too afraid to set up fires lest their position be given away.

Bronwyn huddled in her cloak, her knees pulled up to her chest. "What were those things?"

"Ghosts," replied the knight, "likely conjured by dark forces. They say Lady Penelope is a Necromancer. Perhaps she's the one responsible for them?"

"Lady Penelope?"

"She was the mistress of King Andred. Personally, I believe she controlled him, but I suppose we'll never know for sure. Her machinations led Merceria into a civil war. Now, it seems, she's returned to complete the destruction of us all."

"But why?" said Bronwyn. "What could possibly drive a woman to destroy everything?"

"She's an Elf," said Sir Greyson, "and they live forever. Do you not know any history?"

"Of Elves? Certainly not. Why?"

"They were the dominant race before Humans came to this land, but as the Kingdom of Merceria grew, they ran into the Elven lands. A fierce war was fought, producing heavy casualties on both sides. We Mercerians won in the end, but the Elves are said to have long memories."

"And you believe they plot to retake the land from all Humans?"

"It's only speculation, but I can see no other explanation."

"And these Elves," said the Princess, "are all of them practitioners of Necromancy?"

"Maybe not all of them, but definitely a large number."

"But they have the ability to create spirit armies?"

"So it would appear. There were rumours of it back when we were working with General Fitzwilliam, but I attributed that to mere superstition. I'm sorry. I guess I should have known better."

"It's not your fault," said Bronwyn. "If I hadn't angered the general so much, we might have been kept better informed. As it stands now, there is little choice but to turn ourselves in."

"They'll imprison us, possibly even execute us."

"Better to suffer that fate than be torn to shreds by the spirits of the dead. Speaking of which, you fought them sword to sword. What were they like?"

"They're not spirits in the true sense," said Sir Greyson. "I could feel resistance when my sword hit. It's as if they have a mortal form."

"And did you kill any?"

"I'm not sure if they can BE killed. I caused at least two to... well, I don't know what you call it. I suppose I would say dissipate. It's the only thing that even begins to describe it."

"And was that hard?" pressed the princess.

"You must understand, I've been a Knight of the Sword for years, and I've seen my share of battle, but those... creatures? They are the most formidable things I've ever faced."

"But you did destroy two of them?"

"I did, but our own losses were far higher. If we must trade dead like that, there'll be no living thing left in any of our kingdoms."

THIRTEEN

Summersgate

SUMMER 965 MC

Lady Jane Goodwin paused at the doorway. Inside the room, her son, James, sat with Lord Godfrey Hammond. They appeared to be deep in discussion as they sipped their wine, in all probability plotting their strategy for betting on the upcoming tournaments. With Jack Marlowe off with the army, the jousting trophy was ready for the taking, with no end of challengers to the prize.

She sighed. James was much like his father had been—full of energy but with a willfulness that bordered on obstinacy. As a young man, he had been the toast of the town, but now that he was in his twenties, his efforts had turned more towards politics.

She had intended to ask Lord Godfrey to dinner, but when she saw the two of them so engaged, something told her the interruption would not be welcomed. She backed away from the door, leaving them to their exchange.

"I don't see how?" said James Goodwin. He took another drink, savouring the full-bodied flavour of the wine.

Lord Godfrey Hammond smiled back. "It's pretty simple, really. The earls sit on the Earls Council, that much is true, but the actual power in Weldwyn is the lesser nobles. This includes the viscounts but, more importantly, the barons. Your uncle is a baron, is he not?"

"You know he is, but the title is through my aunt, not my uncle, so I have no hope of inheriting."

"Don't look so glum. Things can change in a heartbeat."

"What's that supposed to mean?"

"People die, James, often without a legitimate heir. There are ways to take advantage of that. Take Lady Lindsey Martindale, for example."

"The viscountess? She's a widow, isn't she?"

"She is, indeed, and, aside from the queen, likely the most influential woman in the kingdom. The point I'm trying to make, however, is she has no designated heir. No son, or daughter, for that matter, or brother or sister, not even cousins to inherit the title."

"And?"

"And she's old, very old. To be honest, I don't know how she manages to carry on, considering her age."

"Even so, she does," said James.

"Look," said the older man. "You crave power. That's something I understand all too well. Were we to speak to the right people, I can all but guarantee that when her title becomes available, it would be yours."

"The way she's going, that's years away."

"Not necessarily. Think back to the invasion four years ago. How many nobles died?"

"Enough to cause problems," said James.

"Precisely. And now the king has gone and gotten himself killed. How many nobles were with him, do you think?"

"Not many, from all accounts."

"Yes, but look at the grand scheme of things. What will Leofric's death mean for the kingdom?"

"A new king?"

Lord Godfrey frowned. Evidently, James did not have the foresight to see the opportunity for what it was, so he decided to take a more blunt approach.

"Whoever destroyed Leofric's army must know it leaves our kingdom weak. One might even say ripe for the plucking. Mark my words, troops will cross our border, and they won't stop until they control the throne."

"You mean the Clans?" said James. "It wouldn't be the first time they tried nor, I suspect, will it be the last."

"All true, yet they now have a golden opportunity, don't they? All of our veterans are gone, James. They all lie dead somewhere off in the Gods' forsaken area north of Merceria. All the Clans must do now is march across the border. Who's there to oppose them?"

"Alstan will be made king, won't he?"

"Of course he will," said Godfrey, "but what has he to work with, the militia? The Clans would brush past that with no trouble at all."

"Are you suggesting we welcome invaders?"

"Don't think of them as invaders, more as brooms, sweeping away the dust of ages past. The Clans can't rule Weldwyn; it's too big for them, and they know it. What they can do, however, is install a ruler who will show them friendship. Imagine how different things would be if Prince Alric had married High King Dathen's daughter?"

"We'd have a peaceful border to our west."

"Precisely. And what did we get instead? Involvement in a foreign war that has cost our king his very life, not to mention destroying the bulk of our army. How many of our warriors died, James? And all to placate the Queen of Merceria!"

"Certainly not our best decision."

"You're right," said Lord Godfrey, "and do you know why those decisions were made?" He waited, but his young protégé apparently had no answer. "Because our Council of Earls is made up of old men. The rule of Weldwyn requires men of action, men like you and me, not those who are near death."

James Goodwin took another sip of wine, clearly mulling things over.

"You have an intelligent mind," continued Lord Godfrey, "and a mind like that is a terrible thing to waste. Imagine all the good we could do?"

"You make a compelling argument. It's obviously something you've given a lot of thought to."

"And I'm not the only one."

James looked up in surprise, and Lord Godfrey smiled, his trap sprung. "There are a great many people who desire change, my friend. I swore myself to secrecy regarding their identities, but I assure you there's a new generation, one that sees a glorious future for our kingdom if we can but break the shackles of our past."

"Yet our traditions are what make us men of Weldwyn, are they not?"

"Traditions are one thing, yet blind obedience to outdated principles is quite another. Look to Merceria, if you will. There they have a young queen who was raised without the interference of court. As a result, their kingdom is now reborn. We can do the same, but not if we cling to the past with such fervour."

"And so we welcome invaders?" James repeated.

Lord Godfrey poured himself another drink, using the interlude to contemplate things further. Finally, he took a sip before looking back at his companion. "Tell me, James, how many lives do you imagine would be lost opposing another invasion?"

"Oh, I don't know. Hundreds, I suppose, maybe even thousands?"

"And if the war could be brought to a halt without such losses, would it not be worth considering?"

"That makes sense," agreed James.

"We, as a kingdom, have seen more than our fair share of loss these past few years. Surely it's our duty to do all we can to prevent further deaths going forward?"

"The earls will all resist."

"That they will," said Lord Godfrey, "but it is to be expected. After all, their very livelihoods depend on blind obedience to the past. What this kingdom needs is fresh blood, and that is best exemplified by men like you and me."

"I like the sounds of that," said James, "but I'm still hesitant about these Clansmen. They've tried to invade us several times over the years and have met with disaster each attempt. How do we know this time they'll succeed?"

"Ah, but that's the beauty of it. They're not the ones planning this invasion."

The younger man leaned forward, his drink all but forgotten.

"If not the Clansmen, then who?"

"What do you know of Elves?"

"Elves? You mean like Lord Parvan of Tivilton?"

"I was approached by one of the woodland folk. It appears they have a particular interest in the politics of Weldwyn of late. They would deem it as a great benefit if someone favourable to them came to power here."

"Are you suggesting the Elves would help conquer Weldwyn?"

"Elves live a very long time," said Lord Godfrey, "and their lot in this land has not changed significantly in centuries."

"But they have a baron!"

"True, but they are also vastly outnumbered by us Humans. Lord Parvan has petitioned the Crown to allow him access to the Earls Council on many occasions, but you know how the earls are. They don't want their power diluted by expansion. Especially when that means the inclusion of an Elf."

"And you would allow something like that?"

"Why not? What is one Elf compared to the five earls we have now, particularly when he might be counted as an ally? Think of it, James. You and I could finally control the destiny of Weldwyn, guiding it to whatever future we desire."

"We'd have to eliminate the old earls first."

"Sometimes sacrifices must be made in order to give the realm a future."

"I'm in," said James. "What's our next step?"

Lord Godfrey smiled, his trap now complete. "Well, here's what I was thinking…"

.   .   .

Queen Igraine clutched a weeping Edwina. At fourteen, she was the youngest of her five children, and the news of her father's death had been particularly hard for the child.

"There, there," she soothed. "Everything will be all right."

"Don't lie to her," said Althea. Though only four years her sister's senior, the elder daughter couldn't have been more different in her outlook. Where Edwina saw only sorrow, Althea raged.

"Someone must be made to pay," she shouted.

"And they will, in time," said the queen, "but at present, there's little we can do about it. In the meantime, we must prepare Alstan to stand in his father's place."

"Then get on with it! Why does this need to take so long—it only prolongs the agony. Alstan should have been crowned the moment we heard the news."

"These things cannot be rushed."

"No? Why not? The kingdom is in turmoil, Mother. A new king would at least give people a sense of hope."

"Do you presume that's not what I want? I have served this realm for my entire life, Althea, and shall continue to do so until I die. We cannot install a new king until the Earls Council has met to approve his coronation, and that takes time."

"Why?"

"The earls must travel to Summersgate, for a start, and until Uncle Edwin's successor is named, his seat on the council will remain empty, necessitating a further delay."

"And in the meantime, the kingdom lies vulnerable."

"A few weeks will make little difference. Word of your father's death is only now reaching the far corners of Weldwyn. How would you expect the Clans to know of it already?"

Althea held her ground. "I didn't say the Clans were a threat."

"No, you didn't, but you were thinking it. For all that, who else would dare to attack us?"

"A powerful presence at our borders would be a good deterrent."

The queen sat back, impressed. Althea had shown little concern for such matters in the past, but ever since her visit to Merceria, her interest had been piqued.

"Let me take warriors to Loranguard." Althea's pleading tone interrupted her thoughts.

"You are a princess, not a commander of troops."

"Alstan commanded troops when he was not much older than I am now."

"That's different," said the queen. "He will soon be the king."

"Precisely why he can't go, but I can."

"You have no training."

"Did Queen Anna have any when she defeated the invasion of Merceria? Or how about the war that put her on the throne—she led that, didn't she?"

"She had a general to command her army," defended the queen.

"I'm not suggesting I'd fight, but at least the presence of more warriors at Loranguard would serve to quell any ideas of invasion the Clans might consider."

"I should never have let you go to Alric's wedding. The Mercerians have put all sorts of strange notions into your head."

"And what am I to do instead, Mother? Master my needlepoint, so a future husband finds me of value? I can fight!"

"I admire your spirit, Althea, but these are dangerous times, and you have yet to lift a sword in practice, let alone in an actual battle."

"But I have, Mother."

Igraine paled. "You have what?"

"Learned to use a sword. I may not be as accomplished as Alstan, but I daresay I could hold my own against a common warrior."

"I never gave you permission to do that!"

"No, you didn't. Thank Malin I took it upon myself to find a tutor."

"A tutor? Who dared to do such a thing?"

"Does it matter?" said Althea. "The truth is I can wield a sword. Face it, Mother. With Father gone, along with Uncle Edwin, who else do we have to lead an army, save for Alstan? And you yourself said he must remain here until installed as king."

Igraine took a deep breath, trying to settle her temper. Althea was at an age where passion often overwhelmed common sense. She remembered her own years as a young woman, of how Prince Leofric had stolen her heart, and then wondered if the same type of thing might have happened to her eldest daughter.

"Even if I were to agree," the queen continued, "the simple fact of the matter is we lack the troops. Your father marched into Norland at the head of almost two thousand men, all of which are now lost. Even if we had the manpower, we don't have armour or the weapons to equip them."

"Then get the smiths to work!"

"Don't you think I've already done so? It takes years to put together an army of that size. One cannot simply replace it in a few weeks."

Althea seemed to calm. "How many soldiers have we left?"

"Not many, to be honest. Aside from the local garrisons, we can field no more than four hundred warriors, and most of those are simple footmen, armed with little more than spears and shields."

The princess was clearly shocked by the admission. "So few?"

"I'm afraid so. Your father also emptied the Royal Coffers in his quest for greatness. There's little left with which to deal with this emergency."

"And leader-wise?"

"You had the right of it earlier. Aside from your Uncle Edwin, Alstan is the only one with any experience other than Alric. But he's off running around Norland."

"Then you must send word recalling him to Summersgate."

"He is consort to a queen," said Igraine. "I have no such power over him anymore. In any event, it would take weeks to even reach him."

"Have you not even sent word of Father's death?"

"Of course I have. The Enchanter, Gretchen Harwell, left some time ago, but I suspect the court of Wincaster is all busy fighting in the north. It will take her a while to travel to them."

"So, in the meantime, all we can do is wait?"

The queen nodded. "So it would seem. It's galling to stand helpless while all around us is chaos, but we have little choice."

"Then allow me to help."

"I would welcome it, but what can you do? As I said, you have no experience leading men in battle."

"True," said Althea, "but I can at least show them we are concerned for their welfare."

"What are you proposing?"

"Alstan has ordered the militia to gather. Let me speak to them. I will give them the impression that all is well."

"You'll do more than that," said the queen in a sudden burst of inspiration. "I shall send you to Mirstone."

"What's in Mirstone?"

"Lord Tulfar Axehand."

"The Dwarven baron?" asked Althea.

"Yes. For years he's been wanting to raise a company of Dwarves to help defend Weldwyn. You will now go there and give him his chance."

"If he was so keen to raise troops in the past, why didn't we let him?"

"It's said Dwarves can be fierce warriors," replied the queen, "but there's more to being in an army than fighting battles."

"What does that mean?"

"An army must march to battle, my dear, and Dwarves are slow of foot. Shall we then hold up the entire proceedings to allow the slowest of warriors to keep pace?"

"That said, why are you willing to use them now?"

"We have little choice in the matter," said the queen.

"And how would they be used?"

"Likely to man the walls of Summersgate, where their slow pace matters little. That would at least free up the current garrison, which we would then use to bolster our field army."

"Very well," said Althea. "I shall go to Mirstone, but I doubt Lord Tulfar will be agreeable to your plan."

"It is not his place to question royalty but rather to obey when summoned. He might complain, but he will do his duty. Of that, I have no doubt."

"What of the Elves?"

Igraine looked at her in surprise. "What of them?"

"Will they not also send warriors?"

"They have never been the type to support military campaigns."

"At the same time," pressed the princess, "Lord Parvan is a baron of this realm, is he not?"

"He is, nevertheless, his relationship with the Crown is strained, to say the least."

"Why?"

"Your brother Alric uncovered some unsavoury news where Lord Parvan is concerned. As a result, they have become withdrawn."

"Withdrawn? You make him sound like a petulant child. Is each baron now able to choose when and if to answer a Royal Summons?"

Queen Igraine's voice grew frosty. "You should learn your history, Althea. The Elves were already here when our kingdom was founded. Only through the allowance for certain... circumstances did we manage to convince them to join Weldwyn."

"So they refuse to fight on our behalf?"

"I have no doubt they'll fight to hold on to their own lands, but I wouldn't expect Elves to be marching to our capital's defence any time soon."

"That is unconscionable," said Althea.

"True, but it's their way, and nothing we say or do will change that."

"Then we must hope Lord Tulfar can raise the warriors we need. When can I leave for Mirstone?"

"First thing tomorrow morning, but before you go, you should visit the Royal Armoury. If you're going to inspire the men, or Dwarves, in this case, you should at least look the part."

Althea appeared highly pleased with herself. "Thank you, Mother. I shall." She turned to leave but then thought of something and twisted to look back at her mother one more time. "I'm sorry, Mother. I truly am. I know Father's death has hit you hard. Have no fear, I will do my duty, and together we'll save Weldwyn."

Igraine smiled as she pulled her youngest daughter from her embrace. "It's time you pulled yourself together, Edwina. We have important things to do. Now, say goodbye to your sister. It may be some time before you see her again."

Edwina stood straight, stifling a sniffle. She took one look at her older sister, then ran to her, wrapping her arms around Althea. "I'll miss you," she said.

"And I, you, but you must promise me you'll listen to Alstan. He'll soon be the king."

"I will."

"Good. Now, I must go and find armour and weapons suitable for a warrior princess." She left the room, missing the look of grief on her mother's face.

FOURTEEN

The Gathering of the Clans

SUMMER 965 MC

"I've never heard anything so ridiculous," said Warnoch. "The fact Dathen is your father gives you no right to claim such a thing."

"It most certainly does," replied Brida, her voice rising. "You yourself claim the right to rule by nature of your bloodline. How is it any different for me?"

"No one here is denying your right to rule your Clan, but the position of High King is not hereditary."

A calm voice interrupted the proceedings. "Then why call him High King?"

Everyone looked at Prince Tarak. His physical size presented an imposing figure, but even more remarkable was the way in which he commanded respect by his mere presence.

Warnoch pressed his case. "With all due respect, Your Highness, our ways are steeped in history and not designed to placate outsiders."

"In spite of this, you name him king, do you not? Such a ruler is, by definition, a hereditary position. I could well understand your argument had your forebearers chosen a title such as High Chief, or maybe Overlord, but being named king sets certain expectations, amongst them the right to hereditary rule."

Warnoch wanted to rebuke the prince but found himself unable to counter the argument.

"It is clear," Prince Tarak continued, "that you, the Chiefs of the Twelve Clans, thought enough of King Dathen to name him High King. Why, then, would you now consider his daughter unequal to the task? Has she not shown leadership since her father's incarceration?" He stared down each

Clan head, but few would meet his gaze. "Could it be you are uncomfortable being ruled by a queen?"

He took a step, watching as several of the esteemed members of the council shrank back in their seats. "For far too long, the Twelve Clans have hidden from their destiny, eking out an existence in this Saints' forsaken place you call home, while the nobles of Weldwyn luxuriate in a life of privilege. Why should they prosper while you suffer?"

Prince Tarak recognized the hungry looks. The Clansfolk had coveted their neighbour's land for generations; however, victory had eluded them.

"Your armies are powerful," he continued, "of that there can be no doubt, yet without a firm hand, you'll once again degenerate into petty squabbles, fighting over scraps of land that mean little in the long run. I say you deserve better!"

Their interest was building, and he noticed greed starting to take hold. "You've been given a gift," he said. "Weldwyn is now on its knees. All that is required is a firm push, and the entire kingdom will topple. Confirm Brida as your High Queen. Let her be the instrument of your victory!"

The room erupted into spontaneous applause. The prince took it all in, noting the less-enthusiastic individuals.

Warnoch stood. "You have given us much to think on, Your Highness. I believe it best each Clan leader now withdraw to seek consultation with their people. I call on this assembly to reconvene tomorrow at first light, there to give final voice to this resolution."

They all nodded their agreement before rising from their seats. Tarak watched them milling around, congratulating each other on a job well done. Warnoch had done his duty, delaying the vote until cooler heads could prevail, but the princes of Kurathia were not known for letting others have their way. Tarak smiled as he thought over his possible actions, then sought out Brida.

The young woman looked extremely pleased with herself, and why not? She fully expected to be named High Queen on the morrow.

"Highness," he said. "I wonder if I might have a moment of your time?"

"Of course," she replied. "Will here suffice, or would you prefer something a little more private?"

"In consideration of those assembled, I should imagine a private audience would be more appropriate."

"Well, follow me, then, and we shall repair to my lodgings."

Tarak breathed in the chill evening air as they stepped outside. "Is it always so cold in these parts?"

"Cold? This is one of the warmer days of summer. Do you not have weather like this back in Kouras?"

"No, Kouras is a much warmer clime. Even on the coldest of nights, a person can wander around the city bare chested."

"And is that a common custom where you're from?"

"Only amongst sailors, but that is simply a practical adaptation to their environment."

"Tell me more of your home."

He smiled. "There's not much to tell. Like most of the Kurathian Isles, it's small, the land completely covered by the city itself."

"Have you no farms?"

"Few. Most of our food comes from the sea. Each morning a fleet of hundreds exits the harbour, intent on spreading their nets for the day's catch."

"So you eat fish all the time?"

"It's the main part of our diet, and we import grain from other kingdoms, then there's the kelp."

"Kelp?" asked Brida.

"Yes, I believe you might refer to it as seaweed."

"And you eat it?"

"Amongst other things, yes," he said, "but we also burn it to produce ash —a very useful substance for making soap and glass."

"I thought glass was made from sand?"

"Usually, but we Kurathians cannot afford to use up our sand. We would soon find we had no islands left." He laughed, and she joined in.

"Well now, that's quite an interesting story."

The sounds of the meeting had quickly diminished as they walked away.

"What was it you wanted to talk to me about?" she said.

"There's still opposition to you. It is something that must be dealt with."

"Dealt with? What are you proposing?"

"Merely that sometimes actions speak louder than words."

"Are you suggesting I become High Queen by force of arms?"

"That would do little other than precipitate a large conflict. We are on the verge of a great invasion, Brida. Would you have your fellow countrymen fall upon each other like a pack of hyenas?"

"What's a hyena?"

"It is a scavenger not found in these parts. You must have something similar here?"

"We have crows."

He laughed. "Yes, that analogy will work just as well."

They halted by a hut, waiting as two guards opened the door for them. Inside, servants stood by, ready to serve food and drink. Brida collapsed into a set of furs, taking a tankard that was offered. Prince Tarak accepted a goblet of wine but remained standing.

"Tell me," said Brida. "Is this anything like your home?"

In answer, he scanned the room. "Not in the least. I live in a Royal Palace, with marble floors and walls of stone. It is a place of light and warmth that stands in stark contrast to what you have here."

"Then why are you here?"

"I beg your pardon?"

"What brings you to our land? I know what Lysandil told us, but there's more to your story. You rule Kouras. Why would you bring your army here to a land you so clearly loathe."

"Loathe is a strong word."

"Even so, it certainly fits. Do you deny it?"

He smiled. "I can see why the Elves thought you useful. You have a keen mind, Brida of Dungannon."

"You still haven't answered my question."

"I am a wealthy man," he explained, "and rule with absolute power back in Kouras. My wife, Princess Olani, is said to be the fairest of all women. On the surface, it would appear I lack nothing, so why, do you suppose, I come all the way here?"

"You mentioned your entire island is a great city. Could you be running out of space?"

He smiled. "I live in a grand palace. Why would I need more?"

"You tell me," said Brida.

"Very well, I shall, but it may surprise you. The Elves, you see, are an ancient people, their civilization rising long before the coming of our own race. Over the years, they've devoted centuries to studying matters Humans can barely grasp."

"Such as?"

"Life, for one thing. Elves are not merely long-lived—they're immortal."

"Are you suggesting they can't be killed?"

"Not at all," said the prince. "They are much like us in that regard. The woodland race can die from all manner of things, be it the point of a sword or even poison, but if left to their own devices, they will never succumb to natural causes. Have you ever met an Elf?"

"Only Lysandil. Why?"

"They are ageless. Oh, I imagine they grow up much as we do, but once they become an adult, the aging process appears to stop for them."

"Why is that?" asked Brida.

"It is one of the greatest mysteries of Eiddenwerthe." He saw the look of confusion. "Have you not heard that name before?"

"No, what is it?"

"Eiddenwerthe is the name we give to this place." He spread his arms wide, encompassing the room.

"You mean the Clan holdings?"

"No, I mean everything. The entire Continent, these lands, the Kurathian Isles, even the great wilderness. All the known lands, as well as the unknown ones, encompass what we call Eiddenwerthe."

"It's a strange name."

"It is from a language long forgotten, yet the name still lingers."

A grief-laden scream echoed through the streets, interrupting their conversation. Brida looked at Prince Tarak to see him smiling, and rose. "That doesn't sound good."

"Do not trouble yourself," replied the prince. "It is of little concern to you."

"What's that supposed to mean? What did you do?"

"Only what needed to be done. Come morning, you will doubtlessly discover all opposition to your ruling as High Queen has been eliminated."

"Are you saying you murdered people?"

"Do people not die in war? How is this any different?"

"Those are the leaders of the Twelve Clans!"

"And they shall continue to be so, providing they support your claim to the throne. These people can't be allowed to stand in the way of your destiny, Brida. You deserve to be High Queen, and no amount of argument can be tolerated."

"But to kill them outright?"

"How many of your kin died in the last invasion of Weldwyn?"

"Hundreds," she said.

"Then what does it matter if a few more perish if it will allow you to take your rightful place?"

"But I can't just kill my countrymen!"

"And I'm not asking you to. I took that burden from your shoulders, Brida, leaving you free to deny any knowledge of it."

She stared back in horror for a moment before a look of resignation settled over her features.

"Yes," said the prince. "Simple acceptance is the best course of action. When all is said and done, you cannot undo the past."

"This time, you killed on my behalf," she hissed, "but you shall never do so again. Is that clear?"

"Abundantly."

He kept his face calm, although inside, he was elated.

"You still haven't answered my question," she said.

"Which was?"

"Why are you here?"

"As I said earlier, I expect to be rewarded by the Elves."

"Surely you have enough gold?"

"Ah, but gold is not what I seek. Instead, I wish to prolong my life, and I believe the Elves possess that ability."

"That's impossible."

"Is it? The Elves are immortal. Why not Humans?"

"For one thing," said Brida, "we age. Would you like to live a long life if you were feeble and old?"

"As long as I lived a life of comfort, why would I care?"

"But you already live a life of luxury. Are you so vain as to assume things can only get better if you live forever?"

"Were I to live on, I could spend my time on pursuits of a more experimental nature."

"Meaning?" she pressed.

"I could learn the use of magic."

She laughed. "You can't learn magic any more than I can. Spellcasters are born, not made. Pursue eternal life if you want. I won't stop you, but don't fool yourself into believing magic is there waiting for you."

He felt the disappointment but refused to let his spirit be dampened. "You have given me much to consider." He passed his goblet to a servant and bowed. "I shall see you tomorrow," he said, "at the meeting. In the meantime, you may rest assured your position as High Queen is secure."

"I wish I had your faith," she said.

"You will, in time."

The overall mood was sombre as the Clan heads met the following day. Brida took her seat, her eyes wandering over the crowd to spot who might be missing. Sure enough, Warnoch's seat was now taken by someone else, and the elderly Erlach was nowhere to be seen.

Prince Tarak entered, along with two of his bodyguards but kept close to the doorway. His eyes briefly met those of Brida, and he nodded but said nothing.

Calindre, Chief of Windbourne, stood waiting as the noise died down.

"I call on this assembly," she began, "to name Brida, daughter of Dathen, as High Queen of the Twelve Clans."

She sat as the other leaders whispered amongst themselves. After some deliberation, Rurik of Halsworth stood. "I second the motion and propose we take a vote."

"I vote yea," said Calindre. "How vote you, Rurik?"

"Yea," he answered.

Each Clan chief followed, taking their turn to give their vote in full view of the assembled witnesses. Even though Brida knew the outcome, it was still exhilarating to watch. She was even caught up in the excitement as the result of the vote was announced.

"By unanimous consent," said Calindre, "Brida, daughter of Dathen, is hereby named High Queen and ruler of all the Clan holdings."

The townsfolk, having gathered to witness this historical occasion, let loose with cheers and Brida smiled. With her position now assured, she was able to muster the might of the Clans and declare war on Weldwyn, something she had longed to do for years.

She searched the room, watching for any sign of her brother, but he was nowhere to be seen. Brida suddenly became aware all eyes were on her. She glanced over at Calindre, looking for some hint of how to continue, but she, too, was surprised by the outpouring of emotion. Calindre stood, raising her hands to still the crowd.

"I know this is a joyous celebration," she said, "but it behooves us to let our new sovereign speak." The din died down, leaving everyone eager to hear Brida's words.

"Thank you all," she began, rising from her seat. "The Crown you bestowed on me is a great burden, one which I hope I shall bear with all the grace and dignity due a High Queen. We, the Clans, have had our fair share of loss and sorrow over the years, but through it all, we valued the bravery and perseverance of our warriors." She took a deep breath, trying to calm her nerves.

"Our forefathers attacked Weldwyn on multiple occasions, and at every attempt, they were repulsed at the border. Today, I stand before you to proclaim this time will be different. We stand this day ready to take advantage of the weakness of our enemy. King Leofric of Weldwyn is dead, and with him, any hope of repulsing our army. Let us, therefore, raise the banner of war and march to rid the land of those who would oppose us!"

The crowd cheered again, this time much louder, and it was unmistakable that the other Clan leaders had no choice but to join in the celebration.

Calindre leaned in to whisper, "Well played, Brida. Well played, indeed, but there's a big difference between riling up a crowd and leading an army. What will you do next, I wonder?"

In answer, the High Queen smiled. "Wait a moment, and you'll have your answer." She raised her hands as she had seen Calindre do.

"I call on all Clan chiefs to return to their domains to raise a force of arms the likes of which has never before been seen. Those of you from the north will muster at Halsworth, while those from the south shall bring their warriors to Banburn. Once assembled, we march eastward into Weldwyn and rid the land of our enemies." She waited again for the noise to abate. "Before dismissing this council, I shall take your pledges of loyalty."

She saw the looks of defiance on some of the faces and counted herself lucky, for now she knew her enemies. Her eyes met those of Prince Tarak, and the Kurathian simply nodded to one of his bodyguards. Moments later, more warriors entered the building, spreading out on either side.

Now, faced with an immediate threat, the Clan leaders quickly fell into place, stepping forward one at a time to offer their heartfelt support and best wishes for a prosperous reign.

Brida couldn't help but feel giddy. She had succeeded beyond her wildest dreams. She imagined herself destroying the city of Summersgate and watching it burn as she released her father from its dungeons. The inner fire of revenge raged within her, and she smiled.

Many pressed close to her, offering her congratulations, but she largely ignored them, concentrating instead on how she would punish those who had opposed her. The face of Prince Alric came to mind. He had spurned her advances, making a fool out of her, and she swore she would exact revenge for the injustice. Her anger spent, her attention returned to the present, where Calindre had just completed her oath of loyalty.

"Come," Brida said, her voice pleasant. "It is time you and I discussed your future."

"My future, Majesty?"

"You command the fleet, Calindre. That makes you of great value to me, far more so than these other fools if truth be told."

Two Kurathian guards appeared at the High Queen's side, ready to escort her through the crowd. "Lead on," she commanded, leaving the building, Calindre in tow.

Lochlan watched from afar, too shocked to reveal his presence. His sister played a dangerous game that could well end in disaster. Somebody had pushed her to it, and his eyes wandered the crowd, seeking the Elf, Lysandil, but he was nowhere to be seen.

A Kurathian warrior shoved him out of the way, and then he knew, at that moment, the fate of his home lay not in his sister, or in the hands of a mysterious Elf, but rather in those of a foreign prince.

FIFTEEN

The Dwarves March

SUMMER 965 MC

"Come," said Agramath. "Let me show you something."

He led Revi Bloom down a hallway that ended at an ornate door carved from ancient-looking wood. The Dwarven mage pushed it open, revealing a balcony beyond that overlooked an immense cavern.

Revi followed him through the door to gaze down at a massive court-yard. Below them, hundreds of Dwarven warriors stood in formation while individuals examined them in detail.

"What's this?" asked the Life Mage.

"The Royal Army," replied his host, "or at least a portion of it. These warriors are preparing for the march. They assembled here only so the king can make sure they're ready."

"To where will they march?"

"To Holdcross, of course. Our king means to put an end to the Norland threat once and for all."

"By my count," said Revi, "you have close to five hundred warriors here, while the enemy numbers closer to nine from what I saw."

"Yes, but they're all Humans. Ours are experienced warriors, well equipped and heavily armoured; you can't simply compare numbers."

"In spite of that, to ignore the superior odds would be foolish."

"Look again," said Agramath. "First of all, you have the heavy foot, those encased in chainmail. Beside them are the arbalesters, whose weapons far exceed the reach of anything the Norlanders have to offer. Now, those there"—he pointed—"with the plate armour are what we call the king's guard, a hundred of the most experienced warriors amongst our number. Lastly, there is the Hearth Guard, distinguished by their gold armour. They fall under the command of Kasri Ironheart herself. You'll note the coloured plumes on the helmets? They're used to identify each company."

"An impressive army, I grant you," said Revi, "but still, they lack a certain... mobility."

"That's where you come in. The job of you and your riders is to keep the enemy horsemen at bay. Do you reckon your men will be up to it?"

"I do, yet I can't help but feel all of this is a little premature. My queen has agreed to no conditions as of yet."

"And King Thalgrun understands that. He is willing to help you defeat Lord Calder if only to get the man off our backs. After that, you can do as you please. Is it so much to ask that you help us here? In the end, it will benefit us both."

"What about the threat of this shadow that lies to the east?"

"We shall discuss that at a later date. King Thalgrun is confident that your queen will be ready to speak of such things once this war is over. The more we do now, the greater the chance she'll be more amenable to our proposal."

"Good enough," said Revi. "I believe I can speak for Arnim on this matter and agree. I do have a few questions, however."

"By all means, go ahead and ask."

"Who will command this army?"

"Why, the king, of course. Is it not so in your own land?"

"No. We have both a marshal and a general to lead our armies."

"An interesting notion, but in Dwarven society, it's the king who bears that ultimate responsibility."

"Has he experience in such things?"

"Certainly. This is not his first foray onto the battlefield, although I daresay, at his age, this is likely to be the last."

"He's fought before, then?"

"Yes, although admittedly not for a century or more."

"Just how old IS King Thalgrun?"

"Close to five hundred years," replied the Dwarven mage. "A ripe old age for a Dwarf, but fear not, he still has his wits about him."

"And Kasri, is she the next in line for the throne?"

"At the moment."

"What do you mean by that?"

"Dwarven rulers are not chosen by bloodline, though that does occasionally happen."

"Then how ARE they chosen?"

"The ruling monarch selects the person they wish to take their place. Considering how long we Dwarves live, that's likely to change over the decades. In Thalgrun's case, he's made it pretty clear Kasri is his designated successor, but if something were to happen to her, who knows who he'd pick as her replacement."

"And the Crown is always passed on in this manner?"

"Of course. It makes perfect sense when you look at it closely. After all, a king wants someone who will keep his policies intact after his death. You can't always guarantee that where a bloodline is involved."

"And is having a queen rare in Dwarven society?"

"Not particularly, although having said that, Ironcliff hasn't had a queen in close to three hundred years."

"You said King Thalgrun was almost five hundred years old."

"Yes," admitted the Dwarf, "but he's only been king for the last hundred since being chosen as successor to his cousin, Grimdal."

"Yes," said Revi. "Kasri mentioned that. Are all your rulers of a similar age when taking the throne?"

"Most, but there are exceptions. If Kasri becomes king, she'll be one of the youngest."

"You mean queen," corrected the mage.

"You must excuse my understanding of your language. Kings and queens are Human concepts. In our language, we use the term 'Vard', which doesn't translate well, though I suppose you might replace it in your tongue with the word 'ruler.'"

"So, in your language, he would be Vard Thalgrun?"

"Yes," said Agramath, "though without your Mercerian accent, of course. Our native tongue is much more guttural than yours, but we seldom use it in the company of outsiders."

"Why is that?"

The Earth Mage smiled. "We are, by nature, secretive and guard our heritage fiercely. In truth, we share much of our ancient language with the Orcs, so if you are familiar with their tongue, chances are you already know quite a bit of ours."

Revi cast his gaze around the immense cavern. "And this? Is it natural, or did you carve it from the stone of the mountain?"

"The cave? Successive generations of Earth Mages shaped it, and then artificers went to work on it, producing what you see now. Naturally, it required a great deal of care. After all, you can't just move rock around and not expect the ceiling to collapse."

"Not something I'd considered, to be honest, but now you mention it, it makes sense. Do all your people live under the mountain?"

"They do, although many travel outside to tend the crops. Centuries ago, we tried growing food underground, but the results were utterly disappointing. There's only so much you can do with mushrooms."

"I had no idea Dwarves were agrarian," admitted Revi, "but I suppose everyone still has to eat."

"Naturally," said Agramath. "Though I must confess we learned that particular skill from the Wood Elves."

"Wood Elves?"

"Yes, they live to the south, in a place we call the Wayward Wood."

"And are Wood Elves the same thing as regular Elves?"

"No, although they are, perhaps, related. Wood Elves stand much the same height as us, though thinner of frame."

"And do they employ Elven bows?"

"No," replied the Dwarf, "they prefer spears to swords and bows. On the whole, they are a peaceful people, but they can fight when needed. They fear the east as much as we do."

"Can you tell me more about this eastern threat?"

"It's not a subject that lends itself to casual conversation, but I shall do my best to be succinct. Beyond the Gap lies the Continent, a sprawling land mass easily ten times the size of our land. If you travelled there, the first kingdom you would enter would be a Human one they call Halvaria. It is this kingdom, more than any other, that represents the greatest threat to our people, not only by its physical proximity but also by its beliefs."

"Which are?" Revi pressed.

"They are supremacists who believe it's both their right and destiny to rule over all people."

"A dangerous foe, from the sounds of it. Are they a large kingdom?"

"To be honest," said Agramath, "I really have no idea. We know only what we can glean from those who live close to the border. Don't get me wrong, the average farmer cares little for such things, but the people who rule there will brook no interference in their way of life. We sent people there with offers of trade multiple times, but our efforts were met with official silence."

"Official?"

"Yes, farmers will talk, naturally. From them, we learned more of this place, but a worker of land has little knowledge of things beyond the boundary of his field. As for their rulers, we've heard nothing at all, not even a refusal."

"So your traders returned empty-handed?" said Revi.

"Or not at all, in some cases. So you can see why we're deeply concerned."

"Have they made any attempts to send warriors through this gap?"

"Not yet, but the king suspects, as do I, it's only a matter of time."

"Then we'd best concentrate on Lord Calder for the moment, before this eastern land becomes more of a menace."

Agramath grinned. "My thoughts exactly."

"I guess I should go and find Arnim. I expect he'll be interested in learning more about this army of yours."

"Didn't I mention it? He already has."

"He has?"

"Yes," said the Dwarf. "Take a closer look below. You might recognize him."

Revi gazed at the warriors yet again, this time spotting the familiar form of Arnim Caster walking right behind King Thalgrun as the Dwarven ruler inspected his army.

"I suppose I should have expected that."

Revi and Arnim rejoined the Kurathians, waiting as the king's army made its way down the massive steps of Ironcliff. On either side, gathered hundreds of Dwarves, cheering them on as they went, giving the whole affair a feeling of a celebration.

At the head of the warriors walked King Thalgrun, his daughter Kasri by his side, followed by the Hearth Guard ready to leap to the king's defence should it prove necessary. The rest of the Dwarves followed, organized by company.

"Aldwin would be impressed by that armour," Revi replied. "What do you make of it?"

"It's impressive, I'll grant you, but I would imagine it's terribly expensive. The Dwarves hereabouts must be swimming in iron to be able to make so much of it."

"Yes," said the mage, "but to a certain extent, that worries me."

"I would think you'd be pleased?"

"That they have it? I am, but Agramath said it's fairly common to the east, and that means we're lagging behind the rest of the Continent in terms of our arms and equipment."

"True," said Arnim, "but we're not at war with the Continent, only Norland."

"You must take a broader view, my friend. We're lucky in that our enemies lack sufficient iron to be much of a threat. The truth is, our advantage over the Norlanders is due to our superior equipment."

"You're wrong, Revi. We succeed because we have the best-trained warriors in the land."

"And how would those warriors stack up against someone armoured like these Dwarves? Our men primarily rely on the sword, Arnim, and such weapons would do little against armour like that."

"Then what do you suggest?"

"Look at those Dwarves—they use poleaxes. Maybe it's time we adopted a similar weapon."

"I understand your concern, but these are long-term goals, are they not? Our present threat is the Norlanders, and they don't wear much in the way of protection."

"True, but we should always look to the future."

"That's your job," said Arnim. "As for me, I'll take care of the here and now. We can deal with army reform AFTER this war is over."

King Thalgrun reached the bottom of the stairs and began marching westward towards Norland territory.

Arnim arched his back, letting out a sigh of relief as his back cracked. "I think it's high time we get moving, don't you?"

"Yes," said Revi. "I shouldn't like to be outpaced by a Dwarf. It sets a poor example."

For three days, they headed west, with the Dwarves, who were slower of foot, marching from sunup to sundown each day. They set a gruelling pace, and Revi wondered how they didn't all collapse from exhaustion. Even the Kurathians found it uncomfortable being in the saddle for such extended periods and took to riding ahead to give themselves a break while they waited for the army of King Thalgrun to catch up.

By Revi's reckoning, they were drawing close to Holdcross. Early the next morning, he sent out Shellbreaker to scout the area. With his familiar confirming their location, they met with the Dwarven king to firm up their plans.

Unlike their Human counterparts, the Dwarves preferred to sleep under the stars, foregoing any tents. Their king adopted a similar philosophy, so they found themselves outdoors by an open fire, planning their next steps.

"The cavalry is billeted to the north of the town," said Revi, "in amongst a cluster of farms."

"And this town," said Kasri, "is it fortified?"

"There's no wall, although I suppose they could put up makeshift barricades, but there's no sign of any at present."

"As I see it," said Arnim, "the real problem here is the approach. As soon as we come into sight, the earl will be able to deploy his troops."

"Good," said the king. "That's what we want."

"Is it?"

"Yes. My warriors can make quick work of the earl's men if they stand and fight." He cast his eyes at Arnim. "It prevents them from running away, you see."

"But that's the problem," said Revi. "If they know their business, they'll let us commit to the attack and then withdraw, leaving us at the mercy of their horsemen."

"Can you not screen us from that?" asked Thalgrun.

"I can try," said Arnim, "but even though we are evenly matched, there's always the possibility they might get away from us."

"What if you lured them towards us?" asked Kasri.

"I would imagine that's the last thing you'd want," said Arnim.

"You forget the arbalesters. One volley of bolts and they'd run, then your lot can chase them down."

"Her plan has merit," said the king. "What think you?"

"I'm willing to give it a try," replied Arnim, "but if it doesn't work, we'd be putting the entire army in great danger."

"Not really. Our warriors can maintain a formation to hold them at bay if it becomes necessary, but I doubt it will."

"I admire your courage," said Revi, "but a battlefield is a place of chaos. All sorts of things can go wrong and usually do."

"I'll admit it's a gamble," said the king, "but I believe we ought to give it a chance, don't you? After all, what else CAN we do?"

"True," said Arnim. "I'll send out the Kurathians to divert their attention while the remainder of the army gets into formation."

Revi watched as the Dwarves started moving into a long line, anchoring the ends with their arbalesters, while the more heavily armoured troops mixed in with the rest. The Hearth Guard remained behind the line, ready to jump into any trouble spots that developed. King Thalgrun was perfectly calm, but Kasri appeared nervous, for she kept fidgeting as she waited.

"What do you see?" asked the king.

Revi closed his eyes, calling on his arcane powers to connect with his familiar, Shellbreaker, who flew overhead.

"The earl has deployed into line in much the same manner as you, placing his archers on either flank, with his horsemen massing to the north."

"And your companion?"

"Arnim is approaching the enemy line to the north. They should notice him any moment now." The mage observed the enemy horsemen through his familiar's eyes. Evidently, they had taken the bait, for they were beginning an advance to the northeast, their intent most likely to chase down the Kurathians. Arnim, for his part, let his men linger for a moment, then broke into a run, eager to put some distance between themselves and the enemy, or at least that's what they hoped the Norlanders believed.

The earl's horsemen drew closer to the Dwarves, and then the mountain folk began moving all over the place. Revi struggled to understand as Dwarves moved left, right, some of them even moving to the rear of the formation. He felt panic rising, barely resisting the urge to flee, but then calmed as he watched them march into their final positions. Though it had looked chaotic, it was, in fact, a highly practiced manoeuvre. The Norland horsemen still advanced, but now they came up against a circle of Dwarves presenting a wall of poleaxes and spears against their opponents.

The king's voice rang out, and then the arbalesters let loose with their initial volley, striking the Norland cavalry formation dead centre. As horses fell beside them, riders pulled back on their reins in a mad attempt to control their mounts, but the force of the charge had been unleashed, and now, full of adrenaline, all they could do was go along for the ride.

A few horses struck the line, only to impale themselves on the polearms. All sense of formation amongst the riders was lost as the Dwarves struck out. Mounts reared up, throwing riders, while Norland cavalrymen desperately tried to regain control of their horses.

Having witnessed the carnage, Arnim turned his Kurathians around, leading them back to charge into what remained of the enemy cavalry. The fight was short but bloody, and then the enemy horsemen, or what was left of them, fled westward towards their own lines. The Kurathians, having completed their task, regrouped but maintained their position, foregoing the opportunity to pursue.

Having watched the debacle, the earl ordered his footmen forward, and the great mass of Norland warriors started their advance.

Not to be outdone, King Thalgrun rattled off more commands, and once again, the Dwarves moved around. Revi watched with fascination as they quickly formed back into a line facing the threat. He expected bolts to sail forth, but Thalgrun ordered the arbalesters to wait.

The enemy drew closer until they were just about to make contact. King Thalgrun raised his hammer on high, lightning dancing around on its head as he smashed it to the ground, sending a trio of bolts flying into the enemy line with a loud crack. Instantly, the Dwarves all advanced, closing with the Norlanders while they were distracted.

Revi kept back, concentrating on Shellbreaker's view. Somehow Kasri had brought her Hearth Guard up to the front, and now they carved through the enemy like a sharp knife through venison. Arnim, not one to waste an opportunity, led the Kurathians north, bypassing the line entirely, his intent to take the enemy from the rear.

The Dwarves were in the thick of it now, swinging weapons left and right, leaving a trail of blood and destruction. The hard-pressed Norlanders fought back, but their weapons did little against their heavily armoured foes. The final straw came as Arnim sent the Kurathians against the rear of the Norland line.

Outmanoeuvred and out armoured, the earl's army began to panic. Soon, men were running everywhere, desperate to escape the carnage. The highly disciplined Dwarves, however, kept up a slow but steady advance through what remained of the Norland army, but it didn't last long.

Revi noted horsemen approaching and recognized Arnim, who led a captive by a rope that he had tied around the fellow's neck. Arnim halted before King Thalgrun and dismounted.

"A present for you, Your Majesty. May I present Lord Calder, Earl of Greendale."

SIXTEEN

Rebels!

SUMMER 965 MC

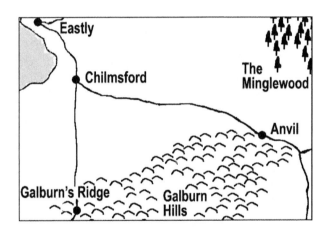

S ir Heward rode through the village of Anvil. His small force had
smashed what little opposition the Norlanders presented, and he was
prepared to continue the advance before word had reached him that all
further marching must be halted. This was a frustrating development,
particularly after his failure in losing the Guard Cavalry at the Battle of
Hammersfield. Shattered by the orders, he now wondered if the marshal
had lost faith in him altogether.

He wandered past the local smith, who waved hello. At first, the arrival
of the Mercerian army alarmed the townsfolk, but under Heward's hand,
the troops behaved well, even earning the grudging respect of the inhabi-
tants. He'd insisted the lives of the commoners be disturbed as little as

possible, even that all local goods required by the army were paid for, something the Norlanders had clearly not expected.

Impossible as it was to keep a close eye on everyone, it was inevitable that a small group of soldiers had seen fit to take out their frustrations on some of the locals. Heward quickly dealt out harsh and public condemnation of the acts, punishing those responsible, and things soon calmed down.

It was with some trepidation he noted the arrival of the rest of the army. The first sign was a gigantic dust cloud to the south, coming up the Hammersfield road.

Kurathian horsemen led the way, followed by a sea of green faces. Heward had seen the Orcs before, having fought alongside them during the civil war, but their numbers here surprised even him. It appeared the majority of their army now consisted of Orcs, many armed with the mighty warbows that had proven so decisive.

The horsemen drew closer before veering to the north, leading the army into the empty fields that would serve as their camp. A small group of riders broke off from the main group, trotting towards him, and he instantly recognized the marshal.

"Lord Matheson," he said. "Welcome to Anvil."

Gerald scowled, and Heward felt the sting.

"Don't worry," piped up Dame Hayley. "It's not personal. He's upset with everything in general at the moment."

The marshal gave her a withering glare before relenting. "Yes. I must apologize, Sir Heward. You've done a fine job. How are things going here?"

"Well, my lord, the footmen are camped north of the town, with the Wincaster bowmen stationed as a garrison in Anvil itself."

"Any trouble with the locals?"

"No, sir," said Heward. "I kept a tight lid on the troops, as per your instructions. The locals are taking things well, all things considered."

"Are they, now? And you've had no trouble at all?"

"Only one or two minor incidents that were quickly rectified."

"Good," said the marshal. "I knew you were the man for the job." He looked over his shoulder at the approaching Orcs before returning his gaze to the Knight of the Hound. "We, unfortunately, did have some issues with the rebels."

Sir Heward's face grew sombre. "That sounds ominous."

"It is. Bronwyn saw fit to turn on us, attacking the Dwarves at Galburn's Ridge before fleeing north with her army. It might be small, but it can still cause us no end of problems."

"Any indication of their present location?"

"Little, I'm afraid," said Gerald. "We know there's a place called Chilmsford around here somewhere, but that could be anywhere from a day's march to weeks. Have you heard tell of the place?"

"I can't say that I have," replied Heward, "but I'll talk to some of the townsfolk and see what we can discover."

"You think they'll help?" asked Hayley.

"I've worked hard at convincing them we're here to liberate, not conquer."

"And has that worked?"

"I think it has. Most of these people were forced to give over a lot of their food to the earl. It came as quite a shock when we offered them coins for it."

"Excellent," said the marshal. "If we keep on their good side, we can prevent the enemy from recruiting them. Now, as the main force is here, I won't need you to command the vanguard."

Heward felt despair welling up inside him.

"Instead," continued Gerald, "I've got something special planned for you, providing you're up to the task."

Hope grew anew. "Special, my lord?"

"Yes. We have all these horses we captured but have no riders. That's where you come in."

"You want me to train horsemen?"

"In a manner of speaking, yes. Actually, I want you to train Orcs to act as cavalry."

Surprise was evident on the knight's face. "Orcs?"

"Yes. I believe you'll find them a quick study."

"Why me?"

Gerald let out a chuckle. "Wait? Are you serious? You're one of our best warriors, Sir Heward. Why wouldn't I pick you?"

"I lost us the Guard Cavalry, sir."

"And defeated a superior enemy in the process. Men die in war, Heward; it can't be helped, but you can't let that get you down. The truth is we're desperately short of cavalry, and you're the best one for the job."

"I would have thought Dame Beverly—"

"Dame Beverly is not my choice for this—you are. Now, are you up to the task or not?"

"I am," said Heward, his confidence restored. "How many will I be training?"

"We'll start with a hundred and see how it goes. You'll draw what men we can spare from the Kurathian horse to assist, but it's no small feat."

"How much time do I have?"

"I can't say for certain. A few weeks, or possibly even as much as a month, but it largely depends on the enemy."

"Are these to be employed as light horse, my lord?"

"No. We need them to be able to charge home against formed troops. Think of them as unarmoured heavy cavalry if you wish. Certainly a contradiction in terms if ever there was one."

"In that case, I shall concentrate on having them charge with spears."

"Excellent," said Gerald. "See? I knew you had it in you. If there's anything you need, see Dame Hayley here; she's my designated second-in-command at the moment."

"I am?" said Hayley. "That's news to me!"

Gerald laughed. "Don't let it go to your head. I need you to keep your wits about you." He looked around the area. "Say, where's that wolf pup of yours?"

"Gryph? He's with the Orcs. Apparently, those wolves Zhura brought with her took a liking to him."

They all shifted their horses, trotting to the side of the road, as the Orcs marched past.

"They're an impressive sight," said Heward. "I suspect they'll be devastating as cavalry."

"Orcs learn quickly," noted Hayley. "It has something to do with their nature."

"Their nature?"

"Yes, most of them possess an ingrained sense of duty, so they take their studies seriously."

"I wish it were true of Humans," noted Gerald. "It would make raising an army so much easier."

Urgon and Zhura walked past, giving a nod of greeting as they went. The sight of the ghostwalker clearly shocked the knight.

"Anything else I should know about?" he asked.

"Yes," said the marshal. "We believe the spirit army to be close. I'm hoping we can pin down Bronwyn before we need to fight them though. I don't much like the idea of taking on two enemies at the same time." He nodded at the pale Orc. "That's Urgon's bondmate, Zhura. She's a ghostwalker. I don't understand all the ramifications of that, but suffice it to say, she has some knowledge of what we're facing."

"Enough to make a difference?"

"That remains to be seen."

. . .

They continued the march the very next day, leaving only a token force to garrison the town. A day and a half later found Gerald sitting on his horse, looking over the terrain as the army marched past.

"See something that interests you?" asked Hayley.

"I do, as a matter of fact."

"Care to fill me in? I AM supposed to be your second-in-command."

"This is where we'll fight," said Gerald.

"Fight? But we have yet to locate the enemy."

"True, but when we do, we may not be able to make a stand right away. If that's the case, we'll withdraw to this location."

She turned her gaze to the flat field before them. "I see nothing of note to suggest this place is better than any other."

"Ah, but that's where you're wrong. The ground here is soft, easy to dig with a minimum of tools."

"Are we to be farmers now?"

He looked at her in annoyance. "Your uncle's a farmer. I'm surprised you don't have more respect for them."

"I didn't intend to demean them, but I fail to see what digging has to do with anything."

"Do you remember the Battle of the Oak?"

"Back in Weldwyn? Yes, of course. Why?"

"Do you know why we won that battle?"

"Superior tactics?"

"No," said the marshal. "It's because I was able to pick the location."

Hayley wore a look of confusion. "I understand the importance of terrain, but these fields are flat. How can that possibly be to our advantage?"

Gerald smiled. "Ah, now I see the problem. Use your imagination."

"To do what?"

"Prepare the ground. Tell me, if you made a stand here, what would you do to get ready?"

"I'm not sure I grasp the problem."

"I should have realized that. You're a ranger at heart, so you're used to using the woods to conceal your positions. I, on the other hand, spent a good part of my life fighting in a line of footmen, so I'm more inclined to consider melee options. If we're going to meet this spirit army head-on, we need to be able to pick a spot of our own choosing: one we can make ready with earthworks."

"You mean digging?"

He nodded. "When King Leofric made a stand at the Battle of the Three Kings, he used his mages to create hills of dirt."

"I remember now," said Hayley. "I believe the spell was called defensive mound. It played quite an important role in holding off the Clans, if I recall."

"It did," said Gerald. "To such an extent that I want to do the same thing here."

"But we lack Earth Mages. Albreda is with Baron Fitzwilliam, and Aldus Hearn is with the queen."

"You forget the Orcs of the Black Raven. They have what they call a master of earth."

"So you'll create a big hill to defend?"

"A group of hills, in fact, with wooden spikes added in to funnel the attack."

"Will that even work against spirits?"

"Remember," said Gerald, "these spirits are anchored to our world by a magical link that gives them a sort of physical form. If we can destroy that, they should be banished back to the realm of spirits."

"Are you sure?"

"Not entirely," he admitted, "but Zhura seems to think so. Look, we can't outmanoeuvre them."

"Why is that?" asked Hayley.

"For one thing, we're extremely short on horsemen. They're also spirits, and, as a result, they never need to rest. Our best hope of making a stand is to hold the ground."

She looked at him with a critical eye. "You're hiding something."

"I am, but I'm not sure I'm ready to talk about it."

"And if something happens to you?"

He thought it over, then nodded. "You make a good point, Hayley. Very well, I'll tell you what I'm thinking. According to Zhura, this creature... what's it called again?"

"A Volgath?"

"Yes, that's it. In any case, this Volgath must be stopped, and the only way to do that is to get as close to it as possible."

"Agreed, but how? Would it not be better to withdraw?"

"No," said Gerald. "We can't retreat forever, and they'd be amongst us in no time—no need to rest, remember? No, I was thinking along other lines. Even if we lose, we should at least be able to inflict SOME casualties."

"Yes, but surely they can simply raise the spirits of the dead afterwards?"

"According to Zhura, Human spirits must be reached within a short time of death. If we hold the field after the battle, we can deny that eventuality."

"But Orcs make up the majority of our army, don't they?"

"I aim to use them at a critical time."

"Which is?" asked Hayley.

"When we make a push to reach the Volgath."

"Don't we need Beverly for that?"

"Naturally. Why do you think she's screening our northern flank instead of marching with us?"

"Now I see," said Hayley. "You want to outmarch them. Pin them in place until Bev can attack the rear. That's a big gamble."

"It is," he admitted, "but I'm thinking the Volgath's attention will be far too focused on the battle to be able to see it coming."

"So we must keep its focus on us."

"Don't worry, it's not the only trick I have up my sleeve."

"Care to share?" she asked.

"Not at this time. I'm still working out the details. In the meantime, I'm hoping we can put the Saurians to use helping to prepare this field."

"Aren't they a bit short for such work?"

"They are, but they have those massive three-horns. They might not be good for fighting, but they can dig up the dirt, not to mention hauling wood for the stakes."

He noted the look of doubt on the High Ranger's face.

"Don't worry," he added. "Some of Urgon's Orcs will be there to help."

"There's still the matter of finding this army. It could be hundreds of miles away."

"No," said Gerald. "Zhura can sense it. I imagine we'll run across it before the week's out."

Hayley felt the hairs on the back of her neck stand up. "That soon?"

"Now do you see why I'm picking out terrain?"

"What if it goes after General Fitzwilliam?"

"That's where the rest of the army comes in. We must offer ourselves as a target to draw them this way."

"You know," said Hayley, "there are some days where I wish I'd just taken up my father's profession."

"Wasn't your father a poacher?"

"He was, but at least he died a quick death at the end of a rope. Somehow, I believe ours will be a little more gruesome."

The very next day saw a rider hurrying to the marshal's side.

"We spotted some warriors, my lord," the man said.

"The spirit army?" asked Gerald.

"No, sir. The rebels, by the look of them."

The marshal turned to Urgon, who stood nearby. "Is your tribe ready for a fight?"

"You need only to give the command," the Orc replied, "and they shall obey."

Gerald turned his attention back to the scout. "How far ahead are they?"

"Just beyond that rise," the man replied, pointing to the west.

"Return to your group and keep an eye on them. Send word if they approach any closer."

The man was about to ride off when Gerald called out.

"Wait a moment," he said. "How many of the enemy did you see?"

"A hundred, maybe a little less."

"And had they any horsemen?"

"They did, my lord, but only about two dozen, by my reckoning."

"All right, off you go." Once more, the marshal turned to Urgon. "Have your spears form a line at the top of that hill," he ordered.

"With archers on either side?"

Gerald smiled. "You've learned our tactics well."

The Orcs started moving while Gerald rode out in front to get a better view of their enemy. The pitiful rebel army sat facing them, the flag of the princess barely blowing in the slight breeze. As he watched, a lone horseman broke away from the enemy line, making directly towards him. There was no mistaking the man's armour or the Mercerian charger he rode. Sir Greyson reined in his horse just shy of the marshal.

"My lord," he said. "I bring word of the spirit army." All thoughts of punishment fled Gerald's head as soon as the words issued forth.

"Where is it?" he snapped.

"We encountered it only a few days ago. It's been on our tail ever since."

"And they haven't destroyed you?"

"No, my lord, although I know not why."

Gerald set his jaw. "I do," he grumbled. "They let you lead them right to us."

"Princess Bronwyn wishes to place herself in your custody," said the knight, lowering his head, "as do I."

The marshal's gaze drifted past the rebels, and then his eyes went wild.

Sir Greyson, mistaking the look, pressed his case. "Do you accept our surrender, my lord?"

"We haven't time for this," shouted Gerald. "Go back to your princess, and tell your men to form up to the right of our line."

"My lord?"

In answer, the marshal merely pointed. Sir Greyson looked over, paling at the sight. Some distance off, a large host appeared, flooding across the land like a plague of locusts.

"Move!" screamed Gerald, then turned his horse around, galloping back to his own lines. He was soon in amongst the Orcs, seeking Urgon. "Deploy your archers in front in skirmish formation," he said. "They are to loose arrows at the earliest opportunity, but ensure they fall back rather than enter melee."

"Yes, Marshal," said Urgon.

"And where's Kraloch?"

"I am here," came the shaman's reply.

"Use your magic to inform Aubrey we made contact with the spirit army. Beverly will know what to do."

"Will she be back in time?"

"Not for this battle," the marshal informed him, "but this is only a holding action."

"You mean to retreat?" asked Urgon.

"Eventually, but not before we get a good view of our enemy. Where's Zhura?"

"Behind us with Hayley and the Human warriors. Why?"

"I'd like her here," said Gerald, "where she can see what we're up against."

"What about the rebels?"

"They're going to take up a position to our right. Your Orcs, on the other hand, will fall back as the Mercerian foot arrives, allowing the Human warriors to replace you."

"And our archers?" asked the Orc.

"Will carry on as ordered. Once they drop back, they are to remain out of the fight. Is that clear? We can't afford to have Necromancers raising their spirits after the battle."

"Understood."

"What of me?" asked Kraloch.

"Did you pass word on to Aubrey?"

"I did. Dame Beverly is on the way."

"Then you'd best stick close," said Gerald. "I may need to send more messages."

What was left of Bronwyn's forces took up their assigned position. Shortly thereafter, Hayley arrived with the Mercerian footmen, who stood ready to face this new threat, but there was fear on their faces, especially as the Orcs withdrew.

Gerald rode out to their front, drawing their attention. "Over there"—he pointed—"lies the enemy you've heard so much about. They're coming for us, all of us, but we have the one thing they don't—the will to live. You were told they're ghosts, that they aren't alive, but the truth is they're prisoners, bound to this realm by dark magic. The power that keeps them amongst the living is a tenuous thread, one that can be cut. And that's our job this day."

He took a breath before continuing. "They outnumber us, but to defeat them, we must buy the rest of our army precious time. Hold this field at the end of the battle, and we will have done our part. Break, and they shall cut us all to pieces. Then, even Saxnor himself won't be able to save your families from this blight."

A strange, keening sound drifted towards them, borne upon the wind. Gerald's skin crawled, and he watched as the faces of his men turned pale. He noted a few familiar faces from Bodden amongst his troops and smiled, instinctively drawing his sword and readying his shield. Without even thinking, he hit the sword's pommel against it, creating a thumping that boomed out in the cool breeze.

The sound echoed out towards the rest of the men. Individuals throughout the army repeated the motion, carrying it farther still. Soon, every warrior joined in, and he saw determination and pride settle once more amongst the faces of the army. The enemy was coming for them, but they were ready.

SEVENTEEN

Fitz

SUMMER 965 MC

Baron Fitzwilliam stared at the distant fortress. "It's an imposing sight."

"That it is," agreed Herdwin, "and it will take some time to bring down that wall."

"How much time?"

"A few weeks, maybe even as much as a month." He looked at his Human companion, but the baron did not appear pleased. "We'll get in, eventually," he soothed.

"I know we will, but every day we're delayed here, is another day the rest of the army is in danger. We must combine our forces if we have any hope of defeating this host of spirits."

"Could we bypass Galburn's Ridge altogether?"

"No," said Fitz. "That only would serve to endanger our supply lines. I just wish there were some way to speed up this siege."

One of the trebuchets took that moment to lob a stone. They both watched it arc high into the air before striking the cliff face with a loud crack. Stone splinters flew from the point of impact but left little visible effect.

"Well, that was disappointing," said Fitz.

"Not every hit removes rock," explained the Dwarf, "but each stone weakens the cliff. You might not be able to see it, but there are fractures beneath its surface. Through the proper application of our siege engines, we can take advantage of that."

"I thought you were a smith?"

"I am," replied the Dwarf.

"How is it you know so much about sieges?"

"I don't," said Herdwin, "but he does." He nodded towards a grizzled, old Dwarf with snowy white hair and bushy eyebrows. "That's Golmar Hengesplitter, one of our finest engineers."

"Has he conducted sieges before?"

"No, but he understands the calculations."

"What calculations?"

"Every building, or rock formation, for that matter, has its own innate set of characteristics. Golmar has spent a lifetime studying anything and everything made of stone. Some call him the stone whisperer."

"So he's an Earth Mage?"

"No," said Herdwin, "merely a scholar with expertise in rock and stone. Show him a building, and he'll tell you its weaknesses."

"He's been advising you all along?"

"Of course. How else would I know all the answers?"

Fitz chuckled. "Well, I believe you have effectively destroyed your own reputation. And here I thought you Dwarves knew everything."

"We might not know everything, but what we don't know, we can find out. Nothing's unachievable if you have enough time to plan and study."

"Yes, well," said the baron. "Unfortunately, time is not something we have in abundance at the moment. Did you ask them to surrender?"

"Of course, but the Norlanders are proving obstinate."

"I can't say I blame them. That fortress is formidable."

"What you see as formidable, we Dwarves see as a challenge."

"And once you bring that cliff down, how do you intend to get up to the fortress?"

"We climb, naturally."

"Through all that rubble?" said Fitz.

"Dwarves have been climbing through rubble for thousands of years. You might say it's in our blood."

"Perhaps, but you'd still need to fight once you get to the top. Won't your warriors be tired after the ascent?"

"Of course," said Herdwin, "but no one wants to climb all the way back down again. They'll do their part; don't you fret."

"Any indication of how many Norland warriors are in that place?"

"You would likely have a better idea than me. In any event, it's enough that they could afford to refuse entry to that traitor, Bronwyn. Speaking of which, do we know where she went?"

"Far from here, it would seem, but I'm keeping sentries posted to keep an eye out for her, just to be sure."

"Richard?" Fitz turned at the sound of Albreda's voice.

"Over here," he called back.

The Druid walked over to them, pausing to look at the distant cliff. "I assume you two are discussing the fortress?"

"We are," replied the baron.

"And what have you concluded?"

"That it will be some time before we can conduct an assault."

"Might I make a suggestion?"

"Of course, my dear. I would welcome it."

She turned her attention to Herdwin. "If I'm not mistaken, your cata-pults are attempting to bring down the cliff, are they not?"

"They are indeed," said the Dwarf, "but it's a slow process."

"What if I could speed it up?"

"Can you manipulate rock and stone?"

"Only in small quantities, hardly enough to make much of a difference here. No, I was thinking of using the power of nature to do the work for us."

"In what way?" asked Fitz.

"Do you remember the first time we met?"

The baron blushed. "I could hardly forget."

"I was referring to how I conjured vines to appear from the floor of your keep."

"Oh yes, of course. Why? Do you believe you could do something similar here?"

"Roots can do significant damage," said Albreda, "especially if they work their way into fissures and cracks."

"How close would you need to be for that?"

"Closer than we are now."

"Difficult," chimed in Herdwin. "Any closer, and you'd be within range of Norland crossbows."

"Then we do it under cover of darkness," said the baron. He turned to Albreda. "Would that work?"

"It makes things more difficult, but we must work with what we have."

"Difficult, how?"

"In order for the roots to do their part, I must be able to see the cracks in the rock. Otherwise, I couldn't correctly target the spell."

"There's a full moon tomorrow night," said Fitz. "Would that suffice?"

"I suppose it will have to," she replied.

"What about you, Herdwin? Can your Dwarves be ready for an assault by then?"

"Easily," replied the smith. He looked back at the trebuchets and the

Dwarves who swarmed over them, preparing for the next volley. "What about those?"

"Simple," said Fitz. "Keep up the bombardment for the rest of the day. We don't want the defenders expecting anything."

Albreda frowned. "Won't they realize something's up when they stop at dusk?"

"They always stop at night," said Herdwin. "After all, we can't judge the effectiveness of our attack in the dark."

"Then it's all settled," she said. "Now, if you don't mind, I shall go and eat. It's likely to be a long night. Care to join me, Richard?"

"Of course! Truth is, I'm rather famished myself."

Herdwin crouched in the darkness, Dwarven warriors on either side of him, their shields slung, their weapons sheathed. The sun had long since sunk in the west, and thankfully, the moon was bright enough to light their way when the time came, but he was beginning to wonder when that might be.

He felt his leg muscle cramp up. "By Gundar's beard, are we to wait here all night?"

Footsteps drew his attention, and he turned to see Albreda approaching from behind. It was odd seeing a solitary woman walking amongst the Dwarven warriors, but the Druid commanded respect by her mere presence.

She halted, her gaze focused on the cliff face, contemplating her next actions. Herdwin knew of her power but had seen little of it up close. Here, she was within ten paces of him, and he found himself wishing there were more room between them. He'd never been a big fan of magic, although he grudgingly admitted it was, at times, useful.

Albreda began muttering something, and he strained to make out the words, but it all came out in a jumble. He swatted away an insect that buzzed nearby, and then the entire area came alive as if a swarm had been awoken.

The Dwarf waited, eager to witness the Druid's power unlocked, but all he saw was the sudden appearance of half a dozen fireflies leaping from her fingers, heading towards the cliff face before sinking into the rock.

"Is that it?" he mumbled.

In reply, Albreda simply looked at him, then pointed at the distant precipice. He heard the rumble first, a low vibration that shook the very ground on which he stood. A small trickle of stones falling echoed back to him, then a sound higher up—a cracking loud enough to startle him.

More stones fell, and then more cracks. The rumble intensified until thunderous crashing drowned out everything else. A massive cloud of dust and debris came towards them, and he felt the sting on his face as tiny bits of stone were hurled in his general direction. Herdwin closed his mouth, desperate to avoid inhaling anything, but the dust was everywhere, stinging his eyes and making breathing difficult even through his nose.

Albreda appeared unfazed by the effects, her eyes glued to the distant wall as her hands were gesticulating once more. She pointed at the ground before her, and small vines appeared, growing longer as she continued with the words of power. They stretched out before her, and Herdwin tried to determine their purpose, for the cliff was still some distance away.

Off into the darkness crept the vines, and then they started to bloom, small flowers sprouting, bathing the area in a pale-green light. The Dwarf watched in fascination as the trail of lights entered the dust cloud. He couldn't see the cliff, but neither did he need to, for the glowing vines climbed the rock wall, illuminating the way.

"Go," shouted Albreda. "The light will guide you."

Herdwin rose, making his way towards the base of the cliff, waving at his warriors to come after him. The cloud hid his destination, but the bright flowers were simple to follow, and soon he was navigating over the piles of rock and stone. He picked a way through, taking care to avoid injury, for it was easy to twist an ankle on the uneven rubble.

The ground sloped up, so he continued until he needed his hands to steady himself. The rumbling had stopped, and now he could hear the sounds of people above him crying out in pain and fear. Reaching up to secure a handhold, he found himself grasping a foot that extended out from the rocks. Unfortunately, it appeared the poor soul had been caught in the collapse. Herdwin's heart went out to this unknown warrior. He knew the fear, for nothing was worse to a Dwarf than experiencing the collapse of stone firsthand.

He briefly thought back to his Great-Uncle Bremel, who'd been a mining supervisor, when a tunnel collapse trapped him deep beneath the mountain. For four days, they'd dug, only to find him trapped beneath a large stone. It was one thing to die in the mines, but his great-uncle had suffered during his last few days, and the memory of it still stung.

He was brought back to the present when a stone crashed against a nearby rock, sending splinters flying everywhere. He turned his head just in time, feeling a piece rebound off his helmet.

Herdwin managed to peer through the dust to spot another Dwarf to his right, wearing a flat-topped helmet, a popular choice amongst the more well-to-do Dwarves of Stonecastle. Still, it did nothing for him as a rock came tumbling down from above, striking the helm full on, crushing the Dwarf's neck, and sending him tumbling off into the distance.

Muscles ached, and fingers strained, but Herdwin kept climbing, using the vines to assist in the ascent. He heard more rocks falling and then the familiar clatter as bolts struck stone. Down below, the arbalesters gave a cheer as a bolt took someone in the chest, and then a body plummeted past him, crashing onto the stones below.

The dust was clearing now, giving him a view of those above. Men stood atop the collapsed wall, hurling stones at those below, while others, now dangerously exposed, used their bows to take out Dwarves climbing up the wreckage of the wall.

An arrow struck his helm but deflected onto his shoulder, its strength spent. He gritted his teeth and made a silent prayer to Gundar to keep him safe. His arms strained, reaching out, again and again, slowly drawing him closer to his enemies.

He had lost all sense of time or distance before he finally hauled himself up onto a ledge only to notice a man's boot. His eyes followed up the leg to see a Norland archer looking down at him in alarm. The defender reached for his long knife, but Herdwin was faster, grabbing his foe by the ankles and pulling with all the strength he could muster.

Down went the archer, scrambling to reach out and grab ahold of something to steady himself. He managed to seize a section of collapsed wall, but the stones came loose in his hands, sending him tumbling down into the darkness.

He struck Herdwin as he fell, and the Dwarf felt his own fingers lose their grip. Down he slid, directly onto another Dwarf, who cursed and swore at him but at least halted his descent.

"Sorry," he called out as he resumed his climb. The top came into view, and then once more he was on the ledge, where he could finally stand. His hands instinctively sought out his axe as he unshouldered his shield just in time to deflect a fist-sized stone hurtling towards him. He tried to run forward, but his legs shook with the strain, so he slowed his pace, ready to cut down any who might oppose him.

He glimpsed an archer to his right, quickly throwing up his shield. The arrow sank into the wood, and he thanked Gundar once again. The bowman nocked another arrow, but Herdwin closed the distance, striking out with his axe, slicing through the forearm before digging into the bow itself. The Norlander fell, screaming, blood pumping out of the newly severed arm.

The Dwarf ignored the man, pushing on despite the fatigue. His blood was pumping now, his body working on pure adrenaline; he felt ready to take on the entire garrison. One of his fellow warriors climbed up beside him, pulling forth a hammer and readying a shield. Herdwin looked at him, and they both nodded before commencing their advance.

Dwarven mail is strong, much stronger than that made by Human smiths, but even Dwarven mail has its limitations. This became evident as a crossbow bolt took Herdwin in the thigh, breaking through the links and digging deep into his leg, sending him to the ground. Right as he fell, three more bolts sailed forth, and his comrade fell backwards, his helmet punctured.

Norland footmen now surged forward, desperate to fight off the attack at the collapsed wall. Dwarves emerged from the rubble, but they were too exhausted to put up much of a fight after such a steep climb.

Herdwin saw dozens go down before it became clear the Norlanders had the upper hand. Spearmen moved forward, stabbing out, and then the entire assault fell to pieces.

Dwarves scrambled to get to safety, but the Norlanders counterattacked with a vengeance. Men with swords followed in the spearmen's wake, stabbing down at any who might offer resistance. They drew close to Herdwin, and he lay still, hoping to convince them he was dead. A sword stabbed down into his back, and he felt the pain as the blade sank in but managed to remain still. The Norlander, satisfied with the results, moved on.

Herdwin remained where he was, counting to fifty before risking a peek around the area. The Norlanders were moving closer to the edge of the cliff now, jeering at the retreating Dwarves. When the wall's foundation had given way, the vast majority of it fell down into the valley below. However, a good portion remained at the top, now in heaps like a stone mason's castoffs. He noted two large sections, leaning against each other, and crawled towards them. Several times he stopped, lest the enemy notice his movements, but in the end, he was able to drag himself into the Gap. He twisted around, feeling pain lance through his body. Stifling a cry, he completed the manoeuvre, then pulled rubble towards him to conceal the entrance to his hiding place.

Baron Fitzwilliam saw the Dwarves streaming back to the camp, their faces distraught. They'd taken heavy losses, yet the fortress of Galburn's Ridge, even damaged, resisted their best efforts. He felt a surge of despair, not for the lost battle but for the many warriors who'd given their lives in this folly.

"For Saxnor's sake," he said. "I never should have allowed this."

"They knew the risks," said Albreda, "and very nearly won through this night. Had we a few more of the stout mountain folk, they might very well have persevered."

"Instead, they are now battered and defeated."

"How many were lost?"

"I don't know," replied Fitz, "but I fear it a great many, and there's still no sign of Herdwin. There are scattered reports he was seen fighting at the top, but there's no confirmation as to his whereabouts at present."

She placed a hand on his arm. "This is not your fault, Richard. I should never have suggested this attack. It was foolhardy."

"You were only trying to help. It would have put an end to this war had it succeeded, but..." His voice trailed off.

"What do we do now?"

"We go back to using the trebuchets."

"And will we assault again?"

"Unless they surrender," he admitted, "we shall have no choice. We cannot defeat Norland without taking their capital."

"And now the war goes on while an army of dead conquers both sides."

"So it would seem, but what else can we do?"

Morning found Fitz once again examining the debris. The light of day revealed just how devastating Albreda's attack was, but also how many Dwarves died in the assault. Sir Preston found him standing there with tears running down his cheeks.

"General?" interrupted the knight.

Baron Fitzwilliam wiped his eyes. "Yes, Sir Preston?"

"I wonder if I might have a word, my lord?"

He turned to the newcomer. "About what?"

"Some of the others and I have been talking, Lord. I believe we may have a solution."

"A solution to what?"

"Galburn's Ridge."

The baron shook his head. "We lost enough warriors this day. I'll not lose anymore."

"You haven't heard our idea."

"OUR idea? Who else is involved in this?"

"The prince and Kiren-Jool."

Fitz stared back, not quite believing his ears. "What is it you're proposing?"

"It requires some explanation," said Sir Preston, "and it would be best discussed with the others present."

"Very well, but I'd like Albreda there to get her opinion on things."

"Of course, my lord. You are the general after all."

"Good. I'm glad someone remembers. Where is Prince Alric?"

"In his tent. We thought it best to keep the plan to ourselves for the moment."

"Then lead on," said Fitz. "I'm eager to learn what it is you propose."

EIGHTEEN

News

SUMMER 965 MC

P rince Alric stared down at the map, drawn in a crude hand, but at least it would serve to illustrate the plan he was about to present.

"General. Sir Preston and I have been talking."

"So I heard," said the baron. "Go on, then. Let's hear what this plan of yours entails. Saxnor knows our last one didn't go over so well."

Alric cleared his throat, nervous but at the same time eager to show he had ideas that could make a difference.

Baron Fitzwilliam, as if sensing his unease, tried to take some of the pressure off him. "There's no need to be shy, Highness. I'm listening with an open mind, not here to condemn you."

"Yes, thank you, Lord Richard. Now, where should I start?" Alric stared some more at the map, trying to organize the thoughts that raced through his mind in a jumble, struggling to slow his thought processes before he spoke. "As you are no doubt aware, last fall, the queen took a diplomatic mission to Galburn's Ridge. Due to a strange sequence of events, the Mercerian delegation left in a hurry, an exit facilitated by the use of a series of underground tunnels running beneath the castle."

"Yes," said Fitz, "and I believe I see where you're going with this, but surely those tunnels have been sealed off by now?"

"Sealed, yes, but not completely filled in. Such an operation would take months, if not years. It is my belief… OUR belief"—he glanced briefly at Sir Preston—"that these tunnels could be used to gain entry once more."

"A fine idea, but how would we find them? Beverly isn't here, nor the marshal. Who could guide us through them?"

The prince looked at his senior knight. "Sir Preston?"

"The flight of our delegation back to Merceria was a long and arduous one, my lord, and many of the Queen's Guards distinguished themselves. They were rewarded with promotion, and, seeing as how the Queen's Guards are a relatively small company, many were given commands elsewhere."

"Are you saying some of them are numbered amongst our own troops?" asked Fitz.

"Indeed, my lord. There are half a dozen amidst the heavy cavalry that forms my command."

"And if the tunnels are sealed?"

"Then we shall take picks to break down any barriers."

"That would make a lot of noise." The baron noted the loss of confidence on Sir Preston's face. "What if you had another way to break through?"

"What might you suggest, Lord?"

"I'm sure Albreda would be willing to accompany you. There's precious little that can stop her magic once she sets her mind to it."

"Then it's all settled," said the knight.

"Not so fast," cautioned Fitz. "I like the idea, but it needs more work."

"Ah," said the prince. "That's where I come in. The intent is to keep the defenders focused on a frontal assault while I lead my men up the slopes."

"The Dwarves already tried that," said Fitz. "What makes you believe you'd be any more successful?"

"I thought to use Kiren-Jool's magic. As an Enchanter, he can banish fatigue."

"How will that help? He can't very well use his magic on the entire assault, can he?"

"No, but it would definitely work on a select few."

"Which select few?" asked the baron, although he suspected he already knew the answer.

"My own guard," said Alric. "Naturally, they won't be mounted, but their heavier armour could prove decisive once we reach the top."

"And the magic would prevent them from tiring?"

"Precisely. I first saw the spell in action back in Weldwyn, although Kiren-Jool wasn't the one who cast it, rather it was Gretchen Harwell. We were in a hurry to get to Anna after she was injured, you see—"

"Yes," said Fitz. "We all know the story, but are you sure our Kurathian friend has that spell in his repertoire?"

"I know he does. I spoke to him about it at length this morning."

"So we have a frontal assault, backed up by a small infiltration team. Anything else I should know about?"

"There is," said Sir Preston. "A third group of mounted men will be on the plain at the top of the cliff, ready to ride in once the gate is secured."

The baron considered the plan carefully. "My first impression is it has merit, but I thought the same for the Dwarven assault, or I wouldn't have permitted it. Before I approve it, I need some time to think things over. If I should agree, how long would it take you to get everyone into position?"

"I should think two full days, my lord," said Sir Preston. "We'd need to get our people into those hills at the top of that cliff, and that would require them to circle around to the south."

"Not necessarily," said the prince. "Couldn't Albreda use her magic to spy out the area to the north?"

"Yes," said Fitz, "and her bird friends might be able to find a shorter route. I'll get her on it right away. As to the rest, I'll give it careful consideration."

He left them, stepping outside to disappear into the camp.

Sir Preston let out a deep breath. "That went better than I expected."

"He's getting desperate," said the prince, "and he has little in the way of options."

"And what of you? Do you believe this will work?"

"It must. We can't afford a protracted siege with an army of ghosts wandering around out there. I'd feel better if we had some idea of how many Norlanders are in that garrison though."

Just then the tent flap parted, revealing the presence of the queen.

"Anna!" said the prince, a smile breaking out on his features. "What are you doing here?"

"I came to see you." She turned her attention to the knight. "Sir Preston, I wonder if you might step outside for a moment and look after Lady Sophie for me? His Highness and I have something to discuss in private."

There was no mistaking the pleasure on Sir Preston's face. "I would be delighted to, Your Majesty."

He rushed from the tent.

"You made his day," said Alric.

"And now I'll make yours," she said with a grin. "It seems we are to be parents."

"You're expecting? That's marvellous news!"

"Is it? I doubt I could have picked a worse time to carry a child, what with the war and everything."

Alric stepped forward, embracing her. "Nonsense," he soothed. "And besides, you can't plan something like this. It's just the way life is."

She broke away, staring up into his face. "And how are things here? Keeping you busy?"

"They are," he admitted. "Sir Preston and I just came up with a plan to take Galburn's Ridge."

"And what's your part in this plan?"

"I'm to lead an assault up the cliff face. We'll see if I can succeed where the Dwarves failed."

"The Dwarves already attempted it?"

"They did," said Alric, "but it was too much for them."

"And what makes you believe you'll do better?"

"We'll have Sir Preston making his way through the tunnels."

He saw a look of fright on her face. "What's wrong?"

"You can't do this," she said. "Not now."

"I must. It's my idea."

"No, you don't understand. You mustn't go into battle."

"Why ever not?"

Tears came to her eyes. "Because you'll die."

"I'll be surrounded by my guard, Anna," countered Alric. "I hardly think—"

"NO!" she cried out. "I saw it!"

"Saw what?"

"You, lying on a battlefield, covered in blood. It was horrible!"

He moved closer, but she backed up, terror in her eyes.

"Where did you see this?" he asked.

"In a dream."

"Dreams are only a manifestation of our fears."

"Albreda might say otherwise."

"Unless I miss my guess, Albreda is usually wide awake when she has her prophetic visions."

The argument appeared to settle her. "I suppose that's true."

"I promise you," he said. "I shall take no chances during this assault. If things are going badly, I'll withdraw. Agreed?"

She nodded. "Very well," she said as she sniffed, and for a moment, instead of a mighty queen, he saw a frightened young woman. He took her hands into his own.

"Now," he said, "we must consider more important matters."

"Such as?"

"Names, for a start. What do you think about Ignacious?"

She stared at him in shock, then noticed his look of mirth.

"Now you're just teasing me."

"I am," Alric admitted, "but in all earnestness, we should choose carefully. After all, one day, Saxnor willing, he or she will be the ruler of Merceria. Would we, for instance, name it after your parents?"

He immediately noticed her distaste. "Sorry. For a moment there, I forgot how you feel about them. Still, we could name a son after Gerald?"

"Maybe a middle name?" suggested Anna.

"There, it's settled, then. And if it's a girl, we'll call her Geraldine?"

She laughed. "What about your parents?"

"I hardly think Leofric a good name for a Mercerian king, do you? As for a girl, I suppose Igraine isn't too bad."

"Your mother would love that."

"Beyond a doubt, but once again, it's not a Mercerian name."

"I only just discovered I'm pregnant," said Anna. "I think we can take a few weeks to choose a name."

Alric made an exaggerated bow. "In that case, Your Majesty, I shall give it my undivided attention."

"No, you won't," she replied. "You have a fortress to capture, remember?"

"Ah yes, I suppose I do."

"Speaking of which, how do you intend to coordinate the attacks?"

"By striking at nightfall."

"Could I suggest an alternative approach?"

"I'm all ears," he said.

"Have Andurak accompany Sir Preston."

"What good will that do? We don't have another shaman to relay details."

"You do now," said Anna. "Urgon's sister, Kurghal, accompanied me."

"I assume she's a shaman?"

"She is, and quite accomplished at that, but she does not speak our language at present. I suppose that means I'll need to stick around and translate for you."

He smiled, a twinkle in his eye. "Are you sure? I know it's a heavy burden."

She laughed. "You're teasing me again."

"The truth is, I think it an excellent idea. In fact, I shall seek out Fitz and propose it this very afternoon."

"In that case," said the queen, "I think I'll accompany you."

"Master Hearn," said Albreda. "I didn't expect to see you here."

The old Druid returned her stare. "I accompanied Her Majesty. We were to recall back to Wincaster, but she insisted on coming here first."

"Yes," added Anna, "and a good thing too. It appears I arrived at an opportune moment."

"Though we are pleased to see you," said the baron, "I'm at a loss as to what brings you here."

In answer, the queen looked at Alric, nodding. The prince let his gaze flow over the entire room before speaking.

"We are to welcome a child," he announced.

A chorus of congratulations sprang forth, so much so that the queen was forced to calm everybody down.

"We are both delighted," she said, "and welcome your best wishes, but do you think we could delay the well-wishing until later? I don't want to distract us from the task at hand."

"Of course," said the baron, turning his attention towards Prince Alric. "You had something you wished to bring up?"

"Yes. Anna pointed out we now have another shaman in our company."

"We do?"

"Yes," said Anna. "Kurghal, the sister of Urgon. She can use her spirit magic to communicate with Andurak, making it possible to keep the two assault parties in touch with each other, providing I'm present to translate."

"This is most welcome news, indeed," said the baron. "And I have some good news myself, or rather Albreda does." He turned to the Mistress of the Whitewood.

"I found another way up to the plains," said Albreda. "One that shouldn't take more than a half a morning to navigate. That means we could carry out the attack in as little as a day, although I would prefer two."

"Why two?" asked Alric.

"I spent a good part of the morning using my magic to look for this path. I should now like to concentrate my efforts on the fortress itself. With a little luck, I can have the entire tunnel system mapped out for you."

"You can?" said Fitz. "How?"

"Bats," she replied.

"Bats?"

"Yes, they are flying creatures that often nest in caves."

"I know what a bat is," said Fitz. "I'm just surprised they would be of use to us."

"And why wouldn't they be? Are they not used to flying in and out of caves?"

"And if Norland soldiers are guarding the tunnels?"

"Do you honestly believe a soldier would care about a bat flying around the area?"

"No," said Fitz, "I suppose not. You make a compelling case."

"Meaning you'll accept the plan?" said Alric.

"I will. Prepare your men, Your Highness. Tomorrow evening, we shall make our move."

"I would suggest the next morning," said Anna.

"For what reason, if I may ask?" replied the baron.

"It will allow the troops to climb under cover of darkness while fighting at the top in the early morning light. There would also be less chance of mistaking friend for foe in the confusion."

"I hadn't thought of that," said Alric, "but I must admit it's a good idea."

"And one we'll adopt," agreed Fitz. "Now, it's time to get moving if we want everything in place in time."

A guard stepped into the tent. "My lord, Your Majesty, you have a visitor."

"Who is it?" said the queen.

"A woman by the name of Gretchen Harwell."

"The Enchanter?" said Alric. "What's she doing here?"

"Let's find out, shall we?" said Anna, turning her attention to the guard. "Show her in."

The guard returned a moment later, the Weldwyn mage in tow.

"Your Majesty, Your Highness," said Mistress Harwell. "I bring grave news. King Leofric is dead."

Those in the room fell into a stunned silence.

"How can this be?" said Alric. "He leads a massive army."

"We have reports an army of ghosts overwhelmed them."

"The spirit army," hissed Fitz.

"Are you sure?" pressed the prince.

"There can be no doubt," the Enchanter said. "Aegryth Malthunen herself witnessed it, as did Roxanne Fortuna, although I regret the latter did not survive the recall to Summersgate."

"For Saxnor's sake," said Sir Preston. "This puts us in a precarious position. Leofric's army dwarfed ours. If he was defeated, then what chance have we?"

"It wouldn't be the first time we were outnumbered," said the queen, "nor do I believe it will be the last. We must trust in the strength of our weapons and our resolve to win at all costs."

"At all costs?" said Hearn.

"There is little choice in the matter. This war is no longer about punishing Norland—it's a fight for our very survival. Should we fail to destroy this menace, both Weldwyn and Merceria will be in peril." Her gaze fell upon the Enchanter once more. "How long ago did this unfortunate episode occur?"

"Some weeks, I'm afraid. I recalled to Wincaster, but when I learned you weren't there, I came north the old-fashioned way. I would have been here sooner had I been more familiar with the countryside."

"At least you're here now," said Alric, "though what your news portends is still open to debate."

"Agreed," said Anna. "Can you tell us of Leofric's last position? That might give us some indication of the location of this spirit army."

"According to Aegryth, they were on the northern shore of the Windstorm Depths. Is that close?"

"Uncomfortably so," chimed in Fitz, "if our maps are anything to go on. Of course, they're notoriously unreliable, so who knows?"

"What about Weldwyn?" asked Alric. "The loss of my father will be keenly felt, but the soldiers, even more so. He stripped away most of the army to send those warriors up here. Now that they're gone, the kingdom's virtually defenceless."

"What about you?" asked Anna.

"Me?"

"Surely you must feel a great sadness at your father's death."

"He and I weren't exactly close. I don't think he ever got over the fact I killed Cuthbert."

"That wasn't your fault," Anna insisted.

"That's exactly what he said, but the loss of a son is a bitter mead to swallow, even if it is justified."

"We are saddened by your father's death," said Fitz. "He was a fine fellow and a staunch ally."

"Thank you," said Alric, "but I would prefer we return to more urgent matters, that of this spirit army. Is it your supposition, Anna, that Necromancers enslaved my father's army?"

"It is," she said. "Did Kraloch send word of what transpired to the east?"

"You mean the arrival of Zhura?" said Fitz. "He did. Why?"

"Zhura talked of something called a Volgath. Do you think that could be King Leofric?"

"Possibly," said the baron, "but the army must have existed before Leofric's defeat, or how else would they have beaten him?"

"Agreed," said Albreda, "and there's still the matter of the missing Ancestors. That would seem to indicate a spirit army comprised of Orcs."

"Could there be two such armies?"

"Let's hope not," said the queen. "It would be hard enough dealing with only one. Gerald thinks they can be beaten, although he'll need to combine all the soldiers we have, to do so."

"All the more reason to take that castle sooner rather than later," said Fitz. "And, from the sounds of it, we don't have a lot of time."

"So we are to proceed?" said Sir Preston.

"Yes. Get your men into position. We'll update you once Albreda has more information. We'll plan the assault for tomorrow night. Andurak and Kurghal will remain in close communications in case there are any last-moment changes. Any questions?"

The Weldwyn Enchanter stepped up. "What would you like me to do? Shall I remain here with you or return to Summersgate?"

"Remain here for now," said Anna. "At least until the attack is over. If we're going to send you all the way back to Weldwyn, we can hopefully pass along some good news."

"And if the attack fails?"

"We'll just have to hope it doesn't."

"I can do more than simply sit and wait," said Mistress Harwell. "I can help prepare the troops for the coming battle. I am an Enchanter after all."

"That would be much appreciated," said Fitz, "though I don't want to put you in any danger."

"I can handle myself."

The baron turned to the queen. "I suppose this means you'll be sticking around here for a few more days, Majesty?"

"Of course, but I'll try to keep out of everyone's way. There IS a war raging across the land."

They were about to break up the meeting when Andurak arrived. Not recognizing the queen, he made his way directly to Baron Fitzwilliam.

"General," he said. "I bring dire news from the marshal. It seems he has found Bronwyn and what's left of her army."

"And the bad news?" said Fitz.

"An army of ghosts followed her."

"By the Gods, they're closer than we thought! Where are they?"

"About three days march west of Anvil," replied the Orc.

"Should we ride to assist?" asked Sir Preston.

"No, we'd never get there in time. I'm afraid Gerald's on his own this time. We, on the other hand, have our plates full trying to take care of these Norlanders."

NINETEEN

Across the Border

SUMMER 965 MC

B rida brought her horse to a halt. Beside her rode Lochlan, looking resplendent in a fine coat of chainmail beneath a crimson cloak.

"Isn't it grand!" she said.

"Grand? What's so grand about it? We're marching to a river we can't cross. I told you this was a bad idea."

"Hush now," she soothed. "The prince assured me his mages would be able to get us across."

"I'd prefer to put my faith in a few sturdy boats than trust that foreigner. And why here, of all places? Couldn't he have picked somewhere a little easier to get to?"

"And where might that be? The same place we crossed last time? Weldwyn would never expect us to make a crossing here."

"You don't know that," Lochlan insisted.

"Yes, I do."

"How?"

"Look for yourself," Brida said. "Do you see any enemy warriors waiting to welcome us?"

"No," he admitted.

"Then there's all the proof you need. We have the element of surprise."

"How do you know he didn't just lure us here to take our cities?"

"Because his army is here as well, or did you forget the three thousand Kurathians marching on our southern flank?"

"Not at all," he said. "In fact, it's the very presence of those mercenaries that has me worried."

"How many times do I need to tell you they're not mercenaries? Those are the household troops of Prince Tarak."

"Household troops? He must have the largest great hall in all the known lands... possibly even the unknown ones as well."

Brida took a breath. Ever since he returned from Glanfraydon, he'd been surly, far more so than was usual for her brother. Her father, King Dathen, had been his guiding hand, but since his incarceration, it had fallen to her to carry out that duty, a duty she despised. It wasn't that she didn't love her brother, but he could be so immature at times.

Those marching before them slowed.

"Ah," said Brida. "We're here. Come, let's take a look!" She spurred on her horse, leaving Lochlan to catch up.

The River Loran, named after the founding King of Weldwyn, emptied into the Sea of Storms at Riversend. Its true source had never been discovered, at least as far as Brida was aware, but everyone knew it formed the western border of Weldwyn. Here the water ran swift and deep, making even a boat's crossing a hazardous experience.

She tried to place their position, thinking back to the crude maps her father had ordered made. They were, quite literally, in the middle of nowhere, something Prince Tarak has assured her would make the perfect place to launch an attack. Now, as she stared at the opposite bank, she wondered if she'd been a bit hasty in accepting his suggestion.

A group of riders came towards them, and she turned, recognizing the Kurathian prince.

"Isn't it magnificent?" said Prince Tarak.

"It is," she replied, "though I would think it more so were we examining it from the other side."

"Something that shall soon be rectified, Your Majesty. If you will allow me, I shall call upon my mages?"

"By all means."

He turned to the riders who followed, rattling off something in his native tongue. After a brief back and forth, three riders dismounted, moving to stand on the western bank of the River Loran, about five paces apart from each other.

Brida had witnessed the power of magic before, but she was utterly unprepared for what happened next. The mages all started chanting, and then each, in turn, stepped forward, touching their hands to the water.

She felt a chill, then saw frost beginning to form on the surface, turning it white before solidifying into ice, yet still, the spells continued.

"Come," said the prince. "The ice will not last forever. We must cross while we can."

They rode forward to discover a sheet of ice crawling towards the eastern bank.

"Will it support our weight?" asked Lochlan.

"Don't be ridiculous," said Brida. "Of course it will. Why else cast it?"

"Your brother is right to be cautious," said the prince. "Such magic is most wondrous, but difficult to control. My mages will require some time to thicken up the ice before we allow the army to cross. However, to prove to you I am earnest, I shall cross my own men first."

"No," said Brida. "I believe a Clan army should have that honour."

The Kurathian bowed. "If that is your wish, then I am happy to oblige you, Your Majesty."

"How long will it take to make it ready?"

In answer, the prince looked at the water once more, then let his gaze drift back to the Clan army. "You may move your men up at your leisure. The river should be prepared by the time they reach its edge."

"Good," said Brida. "We shall start with our lighter horse first, I think, then follow up with our heavier footmen."

"Very well. My Water Mages shall remain here to keep the ice thick, Your Majesty. Is there anything else?"

"No, I believe you've done enough for now."

"Then I shall leave Your Royal Majesty and prepare my own troops to follow yours across."

"And then?"

"Then it shall be up to you to decide where we march next. After all, you're the High Queen." He turned his horse around, galloping off to join his own warriors.

"I still don't trust him," said Lochlan.

"You don't trust anyone."

"That's not true. I trust you, don't I?"

She laughed. "You have no choice there. I'm your older and wiser sister."

"Wiser?"

"All right, I admit that might be pushing things a little. Still, we'll have our entire army across the river before nightfall. Something that would have been impossible mere months ago."

"And then?"

"I thought we might march east. Unless I miss my guess, there lies the town of Walverton. You would know better than I what awaits us there."

"Let's see," said Lochlan. "Walverton, if I recall, is a barony, but the noble who rules there, a fellow named Lord Sherwyn, spends most of his time in Summersgate."

She looked at him in surprise. "How could you possibly know that?"

"You'd be surprised what you can learn from listening in on prisoners. You remember, we still have captives from the last time we invaded Weldwyn?"

"Yes. They were put to work in the mines. I understand they've been most compliant."

"If you mean beaten into submission," he said, "then I suppose they are."

"You don't approve?"

"They're men, not animals."

"They fought against us during the invasion," countered Brida. "Or did you forget that?"

"They were defending their homes. What did you expect them to do, roll over and beg for mercy?"

She gave him a hard stare. "This isn't a game, Lochlan. The warriors of Weldwyn are the enemy. As such, they deserve what we give them."

"Let me guess—death or imprisonment?"

"I might remind you they still hold Father in the dungeons of Summersgate."

"Yes, something you feel a need to mention every single day."

Brida was about to say more but knew it would only lead to more arguments. Instead, she changed the subject. "What lies south of Walverton?"

"Tivilton," replied Lochlan.

"That's the Elven town, isn't it?"

"Yes, astride the Draenor Woods. Mind you, they're not all Elves, but the baron definitely is. Take that town, and it'll open up the road to Riversend."

"And to the north?"

"Loranguard."

"I don't much fancy attacking that place," she said. "It could pin down our army for months."

"Then march farther eastward."

"There are no roads."

"This is not the Clan holdings," said Lochlan. "The countryside of Weldwyn is open and inviting, easy travel for an army."

"And how would we navigate without roads?"

"Walverton lies at the southwestern tip of the Hollow Woods. Follow that forest along its southern border, and when you finally reach its eastern end, you'll be just south of Abermore, which lies on the road to Summersgate."

"Our ultimate prize," said Brida. "It appears your love for maps has served us well. Once the army is across, we'll march for Walverton, sack the town, and then move eastward, destroying crops as we go."

"Destroying crops? I don't think that wise."

"Weldwyn must be made to suffer for what they did to us. We must avenge Father's humiliation!"

"Those crops will be needed to feed our army," argued Lochlan, "and its people to tend the crops. We can't start indiscriminately killing everyone. Now it appears it's MY turn to remind YOU we are here to subjugate the people of Weldwyn."

"And to do that, we must show no mercy."

"Kill them all, Brida, and there shall be no one left to rule over. It would be better if we were greeted as liberators rather than conquerors."

"Don't talk such nonsense," she said, her bitterness rising. "We shall crush their army and then kill every last member of their Royal Family, especially Prince Alric!"

Lochlan shook his head. "You are blinded by your rage, Sister. You're the High Queen now. You must suppress your own feelings for the betterment of the Clans."

"No. I AM the Clans. It is they who must suppress their feelings for the betterment of ME!"

"So you would take your war to Merceria?"

"Merceria?"

"Yes," he said. "You know as well as I that Prince Alric is married to their queen. Do you imagine they will simply sit back and allow us to run roughshod over their allies?"

"Not at all," said Brida. "In fact, I'm counting on it."

"You are?"

"Yes. Alric will, I am certain, persuade his precious queen to send help, and then I shall have him within my grasp."

"There's much to be done before you can spring that trap, Sister. I believe we should first concentrate on taking Walverton."

"You're right, of course. We have yet to take our first town, and here I am talking of revenge. What must you think of me?"

"You are passionate," said Lochlan. "It's what will make you a good queen, although maybe empress might be a better term."

"Why would you say that?"

"If what Lysandil told us is true, you shall end up ruling not only the Clan holdings but all of Weldwyn as well. Surely the ruler of two kingdoms deserves a more fitting title than a mere queen?"

"High Queen," she corrected.

"Even so, it doesn't do justice to the accomplishment."

"And if I were empress, what would that make you?"

"Me? I am content to be a scholar, as you well know."

"Come now," said Brida. "There must be something you desire? If you could have your pick of anything in Weldwyn, what would it be?"

"I would be master of the Dome," he replied.

"The Dome?"

"Yes. Its official title is the Grand Edifice of the Arcane Wizards Council."

"Then why is it called the Dome?"

"For the shape of its roof, which is encased in copper."

"So its roof is sheathed in metal?" she said in astonishment. "What in the name of the Gods for?"

"It protects the stone beneath from the elements. It's also said to be enchanted."

"Enchanted, how?"

"Copper normally turns green as it ages, but the Dome still maintains its original metallic finish after centuries of wear and tear."

"I'm guessing that means powerful magic?"

"One would certainly think so," said Lochlan.

Brida cast her eyes westward to where the army now crossed in ever-increasing numbers. "Prince Tarak has casters of his own. Do you believe they will be sufficient to counter the threat of these Weldwyn mages?"

"Undoubtedly. From what I managed to learn, Weldwyn only has a few fully trained spellcasters."

"And by few, you mean?"

"Less than a dozen, by all accounts, and that's including their students. The prince has three Water Mages, but I understand he has pyromancers amongst his followers as well."

"Pyromancers?"

"Yes, Fire Mages," he said. "Sorry, it's a Kurathian term. I've been reading up on them ever since you told me of his impending arrival."

"And what have you learned?"

"About him, personally? Not much, to be perfectly honest. The records we have on those foreigners are few and far between, mostly gleaned from mercenaries we employed previously. Kurathians have a reputation as being fierce warriors, but I would expect no less. After all, they're soldiers for hire. Their reputation is what makes them highly sought after."

"But you don't believe these stories?"

"Our experiences in the past leads me to believe they are no better or worse than our own warriors. Their one saving grace is, I suppose, their horsemen, which has more to do with their mounts than the actual riders."

"I must admit," said Brida, "your evaluation is somewhat disappointing."

"In what way?"

"I hoped they were more deserving of the reputation they so carefully cultivate."

He laughed. "There's that, but even so, they are here in much larger numbers than in the past."

"The army we have with us this day is even bigger than the one Father used in the last war."

"Yes, and that's not including the prince's warriors."

"There's nothing that can withstand us!" declared Brida.

"That's true at the moment," said Lochlan, "but as we roll across Weldwyn and capture cities, we'll need to leave garrisons behind to hold on to them. That will wear down our numbers fairly quickly."

"You doubt we'll succeed?"

"Not at all. I have complete confidence in the eventual outcome, but conquering an entire nation will not be without its challenges."

"Challenges we will, in all probability, overcome," said Brida, "but let us first go and see how our army fares."

The evening found them camped by the river. The ice had long since melted, leaving Lochlan nervous, for without it, there was no way to retreat. The arrival of Prince Tarak to their tent only served to heighten his fears.

"May I enter?" called out the prince.

"By all means," replied Brida.

The Kurathian stepped in, his clothing immaculate as always. Lochlan wondered how the man could stay so clean but then decided he must simply change his clothes several times a day.

"Have you decided on a strategy, Your Majesty?" Tarak asked.

"Yes," she replied. "After we take Walverton, we shall march eastward, taking Abermore then marching directly on the capital, Summersgate."

"An ambitious plan. Might I ask what inspired it?"

"Lysandil indicated when Leofric was killed, he commanded a large army. That being the case, we have an opportunity to strike while they are short of warriors."

"Assuming he's telling the truth," added Lochlan.

"You may rest assured on that matter," said the prince. "Having known Lysandil a good many years, I have learned to trust him implicitly."

"Summersgate is still a formidable objective," said Brida. "So I thought it best to take it before our army is forced to weaken itself by providing garrisons to the cities that fall to us."

"You show great wisdom, Majesty, but I can assure you such numbers will be unnecessary. If you recall, I have, under my control, weapons of such incredible power that nothing can stand against them."

"And what weapons might those be?" asked Lochlan.

The prince merely smiled. "All will be revealed in due course. For the moment, however, let us concentrate on the military campaign. What do you know of Weldwyn's forces?"

"In what way?" asked Brida.

"What might we expect to face in battle?"

"They tend to employ horse and foot in equal numbers, or at least they did before the loss of Leofric and his precious army."

"And their archers?"

"Mostly bowmen," she said, "although they recently began using crossbows in some companies."

"Interesting," said Prince Tarak. "Do we know why?"

"Likely ease of learning," suggested Lochlan. "A bow takes a lifetime of practice, but a crossbowman can be taught the basics of his trade in weeks, days even. Tell me, Lord Prince, do your own warriors use them?"

"No, they favour the humble bow, a far more practical weapon from a purely military point of view."

"Practical?" said Brida.

"A skilled bowman can loose off many more arrows than someone with a crossbow."

"But a crossbow can puncture armour," insisted Lochlan.

"There is that, but the warriors of Weldwyn have no plate armour, do they?"

"Not that I'm aware, but it's said the Mercerians put armoured plates over their chainmail, a technique that Weldwyn smiths are likely eager to emulate."

"Just to be clear," said Tarak, "are you saying their soldiers wear nothing but simple chainmail?"

"Yes, along with padded jackets, of course. Mind you, that's primarily their horsemen. Their footmen wear only gambesons, aside from their helms."

"Then I see no need to worry about crossbows at this time. In fact, we should be grateful for Weldwyn's use of them. It will slow down their volleys by a significant degree."

"Tell me," said Lochlan, "if plate armour is so effective, why don't all your men wear it?"

"We came here aboard ship," the prince explained, "and storage space is limited. Far better to bring more men than to fill up the holds with armour."

"Could your men not have simply worn it at all times?"

Prince Tarak shook his head. "Obviously, you've never had to wear such armour. Kouras is a tropical clime. If you were so equipped, you would soon succumb to heat exhaustion. Those who are outfitted with it only don their armour for battle or when guarding the Palace."

"But you indicated it's common on the Continent."

"Only amongst knights and those of wealth. Creation of such a suit is an expensive proposition and one that can take months for an armourer to craft. There's also the matter of having high-quality iron available for its construction, along with smiths skilled in its crafting. It's far more cost-effective to arm yourselves in lighter fare."

"Does that go for your cavalry as well?"

"It does. As you've seen, half my army is mounted, and out of that, only a third wears chainmail. The rest make do with padded gambesons and helms, much as you do."

Lochlan thought things over, but something still bothered him. "And if the Mercerians bring their knights into battle?"

"Ah yes, the dreaded Mercerian knights. I was warned about those. While they are, admittedly, better protected than many of their allies, the fact remains they are still relatively few. Should we face them in battle, I am confident our more numerous cavalry will overwhelm them."

"They are rumoured to be the toughest warriors in this part of the world."

"Perhaps," said the prince, "but my men have faced off against some of the finest soldiers the Continent has to offer. These Mercerian knights pale in comparison to the household troops of the mightiest nobles of the Petty Kingdoms."

"I wish I had your confidence."

"It's not confidence, but rather, experience. When I was younger, I was just like you, questioning everything. I thought I was invincible, that I would live forever."

"And?" prompted Lochlan.

"And though I kept my youthful exuberance, it became tempered, in time, with experience. Do not fear the enemy. At the end of the day, they are merely Human, and I haven't met a man yet who was impervious to steel."

TWENTY

Skirmish

G erald stared at the distant horde. They advanced quickly, much faster than he had expected, and he feared they would be upon his army before they were prepared. He checked both sides of his formation to see the last of his archers falling into place.

His orders had, of necessity, been terse and quick. Archers, both Human and Orc, were to take up positions on either flank but avoid engaging in direct melee. His main line consisted of his Mercerian foot, with the Orcs of the Black Arrow standing by behind them, their long spears ready to step in and assist, should it prove necessary.

He stared at the enemy, willing them to slow, to no avail. They came forward as a large mob, making estimates as to numbers difficult. The fast pace of the enemy foot was countered by the slowness of its cavalry, for the spirit horsemen appeared unwilling to gallop. Gerald wondered why this might be the case but could think of nothing that would explain it.

The lead troops were comprised of Humans, likely the remains of Leofric's army, but those in the rear bore pale-green skin, reminiscent of the Orcs. There was little subtlety in the formation, with spearmen making up the bulk of the army, augmented by archers on the southern flank. He tried to spot if there were any to the north but detected no evidence of it. The horsemen, however, were there, ready to try enveloping their flank.

Leofric had the reputation of a seasoned warrior, but Gerald had only seen him in battle once, at the Battle of the Three Kings, back in Weldwyn. At that time, they fought off an enemy much larger than their own. However, this enemy appeared even bigger, stretching down the road as far as the eye could see.

Urgon and Zhura stepped up beside him, following his gaze.

"It is a tremendous sight," said the Orc chieftain. "I fear the numbers are against us."

"Maybe not," said Zhura. "You must remember each of their warriors has to be controlled by a Necromancer's thoughts."

"Or the Volgath's," added Urgon.

"Precisely, and that takes a lot of concentration. I doubt you will see any surprises today. They will probably come at us in one enormous mass and let their numbers tell."

"Can we hold them?" asked Gerald.

"You would know the answer to that better than I," replied Zhura, "but I would suspect so. The real trick to this is holding on to what little space we have. The occupier of this hill will determine the victor this day."

"How can you be so sure?"

"As I indicated earlier, they refill their losses by binding spirits of the recently deceased. If we still hold the hill at nightfall, they will be unable to replace their losses, increasing our strength relative to theirs."

"That largely depends on how many casualties WE take."

"You have some advantages," she said. "For one thing, they lack decent armour."

"Why is that?" asked Gerald.

"They are spirits and thus cannot wear armour."

"And yet they have a physical form, do they not?"

"Only in that their spirits are anchored to those who control them. Scattered in amongst that army are many Necromancers. Kill them, and all under their control will be sent back to the spirit realm."

"You make it sound so simple."

"Not at all," replied Zhura. "In fact, quite the reverse. Getting to a Necromancer is still a far cry from simply spotting one."

"We must trust in our bows," noted Urgon. "Will your footmen hold, do you think?"

"I certainly hope so," said Gerald. "If not, we're going to be facing a terrible retreat."

"Discipline is the key," said Urgon. "Our own soldiers must keep to their lines and prevent the enemy from crossing them. If they can do that, we might yet be successful."

Closer drew the enemy. Gerald spotted Weldwyn's banner, prominent amongst the spirit troops and found himself wishing he were anywhere but here. He'd fought before, of course, but now he doubted his own wisdom in seeking this battle. Was he leading them all to their doom?

The keening grew louder, tempting him to put his hands over his ears before he thought better of it. He must set an example for the army, whose grip on their weapons and shields made such a simple act impossible.

The men looked unsteady, something that worried him deeply. "Let's hear you," he called out. Men started knocking their weapons against their shields, creating a drumming sound that helped drown out the horrible wail of their enemy. It was an old trick to distract his warriors from the fate that awaited them, but it worked.

A typical battle was not about who killed the most, rather who lost their nerve first. Had his opponents been Human, he would be confident in victory but against spirits, who could say?

Gerald spotted what used to be Leofric amongst his ghostly troops, mounted and riding behind the footmen, close enough to keep an eye on them but far enough back as to make an attack against him impossible at this time.

The Orcs on his southern flank were the first to loose their volleys. Under Kraloch's expert guidance, the hunters delivered a devastating barrage. A strange sight befell the battlefield, for when a spirit warrior was hit, one of two things happened: either he continued on, ignoring the hit, or dissipated, fading into nothingness.

There were no hits to critical areas here, merely arrows thudding into... something. Precisely what that was, he didn't know, but he was willing to call it a body for now. The Orcs kept up an accurate fire, switching out their volleys for hand-picked targets. Many of the enemy vanished, but more simply stepped up to take their places.

A lucky arrow must have taken down a Necromancer, for suddenly a whole slew of spirits dissolved into mist, and Gerald felt a grain of hope, a hope soon dashed as the Orcs withdrew, and the army of ghosts continued their advance. The hair on the back of his neck suddenly stood on end as a powerful stench drifted over them—the smell of death and decay.

To their north, Hayley directed archers against the enemy horsemen, and the sight gave him pause. Urgon spotted the source of his attention.

"Why does their horse not outflank us?" the chieftain asked. "They must have the numbers."

"A good question," said Gerald. "Had I that much cavalry, I'd sweep away all opposition. Instead, they advance slowly as if they're not mounted."

Zhura startled them both, coming to stand between them. "It is the Volgath," she explained. "It is unwilling to release its control over them." She turned to Gerald, noticing his confusion. "You rely on other leaders to command those who are some distance from you, but this creature of the spirit realm cannot summon such trust."

"So all he can do is come straight at us?"

"So it would seem."

"That is good news," said Urgon, "though not the type of thing we can take advantage of, given our present situation."

They heard a roar of defiance ripple through the Mercerian army, then the enemy made contact. Up and down the line echoed the sounds of combat, of spear on shield and sword on armour. Gerald moved closer to the action, drawing his trusty sword and shield. He'd elected to fight on foot, preferring to be with his men, but now he second-guessed the wisdom of that choice, for his presence would be lost amongst the swirling melee.

One of the men to his front went down, and a massive Orc spirit stepped into the Gap. Gerald reacted instinctively, stepping forward and stabbing out with his sword. He felt the blade sink into... something, although not the experience he'd been expecting.

His opponent struck back, reaching out with a ghostly spear to stab at him, but the marshal brought up his shield, easily deflecting the blow. Again he struck, this time aiming for the spirit's chest.

"There are no weak spots," called out Zhura, her voice cutting through the din of battle.

"Then how do I kill this thing?" he replied.

"You need only to damage it enough. Aim for the arms or legs if you find that easier."

He sliced his sword into his foe to be rewarded by a solid hit. Had it been against a Human foe, the fellow's limb would have been hacked off, but instead, the spirit exploded into a mist, and Gerald stumbled.

Urgon rushed forward, grabbing him by the belt and pulling him back. "Hold the line," said the Orc. "It is the only way to stay safe."

The marshal fought down the panic building within him. Everywhere there were spirits, reaching out with a wall of spears that stretched as far as the eye could see.

He struck out at another ghost, carving through the thing's face with the tip of his sword. The face deformed, then returned to its original state as the blade came out the other side. Gerald's shield came up again, blocking another spear tip, then he countered, slicing into an arm. A third strike finished the creature off, and it, too, vanished into so much mist.

He stepped back, trying to gauge the progress of the battle. Mist enveloped the entire front line as ghostly forms were cut down left and right. He stared, not believing what his own eyes revealed.

"Are you injured?" came Urgon's voice.

The old warrior watched the melee unfolding before him, then a smile spread over his face.

"What is wrong?" Urgon pressed.

"Nothing," he replied. "I'm fine."

Could his eyes be deceiving him? He looked again until he was convinced he had the right of it. Stepping forward, he struck out, then instantly brought his shield up to bear. The spirit before him stabbed out as he suspected he would. He countered easily, then sliced his blade through the thing's forearm. Two more quick jabs, and the spirit dissolved before his very eyes. Gerald stepped back, now more confident.

"What is it?" said Urgon.

"Watch their attack," urged the marshal. "They always repeat the same moves."

"It must be the Volgath's doing," said Zhura. "He can't manage each individual fight. It would overwhelm him."

Gerald nodded. "So he has them repeat the same actions, over and over, and why not? His numbers will win out in the end."

Urgon pushed past. "Let us see, shall we?" He rushed into the fray, his sword slicing left and right. Spears struck out, as they did against Gerald, but the Orc was quick, dodging and swerving to avoid the tips. He cut down a pair of spirits, then withdrew back to their own line, allowing a Mercerian footman to fill the Gap.

"It is true," said the Orc. "There are limits to his control."

"Useful to know, but we lack the strength to keep this up all day. We must find another weakness."

Just then, the Mercerians to their front went down, and the spirits surged through the Gap. Urgon and Gerald both brought their weapons to bear, ready for a fight, but then something strange happened—the enemy halted.

Gerald struggled to come to grips with it, for all along his line of warriors, the fighting continued. What, then, caused this particular group to halt?

Zhura took a step forward, and the spirits recoiled. "It is me," she said. "They will not suffer my presence." She took another step, and the ghostly spearmen withdrew.

Gerald moved up, taking one out. Urgon, quick to react, did likewise, cutting down the motionless figures.

"Where is the Volgath?" said Urgon.

"Over there," said Zhura. "I can feel his presence. I think it time we threatened him."

"In what way?"

"Gather your men around you, Marshal."

Gerald gave the orders, and footmen ran up to form a wall before the ghostwalker. As a group, they advanced, slowly at first, not quite believing their luck would hold. In their wake came Zhura, Urgon by her side.

All opposition to their advance faded, and then Gerald spotted the banner of King Leofric, its tattered cloth hanging still in the breezeless air. The Volgath, most likely sensing their approach, turned its attention on them, but in order to do so, it relinquished control over much of its army. Captive spirits, no longer having their actions dictated, ceased fighting, and scores of them dissolved into mist as the Mercerians took advantage of the momentary weakness.

Gerald couldn't see Leofric himself, but his banner withdrew and, with it, the rest of this army.

"Hold!" he shouted, causing his men to halt their advance.

"What is happening?" asked Urgon.

"The Volgath is withdrawing, at least for now."

"Should we pursue?"

"No. They still outnumber us by a significant degree. Let them withdraw. We'll return to our own line and see what happens."

His small group started backing up, slowly making their way up the hill, a time-consuming process, made even more so by the need to walk backwards while holding their formation. But eventually, they arrived at their destination. The spirit army let them go, settling instead on forming up some distance away.

"What now?" asked Urgon.

"That's a great question'" said Gerald. "I suppose it depends on what they intend to do." He nodded in the direction of their enemy, then turned to Zhura. "How do we stop those Necromancers from taking the spirits of our dead?"

"You must take the bodies with you," she replied. "Without a corpse, there is no hook for them to retrieve the spirit."

"But they command the Ancestors' spirits, don't they? If what you say is true, then how did they do that?"

"The bodies of your Human allies were used to anchor those spirits, but something else would be required to enslave the Ancestors."

"Are you suggesting the Volgath is not responsible?"

"Likely not. That creature was created by using the spirit of King Leofric, but the Ancestors began disappearing long before the King of Weldwyn marched into Norland."

"Could there be more than one of those creatures?"

"I doubt it," said Zhura. "I would have sensed it as I did the spirit of Leofric."

"I should have Kraloch contact the others," said Urgon. "They need to know of our circumstances."

"Agreed," said Gerald, "and also of what we discovered this day. In the meantime, we must retreat. But tell me, Zhura, can a spirit be called from ash?"

"Not that I am aware of," she replied.

"That would make sense," added Urgon. "For with no body, there would be no connection to the physical world."

"Then that's what we'll do, but not right now. It'll take far too long to collect enough wood. We'll take the dead with us and fall back to our prepared defences."

Aubrey dismissed the spell, breaking contact.

"Well?" said Beverly.

"Gerald has fought the spirit army to a draw, somewhere west of Anvil."

"Did Kraloch say how many there were?"

"As many as two thousand, possibly even more out of sight. They marched down the road, running directly into them. What was more disturbing, though, was their leader."

"Oh?" said the knight. "Who was it? Penelope?"

"No. Leofric, or what used to be Leofric. Apparently, he's been turned into some kind of creature of the spirit realm."

"And they defeated him?"

"No," replied Aubrey, "only fought him to a standstill. His army is still in relatively good shape, although they did sustain casualties. They're withdrawing to prepared defences. Gerald wants us to make all haste to join them."

"I can well imagine. Very well, I'll have Tog pull back his Trolls, and we'll make our way to Anvil. Anything else?"

"Yes," said Aubrey. "Quite a few things, in fact, but I can fill you in as we ride. It's more important to get underway."

Beverly turned Lightning around, heading north. The Trolls still held the northernmost position, watching for any sign of Norland troops, but so far, the effort was largely in vain. As she approached them, she spotted activity farther north, the telltale sign of cavalry on the move.

"For Saxnor's sake," she shouted. "Now is not the time for the Norlanders to be offering battle!"

She reined in her horse, coming to a halt beside Tog. Even standing beside the massive Mercerian charger, the Troll was taller, causing Beverly to need to look up to meet his gaze.

"You saw it too?"

"I did," said Tog, "though it's still too far off to make out any details."

"Could it be Revi and Arnim?"

He stared north, squinting. "I would say yes, but there's far too much dust for such a small group."

"They had Kurathian horsemen with them," she reminded him.

"A fact I am well aware of, but whoever approaches must possess significantly greater numbers to raise that amount of dust into the air."

"Could it be another spirit army?"

"Possibly, but it is most likely Norlanders, considering our location. Was that not the very reason for our presence here?"

"Yes," said Beverly, "but events took on a life of their own. We were asked to rejoin the marshal's force in preparation for a great battle. We can ill-afford to take on another earl at this point."

"We cannot ignore it—to do so could well spell disaster."

"I hate to admit it, but I wish Revi were here. At least he'd be able to send out Shellbreaker, and give us an idea of what we're up against."

"Most of your brigade is made up of archers," said Tog. "Might I suggest we deploy them as skirmishers? Then once they're in range, they can retreat, keeping the enemy at the extreme range of their volleys."

"An excellent idea. I'll keep the horsemen in reserve to counter any enemy cavalry threat, but I'll need the Trolls to maintain their position in the centre of the line."

"Very well," said Tog. "In the meantime, I suggest Aubrey send word to our allies, informing them we've encountered more Norlanders."

"Are you sure?" said the baron.

"There can be no mistake," replied Andurak. "Kraloch was clear enough in his message."

"What now?" asked Sir Preston. "Do we cancel our assault and ride to the marshal's aid?"

"No," replied Fitz. "Much as I'd like to, he's too far away for us to be of any help to him at this time. If he had turned south rather than east, then it might be a possibility, but the last thing we want to do is run into this spirit army in dribs and drabs. We are better served to complete our work here at Galburn's Ridge. What do you think, Your Majesty?"

"I would agree with your assessment, General," said the queen, "though it pains me to leave Gerald hanging out there."

"Wait a moment," said Alric. "Isn't Dame Beverly guarding his northern flank? Surely she'll bring her forces south to support him?"

"Most assuredly," said the baron. "The real question is whether that will be enough. Estimates place the enemy at two thousand or more. Even with Beverly's troops, he'd still be outnumbered."

"True," said Sir Preston. "It appears it's our lot in life as Mercerians to always be smaller in number."

"Gerald will win this," said the queen. "I know he will."

"I wish I shared your optimism, Your Majesty, but I fear he's never faced a foe quite like this before."

TWENTY-ONE

Making a Stand

SUMMER 965 MC

Gerald saw their looks of exhaustion as the men marched past, yet there was no sign of defeat. They had bested an unbeatable enemy, and although they'd been forced to withdraw, their morale remained high.

Hayley rode up from the rear of the column.

"Any sign of them?" he asked.

"Not at present," she replied. "They appear to be content with holding their position. You don't suppose they're summoning more spirits, do you?"

"They can't, remember? We brought our dead with us."

"Then where are they?"

He grunted. "Likely trying to decipher our next move. Tell me, if you were Leofric, or rather that... thing, what would you do?"

"I'd push on. His warriors don't need to rest, but ours do. If he catches us at the end of a long march, he'll have half the work done for him."

"That was my thought, but I can't help but feel we're missing something."

"You think he's attempting to outflank us?"

"No, I have riders out looking for that."

"Then what?" asked Hayley.

"What would you estimate their numbers at?"

"Difficult to say. They were lined up in front of us, but a trail of reinforcements stretched back up the road."

"Of which we never saw the end."

"That's right. Do you suppose he's waiting for more to catch up?"

"It would make sense," said Gerald. "The Orcs tell us all their Ancestors are gone. How many would need to be missing to give that impression?"

"Hundreds, maybe even thousands!"

"Precisely. That could easily double the size of the Volgath's army or even triple it."

"But if that's the case," said Hayley, "why didn't he throw it all at us when we made a stand?"

"I don't imagine they expected to locate us so quickly. Call it a gut feeling, if you like, but I believe this group simply followed Bronwyn's trail."

"And then stumbled into our army. Lucky us."

"It was lucky," he said. "Had they been searching for us, I have no doubt they would have had a larger presence. Mark my words; that army is massing, and when it gets here, it's going to smother us."

"Surely Beverly will come to our aid?"

"I'm afraid not. Aubrey tells us they've turned to face an enemy force. It appears a Norland earl has decided to make his presence felt. Do you ever get the feeling the Gods don't like us?"

"Nonsense," said the ranger. "We are the chosen of Saxnor, the god of strength, and we shall persevere."

Gerald grimaced. "Do you think you could say that with a little more enthusiasm?"

"Perhaps the Gods are testing us?"

"For what? Annihilation?"

"Come now," she said. "You've gotten us out of tighter scrapes before."

"No. This is far worse than anything we've ever faced. Defeat here doesn't mean imprisonment; it means death and lingering enslavement of our spirits."

"We're heading to an area you hand-picked to make a stand. Are you now telling me you're giving up? What would the queen say?"

"I'm not giving up!" Gerald grumbled. "I'm only being realistic. Our chances of coming out of this alive are slim to none."

"Then we shall do our best to take our enemy down with us."

"Easier said than done."

"It's not like you to be so grumpy," said Hayley. "We already beat them once. We can do so again."

He stared at her before finally nodding. "You're right. Listen to me blather on. I've gotten so caught up in this I can't see straight. I need to look at it objectively. What do we know about the enemy?"

"Well, they badly outnumber us, but they appear to be afraid of Zhura."

"Yes, that does seem to be true. What else?"

"From our observations," continued the ranger, "the Volgath appears unable to exercise control over his entire army. If you remember, the cavalry was unwilling to charge us."

"Yes, and I believe that's where we can leverage our strengths."

"Which are?"

"Well, for one thing," said the marshal, "we have several extremely competent commanders, like yourself. That means we're not limited to a single-attack plan like they are. It also makes us more mobile, although I'd be happier if we had more horses."

"I wonder..." Hayley said, staring out over the warriors.

"If you have an idea, spit it out. The worst I can do is dismiss it."

"Do you remember the Battle of Redridge?"

"How could I forget?" he said. "Those blights were nearly the end of us."

"I was thinking more about the mine."

"That's right. You helped the prisoners escape, and then they sacked the enemy camp, but I fail to see how that would help us here."

"When we fought the guards, Kraloch called forth warrior spirits."

"Yes," said Gerald, "but the Ancestors are all gone, stolen by Necromancers."

"But what if they're not?"

"I'm not sure I follow?"

"The spirits, the Ancestors, if you like, are still there." She pointed westward. "Could that same spell steal them back?"

Gerald stared at her for a moment. "I... couldn't really say. We need to consult Kraloch."

"Or Zhura," suggested Hayley. "Better yet, both of them."

"Then come," said Gerald. "It's well worth looking into."

"Your idea has some merit," said Zhura, "but I have no way of knowing whether or not it will work."

"But it MIGHT be possible?" pressed Hayley.

"I thought the spirits were bound to the Volgath," said Urgon.

"That vile creature controls them," said Zhura, "that much is true, but it is incapable of summoning them. A Necromancer is needed for that."

"How does that help us?" asked Gerald.

"If I am not mistaken," said Kraloch, "a Necromancer pulls the spirit into the physical world, anchoring it using their magic. It is then up to the Volgath to control that which is enslaved."

"That would be my belief as well," said Zhura.

"When I summon warriors of the past, it also forms an anchor of sorts, connecting them to the physical world."

"So you control them?" said Hayley.

"No, at least not in the same way a Necromancer would. Once conjured, they fight of their own free will. They do, of course, realize they are only summoned in the most dire of circumstances."

"So the question is," said Gerald, "which anchor wins out, yours or the Necromancers?"

Kraloch nodded. "Precisely."

"I suppose that means we have no way of testing out your hypothesis?"

"Not at the moment, no, but once the battle is joined, a simple casting of the spell will reveal if we have the right of it."

"Even if it works," warned Zhura, "there is a limit as to how many can be called. Kraloch is our most powerful shaman, yet even he could not manage more than twenty."

"Hold on a moment," said Urgon. "We are assuming he wants them to fight for us. What if he calls them and then simply dismisses them? Would that not send them back to the spirit realm?"

"It should," said Zhura, "though the Necromancers could then call them again."

"Yes, but that would take time. What do we know of the dark magic that enslaves them?"

"It is a ritual," said Kraloch.

Hayley was taken by surprise. "How can you possibly know that?"

"It is simple. The spell accomplishes two tasks: that of summoning and then of binding to their will. It is, therefore, of necessity, a ritual, and that typically involves a lot more concentration."

"How much concentration?" asked Gerald.

"Far more, I would think," said the shaman, "than might be achieved in the midst of a battle."

"So the more shamans we have," said the marshal, "the more spirits we can... liberate?"

"Only if it works," cautioned Zhura, "and Kraloch is the only shaman we number amongst our ranks at present. How would you propose we get more on such short notice?"

"It was only an idea," said Hayley, her mood souring.

"It's a good one," piped up Gerald, "but of little use for us today. I do believe, however, it might prove to be the weapon that saves us in the end."

"How?" she replied.

The marshal smiled. "I'm thinking long term here, but I have a few questions first."

"Go on," urged Zhura.

"First of all, we need to test this theory. We'll turn and fight, but only long enough to see if it works. If you're willing, Kraloch, I'd like you lined up with the rest of my warriors."

"Not with the Orcs of my tribe?"

"No. Unless I miss my guess, Leofric's spirit will be keen to come to grips with our Human soldiers."

"Why would you say that?"

"I knew Leofric," explained Gerald. "I'm sorry to say he's never been one to trust in non-Humans, but I believe that's to our advantage in this instance. The Volgath retains all its life memories, doesn't it, Zhura?"

"It does."

"Good. That's what I was hoping. He considers Humans the ultimate warriors, and he knows they must reap the spirits quickly after their death. I think he'll target the Mercerian foot in order to maximize his crop, if you get my meaning."

"A reasonable assumption," said Zhura, "but I see a flaw in your plan."

"Which is?"

"If he sends his Human spirits against you, Kraloch's magic will be of no use."

"Ah, but he won't," said Gerald, grinning.

"How can you possibly know that?"

"Human spirits are harder to replace. The Necromancers couldn't bind new Human spirits for him after the last battle because we took the bodies with us. Orcs, on the other hand, are likely to be seen as replaceable."

"That makes sense," said Zhura. "Orcs linger much longer in the spirit realm, making them easier to replace."

"Of course, I could be wrong about all of this."

"That doesn't matter," said Hayley. "If Kraloch is right behind our line, he can move to where the Orc spirits are."

"As long as they get close enough," added the shaman.

"I doubt that will be a problem. He hesitated last time to press his attack. It's unlikely he'll make the same mistake twice."

"I would agree with her assessment," said Gerald. "This coming battle will differ greatly from the last, as we can use the prepared defences to funnel the attack. If we keep them concentrated on a single point, we should be able to hold them off, but if they manage to flank us, we'll be in trouble."

"How much farther until we reach these defences?" asked Kraloch.

Gerald glanced skyward. "I would suspect we'll be there by nightfall."

"And if the enemy does not follow?"

"They will. Leofric knows if he can hit us right now before anyone can come to our aid, he'll be able to leverage his numerical superiority."

"Let us hope Kraloch's spell is a success," said Zhura. "For without it, we have little hope of defeating the army arrayed against us."

· · ·

Sir Heward led his riders past the wooden spikes that had been dug into the dirt, their pointed tips facing west, menacing any enemy that might approach. He wondered if spirits housed a fear of such things, then shook his head. Idle speculation would do no good, and he must concentrate on more important matters.

The terrain hereabouts had been altered considerably. Now, instead of a gentle, sloping hill, there stood a steep incline, with these wooden spikes set on either side to funnel the enemy into a short, well-defended area. It had been a tough job, but the Saurians proved equal to the task, using their massive three-horns to drag heavy timbers into place at the top of the hill, providing a sturdy wooden wall to help the defenders.

Would it be enough, he mused? Part of him had doubts, but as a Knight of the Hound, he would do his duty, giving his life, if need be, to protect folk back in Merceria.

"*Commander?*" The deep bass of Morgash, the Orc cavalry commander dragged his attention back to the riders.

"*Yes?*" he replied, using their language.

"*Will we be ready enough to take part in the coming battle?*"

"*That is not my decision to make. Though your hunters have become comfortable in the saddle, you still lack the training a true cavalry unit requires.*"

"*But the army has few horses. Will they not need us?*"

"*Likely,*" said the knight, "*but I suspect your duties will be confined to more mundane things, like scouting, at least for the present.*"

Morgash persisted. "*But we are ready to fight!*"

"*And I applaud you for your eagerness, but there is more to fighting a battle than simply killing the enemy. You men, or rather Orcs, will serve as the eyes and ears of the army. Without you as sentries, we could be caught unawares, leading to disaster.*"

"*Understood. We shall do our duty.*"

"*Excellent. You've made good progress over the last little while, and one day you'll make a fine addition to our heavier cavalry, but such things take time. Meanwhile, we must play to your strengths.*"

A horn sounded off in the distance, drawing their attention. Heward looked to the west to see riders approaching. "*It's the marshal,*" he said. "*It looks like he's finally returned. Continue on with the patrol. I need to go and fill him in on our progress.*"

"*As you wish, Commander.*"

Morgash rode off as Heward steered his mount towards the distant riders. As he approached, the marshal angled towards him.

"Sir Heward," Gerald called out. "You've certainly been busy."

The knight pulled up alongside him. "We have indeed, my lord. As you can see, the stakes will dissuade the enemy from trying their hands at our flanks. You can't see it from here, but at the top of that hill, we've put in a large half wall of timber, the better to protect the defenders."

"And steepened the hill, I see. How in the name of the Gods did you move so much dirt?"

"The Saurians, sir. They seem to have a knack for it, and those three-horns of theirs proved most useful."

"I'm surprised you could speak their language. I've never been able to make head nor tail out of it."

"I can't either," said Heward. "Luckily, Lily understands our language well, even if she can't speak it."

"Well, you've both done an outstanding job. How is the Orc cavalry doing?"

"They've taken to riding quickly, but I'm afraid there's much to do yet to prepare them for combat. I thought, in the meantime, we'd utilize them for scouting and picket duty. They're a bit slower than our Kurathians, but that can't be helped. It's their size, you see. They're heavier than the horses are used to carrying."

"That's fine. I doubt cavalry will prove decisive in our next engagement anyway."

"So we are expecting a fight?"

"We are indeed," said Gerald. "We fought them only two days ago and managed to hold our ground, but their army only gets bigger with time."

"And can we expect anything in the way of reinforcements?"

"I'm afraid not. Beverly has her own problems in the north, and Fitz is still trying to take Galburn's Ridge. This one is going to be up to us to deal with on our own."

"I can't say that encourages me, my lord," admitted Heward.

"I know it sounds bad, but we have a plan. The fight here won't defeat them, or the next, but we will get the measure of them. I swear."

"If that's true," said Sir Heward, "then why not retreat farther east and delay battle until we can get reinforcements?"

"Two reasons. First of all, the enemy moves faster than we do. They're not following hot on our heels at the moment, but spirits don't tire. Once they decide to come after us, they'll move quickly. The second reason, likely more important of the two, is that we need to develop tactics to defeat them."

"Those tactics won't be much use to us if we're all dead."

"You're correct," replied Gerald, "but I deem it worth the gamble.

Speaking of which, you should know I chose Hayley as my second-in-command. If anything happens to me, you're to follow her orders. Baron Fitzwilliam will assume the role of marshal, subject to the queen's approval."

"Understood," said Sir Heward, "but just so we're clear, I have no intention of letting you die in battle."

"Nor do I intend to, but arrangements must be made, nonetheless."

"What can I do to help?"

"You can get back to training those Orcs. The sooner we have more cavalry, the better. I'd also be interested in your thoughts as to how we might equip them in the future."

"Future?"

"Yes," said the marshal. "Once this war's over and we have time to make more permanent changes."

"I suppose some armour wouldn't go amiss."

"And should we keep them as light troops?"

"No," replied the knight. "I believe they'll be better suited to melee."

"I'm surprised to hear you say that. I assumed, as hunters, they'd make excellent scouts."

"The problem is their size. Physically, the Orcs outweigh Humans by a significant degree, and as a result, the horses are slowed. I fear that reduction in speed would allow their opponents to outride them."

"A good observation," said Gerald. "Do you think they'd be able to handle Mercerian Chargers?"

"Not yet, but given enough time, anything is possible. If we mounted them on larger horses, we'd need to armour them too."

"Given enough time, I'm sure our armourers could create Orc-sized chainmail. I think the real question is whether or not they'd wear the stuff?"

"I imagine they would," said Sir Heward, "but that's probably a question best left for another day. It appears there's a more immediate issue."

"Which is?"

"Your army has arrived."

Gerald looked over his shoulder. "Ah, yes, finally. Well, I guess I'd best let you go, but before I do, where did you set up camp?"

"To the east," replied the knight, "behind that hill. You'll find spots already marked out for you."

"You HAVE been busy."

"I just believe in being prepared. Might I ask when you expect the enemy to make an appearance?"

"That's a good question," said Gerald. "One to which I wish I had an answer. The truth is, we don't honestly know, but I'm sure they'll show up sooner or later. When they do finally put in an appearance, I'll want you at the centre of the line. It'll take everything we've got to keep the men steady in the face of overwhelming odds."

"Understood, my lord." Sir Heward was about to ride off when he spotted a familiar figure. "Is that Sir Greyson?"

"It is, both he and Bronwyn surrendered to us."

The knight scowled. "They turned against us, my lord. What would ever convince you to allow them to stand with us now?"

"Bronwyn is under guard," replied Gerald, "but as for Greyson, we need every sword we can muster, and like it or not he's a fine cavalryman. Better for him to die in battle than hang from a noose."

"Are you asking me for a favour or just thinking out loud?"

Gerald laughed. "If I was asking, it wouldn't be until AFTER the battle."

TWENTY-TWO

Conspiracy

James Goodwin entered the room, crossing to pour himself a drink.

"I shall be out late, Mother."

"And where are you off to this time? Not the gambling halls, I hope?"

He turned to confront her, his face betraying none of his irritation. "I haven't gambled in years. Why do you persist in perpetuating that myth?"

She put down her book, allowing her gaze to meet his. "As head of this household, I am fully aware of your recent expenditures. You're going through your inheritance at an unsustainable rate, yet you tell me you're not gambling. How do you explain your spending?"

"I am entertaining, if you must know. It is a necessary expense if I am to advance in society."

"Then maybe you might consider hosting your precious meetings here, rather than throwing away coins at taverns. At least then you would reduce the cost."

He stared at her a moment before downing his drink in one gulp. His mother could be difficult from time to time, but he had to admit she occasionally made sense.

"I shall consider it," he said, "but I must hurry. They're expecting me."

"And who are they this time?"

"The usual group," replied James. "You know Lord Godfrey, of course, but I doubt you'd recognize the others."

"And would these others include women?"

"I'm not visiting whores, if that's what you're suggesting."

"Then what is it that consumes you so thoroughly of late?"

"I am attempting to elevate our position in society, Mother, but you wouldn't understand such things."

He stormed out, his mind clouded by anger. The fresh air of the street offered a slight reprieve, and he was grateful for the cool summer breeze that caressed his face. The carriage waited for him as usual, so he climbed inside.

"Let me guess," said Lord Godfrey Hammond. "Your mother objected to something?"

"Of course. It's her way of late."

"Don't let it trouble you. We are embarked on a grand adventure, you and I. Your mother cannot even begin to comprehend the magnitude of it."

"I told her as much."

"Did you indeed?" Lord Godfrey smiled. "You've come a long way, James. Standing up to your mother shows true growth." He rapped his knuckles on the top of the carriage, and it began rumbling down the street.

"Where are we off to tonight?" said James.

"A place called The Crow. Are you familiar with it?"

"It's on the south side of the city, isn't it? Hardly the place for two such as us."

"It's a favourite of soldiers."

"Is that why we're going there?"

Lord Godfrey smiled. "You are perceptive, as usual. Yes, that is precisely the reason for our visit."

"Might I enquire to what end?"

"We shall be meeting a captain of the guard. The recent death of our dear king was a shock, but of even greater significance is the loss of the army that he commanded."

"And what is it that this captain wants?"

"Merely a compassionate ear to listen to his grievances."

"Come now," said James. "I know you, and you're hardly the type to simply sit back and listen. What are you really up to?"

Again, the telltale smile, a sure indication he'd hit the mark. Lord Godfrey leaned forward, lowering his voice despite the absence of anyone else in the carriage.

"In order for us to advance our cause, we must make allies," he said.

"And you believe this captain might be useful to us?"

"Precisely. There are precious few soldiers left in Summersgate and even fewer captains. He is one of only four that remain in the capital. If we can secure his loyalty, we shall hold sway over almost a quarter of the garrison."

"ALMOST a quarter?"

"Yes. You must remember the Royal Bodyguards are more numerous than their more mundane counterparts."

"I thought they were all companies?"

"They are," said Lord Godfrey, "and a company typically numbers about fifty men, all told, but the bodyguards number almost seventy-five. Mind you, they can't field that many since their primary responsibility is guarding the Palace. Even so, their numbers are an important part of the equation."

James Goodwin sat back, revealing a smile of his own. "I understand now," he said. "Perhaps better than you think."

"Oh? Do enlighten me."

"Aside from the aforementioned bodyguards, the companies of the local garrison are tasked with guarding the gates to the city. If this captain proves amenable to our cause, as I suspect he will, then you'll have unrestricted access—access the Crown will know nothing about."

"Very good. Looks like the pupil has become the master."

"Hardly," said James, "but I know you well, and you wouldn't be meeting this man if you hadn't thoroughly looked into his background first. What I don't know is why you want control over the gate? Is this something to do with the Clans?"

"It is. My agents inform me a host has already crossed the border."

"We are invaded? Why hasn't the alarm been sounded?"

"They crossed the river well beyond the sight of our troops. Word will arrive soon enough of their progress, but by then, it'll be too late."

"Do you mean to allow them entry to Summersgate?"

"I do," said Lord Godfrey. "It's the best way to accomplish our aims."

"How do you know you can trust them?"

"This is not the first time I've dealt with them."

"Meaning?" pressed James.

"For years, my agents have traded with them. Who better to rule over a conquered land than someone they've trusted for so long?"

"You intend to make yourself king?"

"King, earl, governor—the title itself does not matter so much as the power that title confers."

"But surely such power would be curtailed under Clan rule?"

"Initially, of course," said Godfrey, "but I'm confident that, given time, they will see the wisdom in reducing their hold. After all, Weldwyn is a prosperous land, and trade can fill the coffers of even the greediest of men. Only a fool would burn it to the ground."

"I don't imagine they're too happy with their High King rotting away in a Weldwyn dungeon."

"Naturally, which is why I've gone to great pains to paint us as the alternative to Leofric's ancient Council of Earls."

The carriage rolled to a stop.

"Ah," said Lord Godfrey. "It appears we have arrived. Come, let us see what this fellow is about, shall we?"

Althea's horse slowed as the town came into view. It was a strange sight, for unlike most of the cities of Weldwyn, Mirstone used the rough terrain to its advantage. The Dwarves who lived here, amongst the Obsidian Hills, were a hardy folk, known for their great skill at mining. A fact that became all too evident gazing at the houses built into the sides of the great cliff. Out from this was a low wall, the height of a man, used not for defence, but to keep animals at bay.

She urged her horse to greater speed, and her guards followed suit. Her mother had wanted her to take a carriage, but the young princess thought the display of wealth too ostentatious. Instead, she'd settled for horseback with a modest accompaniment of half a dozen guards.

As Althea approached the town's gates, a horn sounded, and then the doors opened to permit her entry. Her eyes met the guards who watched her ride past, but she detected only curiosity. She followed the road as it wound through the fields, ending before an impressive stone structure jutting out from the cliff face.

Lord Tulfar Axehand soon made his appearance.

"Highness," he said. "This is a pleasant surprise. What brings you to Mirstone?"

"My mother sent me," she replied. "There are things that are best discussed in person."

"Of course. Let's get you inside, shall we? I'm sure a drink wouldn't go amiss, and maybe some food? You must be famished after your trip."

"That would be nice, thank you." She dismounted, passing the reins to one of her guards. "You men can wait out here."

"We are not to let you leave our sight, Highness," the guard responded.

"In spite of that, I am commanding you to stay here. Will you then argue with a princess?"

The man backed down. "No, Highness, of course not."

"As I thought." Althea turned to the Dwarf. "You may lead on, Lord Tulfar."

The baron led her inside. She'd expected rough stone walls and a cold floor, but the interior was much grander than that, with a thick carpet lining an entrance hall that was flanked with intricately carved stone statues depicting Dwarven warriors, each keeping a vigilant eye on any who might tread these halls.

"Your town is impressive," said Althea. "I've read all about it, but it's quite another thing to actually see it."

"It's grand, isn't it?" said Lord Tulfar. "It even predates the founding of Weldwyn."

"For all that, your ancestors chose to become part of the realm."

"Of course. After all, there's strength in numbers, and the kingdom provides a ready market for our goods."

He led her into a side room, obviously a place of comfort in which to relax. "Would you care to take a seat?"

"Thank you. I believe I shall." She sat, her eyes roaming the room's contents. "I see you have a library. Do you read much?"

"As much as I can," he replied, sitting opposite her, "but the mine keeps me busy."

"What exactly do you do with all that obsidian?"

He looked at her in surprise. "What makes you presume we mine obsidian?"

She blushed. "I'm sorry. I merely assumed that's how this region got its name. It IS called the Obsidian Hills, is it not?"

"Oh, that," said Lord Tulfar. "I'm afraid to say that's merely the result of a poor translation, many years ago. We mine iron here, but the rocks that make up these hills have large concentrations of basalt, giving the region a dark appearance. I suppose that contributed to the error."

"And you didn't see fit to correct it?"

"Why would we? We're a pragmatic people, us Dwarves. Names matter little to us, so long as the market is served." He stared at her a moment before continuing. "But you didn't come here to talk about mining."

"No," said Althea, "I didn't. No doubt you heard the news of my father's demise."

"I have," replied the baron, "and you have my sympathies."

"My brother, Alstan, will doubtlessly be crowned soon, but of more immediate concern is the loss of our army in the north."

"Ah, now we get to the crux of the matter. I'm guessing you've come asking for warriors?"

"I have. I'm told you sent requests to the king on several occasions regarding the raising of troops, only to be rebuffed."

"Your father was a stubborn man," he replied. "No offence intended. The only time we were permitted to raise warriors was during the last invasion of the Clans, and even then he was loathe to accept them."

"I know he could be difficult at times, but he had his reasons."

"Yes, but you must see past that if we are to continue moving forward."

"Moving forward?" said Althea. "I'm not sure what you mean?"

"The very fabric of this kingdom is changing," said Lord Tulfar.

"The army can be replaced."

"So it can," he agreed, "but that is not what I am referring to."

"Then what is?"

"When your brother married the Queen of Merceria, he set in motion a chain of events that are having a profound influence on... well, everything. The Dwarves of Mirstone can no longer sit idly by and allow others to decide our fate. We want representation. A seat at the table, if you will."

"What are you proposing?" asked the princess.

"That your brother, Alstan, make adjustments to the Council of Earls."

"Are you saying you want to be elevated to an earl?"

"No, but a voice on the council would be appreciated."

"And is he to do likewise with all the other barons?"

"That is of little concern to me," said Tulfar. "I speak for my people, not theirs."

"I am not empowered to act in this regard."

"But you could bring it to the attention of your brother?"

She thought it over, choosing her words carefully. "I shall speak to him of your concerns, but I cannot make any promises."

The Dwarf smiled. "That's all I can ask."

"And in return, would you be willing to raise troops?"

"I would. In fact, I already started."

"You have?"

"Of course. When we heard of Leofric's death, many were concerned that an invasion might follow. I called up the militia, and the forges have been busy producing weapons and armour."

"How many warriors do you have?"

"Nigh on two hundred, half of which are trained with arbalests."

"How long until they're ready to march?"

"Ah, well, that's the bad news, I'm afraid. Weapons are no difficulty, but it'll likely be a few weeks before we have all the armour we need. If you like, you can remain here in Mirstone until they're all outfitted, then take them back to Summersgate with you."

The princess thought it over. Her mother's instructions were somewhat vague, no doubt due to the demands of her position as queen. Althea had been ordered here to arrange warriors for Summersgate's defence. Who was to argue if she should insist on accompanying them herself?

"Very well," she said. "I shall accept your offer, providing you allow me to see how their training progresses?"

A broad grin spread across the Dwarf's face, a grin that Althea found infectious. "Of course," he replied. "We shall be honoured to have you here. After all, it's not every day we get a visit from the Royal Family." He paused a moment. "Come to think of it, I don't believe we've ever received a visit from a royal, at least not in my lifetime."

"Really? I find that hard to believe."

"It's not too surprising, considering we're primarily a mine. I don't suppose many royals want to get their hands dirty."

"I do," said Althea, maybe a little too hurriedly. She blushed. "Sorry, I didn't mean to interrupt."

"Not at all. It's nice to have someone show an interest in us. Would you care to see the warriors now? They should be training in the great hall. Not all of them, naturally, but enough for you to get a feel for them."

"I'd love to."

They both rose to their feet just as the door opened, revealing a pair of servants carrying platters on which sat food and drink.

"Not now," said Lord Tulfar. "The princess and I are on our way to the great hall." He pushed past them but then halted, his nose smelling the food. "On second thought, follow us. We can eat in there"—he turned to Althea —"if that's all right with you, that is?"

"I think that a marvellous idea," she replied.

"Good. Then come along, Highness, and let me show you what we've been up to."

He led her deeper into the cliffside, into a large subterranean chamber. "This," he explained, "was carved out from our first mine."

Massive columns supported the ceiling. Someone had gone to great pains to carve a mural into the walls, giving the whole place an elegant look. The perfectly smooth floor was so highly polished Althea took it, at first, to be tiled.

"How long did all this take?" she asked.

"Oh, well, the room just sort of grew over the generations. The original mine was less than a quarter of what you see here, but as time went by, we raised the ceiling and put in columns for extra support."

"Why is it so high?"

"We Dwarves like it that way. I suppose it's our way of compensating for not being outside all the time." He led her to a long stone bench that lined the eastern wall. "Have a seat," he said, "and you can watch the warriors practice their art."

Althea sat, her eyes glued to the Dwarven troops who stood waiting for commands. Their leader turned to Lord Tulfar and waited.

"You may begin," said the baron.

The Dwarf captain turned back to his troops and started issuing orders. Clearly, he spoke in the Dwarven tongue, for Althea could understand nothing of what the fellow called out, but the effect was instantaneous. The warriors lifted up their strange rectangular shields in unison, locking them together. Another order and more shields appeared above, encasing them in metal.

"Astounding," she said. "It's like a giant tortoise."

"We call it the drake," said Tulfar. "In that a drake, when coiled, only shows its armoured side."

"How sturdy is it?"

He rose. "Come and see for yourself."

She got to her feet and followed him to where the rest waited.

"Go ahead," he said. "Climb on top."

"How am I to do that?"

Lord Tulfar turned to his captain. "Would you oblige?"

The Dwarf leader knelt, holding his own shield to form a ramp, then the baron took Althea's hand and guided her up onto the top of the formation.

"This is remarkable," she said, walking across it. "How long can they keep this up?"

"All day if necessary," he replied. "The shields are sturdier, much more so than those the king's soldiers use. They also have grooves on the side to allow them to lock into position with their neighbours."

Althea climbed back down, thoroughly impressed. "And all your warriors can perform this manoeuvre?"

"Only the foot, and even then, it takes a lot of practice. In fact, it's an old technique, first used over a thousand years ago."

"May I see one of those shields?"

The captain offered his, but as she took it, it quickly became evident it was too heavy. Its base soon smashed against the stone floor, resulting in a loud echo reverberating throughout the chamber.

She looked at the baron in embarrassment. "Obviously, I would make a poor Dwarf."

"Don't be so hard on yourself," he replied. "These warriors have been building up their strength for years."

"Would the weight not work against them?"

"It would if they were fighting in individual combat, but we discourage such things. Dwarves live and die standing side by side—we expect no heroics here."

"I'm told my father believed your people would slow down his army."

"A common belief, but hardly true. Yes, we march slower than Humans do, but we more than make up for it with our stamina. Our warriors will march from sunup to sundown with little rest, covering a much greater distance than your father's footmen ever could."

"Evidently, he never took the time to appreciate what you have to offer."

Baron Tulfar, clearly pleased by the compliment, bowed. "I am humbled you think so."

"Do you know Lord Parvan?"

"I know OF him," said the baron, his tone neutral. "Why?"

"It occurs to me the Elves, much like the Dwarves, have no representation within our army."

"Ah, well, he wouldn't, would he?"

"Meaning?"

"The Elves are a relatively isolated community. The only reason they joined the kingdom was to let you lot defend them." He saw her look of surprise and blushed. "I'm sorry. I spoke out of turn."

"Not at all," said Althea. "Feel free to speak candidly. Do you not like the Elves?"

"I have nothing against the Elves as a race, but Lord Parvan is definitely not someone I'd choose to call an ally."

"Why is that?"

"He comes across as a shifty individual. I'm not one to spread gossip, but I believe he had an altercation with your brother, Alric."

"I'd heard that," confirmed Althea, "but I'm afraid I'm not familiar with the details. I suppose, in retrospect, it matters little, for Mother sent me here, to Mirstone, not off to Tivilton."

"In that case, let's put the whole Elven conversation behind us, shall we? Now, if you'd like to follow me, I'll take you outside and show you how our archers are progressing."

TWENTY-THREE

The North

SUMMER 965 MC

Lightning came to a halt, and Beverly cast her eyes over the distant troops. Banners were raised, but the still morning air left them limp and unrecognizable.

"Whoever it is outnumbers us," said Aubrey.

"I don't believe that's an issue," replied Beverly, a smile breaking over her face. "Those are Dwarves."

"Are you sure?"

"Positive, and unless I miss my guess, those horsemen are the same ones who accompanied Revi and Arnim."

"Naturally. Only Revi would come back with more soldiers than when he left."

Beverly stifled a laugh. "Looks like he finally made that monumental discovery."

"Saxnor's beard, Cousin. You've developed quite the sense of humour. Is that Aldwin's influence?"

"I suppose it must be," replied the knight. "Come on, let's go and meet our new friends, shall we?"

They rode northward and soon saw a small group of riders break off and come towards them.

"Dame Beverly," called out Arnim. "What brings you this far north?"

"I'm screening the army. Gerald was concerned there was still an earl on the loose somewhere around here."

"He'll trouble you no more, thanks to King Thalgrun."

"I assume that's the Dwarven king?"

"It is indeed. Shall I take you to meet him?"

"If you would be so kind."

"Then follow me," said Arnim.

He led them closer, and Beverly was immediately struck by the Dwarves' armour. She halted, not quite believing her eyes.

"Those warriors are completely encased in metal," she said.

"Yes, they call it plate armour. We saw it in action against Lord Calder— it's quite effective. These Dwarves might be slow, but get them into melee, and there's no end to what they can accomplish."

"Are they all equipped like this?"

"No, these are the King's Guards. Many of the Dwarves still use chain-mail, like Herdwin's troops." Arnim slowed to a halt before dismounting, his guests doing likewise.

Some of Arnim's Kurathians were there to take the horses, then Lord Caster led them to the centre of the camp where the Dwarven leaders waited.

"Your Majesty," he said. "May I introduce Dame Beverly Fitzwilliam and Lady Aubrey Brandon, Baroness of Hawksburg."

"Greetings. I am King Thalgrun Stormhammer, and this is my daughter, Kasri Ironheart."

Beverly took in the golden-clad warrior, noting the matching armour of some of the guards.

"It's an honour to meet you both," she said.

"Who's this now?" came a rough voice.

She turned to see a Dwarf carrying a large staff, topped by a green emerald. Tufts of red hair poked out from beneath his hooded cloak.

"This," said the king, "is Agramath, our master of rock and stone."

"A fellow redhead, I see," grumbled the Dwarf. "I understand it's rare amongst Humans."

She was about to reply, but then the newcomer turned his attention to Aubrey.

"You don't have the look of a warrior," he said.

"Good," she replied, "because I'm not. I'm a Life Mage."

"Ah, like Master Revi Bloom. Most excellent! Tell me, did you train under him?"

"I served my apprenticeship under his tutelage," said Aubrey.

"Yes," added Beverly, "though she has improved her skill considerably since that time."

"Speaking of Revi," added Aubrey, "where is he?"

"He'll be along shortly," said Arnim. "He's been using Shellbreaker to scout out the area."

"We should get down to business," said the king. "How large is your army?"

"My army," said Beverly, "or the entire Mercerian forces?"

"Let's start with your own command, shall we?"

"Only about four hundred. Why?"

"That matches our numbers, if you don't include Lord Arnim's horsemen. Your wizard tells me you face a supernatural foe."

"We do," agreed Beverly, "and now that Lord Calder is out of the way, we can concentrate on destroying it."

"Have you a strategy in place?"

"Not at the moment. Our marshal, Lord Matheson, has some ideas he's been working on, but we have yet to test them."

"And where is this marshal of yours?"

"Some distance away, I'm afraid. We were just about to march to his aid when you showed up."

"If I had realized that," said King Thalgrun, "I would have sent word in advance."

Beverly looked skyward. "I don't suppose it matters much. We'll soon be losing the light anyway, and that means it's time to make camp."

"Might I suggest tomorrow we march together?"

"You mean to go south?"

"Aye," said the king. "Your people helped my folk rid themselves of an enemy. The least we can do in return is to help you defeat this spirit army. Provided you have no objection, of course."

"None at all, Your Majesty."

"Good. Then I'll have my warriors march over at first light. Until then, I shall bid you good night, General."

"It's commander," said Beverly. "My father's the general."

"Your father?"

"Yes, Lord Richard Fitzwilliam, Baron of Bodden. He commands the second army."

"Then what do you call your lot?"

She smiled. "Simply an independent command."

"But, in spite of that, you have the look of a veteran warrior."

"I'll not deny I've seen my share of battles, but I'm content to follow Marshal Matheson. He's the true military genius."

"Genius, is it?" said the king. "High words of praise, indeed." He turned his attention to Aubrey. "And what of you? Seen much battle?"

"More than I like," she admitted, "but I'm more inclined towards healing injuries rather than inflicting them."

"You don't look old enough to fight, although I'll admit I find it difficult to judge Human ages."

"My cousin is still young," said Beverly, "but has already seen the horrors of war."

"Cousin, is it? I must admit it's nice having family close by in times of trouble. I don't know what I'd do if it wasn't for Kasri here. She's also the captain of the Hearth Guard."

"Are those your most elite warriors?" said Aubrey. "I only ask because Beverly's last command was the Guard Cavalry."

"And what is that?" asked Kasri, finally speaking up. She stepped forward, her eyes examining Beverly's armour. "That's fine work, although a bit dated. Your smith is skilled."

"Thank you. I'll be sure to let him know."

"She has a hammer, Father, just like you."

Beverly's eyes swivelled to the king. "You use a warhammer?"

"That's why they call me Stormhammer." He turned briefly to one of his guards. "Go and fetch me my hammer, would you?"

In response, Beverly drew her own weapon, holding it out for King Thalgrun to examine. "This is Nature's Fury," she explained. "It was forged from skymetal and empowered by Albreda, Mistress of the Whitewood."

"The White Witch? Your friends mentioned her earlier, but I thought they were only trying to impress me."

"Not so. We've been on good terms with her for many years."

"Yes," added Aubrey, "and Beverly's father has known her for decades."

"Then you've made far more powerful friends than I," said the king. "I'm surprised you've heard of her. The Whitewood is hundreds of miles from here."

"I try to keep up to date on the happenings of the western kingdoms."

"Western kingdoms?" said Aubrey.

"Yes, although I believe you refer to them as the Four Kingdoms, or at least Master Bloom does."

"My ears are burning," came a voice. "Did somebody mention my name?"

"Revi!" said Aubrey. "I was wondering when you were going to show up." She noted the look on the mage's face. "Is something wrong?"

"You might say that. I had Shellbreaker searching far to the south. It looks like Gerald is going to make a stand against the spirit army."

"But he's outnumbered, isn't he?"

"I suspect so," said the mage, "though I can only report what my familiar has seen."

"He likely has no choice," said Beverly. "The enemy doesn't sleep, so he can't get away."

"We must march right away," said Aubrey. "Surely he needs us?"

"Likely he does," said Revi, "but I'm afraid we're far too distant to be of use to him at the moment."

"This marshal of yours," said the king. "You say he's your most capable leader?"

"Yes, our finest," replied Beverly. "Still, I can't help but feel this time he's outmatched."

"Then all the more reason to march to his aid. My warriors rise early. Shall I then have them go due south?"

"Yes," said Beverly. "I can have the cavalry lead them."

"And what of our Kurathians?" asked Arnim. "Do you want them screening the advance?"

"I think that would be best," replied the knight.

"Well then, that being the case, I'll take my leave of you, Dame Beverly. It looks to be a long day tomorrow, and I don't know about you, but I function much better on a good night's sleep."

Lord Arnim left them, making his way back through the camp. Beverly was considering doing something similar when the Dwarf guard reappeared. "I have Stormhammer here, my liege."

The king took the weapon, holding it out for Beverly's inspection. "A master of air imbued it centuries ago, and it has been handed down for five generations. One day, I'll be too old, and it'll fall to Kasri to carry on the tradition." His eyes shifted to Beverly. "Tell me, do you have someone to carry on the traditions when you age?"

"Not yet," she replied. "One day, perhaps, but I'm in no hurry."

"You're in need of a husband." The king glanced briefly at his own daughter, leading the knight to wonder for whom the question was truly intended.

"I have one. The very same smith who forged Nature's Fury, but I'm not ready to settle down and have children. There's a war to finish first."

King Thalgrun nodded. "A wise choice, I suppose, given the circumstances. How long have you been forged, if I might ask?"

"Forged?"

"He means married," explained Kasri. "I'm afraid he's too entrenched in our customs." She turned to the king. "I told you before, Father, they have different traditions from us."

"But a female must still choose a partner," the king argued. "It is our way."

"It is not MY way," his daughter replied.

The look on both their faces made it clear this was a common argument. The king, red-faced, turned to Beverly once more.

"I apologize if I upset you. In our society, females are rare, and for this reason, forging has become an important ritual in our lives."

"For some," added Kasri.

The king shot her another look. "In any case, I believe we've kept you enough for now. I suggest we all take Master Arnim's advice and get some sleep."

Beverly and Aubrey climbed into their saddles, ready to ride back to the camp, but a voice called out in protest.

"May I have a word?" They both recognized the distinctive voice of Kasri.

"You wanted something, Highness?" said Beverly.

"I'm no highness," replied the Dwarf.

"Are you not the daughter of the king?"

"I am, but that holds no sway in Dwarven society. Only the king or queen is given honorifics."

"In that case, what can I do for you, Kasri?"

"I wanted to learn more about your warriors. Lord Arnim Caster tells me you employ quite a few different races."

"That's true, although you won't find any of your own race amongst my warriors."

"Why is that?"

"The Dwarves of Stonecastle are with my father's army. I do, however, have Orcs, Humans, and Trolls."

"Trolls?"

"Yes, you've heard of them?"

"Of course, but they're swamp-dwelling creatures, aren't they? Wherever did you find them?"

"They fought against us in Weldwyn."

"So you enslaved them?"

"No," said Beverly. "We offered them a home in return for their service." She saw the look of confusion and decided to elucidate. "There's a great swamp that lies along the south coast of Merceria. It's largely uninhabited, but it's perfect for Tog and his people."

"I hear they're immense," said Kasri.

"They are, but they've proven effective in the past, especially when they work with the rangers."

"Rangers? I don't believe I'm familiar with the term."

"The Queen's Rangers are normally tasked with keeping the roads of

Merceria safe for travellers. In times of war, we use them to augment our archers. They're particularly skilled in things like tracking and hunting."

"I can see why you would employ them. We have our own specialist warriors but of a far different ilk."

"Your father mentioned the Hearth Guard. I assume those are your most elite warriors?"

"They are—each and every one of them a hand-picked veteran. Even to be considered for entry, a warrior must have battle experience."

"You've seen that much battle?"

"Between beating off attacks from Norland and the incursions of the men of the east, we keep fairly busy."

"Men of the east?"

"Yes, through the Gap lies a kingdom that has been a constant thorn in our sides. One day, they'll attack in great numbers, and my father is hoping you'll come to our aid."

"Ah," said Aubrey. "So that's the price."

"It's as good a reason as any to help us," noted Beverly. "And as to you learning about our warriors, I'd be happy to show you around our camp, although this evening is not the most opportune moment to do so."

"I'll take you up on that offer," said Kasri, "and in return, I'll let you inspect the Hearth Guard. Then we can sit down and share our thoughts on tactics and strategy."

"I would like that."

"Excellent. In that case, I shall let you go."

Aubrey lay awake, her mind racing. "We should have heard something by now, surely?"

"I'm trying to sleep," replied Beverly. "As you should be."

Her cousin sat up. "Gerald fought today. It's not like him to remain silent."

"Then use your magic to contact Kraloch and find out how they fared."

"No, it's late. I don't want to disturb him. He's probably far too busy healing the injured. Morning will have to do." She lay back down but kept fidgeting.

"Are you quite finished?"

"How can you be so calm?" asked Aubrey. "A major battle was just fought; aren't you curious as to the outcome?"

"Maybe he didn't fight?"

"Why wouldn't he?"

"There could be any number of reasons," said Beverly. "Perhaps the enemy didn't follow him? Or they waited on reinforcements to continue their advance?"

"That IS possible, although I can't shake the feeling something's... I don't know, off, I suppose?"

"Off?"

"Yes. I just have a bad feeling."

"You've been hanging around Albreda too much. Her visions are starting to rub off on you."

"I could be so lucky."

"So you DON'T have a bad feeling, now? Look, you're a smart woman, Aubrey, possibly the most intelligent I've ever met, but in this case, I think you're getting yourself worked up about nothing."

"I guess you're right, Cousin. After all, I'm a fully trained Life Mage now, capable of making intelligent, rational decisions."

"Yes," agreed Beverly, "you are. Now, get some sleep. It promises to be a busy day tomorrow."

"Only, what if this feeling is my mind looking at this from a purely logical viewpoint?"

"All you're doing at the moment is running in circles, and that's not going to help anyone. Use your magic to contact Kraloch in the morning. I'm sure he can set you straight on what's been happening."

"All right, I'll try to get some sleep."

"Finally!"

"Good night, Beverly."

"Good night!"

Dawn came far too early for Beverly's liking. Her own light cavalry was up before the sun and well on the way, leading the Dwarves south towards the marshal's last reported position. Tog followed with the Trolls while the Humans and Orcs amongst their ranks came next. The rangers rounded out the column, spread out on either side, with the heavy cavalry bringing up the rear.

Beverly had always been, primarily, a mounted warrior, first as a member of the Bodden Horse and then, on that fateful day back in fifty-two, she'd saved the king's life and been knighted. It wasn't until the emergence of Princess Anna, though, that her career finally took off. She was the original Knight of the Hound and now a commander of horse. Would she one day follow in her father's footsteps and become a general? She hoped so but knew in her heart it was likely some time yet before she could achieve such a goal. In the meantime, she would learn all she could from Gerald and her father while honing her skills as a leader of warriors.

By noon, the Dwarves were trailing, their shorter gait slowing their overall progress. Beverly had seen it before. During the civil war, the Dwarves of Stonecastle had marched all day long, leaving camp before sunrise and arriving well after dark. Their stamina was incredible, and these Ironcliff Dwarves proved equally resilient, eating on the march, only stopping for brief rests to water themselves.

She had the Kurathians fall back to keep an eye on them, riding to the rear herself to check up on them on occasion. She pulled Lightning up beside Kasri, who marched ahead of the Hearth Guard.

"Don't you tire?" the knight asked.

"I could ask you the same thing," replied the Dwarf. "I haven't seen you out of the saddle all day."

"Do you get hot in all that metal?"

"It's warm, I'll grant you that, but we Dwarves are used to the heat."

"And what of your feet? Do they not get sore?"

Kasri laughed. "Our feet? No, why would you suggest such a thing?"

"It's the most common complaint amongst our foot troops."

"Ah, well, we Dwarves don't tire so easily. This armour also does an excellent job of distributing the weight so as not to wear us down. Yours, on the other hand, looks quite uncomfortable, what with all the padding you wear beneath it."

Now it was Beverly's turn to laugh. "You mean the gambeson? Yes, it can be uncomfortable at times, but that's the price we pay for all this protection."

"Your smiths should learn to make plate armour."

"I'm sure my husband would love to, but, as iron is scarce in Merceria, the price remains high. I can't even imagine how much armour like that would cost."

"Really?" said Kasri. "We have so much iron we don't know what to do with the stuff. I'm certain my father would be willing to sell it to you for next to nothing. Of course, you'd need to send your smiths to Ironcliff to learn how to make it, although I doubt our artisans have worked with Human sizes before."

"I'll be sure to mention it to Aldwin."

"Is that your husband?"

"Yes."

"Might I ask how you met?"

"My father found him while out on patrol, travelling with others in a wagon that was attacked by Norland raiders."

"And was he a smith in those days?" asked the Dwarf.

"No, my father made him an apprentice to Bodden's smith, a particularly grumpy fellow named Grady."

"Well, if your armour is any indication, Grady must have been quite the master."

Beverly laughed. "I would say it's more like Aldwin taught himself." She blushed.

Kasri watched her with interest. "I'm guessing something inspired him. Was that you?"

"I suppose it was. We were just friends in the beginning, but as we grew older, we developed this bond. What about you? Have you ever felt that way?"

"I can't say that I have. I'm not against forging, but you need to understand the pressures on a Dwarven female."

"I'm not sure I understand?" said Beverly.

"Only one in five of us is female. That means there's a lot of people pushing for you to have children."

"For all that, you've resisted it."

"I have. In our society, we females have all the power when it comes to such things. Of course, that doesn't prevent us from getting all the steely glares for not forging. The males fall all over themselves trying to impress you while the other females look down on you for not doing your duty."

"But you're the king's daughter. That must account for something?"

Kasri grimaced. "That only makes things worse. Don't get me wrong, I love my father, but sometimes he can be set in his ways. What of your parents? Did they push you to wed?"

"I never knew my mother. She died when I was born, and my father… well, he didn't agree with my friendship with Aldwin."

"Why is that?"

"He was a commoner, and I a noble. It wasn't until Father thought he'd lost me, he reconsidered. Listen to me ramble on. I must sound ungracious. My father loves me dearly, always has, but part of him still clings to the past."

Kasri nodded. "It seems our fathers are not so different after all."

TWENTY-FOUR

The Minglewood

SUMMER 965 MC

"Saxnor's beard," said Gerald. "Look at them!"

The entire horizon swarmed with ghosts. He had deployed his foot troops along the top of the prepared defences, with Orc archers in the trees to the north and south. Now he wondered if his attempt to hold off the enemy here wasn't a fool's errand.

"It is too late to change your mind now," said Zhura. "All we can do is stand, fight, and hope the Ancestors look on us with favour this day."

The spirit army drew closer, slowly closing the range. Gerald watched as arrows flew into the air, wondering where they were coming from. Shielding his eyes against the afternoon sun, he searched the horde before him.

"It looks like they deployed archers," he said, "but they appear to be relatively ineffective. Their arrows are going everywhere."

"Likely the Volgath cannot direct them."

"But spirits can still think, can't they?"

"Not as we do," said Zhura. "They are enslaved, and that means their will is suppressed, along with their independent thought."

"I doubt it matters much. Once they get close enough, they won't be able to miss."

"Not so," said Zhura.

"Why would you say that?"

"The warriors are spirits, but the arrows are real. Like us, they do not have an inexhaustible supply."

"Yes," said Gerald, catching on. "And they started their volleys far too

early. I suspect Leofric considers them much like his Weldwyn archers, yet
their range is much less."

Even as he spoke, his own Orc archers unleashed a volley from their
warbows, tearing into the enemy. Some of the ghosts dissolved into mist,
but it made little difference in the grand scheme of things.

Urgon's hunters kept up a steady stream of arrows, but to the south, he
noticed Hayley and the Orcs of the Black Raven falling back. They were
taking their time, withdrawing in waves, occasionally pausing to turn and
loose arrows.

"Shall I ready my spell?" asked Kraloch.

"No," said Zhura. "They are not yet close enough."

Gerald watched the enemy archers. The frequency of their volleys had
decreased significantly. Nevertheless, they still flew forth, now striking the
Mercerian line. With shields raised, the arrows would do little damage, but
he was more worried about the effect on morale.

"Hold tight and draw your weapons," he called out.

Seeing the blades flashing in the afternoon sun, he was reminded of his
time in Bodden. There, he had fought many times, yet never against an
army of this size. He drove the memory from his mind, concentrating
instead on the here and now.

"They have put the Orc spirits in front," noted Zhura.

"Yes, I noticed that," said Gerald. "Precisely what we wanted."

"It does, however, make it harder to reach Leofric."

"He's not the main objective this day."

"Despite that," she continued, "we must still survive the encounter if we
are to fight another day."

The volleys ceased, and then the spirit archers ran forward, engaging the
Mercerians. Weapons and shields clashed as the lines met, and Gerald swore.

"I didn't see that coming," he said. "I would have expected the skirmishers to withdraw."

"They are no longer archers," said Kraloch. "As Zhura indicated, they are
unable to replenish their arrows."

"Thank the Gods for that," said Gerald, "or the Ancestors, if you prefer."

The central mass of spirits now pushed towards his southern flank,
following the road that led to Anvil. There, Hayley fell back, her small
command making every arrow count.

To the north, Urgon also attempted to do likewise, but some of the spirit
skirmishers had made contact with the Orcs, and a fierce melee was
developing.

Gerald looked to his front, where the Mercerian warriors held their positions. Men fell, but there was enough of a reserve that their spaces were quickly filled by others.

"Send the signal to Heward," he ordered. "Send him to the southern flank." A horn sounded, then echoed down along the line.

~

Sir Heward sat astride his Mercerian Charger. He towered over the other horsemen, yet he would never deign to give up his steed. Not only did it represent his elevation to the exalted Order of the Hound, but it gave him a distinct advantage in battle, an advantage he would need to put to the test this very day.

The marshal had lumped the Kurathian horsemen in with what remained of the rebel cavalry. They were behind the hill, out of sight of the enemy, but from the sounds of battle, it was clear where the spirits were heading. His theory was confirmed as the horns sounded. He waited for them to repeat, then nodded.

"Well then, south flank it is." Heward ordered his men forward, moving at a brisk trot. The sounds of fighting grew louder now, but a quick glance to the hill told him the line still held. He slowed his men, bringing them to a halt beside the massive three-horns and the rest of the Saurians. He detected the enemy coming around the southern end of the hill, attempting to outflank the Mercerian defences, but some Orcs had moved up to present a solid wall of spears.

He couldn't help but smile. Gerald's idea of training the Orcs in close order tactics and arming them with spears had been inspired by some ancient ruins they'd found near Queenston and had served them well during the civil war. Even against this particular enemy, the tactic worked as wave after wave of ghosts impaled themselves on the spear tips before dissipating into mist.

Heward knew this was a battle of attrition. They were greatly outnumbered, and simply trading casualties would not suffice. He caught a glimpse of Dame Hayley and her Orcs falling back, but they were soon engulfed by the spirits.

He turned to Sir Greyson. "We must help Dame Hayley, else Master Bloom will never forgive us."

In answer, the Knight of the Sword nodded, then lowered his visor. They advanced, running parallel to the enemy's line until they were at its southernmost tip, then turned westward. Heward swept down his sword, sending them into a charge.

They sliced into the enemy army with little opposition, at least initially.

Sir Heward noted their delayed response as if they hadn't seen the approaching horsemen. They were halfway to Hayley's Orcs when the tide suddenly turned, and the Orc spirits swarmed them.

Heward swung out, his great axe tearing through the ghostly images. His horse kicked out, its powerful hooves tearing into their physical form even as the knight's weapon sought out new targets.

He heard the screams of his men, and then a powerful stench threatened to overwhelm his senses. He fought it down, determined not to fail his marshal. His thoughts drifted back to Hammersfield where he'd lost the Guard Cavalry, pride of the Mercerian army. He would not fail again!

Heward let go of his reins, using his thighs to guide his steed while he took up his shield to help protect him. His axe sliced down, and he had the satisfaction of feeling something part beneath its blade. It wasn't flesh, exactly, but there was resistance as if he were splitting wood rather than bone.

A brief glimpse behind allowed him to spot Sir Greyson, pressed in on all sides, his sword rising and falling with precise cuts and thrusts. He appeared to be holding his own, but then his horse, skewered by a spear, went down, and the Knight of the Sword disappeared in amongst the mob.

～

Lily watched the ghosts draw nearer. She and her fellow Saurians stood ready, and as the spirits closed, they let loose with their razor-sharp darts. The weapons had proved extremely effective against the Norland invaders at the Battle of Uxley, terrifying the enemy and causing panic, but against spirits, they were of little use.

She called forth her mist, blanketing the area, but it, too, proved ineffective, doing little other than hiding the desperate fight that was evolving.

Ghostly Orcs emerged from the fog, and then the battle was upon them. Saurians, armed with bone-tipped spears, stabbed out, but the diminutive beings were ill-equipped to face their larger opponents. Lily watched in horror as her fellow lizardfolk fell beneath the onslaught, and then the survivors began streaming to the rear, overcome with dread.

She pushed through her retreating compatriots, and a large object loomed in the mist. Recognizing the outline of a three-horn, she altered her course, twisting quickly to avoid being speared by a spirit.

The massive creature was wide-eyed, staring at the chaos threatening to engulf it. By its feet lay a baton, one of the padded sticks used to control the great beasts. Lily snatched it up, then used it to tap the back of the three-horn's leg.

It knelt, its training overcoming its fear, and she climbed up its leg and onto the neck. Another tap saw it rising once more. From her new perch, she was above the mist, giving her an unobstructed view of the enemy. To her south, the Mercerian cavalry was surrounded, the spirits too numerous to count. She briefly considered escape, but the thought of her friends dying on the battlefield was too much to bear.

Reaching behind her, she tapped the three-horn on the back. In response, the creature lurched forward and Lily, caught slightly off guard, had to scramble to grab hold of its neck. She intended to move the three-horn forward slowly, cutting across the front of the Saurian line to drive back the invaders, but the giant creature had a mind of its own. It took three steps before the panic that had been building up inside of it was loosed, and then it tore into a frenzied rush, charging directly into the enemy horde.

Lily ducked down behind the bony frill that protected the creature's neck. Ghost warriors were shoved aside by the sheer mass of the three-horn, with several trampled beneath its hooves. A line of spears stood before them, threatening death, but the great beast simply lowered its head and charged into them, knocking them aside as easily as blades of grass.

Hearing a rumble, she looked behind her to spot more beasts following. Lily thought the other riders had copied her actions for a brief moment, but then she saw they lacked any such control. It then dawned on her she had initiated a stampede. Her small hands clung to the creature's neck with all the strength they could muster.

~

Gerald noticed the line wavering. The men, worn down by the constant fighting, were tiring. The enemy, being spirits, suffered no such impediment, so wave after wave of tireless warriors pushed the Mercerians back.

He turned to the Orcs. "Cast your spell while you can, Master Kraloch."

In answer, the shaman looked forward and started chanting. The air came alive with energy, and Gerald felt the familiar buzz as the magic built. Kraloch pointed to an area just to the Mercerians' front, and then a dozen of the Orc spirits halted before turning on their former compatriots.

"It worked!" shouted Zhura.

Kraloch, not content with only one spell, now cast another. However, this time, he raised his hands into the air, looking skyward, the magic spilling out of him. He glowed for a moment before the light shot into the sky and vanished. Moments later, it reappeared, smack in the middle of his conjured warriors, striking an enemy warrior. Before everyone's eyes, the thing morphed into a large Orc, armoured in chainmail, wearing an iron helm. His hands gripped a pair of axes, and he rushed forward, twirling the weapons, dealing out death and destruction.

Kraloch's other spirits formed up behind their new leader and pushed into the enemy. The ghostly warriors, unable to tell friend from foe, ceased their fighting for a moment.

"They are confused," said Zhura. "The Volgath's attention is captured."

"Move forward," shouted Gerald. "Zhura, Kraloch, with me!"

His warriors took advantage of the temporary lull, flooding down the hill in the wake of Kraloch's ghosts. All along the line, the men of Merceria struck out against a now defenceless foe.

Urgon, on the northern end of the line, noticed the spirit army suddenly standing still, motionless for some reason. He didn't hesitate, calling on the Orc cavalry to advance. His own hunters, now devoid of arrows, he sent forward into melee, their axes ready to exact some revenge for the losses they'd endured.

They struck the enemy line like a scythe through wheat. Dozens of ghosts were destroyed, converted into mist, and soon the entire area became difficult to navigate. Urgon lost sight of his other hunters, but then the spirits started fighting back.

The Volgath, evidently having adapted to this strange turn of events, directed his warriors once more. The Orc chieftain was now cut off from his hunters and fighting for his very life.

A spear struck out at him, and he realized with a shock these were now Human ghosts he fought. He cursed, for in his rush to engage the enemy, he'd failed to note the presence of the spirit cavalry. Horsemen bore down on him, their mounts a macabre mix of horse and some ghastly denizen of the Underworld.

He struck out with his magic sword, sinking it into one of these strange creatures. The blade struck deep, digging into the thing's head. The wound exploded outward, spraying pus and ooze around the area. Urgon felt the stuff hit his arm, then some of it dripped down his chainmail links, running onto the back of his hand and burning it.

A roar erupted from his mouth, and then he ducked, allowing a sword to pass over him. He brought his weapon up and stabbed out, knocking aside a second strike before driving it into a leg. It met resistance, and he was reminded of chopping wood. More flesh parted, and then the beast went down, taking its rider with it.

Amongst all the riders, one stood out. The high-peaked helm and winged shoulder guards told him this was no ghost. Instantly, he knew it was an Elf, with hands out, tracing intricate patterns, focusing on a group of warriors off to Urgon's right.

The chieftain rushed in, eager to close the distance before his presence was detected. One swing of his blade cut into the Elf's mount, taking out a leg. The creature rose up, spraying green ichor as it fell. The Elf, taken by surprise, fought to remain in control, but they crashed to the ground, the weight of the steed pinning him in place.

Urgon jumped on the carcass and brought his sword down onto the Elven helmet, his magical blade making quick work of the filigreed steel.

~

Hayley fended off another axe, using her sword to knock the blow aside.

"Back!" she yelled, then looked left and right to see the Orcs of the Black Raven still fighting. She cursed herself. "*Back!*" she yelled again, this time in Orcish.

Her hunters retreated, their pace measured, their fronts to the enemy. She spotted a group of trees to the east of her position and led them towards it.

The spirits surged forward, thirsty for blood. An axe sailed past her head, burying into one of her hunters. All around her, Orcs fell, but the spirits kept coming, their axes and spears reaching out, bringing down all in their wake.

The retreat soon became a rout, with hunters throwing all caution to the wind, fleeing with all the speed they could muster.

~

Gerald struck out with his sword, the steel meeting resistance, but for every opponent he felled, two more rushed forth to take their place. His arms were weak, his legs beginning to fail, and he could tell his men were being worn down.

Even Kraloch's spirit warriors had suffered, now reduced to only three, one of which was his conjured hero. The aged warrior, blocking with his shield, was driven back, bumping into Kraloch.

"It is no use," said the shaman. "There are too many of them."

Only Zhura had remained somewhat safe, for the ghosts would not touch her. At first, they'd kept their distance, but now, as the fighting intensified, they were less inclined to give her space, moving gradually closer with each successive assault.

Gerald found himself bereft of opponents and struggled to understand why. Moments later, a gap appeared in the enemy mass where an armoured foe emerged, dressed in a decorative breastplate with a tall, conical helm apparently made of gold. Chin guards covered the ears, but there was no mistaking those Elvish eyes.

Around the marshal, the fighting ceased, although, in the distance, the battle still raged on. The new arrival held out a hand, pointing at Gerald, and black tendrils snaked out, wrapping around him like a vine. The Elf made a fist, and the inky coils tightened around Gerald, pinning his arms to his sides as it lifted him off the ground. He hung there, unable to move, his eyes glued to this newcomer.

"So, this is the famed Mercerian general," said the Elf, his voice mocking. "Nothing but an old man." He moved his hand in a downward motion, and Gerald found himself flung aside, the wind knocked from his lungs as he hit the ground. Kraloch stepped forward, ready to intervene, but before he could even begin to cast, three more Elves appeared, swords at the ready.

"Who are you?" shouted Gerald.

"Ilarian, though I doubt that name has any meaning to you. I serve Queen Kythelia and have done so for more than a thousand years." The Elf advanced, his warriors forcing Kraloch back at the point of their swords. "Did you honestly believe your ragtag alliance would have any chance of defeating the Dark Queen of Estlaneth?"

He was about to say more when he noticed Zhura. A look of distaste washed across his face, and then he sneered. "What have we here?"

The ghostwalker stood her ground. Ilarian stepped closer, but something stopped him, although whether it was some force of magic or mere revulsion was anyone's guess.

"You are an abomination," he spat out. "Were it within my power, I would see you destroyed."

"No!" said Kraloch. "She is the bridge between this world and the next."

"Do not speak of things you do not understand. Only Kythelia can bridge the worlds of the spirit and the flesh."

"It is you who do not understand," said Zhura. "For centuries, you remained hidden from the world, wrapped in your cloak of darkness while the other races thrived. Did you imagine others could not learn to unlock the secrets of the world?"

Gerald watched the Elf grow pale. Zhura had clearly hit a sore spot, but Ilarian recovered quickly.

"Take them away," he snapped. "Kythelia will want to interrogate them."

The guards moved up, seizing Kraloch by the arms. More Elves came forward, although from whence they came was anybody's guess.

The spirits moved on while the fighting continued to the north. Without the enemy army blocking his view, Gerald could now see the real power behind this threat—an Elven host, the likes of which had not been seen for thousands of years.

TWENTY-FIVE

Galburn's Ridge

SUMMER 965 MC

P rince Alric glanced at his men, advancing alongside him, each of them wearing looks of grim determination. It was one thing to propose this assault, quite another to carry it out. The ground sloped up, but Kiren-Jool's enchantment proved its worth, making it no more exhausting than a stroll through the Palace Grounds.

The prince well remembered the first time such a spell had been used on him. Years ago, he'd needed to ride to Anna's aid, bringing a Life Mage after an assassin had almost killed her. He'd revelled in the newfound energy but had paid the price once the ride was done, sleeping for what felt like days. In all likelihood, it would be the same here, but if they managed to take the fortress, at least he could look forward to a soft bed to sleep in.

Rocks slid by him, loosened by his climb while his mind drifted once again, this time to his wife. His first impression of Anna had been one of annoyance, yet within the year, he could think of no one else. Now, their family was growing, and he couldn't help but feel immense pride.

"Watch your step there, Highness."

He glanced to his right to spot Jack Marlowe making his way up the incline. It grew steeper, forcing the cavalier to begin truly climbing, using hands as well as feet to make headway.

Alric copied his motions, reaching out to take hold of a rocky outcropping, but it broke loose in his hands, sending more stone tumbling and almost knocking him from his perch. He scrambled to find a new handhold and then paused, taking a breath to calm himself. Jack was now outclimbing him, leading the rest of the prince's personal guard up what was fast becoming a steep incline.

"This is getting difficult," the cavalier complained. "Where is that Earth Mage?"

The prince looked below, quickly spotting the old Druid, Aldus Hearn, waving his hands around, no doubt uttering those strange words that powered his magic. Several tiny lights drifted up, settling into the rock ahead of them.

"Hold on," Alric urged. Those around him stopped climbing, clinging to the rock as best they could. The whole cliff face seemed to rumble, and then green sprouts shot out of the rock, climbing upward, dislodging dust and dirt as the vines grew thicker. The vibrations finally ceased, and Alric looked up to see a lattice of green above him. He reached out, grasped the thick tendrils, then hauled himself upward.

"Well," came Jack's voice, "that wasn't so bad. Why couldn't he have done that sooner?"

"He doesn't have the power," replied the prince.

"Albreda did it easily enough."

"True, but she's a wild mage and possibly the most powerful in the entire land."

"Possibly? Who else might match her skill?"

"We have some powerful mages in Weldwyn," said Alric. "As well you know."

Jack shook his head, although whether in disagreement or simply to get the dirt and rock dislodged from his helmet was anyone's guess. "I doubt any of our mages could hold a candle to her. I heard she can open up the ground and swallow men whole."

"Is this really the time to be having this discussion?"

"Why not? Have you something better to talk about?"

"We're climbing a cliff!" said the prince.

"We are, but that only needs arms and legs, not your ears. Now, tell me, have you picked out any names yet?"

∼

Herdwin cursed as his leg spasmed. It felt like he'd been hiding forever, yet he knew it had only been a couple of days. His stomach growled, and he rolled over onto his side as best he could to fish through his pack, finally digging out something that looked like coal.

"Ah, my last stonecake," he said, popping it in his mouth. He expected his saliva to soften it, but none was forthcoming, his mouth having dried up sometime in the night. He spat it out, cursing once more.

"Well, isn't that grand," he grumbled quietly. "I can't even work up a spit. Next thing you know, I'll be talking to myself."

He heard shouting and lifted his head, peering out of his cover. Norland troops had sounded the alarm and were rushing to the collapsed wall, ready to fight.

"What's this, now?" said Herdwin, shifting forward slightly, trying to get a better view. As he watched, men started picking up debris and hurling it over the cliff. Apparently, the Mercerians were assaulting yet again, and the Dwarf wondered how he might be of assistance.

He sat up, examining his leg. He'd pulled out the crossbow bolt and bound it as best he could, but it still throbbed, and he had to wonder if it would still take his weight. His back wound had troubled him through most of the first night but had since softened to more of a dull ache.

"By the forge of Gundar, I've had enough of this!" He stood, immediately regretting his decision as his helm struck rock. He shook it off, then drew his axe. The Norlanders were little more than twenty paces from him, but of more immediate interest to him was the discarded shield halfway between them. If he could reach that, he had no doubt he could survive long enough to get into melee with them.

He knelt and started pushing away the rock and debris that blocked him in. His actions went unnoticed as more stones were hurled down the cliff. Herdwin ceased his digging and squeezed through the Gap, halting a moment in case anyone cried out at his emergence. All was clear, so he moved forward cautiously. He debated the idea of rushing at full speed but finally settled on the slower pace, lest his leg give way.

The Dwarf finally reached the shield and knelt, grasping it by the handle, lifting it to feel the reassuring weight on his left arm. There was an old saying that a Dwarf and his shield are seldom parted. Herdwin had never given it much thought in the past, but the feel of the familiar weight gave him hope.

He advanced towards the Norland line, axe held ready. Closer and closer, he came until he was swinging, his deadly blade descending on the first warrior's helmet, splitting the thing in twain and sinking into the man's skull.

Herdwin gave his best battle cry and struck out with his shield, smashing it into the back of someone's knees, toppling the fellow. The poor sod fell backwards, narrowly missing the Dwarf, and then Herdwin followed it up with an efficient strike to the chest, finishing him off.

Others had taken notice of him by now and were scrambling to drop their stones and draw weapons. He took the opportunity to step forward, smashing his axe into a man's chest. It made a dull thud, and then he felt his victim falling backwards, threatening to take the axe with him. A tug was all it took to dislodge it, and then it was swinging out again, taking an opponent in the forearm.

～

Sir Preston edged forward, his torch held high. "How in Saxnor's name are we ever going to find our way through this maze of tunnels?"

"Leave that to me," said Albreda. She closed her eyes, allowing the magic to build within her. The air around her buzzed before she uttered a single word, and then silence fell.

"Is that it?" said the knight. "Nothing happened!"

"Have patience."

He waited, growing more anxious with each passing moment until he heard it—a tiny, scrabbling noise as a rat ran into the tunnel, pausing at Albreda's feet. She stooped to scoop up the animal, holding it to her forehead before she set it back down, and the creature ran off.

"This way," she said, following in its footsteps.

Sir Preston followed while the other knights spread out behind him. They turned this way and that. He struggled to remember how many turns they made, but the entire thing was simply too complex to keep track of. They finally halted at a wall.

"It's a dead end," he said.

"Not so," said Albreda as she knelt, examining a small hole at the bottom of the wall of rock. "It appears our new friend has found a way into the castle."

"Can you shrink us down to allow entry?" asked one of his knights.

Albreda frowned. "Don't be absurd. Such a thing is impossible. Have you no concept of mass?"

"Mass?"

"Never mind," she snapped.

"Have you a way through?" asked Sir Preston.

"I do. Several, in fact. I'm just trying to decide which method to use."

"What are the choices?"

"I could simply insert a vine through that rat hole and let it expand, cracking the stone in the process. The only problem with that approach is it would be quite noisy."

"Or?" pressed the knight.

"I could soften the wall to the consistency of clay and then dig my way through. That would be quieter, but I fear it would take much longer."

"How much longer?"

"Possibly half the afternoon?"

"That would be too late," said Andurak. The Orc had remained quiet for most of the trip, but now he came forward. "I have been in contact with Kurghal. The main assault has already commenced."

"Then we need the fastest technique you have," said Sir Preston.

"In that case, stand back," said Albreda. "Oh, and you might want to draw your weapons. This is likely going to draw a lot of attention."

She began casting, the air around her quickly whirling into a frenzy. She lifted her hands straight out to her front, her sleeves whipping around as if she were in the midst of a tempest. She then placed the flat of her palms against the stone, and an invisible force vibrated the very air, shaking the wall. She paused the magical litany, shaking her hands and waiting as the power built within her. Again she touched the wall, and this time enormous cracks appeared, radiating out from her fingers.

Albreda shook her hands once more, and the knight noted blood emanating from her fingernails. She pressed her hands to the stone a third time, and then there was a loud booming noise. Chunks of rock exploded away from her as if a god had breathed.

The dust and rock settled to reveal a corridor before them. Albreda pointed to the right. "Up that way, Sir Preston, and be quick about it before the enemy can react."

He led his men through the Gap, flooding the hallway, then turned right, rushing down the corridor, his sword drawn. The occasional sconce lit the way as the hallway curved, revealing a set of stone steps leading up to a doorway. Sir Preston didn't hesitate, shouldering the door to shove it open into the room beyond which was obviously a kitchen full of servants.

"Stand aside," he shouted, then rushed past, his men following. Into the fortress they went, seeking vengeance. Albreda stepped into the kitchen to be met with startled looks.

"How do you do?" she said, pausing by a large pot before taking a sniff. "That smells good. What is it?"

"Pottage, my lady," answered one of the servants, a cook by the look of her apron.

"I'm no lady. My name is Albreda, also known as the Witch of the Whitewood."

The servant grew pale.

"I'm not here to hurt you," she said. "Any of you, for that matter, so long as you don't interfere."

"We wouldn't dream of it," replied the cook. She hesitated for a moment before adding, "Would you like something to eat?"

The Druid surveyed the room. "Actually, I believe I just might take you up on that offer. My recent casting has left me with quite the appetite."

A young girl stepped forward, pointing at her. "Your fingers are bleeding," she said.

"So they are," Albreda agreed. "Where is that shaman of ours? You didn't see an Orc go through here, did you?"

"A big, green fellow?" said the young girl.

"That's him."

The girl pointed at the far door.

"Ah, well, I'll catch up to him eventually."

The cook ladled out a bowl of food. "Should you not go with your... friends?"

"They're more than capable of dealing with the rest on their own." She took a seat at a nearby table, and the cook set the food down before her.

"Please join me," said the Druid. "We can share a meal while you tell me all about this place."

∾

"The rocks," said Jack. "They've stopped."

Alric looked up. "Something must have disturbed them. We're almost at the top. Time to push on." He rushed up the last few feet then emerged onto the remains of the collapsed wall. A group of warriors stood around something, whaling away at it with their weapons. He drew his sword and rushed forward, striking out with the tip of his blade, plunging it deep into a Norlander's back.

Jack appeared at his side, his sword descending onto a helmet. The other Norlanders turned to face this new threat, but Alric's guard now surged onto the wall and rushed forth, venting their rage on those who had so mercilessly attacked them with rocks and stones.

The Norlanders soon broke, fleeing the remains of the wall and falling back into a courtyard where other soldiers had formed up. Alric saw movement beneath the dead Norlanders and pulled a body aside, revealing the crouched form of a Dwarf.

"Herdwin? Is that you?"

The smith was hunched up, his shield held over the back of his head. It appeared the enemy had swarmed him, but he seemed none the worse for wear.

Herdwin grinned up at the prince. "Dwarven mail," he said as if that was all the explanation needed.

"Your leg," said Alric.

"Oh, that was injured in the original attack." He held out his hand, and the prince took it, helping him climb to his feet. The Dwarf arched his back, grimacing. "I'm looking forward to a proper bed," he said. "This Norland hospitality leaves something to be desired."

"I'd love to chat, but I've got an attack to follow through on."

"Of course, Highness."

"Come, Jack. There's work to be done!"

They rushed to the courtyard, straight into the waiting enemy's ragged line. As a prince of Weldwyn, Alric had trained in swordplay from a very early age. As a result, he considered himself a master of the weapon, yet now, faced as he was by a numerically superior force, he was hard pressed to hold his own. His initial rush took down two men, but even with the help of his own troops, they were severely outnumbered.

His blade moved up to guard position, his arm going numb as a great axe struck the edge. Jack stabbed out, taking the axeman in the armpit, the weapon falling to the cobblestones with a clatter. Alric finished the fellow off with an efficient stab to the heart, yet was immediately parrying once more.

Sir Preston charged the door, throwing aside the drop bar and pushing his way through to find himself staring at the main courtyard. It took but a moment to take it all in.

"The gates," said Andurak.

The knight ran across the cobblestones, ignoring the melee raging close by. He desperately wanted to join the fight but knew the gate held the key to success this day. Open it, and the fortress would fall—fail, and they would all die.

A yell to his left caught his attention. Some of the Norlanders had broken off from the fight and now rushed towards him. Sir Preston slowed, waving his men on.

"Go," he commanded. "Seize the gate. I'll hold them off."

He unslung his shield and absently noted the kerchief tied around his forearm, a gift from Sophie. He swore to himself if he survived this day, he would ask for her hand.

The enemy came closer, half a dozen of them, all in a rush. Rather than waiting, Sir Preston counostycharged, smashing into them with his shield in front, his weapon held high.

He knocked one to the ground with his first assault, then struck down,

cutting deeply into another's shoulder. His blade drew back, and he struck
again, feeling resistance as he cut flesh.

A great weight hit his shield, forcing him backwards, and he leaned into
it, eager not to lose his balance. He twisted to the side, and the Norlander
who pushed against him lost his balance. A quick jab to the neck was all it
took to finish him off.

An axe careened off his shoulder, ringing out as the armour deflected it.
He countered by going into a crouch and then striking out but encountered
only air.

He tried to remember how many men were left, but his helmet gave him
only a limited view of the fight. Something bounced off his head, and he
attacked again, slicing into a hand. He heard a grunt as blood sprayed out,
causing him to flinch involuntarily. The action saved his life as another axe
came down, narrowly missing his head. Stepping into the attack, he reached
out with his mailed fist, his sword pommel only adding to the power of the
punch. It struck a face, and a Norlander fell back with a scream.

Sir Preston spared a glance for the gate, but before he could fully turn, a
spear bounced off his shin. He responded in a fury, smashing out with his
shield and then pushing with his legs, overwhelming his opponent.

His foot slipped on blood, and they both tumbled to the ground. Down
came his sword, pommel first, smashing into his foe's chest, driving the
wind from his lungs.

"I surrender!" came the breathless response.

The knight climbed to his feet only to hear horses. He looked up to see
Mercerian horsemen streaming in through the gate.

Faced with this new threat, the melee in the courtyard soon came to an
end. Norland warriors backed up, tossing their weapons to the ground, and
then cheers erupted, drowning out all else.

Baron Fitzwilliam stared at the distant fortress.

"Any word?" he asked.

The queen looked at Kurghal, changing to the Orcish tongue. "*Anything?*"
she asked.

"*Not as yet,*" replied the shaman.

Anna returned her attention to the baron. "Andurak has yet to report on
their progress."

"I wish I knew whether to take that as good news or bad."

"You must have confidence," said the queen, although her face betrayed
her anxiety.

"I'm sure the prince is fine," he said.

"I wish I had your faith, but I fear my vision has come true."

"Vision, Your Majesty?"

"I had a dream," she explained. "I saw Alric lying on the ground, all covered in blood."

"Dreams are merely a reflection of our fears," soothed the baron, repeating what her husband had said earlier. "You should pay them no heed."

"Maybe, but I'd feel a lot better knowing he's safe."

"It is always difficult, thinking of our loved ones putting their life in danger."

"How do you deal with it, Baron? Especially considering some of the battles Beverly has fought."

"Beverly has spent her entire life preparing for such things," he replied. "And I have complete faith her training has suitably prepared her. After all, Gerald trained her. Do you doubt his skill?"

"No, of course not, although I'd feel better if he were here. No offence to you, Baron."

"None taken, Majesty..." His voice trailed off, and then a big smile spread across his face.

"It appears we are successful," he said, pointing. "Look!"

The queen swept her gaze to the fortress of Galburn's Ridge. A warrior had climbed onto one of the towers and now waved a flag. Her face broke into a smile at the red-and-green pennant, the flag of Merceria.

TWENTY-SIX

Preparations

SUMMER 965 MC

Prince Alstan looked over the men who'd gathered at the tournament grounds, and although they numbered some four hundred strong, the sad reality was less than a quarter of them were properly equipped.

"This is not encouraging," he grumbled.

"You must make do with what we have," replied Queen Igraine. "These men are willing to give their lives to protect us, Alstan. That's no small sacrifice."

"Agreed, and yet how am I to defeat the Clans? This group would be hard-pressed to hold on to Summersgate, let alone marching out to face the enemy. Why, half of them are armed with little more than pitchforks."

"Nevertheless, you must give them hope."

He turned to take in the seriousness of her expression. "You're right, of course. How would you suggest I proceed?"

"Talk to them. And I don't mean from on horseback. Walk amongst them; show them you have faith in their abilities."

"And if I don't?"

"For Malin's sake, you are to be king, Alstan. Start acting like one."

Suitably chastised, Alstan dismounted, passing the reins to a nearby guardsman. He walked towards the men, taking his time to give himself a chance to think things through. His father, King Leofric, had always brought out the best in his warriors, and they adored him for it. Alstan's history, however, was far more troublesome. He'd taken the field in the last Clan invasion only to be defeated in his first battle. To make matters worse, he'd been captured and paraded before Weldwyn's enemies. How did he overcome that shame?

The warriors were organized into eight companies, each numbering fifty men, more or less. He started with the most seasoned, comprised of the men who guarded the gates of the city. They were the closest thing the kingdom had left to veterans, for although they'd seen little battle, they at least had proper training and chainmail armour.

He chatted amiably with their captains, but to his mind, it was a strained conversation, his men seeming uncomfortable with the forced familiarity. Alstan moved on to the next group, a local militia by the look of them, equipped with spears and shields. Many wore older, thick leather jackets, but he doubted they would provide much protection in battle. It did, however, serve to give them a sense of security, so he made comments on the usefulness of their attire, if only to encourage them.

At last, he came upon the farmers who had no armour at all, their weapons essentially just farm implements, commandeered for the purpose of fighting. These men made up half his army, and he knew, in his heart, they would likely run rather than face the enemy.

Alstan joked with them, pointing out the tall and short individuals, making small talk about their size. To him, his words felt uninspired, yet he could see their faces hanging on his every word.

He finished his inspection and returned to his horse. As he put his foot into the stirrup, the men of Weldwyn cheered, and he was so surprised, he almost lost his balance. Queen Igraine waited until he was mounted once more before commenting.

"It seems you made an impression," she said.

"I doubt the enemy will think so. Our men will be slaughtered."

"Things will look better when Althea returns."

He looked at her in surprise. "Returns? Where has she gone?"

"I sent her to Mirstone."

"To what end?"

"To bring back warriors," replied the queen. "Lord Tulfar sent arbalesters to aid us in the last invasion."

"None marched with me. They must have accompanied Father."

"No, I sent them with General Matheson. He seemed to have appreciated their presence. I understand they proved instrumental in the final battle that saw an end to King Dathen's army."

"And you sent Althea to fetch them?"

"Someone had to go, and you are needed here, or did you forget you are soon to be crowned king?"

"I forgot nothing," insisted Alstan, "but I hardly think sending a young girl would encourage the Dwarves."

"I might remind you your sister is now older than Queen Anna was at the Battle of Riversend."

"That hardly qualifies her to lead warriors."

"She knows she is no leader. Instead, she is taking on the role of diplomat, soothing egos and convincing the Dwarves to send all they can spare. We all have parts to play during this time of crisis. Allow her the satisfaction of knowing she is helping the cause in some small way."

He nodded. "Of course, Mother. I shall, but I will not permit her to be put in harm's way."

"We are facing invasion," said the queen. "You might not have any say in the matter."

Edwina stood on the city's ramparts, staring off to the west.

"The Clans are out there, somewhere," she said.

Tyrell Caracticus nodded. "Likely, Your Highness, yet I doubt they've gotten far. We'd have word of them."

She turned to the Water Mage. "Shouldn't you be back at the Dome, preparing for battle or something?"

"I came seeking you."

"Me? Why in Malin's name would you be looking for me?"

"Your mother is concerned. You haven't been yourself since the news of your father's demise."

She locked her gaze on the distant sky. "Demise—such a polite way of saying death."

"Death is a natural part of life, Highness. Life carries on, as must we all."

"Easy for you to say. It wasn't your father who fell in battle."

"Actually," said Tyrell, "he did."

Edwina turned in surprise. "Pardon?"

"My father was a warrior. He died in a border skirmish with the Clans many years ago."

"I thought he was a mage?"

"No. I inherited that ability from my mother."

"Was she a Water Mage as well?"

"Of course. How else would I have that power?"

"And did she train you?"

"She did," replied Master Caracticus. "We lived in Southport at the time. I didn't come to the Dome until well after my training was complete."

"Isn't that where all mages train? How is it you didn't?"

"A Water Mage draws inspiration from the sea, something my mother understood quite well."

"I would have liked to have met her."

"And you would have, had she not died. She was a good friend of your mother's."

"She was?"

"Indeed, their two family's histories are intertwined."

"It's your family too, isn't it?"

He frowned. "I never considered it as such, preferring to trace my lineage through my father."

"That's just plain ridiculous."

The mage looked taken aback. "It is the way of things, Highness. Lineage is always traced through the males."

"Not in Merceria," said Edwina.

He struggled to counter the argument. "Well," he finally said. "Each to his own, I suppose, although I might point out even Queen Anna's claim to the throne is through her father."

"No, it's not. King Andred is not her actual father."

"How in Malin's name do you know that?"

"Alric told me."

"You've spoken to Prince Alric?"

"He sends me letters from time to time," said the princess, "although I've heard nothing since the campaign in Norland began. I wish he were here, now. He'd know what to do."

"What to do with what?"

"The army, of course. Alstan means well, but he lacks the experience Alric has. He's been studying under Marshal Matheson, you know."

"Has he now," said the mage. "How interesting."

Edwina looked skyward. "It's going to rain."

"Don't be silly, child. The sun is out."

"For now, but the clouds will soon roll in."

"How can you possibly know that?"

"I can feel in it my bones."

Master Caracticus laughed out loud. "You're a young girl, not an old crone. I would have expected better of you."

"I'm being serious," she said. "I have a way with such things."

The grave response sobered him. "Has it always been so?"

"No," said Edwina, "but I have come to find it these last few months."

The mage gasped, causing her to stare at him. "What is it?" she asked.

"I… cannot be certain. Tell me, have you noticed anything else of late?"

"Like what?"

"I don't know," said the mage, "possibly some strange feelings or unusual events that might have struck your fancy?"

"I haven't a clue what you're talking about. In any event, I believe I shall retire to the Palace. I don't want to get caught out in the rain. Your pardon, High Mage, if I don't stay here and chat."

He watched Edwina run down the ramparts, heading back towards the gatehouse.

"Curious," he muttered.

Lightning flashed, soon joined by the distant rumble of thunder.

"It's quite the storm out there," noted Aegryth.

"So it is," agreed Tyrell Caracticus.

"Surprising when you think about it. Here, it's pouring down by the bucketful, when just this morning, it was bright and sunny. Some might say it's an omen."

"Come now, you're a mage. Don't tell me you believe in such superstitious nonsense."

"Well," said Aegryth, "you didn't see it coming, did you?"

"No," he agreed, "but Princess Edwina did. I saw her on the city walls this morning, and she told me it was going to rain, but I didn't believe her."

"Are you sure?"

"Yes, positive. Why?"

"Do you suspect she could be manifesting?"

"I thought of that, but she shows no other signs."

"Of course not," said Aegryth. "She doesn't know what to look for."

"But there's no mage blood in her family."

"That we know of."

"Come, now," insisted the High Mage. "She's from a proud line of nobles, her family well documented. We'd know if there was a spellcaster amongst them."

"Only if they were trained."

"What are you suggesting?"

"Magic occasionally skips a generation, but what if it could lie dormant for long periods? You know as well as I that without training, a person with the gift is no different from anybody else."

"But surely they would have manifested? We know such individuals display unusual control over their environment as they become adults."

"Who's to say they didn't?" said Aegryth.

"But if that's the case, why wouldn't they reveal it?"

"They're nobles, Tyrell. If they ever hoped to rule, they can't admit their magical potential. It's one of the most fundamental laws of Weldwyn—the separation of magic and state. Igraine could never have married Leofric if something like that were discovered."

"But Igraine has no magic!"

"That does not prevent her from carrying it in her blood."

"This would be so much easier if there were some way to detect such power."

"Agreed," said Aegryth. "Yet there's little we can do about it at present."

"So what do you suggest we do about this?"

"What, Princess Edwina? She's definitely of the right age to start manifesting. I suppose I could keep an eye on her for a little while."

"And if she does show signs?"

"Let's not get ahead of ourselves," said Aegryth. "After all, her prediction of this storm could merely be wishful thinking."

"Halt!" called out Althea. The Dwarven arbalesters ceased moving. "Load!" she shouted. Each archer turned the crannequin that pulled back the metal arms. With the crossbows cocked, they raised weapons and placed bolts, ready to loose.

"Take aim," she yelled, pausing for a moment before continuing. "Let fly!" A volley of bolts flew downrange, striking their targets with a noisy clatter.

"Excellent, Highness," said Lord Tulfar. "We'll make a Dwarf of you yet."

She smiled at the compliment. "You have fine troops, Baron. I wish those in Summersgate were as dedicated."

The Dwarf stared at her. "There's something wrong here," he said at last.

"Nothing I've done, I hope?"

"No, not at all. It's just that your... attire is unsuitable."

"This is chainmail from the Royal Armoury," replied Althea.

"Ah, that's the problem! We need to get you some Dwarven chainmail."

"How is that any different?"

"We use a special smithing technique to harden the steel rings. Few weapons can penetrate such armour. Mind you, it won't save you from bruising, but it'll keep your skin intact."

"And you have such armour just sitting around?"

"No, of course not," said the baron, "but I'm sure our smiths can adapt something for you."

"I shouldn't like to delay the armouring of your own warriors."

"Don't worry, it won't." He walked around her. "Now, let's see. You're skinny, even for a Human, but I believe we can make it work."

She blushed, and he laughed. "Sorry, I meant no disrespect. It's just that we Dwarves are stockier than you Humans. I think we might have a youth's chain shirt though. I'm sure our smiths can lengthen it and bring in the arms a bit."

"I should appreciate that a great deal," she said.

"Have you a helmet?"

"No, I didn't think to bring one, although I'm told there's plenty in the Palace Armoury."

"The Palace Armoury? No, that won't do, that won't do at all. If you're going to lead Dwarven warriors, you need something that will inspire confidence. Come with me, and we'll see what we can find you." He turned to the arbalest captain. "Carry on, Haldrim."

Althea followed the baron out of the great hall and down a sloping passageway. The corridor felt like it went on forever before it finally veered right, opening into a large chamber.

"Another old mine?" she asked.

"Yes, but for the last century, it's been our armoury." He halted at a door, where stood a sentry. The guard pulled a key from around his neck and inserted it into a lock, turning it to produce a series of clanking noises.

"There we are," said Lord Tulfar. "Now, let's see what we have to offer you." He stepped inside, leaving her to follow. The room beyond held several suits of armour on display for all to see. The baron halted by a shelf and picked up a conical helm, holding it up to the light.

"No, this won't do," he muttered, discarding it. He rummaged through some more, then produced another with a flourish. "Here we are."

The helmet had a flat top with a visor that swung down to cover the face. Although made of steel, it was a dark blue in colour, accented with gold scrollwork around the eyes.

"What do you think?" he asked.

"Truly a work of art," said Althea.

"Yet fully functional. All of this armour is, to tell the truth. We Dwarves make armour to protect a person, but that doesn't mean we can't make it pleasing to the eye. Do you want to try it on?"

"May I?"

"Certainly. Why not?" He saw the hesitation. "Don't worry, Dwarven heads are not so dissimilar to those of Humans."

Althea took the helm, examining the workmanship. "It's beautiful." She lifted the visor. "It's hinged!"

"Yes, so you may be recognized if need be. Go ahead, try it on for size. It won't bite you."

She pulled it over her head, only to find it covering her eyes. "It's a little large."

"That's easy enough to fix. We'll just make a new liner. How does it feel, from a weight perspective?"

"Much lighter than I expected."

"It's the tempering—one of our secrets. The same one that makes it blue, actually." He walked around her, looking at the fit. "You'll need a coif to go with it, else your neck will be exposed. That'll need to be custom-made. Yours is much longer than a Dwarf's."

"This is too much," objected the princess. "Why, the cost alone—"

"Bah," said the baron. "Don't you worry about the cost. Most of this armour has sat here for generations. We might as well put it to use. Now, I noticed you use a sword. Any other weapons you're familiar with?"

"Such as?"

"Oh, I don't know," said Lord Tulfar. "An axe or a hammer? On second thought, those might not be the best choice for one of your slight build."

"I only have training in the sword," she replied, "and a fairly short one at that."

"There's nothing wrong with that. Why, the Queen of Merceria herself uses a short Dwarven sword, although I wonder if you might find a mace more to your liking?" He wandered over to a rack full of weapons, picking through them. "Here's one with a nice grip." He pulled it forth, passing it to her.

Althea removed the helmet before taking the weapon in hand, testing its weight. Swinging it around, she noticed it had a flanged head attached to a metal shaft in a way that made it feel perfectly balanced.

"You use it much like a club," said the baron.

"I'm afraid I've never even used a club."

"It's easy enough to handle. You more or less just swing it back and forth."

"And is this a Dwarven mace?"

"Of course. What else would we keep in our armoury? Bring it outside, and I'll show you how effective it can be."

She followed him from the room. The Dwarf, despite his shorter stature, set a brisk pace, and by the time they reached the great hall, Althea was almost out of breath.

"I came to Mirstone seeking assistance," she admitted. "I never thought I'd end up doing all this."

"War has come to Weldwyn," said the baron. "We can't have you wandering around the kingdom unable to defend yourself, now, can we?"

"No, I suppose not."

"Now, let's start with the basics, shall we..."

.   .   .

Althea collapsed into bed, her arms aching so much she swore they were about to fall off. The day had been a busy one, made even more so by the necessity of sending correspondence to the capital. She reported on the Dwarves' training progress but decided against informing her mother of her own development. The letters had gone out right before dusk, and with any luck, would arrive in Summersgate by week's end.

She wondered, briefly, how Alstan was coping with his new responsibilities as king, but her eyelids soon drooped, and she nodded off.

A loud noise woke the princess with a start. She sat up, straining to hear more when the clatter of armour drew her attention. She made her way to the door, pressing her ear up against it. Silence greeted her investigations, so she pulled it open to reveal the back of a Dwarf.

He turned around at the intrusion. "Sorry, Highness," he said. "Didn't mean to wake you."

"Who are you?" she asked.

"The name's Brogar Hammerhand, at your service." He bowed deeply.

"What in the name of Malin are you doing out there?"

The Dwarf blushed. "Why, guarding you, of course. Did Lord Tulfar not inform you?"

"Why would I need guarding?"

"Well, that's just it, isn't it? I mean, you wouldn't, here in Mirstone, but you won't always be in such a safe location. Me and the others were instructed to accompany you at all times."

"Others?"

"Aye," said Brogar.

"And how many of you are there, exactly?"

"Twelve," he replied.

"And are you their leader?"

He puffed up his chest. "Aye, I am, and a great honour it is too."

"Then I thank you," said Althea. "It's comforting to know you're here to protect me." She made to close the door, but Brogar raised his hand.

"Pardon me, Highness," he said, "but I wonder if I might have a quick word about something?"

"By all means."

"Have you a standard?"

"No, I'm a princess, not a warrior, or so my elder brother keeps telling me."

"Perhaps we could change that?"

A grin spread across her face. "I like your idea. What would you propose?"

TWENTY-SEVEN

Prisoners

SUMMER 965 MC

K raloch tried to move his hands, but the bindings dug deep, leaving him little wiggle room. Tied as they were, behind his back, it was a simple yet effective method of preventing him from using his magic. He looked over at Zhura, who sat across from him, but her attention was on the guards.

"*These bindings are digging into my wrists,*" he said in his native tongue. His gaze swept the area, coming to rest on Gerald. The Human's head was down, and he sensed a great sorrow.

"What is wrong?" he asked, switching to the common tongue.

"This is all my fault," replied the marshal. "I never should have ordered the charge down that hill. It cost us the battle."

"Nonsense. Without reinforcements, we were doomed."

"Then I should have withdrawn until the rest of our army could gather."

"And how would you do that?" asked Kraloch. "The spirits do not tire, Gerald. They would have overwhelmed us. It was a far wiser decision to stand and fight in a position of our own choosing."

"Yet now we are prisoners, and the entire land is ripe for these Elves to swoop in and take everything."

"You had no way of knowing that. Had the enemy held only the spirits, we might have succeeded. Even though we were defeated, we did manage to reveal the true nature of our foe."

Gerald nodded. "That's true. I won't deny it, but I should have seen it coming. Lord Greycloak once told us Elf didn't kill Elf. I thought he meant Penelope, but now, looking back on it, I think he knew this Elven army was out here, somewhere."

"It matters little, now," said Kraloch. "The simple matter is we are prisoners, although I must admit to some confusion over why they haven't already killed us."

"What do you know of Elves?"

"Not much, to be honest. Like all shamans, I learned of the Great War where they destroyed our cities and drove us to the edge of extinction. Our ancestors wandered the land, scraping out an existence by never remaining in an area for too long. Eventually, they began to rebuild, living in small villages, although some kept up their wandering ways."

"Like those in the Netherwood," said Gerald.

"Yes, as well as some on what you would call the Continent. We had little interaction with Elves since aside from those we fought beside under the Mercerian flag."

"I was always under the impression the war decimated the Elves, yet here they are with a significant force."

"Yes," agreed the shaman, "and, it would seem, a leader who is a Necromancer. Why do they permit such an atrocity?"

"Who can say?" replied the marshal. "That general, Ilarian, said he had served her for more than a thousand years. What if she wasn't always a Necromancer? On the other hand, we know almost nothing of their society."

"Meaning?"

"They may have different attitudes towards the magic of death."

"Yes," came Zhura's voice. "Elves are immortal, and for that reason, death holds no sway over them."

"But they can still die whether it be by illness or the sword," insisted Gerald.

"Yet they carry the burden of immortality. You Humans are similar to us Orcs in that our lives are relatively short. That brief life gives meaning to all we do. Imagine if your life were to continue with no end? What thoughts would then occupy your mind?"

"What are you suggesting?" said Kraloch.

"The mind seeks knowledge. It is as true for us as it is for the Elves. It is, therefore, inevitable that such a long-lived people eventually turn their attentions to the very matter of life itself. Maybe they wished to know why they, of all the races, were granted immortality?"

"I see, now," replied the shaman. "Their quest to understand death would quite naturally lead them to the study of Necromancy."

"But why?" asked Gerald. "Surely Life Magic would make more sense?"

"To use a Human phrase, the magic of life and death are but two sides of the same sword," said Kraloch. "It is a lesson Orc shamans learn early on in their training. We are taught to resist the temptation of using dark magic. In this, our Ancestors guide us."

"Don't the Elves worship their ancestors?"

"Not in the same way as us," said Zhura. "Orcs learned to communicate with those who have passed on. Our knowledge of Life Magic is said to be the greatest of all the races. As a result, we seek guidance from those who came before. The Elves, on the other hand, venerate their dead, seeing them as shining examples of their beliefs."

"So they see them as gods?" said Gerald.

"In a sense, yes," she replied. "But they are gods who do not speak directly to them. In this, they are like you Humans. Tell me, does Saxnor talk to you?"

"No, of course not."

"And yet you live your lives trying to emulate his beliefs, showing strength in all you do."

"That's different. Saxnor's a god."

"The Elves think of their forbearers no differently. In their minds, they are living on in the Afterlife, looking down on them like gods, guiding them to their destiny."

"Great!" said Gerald. "Not only must we face a horde of ghosts, we also need to defeat an army that's had thousands of years to prepare."

Zhura smiled. "You already took the measure of the spirit army, Gerald Matheson. Its defeat is no longer in doubt."

"How can you say that when we're sitting here as prisoners?"

"It is a setback, to be sure. We may die, but we laid the groundwork for the others to put an end to this menace once and for all."

"And the Elven army?" pressed Gerald

Now it was Kraloch's time to answer. "Do you remember the ruins beneath Ravensguard?"

"I do. They were very similar to those we found near Queenston. Why?"

"The murals we found depicted the Great War between the Orcs and Elves."

"I remember now," said Gerald. "It's what gave me the idea to use the wall of spears, but I don't see the significance."

Kraloch lowered his voice. "The Elves we see here wear the same armour depicted in those carvings."

"Meaning?"

"They have likely been in hiding for centuries. I doubt their knowledge of battles has changed over time."

"How does that help us?"

"You must see the long-term here," said Zhura. "Look at this objectively, instead of wallowing in your guilt. You are a great leader, Marshal Gerald. Urgon calls you the Wolf of Merceria. You use your warriors as a wolf uses its pack, coordinating its efforts for the greater good. Drive all emotion from your heart, and set your mind to the task at hand."

"I'll give it a try," said Gerald, risking a glance at the guards. "Their armour's decorative, but the truth is, it's just chainmail. Their warriors also favour swords, not as effective against heavily armoured opponents."

"Did you notice any cavalry?" asked Kraloch.

"No," said Gerald, "but the carvings did show horses, so they must have had them at some point. I'm guessing they use them purely for scouting, as they didn't appear to be wearing any armour. Mind you, they might have learned a thing or two since that war. It has been thousands of years."

"Do not think of them as Humans," urged Zhura. "They are Elves, inca-pable of adapting to change. They won the war. They would take that as proof of their supremacy in matters of battle."

"Then I doubt their cavalry would offer much opposition to us, but their bows are quite another thing. I've seen Elven bows in action, and I don't fancy the idea of going up against them. Mind you, those warbows your people use are pretty effective as well."

"Yes," agreed Kraloch, "and we now have them in abundance."

"So those, along with the Dwarven arbalests, could effectively neutralize that threat." Gerald nodded his head, looking at Zhura. "You're right. We can beat them, but not here, tied up as we are."

"Overcoming our fear of the enemy is the first step," said Zhura, "and you have now… Humanized them. Is that the right word?"

"Yes," said Gerald. "I suppose it is."

"Good. Now, let us put our minds to our current imprisonment."

Gerald woke to a star-filled night sky. A group of Elven guards had come to visit, amongst them a female wearing immaculate robes.

"These are the prisoners?" she stated. "I expected something a little more impressive."

"The Human is a great general," said the captain, "said to have many victories beneath his cloak."

"Is he, now? I wonder if he might make a nice Volgath?"

"I thought only the queen held such power?"

"Is she not coming to see them?"

"No, Your Grace. She is far too busy to the west."

"Then perhaps a lesser spirit? Let me see what I can do. Get him to his feet."

Two guards moved forward, grasping Gerald by the arms and lifting him upright. He stared back, determined to show defiance to the end.

"Release him," she commanded, "then stand back, but keep a close eye on these other two."

She started grasping the air as if gathering thread from an invisible spider web. Words issued from her mouth, and then the night sky somehow grew darker still, the very air becoming oppressive before a foul stench drifted towards the prisoners.

The Elf mage pointed at Gerald, wispy grey tendrils leaping from her hands to wrap themselves around him. She kept up a litany of magical words as he felt the coils pierce his flesh, reaching into his very soul with a gut-wrenching pain before everything went black.

⌇

Kraloch watched in horror as the Elven Necromancer plied her trade. "Witness the power of my magic," she screeched as she clenched her fists and pulled back on the wispy rope.

He imagined she'd expected to pull out a spirit, but what came forth took her by surprise, for instead, a grey wolf emerged, lunging at her with a suddenness that left no time to react.

Closing the distance quickly, it sank its teeth into her throat while the other Elves looked on in horror, unable to tear their eyes from the grisly sight.

"*It is the grey wolf!*" yelled Kraloch, reverting to Orcish.

The Necromancer fell back, her screams soon silenced. The grey wolf released its prey, letting the body drop to the ground. It prowled the area, snarling at the Elven guards who backed up, their faces betraying their fear. Drawn by the Necromancer's screams, Ilarian appeared.

"What is this?" he demanded.

The guard captain regained his senses. "Nerenya tried to pull the Human's spirit from his body to enslave him. This creature emerged instead!"

"Bring bows," ordered the Elven lord, "and we shall put an end to this Human once and for all."

"Do that," said Kraloch, "and you shall release the wolf to roam freely. Are you so eager to see the beast decimate your army?"

"It is only a spirit," said Ilarian.

"No. It is far more than that. This creature has been imprisoned in his body for years. It is what gives him his power on the battlefield."

"Make it go away."

"That I cannot do. The wolf is bound to the Human and remains locked away only so long as his master lives."

"Then use your magic to heal him!"

"When my arms are bound?"

Ilarian looked at his guards. "Untie him."

His warriors took a step but hesitated.

"Do it!" screamed the Elven lord.

They moved forward, one of them drawing a dagger to cut away the ropes while the other held a sword to the Orc's chest.

Now released from his bonds, Kraloch raised his hands and then paused. "I will only do this if you give your word not to execute us."

"You are in no position to dictate terms," countered the Elf.

Kraloch lowered his arms. "Then I shall not cast. Instead, I will let the wolf wander your camp, stealing your spirits."

Ilarian paled. "Very well, I shall guarantee your lives. Now, cast your spell and be quick about it."

Kraloch started incanting the spell of healing, the words tumbling from his mouth with little effort. His hands glowed with magical energy before he placed them on Gerald's arm, watching as the colour bled into him.

The marshal's eyes slowly opened.

"What happened?" he asked.

The Elves looked around, but there was no sign of the wolf.

"I shall tell you later," said Kraloch. "For now, you must sleep. You have been through quite an ordeal."

Ilarian, content the beast was gone, turned and stomped off, leaving only a few guards to keep watch. The shaman sat, rubbing his wrists where they'd been rubbed raw.

Zhura looked at him with a new sense of respect. "*Tell me, my friend,*" she said, using the tongue of the Orcs. "*We have known each other for years. How did you learn so much about the wolf?*"

Kraloch smiled. "*I did not.*"

"*You lied?*"

"*I... bluffed. It is a Human concept, a mis-truth to throw the enemy off the scent.*"

She nodded her head sagely. "*You learned much from these Humans.*"

"*As they have from us,*" said Kraloch.

Kraloch opened his eyes just as the sun was rising. However, it was not the light that awoke him but a magical summoning. He glanced at the guards, yet none appeared to be taking an interest in him. He turned his attention to a slight distortion of the light, and then the ghostly image of Aubrey appeared before him.

"Kraloch," she said. "Where are you? What's happened?"

"We fought a battle," the Orc replied, keeping his voice low, "but the army of spirits proved too much for us. I am now a prisoner of the Elves, as are Gerald and Zhura."

"The Elves?"

"Yes, there is an army of them following in the spirits' wake. It is they who are the greater threat."

"What of the others?"

"I have no word. When last I spotted him, Urgon was to the north of the line, and Hayley to the south. They may have escaped destruction, but I cannot say for sure."

"I'll have Shellbreaker scour the area," replied Aubrey.

"Send word to the queen," said Kraloch. "It is important she be kept abreast of these developments."

"She won't like her marshal being captured, or you, for that matter, not to mention Zhura. Are you in danger, do you think?"

"No, they look content for now to hold us prisoner. Their leader, Queen Kythelia, is not with them. Apparently, she has more pressing business to the west."

"Bide your time, my friend. We shall do what we can to rescue you."

"No," the shaman replied. "It is far too dangerous. Better you plan the defeat of this army before it can reach the borders of Merceria."

Aubrey looked aside, clearly talking to someone out of sight. "I'll try to contact you later," she said.

"Very well, but be aware I may not be able to answer without letting the Elves know."

"In that case, I shall be sure to communicate things that can be answered with a nod or a shake of the head."

"A good plan," said Kraloch. "Now, you must let me go before they grow suspicious."

"Good luck, Kraloch. May the Ancestors watch over you."

"And you," he answered.

Aubrey's image faded.

"*That was interesting,*" said Zhura in her native tongue.

"*You saw her?*"

"*Of course. I see all spirits. Why should your spell be any different? It was, after all, Aubrey's spirit that travelled here.*"

"*So it was. You must excuse my confusion, Zhura. It has been some years since I have been in your company.*"

"Yes, far too long, my old friend, but let us not use this time to become overly sentimental. Do you believe she will truly help us?"

"Undoubtedly. Once the queen hears of Gerald's captivity, she will stop at nothing to see him freed. What form that help will take, however, is anyone's guess."

"Then we must put our faith in the Mercerians."

Aubrey let the spell dissipate.

"Well?" said Beverly.

"There's been a big battle, and Gerald's army was defeated. He, Kraloch, and Zhura were captured."

"And the rest?"

"We have no word. Kraloch thinks Urgon and Hayley may have survived, but it's only a guess at this point."

"This is catastrophic."

"There's more—a host of Elves backs the spirit army."

"Oh, great," said the knight, "because we didn't already have enough troubles without all that!"

"What do we do now?"

"We'll start by contacting the queen. My recommendation is we move south, as far back as Hammersfield."

"To what end?"

"If my father can move eastward, we can join forces."

"What about the capital?" Aubrey asked.

"That's a good question. If it were up to me, I'd abandon it, but then again, even a small garrison could defend it."

"So we just retreat?"

"If we want to survive to fight again, yes. In the meantime, I'm open to suggestions about how we might rescue Gerald and the others. You know the queen is going to insist on it."

"First, I'll contact Andurak and get word to the queen," said Aubrey. "I understand she's with your father's army at present."

"Good, and while you're doing that, I'll go and talk to King Thalgrun. He may need to reconsider things after our defeat."

Aubrey stared at her cousin. "We will get through this, Beverly."

"I'd like to believe you, but the facts say otherwise. We're dangerously exposed here in the north, with a powerful enemy likely as close as only a few days' march. It's going to take everything we have to meet up with the rest of our army, not to mention locating any stragglers from Gerald's forces."

"Revi can help."

"Yes," said Beverly. "That's an excellent idea. I'll have him send out Shell-breaker. At the very least, he ought to be able to locate some survivors. Maybe then, we'll have a better idea of what happened."

"Anything, in particular, you want me to pass on to the queen?"

"Make sure you let her know Gerald is alive. That's the main thing, and don't forget to assure her we'll send word if we learn anything new."

Urgon knelt in amongst the underbrush, watching the spirit army off in the distance. Not willing to take any chances, he'd personally taken command of the rearguard, ready to lead the enemy astray should they choose to pursue. He turned to the young hunter, Bagrat.

"It appears you would have been better off to have stayed with Zhura," he said, "or at the very least with my sister, Kurghal."

"No, my place is here, beside my chieftain. And in any case, the wolves have proven to be of great use."

Urgon turned his head to take in the three animals. They'd travelled all the way from Ord-Dugath, accompanying Zhura and Kurghal on their pilgrimage. However, during the battle, they had joined the northern flank, helping the hunters maintain their concealment. It wasn't as if they had any magical ability, but they were quick to recognize the enemy's approach, giving the Orcs far more warning than simple scouts could. At the moment, they sat peaceably, showing none of the signs that would alert them to danger.

"What do we do now?" asked Bagrat.

"We travel east. Then, if we are not pursued, north to try to locate the army of Redblade."

"Redblade," said Bagrat, the very word inspiring confidence in the young hunter. Urgon, content not to dissuade his comrade, let him have his moment.

"It is true she is a great warrior," the chieftain said, "but even more importantly, the marshal trained her himself. If anyone can find a way to defeat this great evil, it is she."

TWENTY-EIGHT

Alric

SUMMER 965 MC

Queen Anna took the news remarkably well, remaining stoic despite learning of the events that had taken place.

"And we know them to still be alive?" she asked.

"Yes," Andurak assured her. "According to Lady Aubrey, they were in good health. It appears the Dark Queen is content to simply let her people hold them prisoner at this point."

"Her people?"

"Kraloch reports Kythelia is not with the Elven host. Something to the effect she's busy in the west."

"The west?" said Prince Alric. "That can only mean one thing—they're planning a move against Weldwyn!"

"Yes," said the queen, "with Leofric's death and the loss of his army, the kingdom is in a vulnerable state."

"Ripe for the Clans to attack anew," agreed the prince.

"Is that likely?" asked Baron Fitzwilliam. "After all, their High King, Dathen, is still in a dungeon, isn't he?"

"He is, but then again, the Clans are known for turning on each other. The real question is whether or not they have the numbers."

"Of course they have the numbers," said Albreda.

Queen Anna looked at the Druid. "What makes you say that?"

"It's obvious, isn't it? This whole thing was carefully orchestrated. The Dark Queen isn't content just to take Merceria—she wants Weldwyn and Norland as well."

"To what end?"

"Who knows? These are the Elves we're talking about. Few can understand the machinations of that race."

"Come now," said Fitz. "You can't lump all Elves together. Did you forget
how Telethial gave her life to help protect Merceria?"

"I stand corrected," replied Albreda, "but I still believe it's clear Penelope
or, rather, Queen Kythelia, since that's her real name, has been planning
something like this for centuries."

"Then how do we stop her?" asked the baron.

"We do as Beverly has suggested," said the queen. "We'll leave a token
garrison here at Galburn's Ridge, and then march the rest south to
Oaksvale. From there, we'll head eastward, with the ultimate goal of joining
up with Beverly's forces."

"Who do we leave as a garrison?"

"I volunteer the Dwarves," said Herdwin. "We know how to defend a castle,
and while we wait, we can see about repairing that damaged section of wall."

"If the enemy shows up here," said Fitz, "you'll be hard-pressed to hold
them back."

"Nonsense. Dwarves can defend stone better than anyone. They might
overrun us given enough time, but don't you worry, we'll make them pay
for the privilege."

"Excellent," said Anna. "The Dwarven brigade will remain here in the
capital." She shifted her attention to the baron. "How long before you can
begin the march?"

"My men can be on the road first thing tomorrow morning."

"I should go with the lead elements," suggested Kiren-Jool. "I can use a
spell of scrying to keep an eye out for the enemy."

"How far can you see with such a spell?" asked the queen.

"A hundred miles or more. Why?"

"I might need you to locate Gerald. Is that something you can do?"

"I can," replied the Enchanter. "And since I know him well, it shouldn't
prove too difficult to find him. Are you planning a rescue?"

"If possible, but we can't even consider something like that if we don't
know his location."

Sir Preston stepped forward. "Your Majesty, is that wise?"

Everyone in the room looked shocked at the mere suggestion they
abandon the search, but the queen took it in stride.

"Speak your mind, Sir Preston. I shan't hold it against you."

"I have great admiration for the marshal, Majesty, but we are facing an
enemy who will require all the effort we can muster. Diverting any of our
warriors to a rescue operation would only serve to weaken us."

"I disagree," she replied. "If we are to face this threat, we need our greatest leader, and that's Gerald."

"In that case," continued the knight, "may I volunteer to lead the rescue operation myself?"

"I thought you believed the rescue a foolish errand?"

"I do, but that doesn't mean I won't give my all to the cause."

"Fine. I accept your offer, although we don't, as yet, know the nature of that rescue." She turned to the rest of the group. "Anything else anyone would like to bring up?"

They all looked down at their feet, lost for words. The loss of Gerald was a terrible blow, not only to the army of Merceria but on a more personal level to the queen herself.

"You are dismissed," she said. "Though I wonder if Kiren-Jool might remain a moment?"

They filed out, leaving the Kurathian Enchanter in the company of the queen and Prince Alric.

"You wanted to see me, Majesty?"

"How long will it take you to use your magic?"

"It is a ritual, Your Majesty, requiring the casting of two separate incantations, but aside from that, there are no special requirements. Did you wish me to do so now?"

"You don't need time to prepare?"

"Not at all."

"Then, yes," she said. "If you would be so kind, I would have you try to locate the marshal."

"Ordinarily, I would use a crystal ball for such a spell, but a mirror will do in its place." He wandered over to a side table, selecting a hand mirror. "May I?"

"By all means."

He held the mirror up, closing his eyes to call on the magic that lay within him. The air began to buzz, and then the mirror glowed slightly.

"I found his location, Majesty. Now I must establish the visual connection." More words poured forth while the very air felt like it came alive. The Kurathian's hair stood on end a moment before the mirror's surface pulsed with power, rippling as it showed the mage an entirely different view.

"I see him," said Kiren-Jool. "Though the connection does not allow us to speak to him."

"Can he see us?"

"No, though one skilled in magic might detect the presence of scrying in the area. For this reason, I shall keep my point of view at a suitable distance."

"What can you see?"

"It is, I fear, much as Aubrey described it. The spirit army is in the distance, but the Elves are close by. Give me a moment, and I shall pull farther back."

He stared into the mirror as Anna moved to look over his shoulder, but she only saw a regular reflection. Apparently, no one but the caster could see the results, a notion she found most frustrating.

"I see hills, Majesty, lying to their south and, if I'm not mistaken, a road that runs roughly east-west, possibly to Anvil. That was, I believe, their last reported position?"

"It was," she confirmed.

Kiren-Jool turned around, rotating in place, the mirror still held before his eyes. "Wait, there's movement up in the hills. I'll try and get closer."

"How well do you see through such a spell?"

"Remarkably well. It has often been compared to a bird's eyesight, though that, of course, would be more appropriate to an Air Mage. By the Saints, look at the size of that thing!"

"What thing?" she asked.

"Oh, it's one of those three-horns. A Saurian is guiding it through the hills, and it looks like some Orc hunters are leading them." A smile broke out. "I see the High Ranger. She must have led some survivors into the hills."

"Are they in danger?"

"No, they're well back from the enemy army. If I hadn't had a height advantage, I never would have noticed them. They appear to be heading south, deeper into the hills."

"If we can get word to them," said the queen, "we might be able to arrange a rendezvous."

"I'm afraid I have no spell that will help with that."

"Could Albreda not send a bird," suggested Alric, "or Revi Shellbreaker? Hayley would at least recognize him."

"Yes," agreed Anna. "You did well, Master Kiren-Jool. I'll be sure to call on you again if I have need."

The Enchanter let the spell dissipate before putting down the mirror. "Of course, Your Majesty. I am ever at your service."

He backed from the room. Alric thought it a strange custom, but he was told it was something the Kurathians had practiced for centuries.

As the door closed, Anna turned to him, tears in her eyes, her regal pose of earlier now replaced by a frightened young woman. He held on to her, letting her sobs come freely.

. . .

Anna sat on the bed as Sophie combed her hair, while nearby, Alric read through reports.

"You should go to Weldwyn," suggested the queen. "Your people need you."

"I'm needed here, by your side."

"But if the Clans attack—"

"The Clans have threatened invasion for years. And in any case, we have no warriors to spare. Am I to then ride home to face capture by the enemy?"

"No, of course not, I just thought..."

"You are thinking of me," said the prince, "I understand that, but when we married, you gave me a sword to defend our hearth and home, and that's what I intend to do."

"All right, but once we defeat this menace, you shall lead an army westward to Weldwyn's aid. You have my word."

"Providing we have an army left."

"You doubt our chance of victory?"

"No," said Alric. "I've seen you Mercerians win against impossible odds too many times in the past to give up hope."

"Now THAT's the prince I fell in love with."

He smiled. "It's pretty simple. All we need to do is get Gerald back."

"What makes you say that?"

"Come now, I know your history. You two are unbeatable when you're together. Why, if you'd been with him at this last battle, the two of you would have chased the enemy clear back to the Windstorm Depths."

Anna smiled, but he could tell it was forced.

"We will get him back," he said. "I promise you."

"How?" she asked. "He's in the middle of an enemy army, for Saxnor's sake."

"I have an idea, but I need to give it some further thought." He rose from his chair. "I'm going to find Sir Preston. I value his opinion." He looked at the queen's maid. "Don't worry, Sophie. I won't keep him long."

He left the room, turning in the doorway to look at her one last time. "I shall be back soon, my love. I promise."

Albreda picked at her food.

"Something troubling you, my dear?"

She glanced up to see the look of concern on Baron Fitzwilliam's face. "It's nothing, Richard."

"Come now. I've known you long enough to know that's not the case."

"It's this spirit army. It's just so… unnatural. It goes against everything I believe in."

"We all feel that way," soothed Fitz.

"No, you don't understand. I'm connected to the Whitewood, a part of it, if you will. This army of spirits is an abomination. This is the world of the living, Richard. Yes, spirits may roam here from time to time, but they have their own place. The Elves have always lived amongst the woodlands of Eiddenwerthe, respecting nature; at least that's what I thought."

"Eiddenwerthe? What's that?"

"You're well-read; I'm surprised you don't know. It's the ancient name for this world of ours."

"Of ours?" said Fitz. "Do you mean to say there are other worlds?"

"That, I cannot answer. The great scholars of Shrewesdale debated the concept for centuries. I remember reading about them when I worked there."

"You worked in Shrewesdale?"

"Yes, at the Library of Kendros."

"I knew you'd visited it, but I had no idea you worked there."

"I did. It's how I managed to learn the magical runes."

"Astounding. Is that where you learned about Elves?"

"Some, although the scholars know little about the woodland race. I learned more from Telethial than I ever did from the library."

The baron refilled his goblet, offering some wine to her.

"Now, why do you suppose the Elves called on this army of ghosts?" he asked.

"That's clear, isn't it? They need the warriors. If you remember, the Elves were decimated in the Great War with the Orcs."

"Yes, but wasn't that close to two thousand years ago? They must have increased their population by now?"

"Ah, but they haven't, don't you see?" she said. "The Elves are no longer able to bear children."

"Why do you think that?"

"It first came to light in Tivilton. The queen noted the lack of Elven children there, and then, when she visited the Darkwood, she came to believe they were barren."

"But what of Telethial?" Fitz asked. "She's Lord Greycloak's daughter, so he obviously had a child."

"Yes, she's from a younger generation, yet I believe she was, by our terms, extremely old—a thousand years, at least."

"She DID claim they were born AFTER the war."

"She did," agreed Albreda. "Aubrey thinks there might be a means to cure them of their plight, but that is neither here nor there. This Queen Kythelia—"

"You mean Penelope?"

"Yes. She may have delved into the foul magic of Necromancy, seeking a way to once again make it possible to bear children."

"With Death Magic?" said the baron. "Wouldn't the magic of life be more appropriate?"

"I cannot speak to their mindset, but what if that's all they could master?"

"She must be powerful if she's thousands of years old."

"Indeed," said Albreda, "but I believe my power may be greater."

"What leads you to suspect that?"

"Mine is tied to the very ground beneath our feet."

"I thought magic came from within?"

"It's complicated," she replied, "and I fear you would find it difficult to understand if I tried to explain it to you."

"I'm willing to listen if you're willing to try."

"Well, as you know, I am a wild mage, a caster of magic which is self-taught. The magic of the Whitewood released my power, unlocking something inside me—amplifying it, if you will."

"Is that what makes you so powerful?"

"I believe it is. When I call upon the magic of the woods, I can feel the power flowing through me as if a part of nature coursed through my veins. Traditional mages are taught in a strict manner, a manner which places mental limits on what they can achieve."

"But my niece Aubrey has done quite well for herself," said Fitz.

"Yes, likely due to my influence. I taught her to abandon some of her preconceived notions about magic, allowing her to expand her power considerably."

"Still, if the Elves had thousands of years, wouldn't that make them even more powerful?"

"The power of the living world is all around us," said Albreda. "Think of it as an energy that amplifies the power within me. On the other hand, Death Magic takes more direct action, drawing from the power within."

"What about Blood Magic?"

"Yes, that's powerful, too, because it draws on the power within another living entity."

The baron took a sip of wine, mulling things over before he finally shook his head. "I'm afraid you've lost me there."

"Imagine that goblet is a mage, and the wine within it the power of magic, their energy, if you will. A typical mage can call upon their own cup at will. However, Blood Magic can use a second cup, stealing the energy from another individual, but there is a cost."

"The cost being the person's life?"

"Exactly."

"But why is that any more powerful?"

"When a mage uses up their reserves of energy, they can draw on the body itself. The primary evidence of this is typically a nosebleed or even ears that drip blood. Take it too far, and it can consume the entire body. In Fire Mages, this is known as self-immolation. Blood Magic consumes not only the contents of the cup but the goblet itself, thus doubling the available energy. Of course, the sudden release of energy is utterly destructive."

"Accounting for the decaying flesh Beverly and Aubrey found."

"Precisely. But, you can only use such magic as long as there is a living creature nearby to supply the energy. As far as I know, our enemy has so far used animals to achieve their aims, but it's only a matter of time before they turn to us Humans."

"Saxnor's beard," said Fitz. "Are you saying they want to harvest Humans for Blood Magic?"

"It's a distinct possibility."

"And is there a limit on what they can do using this technique?"

"I have no idea, and I can't say I'm eager to find out."

Fitz set down his drink. "These Elves must be stopped at all costs!"

A guard opened the door. "You have visitors, my lord. Prince Alric and Sir Preston. Shall I show them in?"

"Of course, of course," said the baron. He turned to Albreda. "I wonder what brings them here?"

Prince Alric stepped into the room, the knight following. "Lord Richard, Lady Albreda. So good of you to see us on such short notice."

The baron laughed. "One can hardly refuse a prince! Come, sit. What can I help you with?"

"Truthfully, it's Albreda we came to see."

The Druid looked up in shock. "Me? Whatever do you want me for?"

"Sir Preston and I were discussing Gerald's predicament. He had a notion you might have some thoughts on the matter."

She turned to the knight. "Whatever made you assume that?"

"You were of great assistance during the assault on Galburn's Ridge," Sir Preston replied, "and the Orc shaman, Andurak, came all the way here to seek you out. It's clear you're meant to be in the thick of things."

"Meant?" she replied. "No one is 'meant' to do anything. We live in a world of free will, Sir Preston, not subject to the whims of fate."

"And yet you yourself have visions," countered the prince. "Ones most would describe as prophetic."

"That is beyond my control."

"Perhaps, but the truth is you know more about magic than anyone else in Merceria."

"You have my attention. What is it you seek, Sir Preston?"

The knight cleared his throat. "I wondered if you might be able to summon gryphons?"

"If by that you mean do I have the power, then certainly, but to what end?"

"I thought we might ride them to rescue Gerald and the others."

"Have you ever seen a gryphon up close?"

"No," replied Sir Preston. "Why?"

"If you had, you would know they are quite incapable of carrying a person."

"Even a large one?"

"I could summon the largest gryphon in existence," explained the Druid, "and yes, you might be able to sit upon its back, provided it allowed you to do so, but that's a far cry from being able to fly with a rider."

"So," said the knight, "that's a no to the flying, then?"

"Clearly."

"Well, so much for that idea."

"Is that it?"

"Not quite," said Alric. "Thanks to Kiren-Jool, we can easily locate Gerald whenever we need to, but coming up with a way of getting him away from the Elves is proving troublesome."

"You need a diversion," said Albreda. "Something to keep the Elves' attention elsewhere."

"Such as?"

"A show of force?"

"An excellent idea," noted Sir Preston. "If we could draw them north, maybe Hayley and the others could effect a rescue?"

"A reasonable assumption," said the baron, "but the Elves already beat them once. What makes you believe they'd be eager to fight them again so soon?"

Albreda abruptly stood. "I must go," she said.

"Go where?" said Fitz.

"Why, to help rescue Gerald and the others, of course."

"You can't go by yourself. It's far too dangerous."

"Then I shall take some Dwarves."

"Dwarves?" said Sir Preston. "Won't they slow you down?"

"I intend to cross the hills. Who better to navigate that rough terrain?"

"But how would you find them? You'd need Kiren-Jool and his scrying, surely?"

"I can call on the birds to guide me," Albreda reminded him. "I have no fear treading the wild, Sir Knight. It holds little danger for me."

"And what are we to do in the meantime?"

"March with the queen," she replied. "I shall take care of liberating our friends from the clutches of the Elves."

"I can't say I'm comfortable with this," said Prince Alric.

"That's not my concern," she snapped. "Now, I shall go and confer with Master Herdwin. We will likely head out first thing in the morning."

"Just like that?" said the prince.

The baron chuckled. "You might as well accept it, Highness. Once Albreda makes up her mind, there's nought that can dissuade her."

TWENTY-NINE

Revelation

SUMMER 965 MC

Gerald rose as Elven spears prodded him to his feet. They'd marched all day, and he'd thought this stop was the end of their efforts, but he was obviously mistaken. By his estimation, they were close to the town of Anvil—did their captors intend to take them there? Further thoughts were cut off as their guards parted, revealing a new visitor.

"Princess Margaret?" he said.

The dark-haired woman smiled, clearly pleased by the recognition. "Gerald Matheson, it appears we are destined to meet again."

"I thought you a prisoner?"

She held out her hands to the side, displaying her ornate robes. "Do I look like a prisoner?"

"Who is this?" asked Kraloch.

"The queen's sister," replied the marshal.

"But this woman is older than Queen Anna?"

"Yes, but she disappeared after the war. We assumed Penelope took her hostage."

"You mean Queen Kythelia," corrected Margaret.

"Why would you serve her?" asked Gerald.

"Why wouldn't I? She is a Necromancer of the highest calibre. Her power far exceeds anything your precious mages could control."

"She has warped your mind."

"Has she? Or has she liberated it? I learned one's magic can grow considerably more powerful if you're willing to throw off the constraints of traditional beliefs."

"Meaning?"

"I am a full-fledged master of the dark arts now. Such things would have been inconceivable without Kythelia's tutelage."

"Why are you here?"

"I've come to make you an offer, old man."

"Which is?"

"Bow down before Queen Kythelia. Accept her rule over the kingdoms of man, and she shall be merciful to you and your friends."

"And the Orcs?"

Margaret turned her gaze on Kraloch and Zhura, her distaste evident. "They will be annihilated, as they should have been two thousand years ago."

"What is your fascination with them?" asked Gerald. "The Great War almost eliminated the Elves, yet still they wish only to destroy."

"Is that what you think? I'm afraid you do not see the grand scheme here."

"Then I assume you're going to explain it to me?"

She smiled, a look of mischief coming over her face, and suddenly her likeness to Anna was incredible, save for the colour of her hair.

"No," she said at last. "I believe I'll let you wonder about it for the rest of your life, however short that may prove to be."

"You're wasting your time. Anna won't agree to your proposal, and she won't stand by while you try to exterminate the Orcs."

"Then you'll all die fighting. In the end, it will matter little, for Kythelia will rule over Merceria, one way or the other."

"It wouldn't be the first time she tried, would it?" Something in his words hit a sore spot, causing Margaret to scowl.

"You're fools," she said. "Can't you see this is the only way for you to survive? Queen Kythelia is merciful, but even she has her limits. Refuse this offer, and your only reward will be a slow, lingering death."

Gerald looked at the others, but they simply nodded in agreement. "So be it," he said.

"Don't say I didn't warn you."

She turned to leave, but Gerald pressed forward. "Have you forgotten how we saved you at Alfred's funeral?"

"I forget nothing," she said, her back kept to them, "but there's no point in dwelling on the past. We must move forward if we are to achieve greatness."

"Oh, and what greatness would that be? Serving an Elven queen? She enslaves you, Margaret. You don't see it because you're enamoured of all the supposed power she's given you, but you are as much a prisoner as us."

The woman stood there, and Gerald wondered if she might have changed her mind, but then she stormed off, fleeing the location as swiftly as her feet could carry her.

"Are you sure this is the right direction?" asked the Orc Shadra.

"Of course," replied Hayley, *"but what I don't know is the distance."*

"It might be better to travel eastward and try to get to Anvil."

"No, the enemy has the road. They'll be there long before we ever could. Our best chance lies in getting to Galburn's Ridge. If we follow the edge of these hills, we'll arrive, eventually."

Hearing a loud huff, she turned to see the three-horn, its breathing laboured, its skin dried and cracking. Upon its neck sat Lily, the poor Saurian looking equally worn out.

"We must find water soon," said Hayley. *"The Saurians are used to living in the swamp. This area is far too dry for them."*

"These hills are much like my home," said Shadra. *"There is a plant there whose roots hold water. Do you know it?"*

"Yes, moistroot, although Gorath tells me you call it Nargun's thumb."

"If you find some, we can make it into a paste and rub it into their skin."

"You think we could find enough to help a three-horn?"

"Likely not," said the Orc, *"but the Saurians would not require nearly as much. I would imagine a plant or two would yield sufficient quantity for an individual. Shall I go out in front and search?"*

"Yes," replied the ranger, *"but remain alert. We have no idea what dangers may lurk in these hills."*

The High Ranger watched as the Orc hunter ran off, soon disappearing over the next rise. Hayley waited as the other Orcs trundled past before the remaining five three-horns came into view, the rest having been scattered after the battle. She briefly wondered how such beasts could survive in this environment, used to living in the swamp as they were, but then pushed such thoughts from her mind. The game now was simply survival, and if getting thirsty was part of that, then so be it.

She'd needed to survive in the wild all her life, first as a poacher and then as a King's Ranger. Her being here in these hills was no worse than any other trip she'd made. No, that wasn't entirely true. Survival was not the objective here. Rather, it was avoiding the gaze of the enemy. If it had only been herself, or even just the Orcs, she could have managed, but keeping a three-horn from being seen was an altogether different challenge. Luckily, the chaos of battle, and the nearby hills, saved them. While others fled east and north, Hayley had led her own small group south into the cover of rougher terrain.

It had been tough going at first, trying to find a way through this unyielding landscape, but that all changed once Hayley got the lay of the land. In truth, it wasn't so different from the Artisan Hills. Years ago, while still serving in King Andred's rangers, she'd come across a gryphon in similar terrain. She smiled at the memory and then mused whether or not there were gryphons in these parts.

Movement off to her right drew her attention as her wolf made an appearance. Gryph, as she called him, was still technically a pup, but he had grown significantly, so much so, he now loped around on his own. At the moment, he watched the weary warriors make their way westward, a small rodent held in his mouth.

"My goodness," said Hayley. "What do you have there?"

In answer, the wolf came closer, dropping the dead animal at her feet. She picked up the carcass, examining it closely. It looked like some type of rat, yet the legs were longer, and the tail furry instead of bald.

"Don't believe I've seen one of these before. I tell you what, let's save it for later, shall we?"

Gryph appeared content to let her have it and turned, padding off into the hills once more.

Urgon crouched, peering off into the distance. "*There is someone out there,*" he said, "*but I cannot see who or how many at this range.*"

"*Is it the enemy?*" asked Bagrat.

"*Unlikely. We moved swiftly and have seen no indication of pursuit. There are also the wolves to consider.*"

"*True. They are not reacting as they did with the spirits. Who do you think it is? The Mercerians?*"

"*Either that or Norlanders,*" said the chieftain. "*The last we heard from Dame Beverly, she was preparing to engage a foe.*"

Without warning, he rose, moving out into the open.

Bagrat, surprised by the sudden action, called out, "*Are you sure it is wise to reveal your location?*"

"*You may relax,*" said Urgon. "*It is the army of Redblade after all.*"

"*How can you be so sure?*"

He grinned. "*I can see the Trolls.*"

The army came closer before a group of horsemen broke off, riding towards them. Urgon recognized the Kurathian captain, a man named Caluman.

"Greetings," the chieftain called out.

The rider slowed his horse and bowed. "It's good to see you, Chief Urgon. We thought you might have perished in the battle."

"I survived and managed to save a number of my hunters. Does Redblade still command?"

Caluman grinned. "So she does. Shall I take you to her?"

"If you would be so kind."

"Come then. She is with the column."

The horseman led Urgon and Bagrat towards the distant troops.

Beverly rode in front, Aubrey at her side. They both moved off the road at the sight of the approaching Orcs, allowing the warriors to pass them by.

"Chief Urgon," said Beverly. "It does my heart good to see you well."

"And mine," replied the Orc. "Have you heard from Kraloch?"

"I have. Both he and Zhura are alive, but I'm sorry to report they're prisoners of the Elves."

"Elves?"

"Yes, led by our old nemesis, Lady Penelope, or Queen Kythelia, as she's now known."

"Kythelia?" said an astonished Urgon. "She is the one who destroyed Gar-Rugal, the city of the Ravenstone."

"Indeed, but it gets worse. We learned a great Elven host follows in the wake of the spirit army."

"Do we know their numbers?"

"I'm afraid not," said the knight. "Might I ask how many of your hunters survived?"

"I have close to a hundred with me, but more are likely to be found. The enemy shows little inclination to spend the effort to chase down fugitives."

"I believe there's a reason for that," said Aubrey.

"Care to explain?" asked Beverly.

"I suspect the Volgath has a limited range. Beyond that, he can exert no control over his minions."

"That is borne out by what we saw at the Minglewood," said Urgon. "He had cavalry available and yet chose not to use it to outflank us."

"Interesting," said Beverly. "How DID he use it, then?"

"Much like his foot—advancing to melee at a slow pace."

The knight turned to her cousin. "How do you explain that?"

Aubrey considered the implications. "We know spirits don't tire, so theoretically, they could have rushed into battle without any trouble at all. Having them fight likely requires a greater degree of concentration, and as a consequence, they move slower."

"I'm not sure I understand. I've fought alongside warriors of the past when Kraloch called them at the Battle of Uxley. They showed no inclination to slow down at all."

"The difference, in this case, is free will, or rather lack of it. When an Orc shaman calls on the spirits to assist in battle, they do so of their own free will. That thing out there, though, has to dominate the minds of the spirits. Think of your own warriors. Commanding a company to advance is one thing, but imagine how much more demanding it would be to direct each individual melee?"

"Yes," said Beverly, "I see now. It's a common trap for a commander—spend too much time on the minor details, and you lose sight of the overall battle." She smiled. "Thanks, Aubrey. You've given me the key to victory."

"I have?"

"Yes, but it won't be easy to arrange." She turned to Urgon. "Do you have wounded?"

"Yes, although none serious enough to impede their progress."

"Aubrey, I wonder if you might see what you can do for them? We're going to need every spear we can muster."

"My hunters use bows," said Urgon.

"My pardon," said Beverly. "It was merely a figure of speech. Captain Caluman?"

"Yes, Commander?"

"I want your men searching south and west. If there are survivors out there, I want them rounded up."

"Yes, my lady." The Kurathian rode off at a gallop.

Urgon sent Bagrat off to retrieve his hunters. "Is there anything else, Dame Beverly?"

"Come seek me out once we set up camp. I shall need your counsel. In the meantime, talk to your hunters and find out as much as you can. Any detail of the battle, no matter how small or seemingly insignificant, may prove decisive in the long run."

"I shall do as you ask."

Beverly watched him go, following in Bagrat's footsteps. Lightning gave a snort, and she reached forward, rubbing her hand between the horse's ears. A hawk flew overhead, and she gazed up at the sky to see the sun breaking through some clouds.

"A good omen," she said. As if in answer, Lightning neighed.

That evening, they all gathered by a fire.

"This," said Beverly, by way of introductions, "is King Thalgrun of Ironcliff."

"I saw his warriors," said Urgon. "They are most impressive. It will be an honour to fight beside the mountain folk once more."

"Once more?" asked the king.

"Yes," explained Beverly. "Urgon here has fought beside the Dwarves of Stonecastle on multiple occasions."

"Has he now? I would be most interested to hear how our two fighting styles complement each other."

"Perhaps later," said the king's daughter. "I'm Kasri, by the way, Kasri Ironheart."

"Greetings," replied the Orc. "I am Chief Urgon of the Black Arrows."

"Your fame precedes you," she replied. "Dame Beverly speaks highly of your tribe."

A deep voice rumbled across the fire. "Perhaps we could refrain from such pleasantries for the time being. There are more pressing matters to discuss."

"Tog is right," said Beverly, sparing a quick glance at the massive Troll. "I brought you all here to get your opinions on something I've been giving considerable thought."

"By all means," said the king. "What is it that vexes you so?"

"We have two threats before us—an army of spirits and one of Elves. Of these, I believe the Elves to be the greater threat. Unfortunately, the tactics that would allow us to defeat the former would only make us more vulnerable to the latter."

"What have you got in mind?" asked Kasri.

"Based on what we've learned so far, it appears the Volgath's control of the spirit army has some limitations."

"Such as?"

"I could be wrong, but I think it requires a great deal of its concentration to command the spirits. If I'm right, this is its greatest weakness, a weakness we can exploit."

"How?" asked Urgon.

"By attacking from multiple angles simultaneously."

"We don't have the troops for that," warned Aubrey.

"Not yet we don't, no," said Beverly, "but once we rendezvous with my father's army, we'll have the means to carry it out."

"Are you sure that's wise?" asked the king. "We Dwarves have always been about concentrating our forces."

"Bear with me. By hitting the enemy from different angles, we force the Volgath to stretch his concentration, hopefully to the point of breaking."

"And what, precisely, would that look like?" asked Kasri.

"Likely one of two things," said Aubrey. "Either he'll lose complete control, or more likely, he'll be forced to concentrate on one or two spots at a time, leaving the others vulnerable."

"But the spirits would still fight, wouldn't they?"

"I'm not sure they would," explained the Life Mage. "You see, Necromancers created this army of theirs, pulling spirits from the Afterlife and tying them to this mortal realm, but it's the Volgath who controls them, guiding them in battle."

"That's true," said Urgon. "I took down a Death Mage, and the spirits around him were released."

"How many were affected?" asked Beverly.

"Two dozen, maybe more."

"Then that's how we fight them," said Kasri, "by targeting their spellcasters. Much more efficient than taking them down one spirit at a time."

"Easier said than done," said the chieftain. "I fought dozens of spirits but only found one caster."

"The true target here is the Volgath," said Aubrey. "If we can send that creature back to the realm of the dead, the rest of the spirits should be released."

"But wouldn't the Necromancers still bind them?" asked Urgon.

"True, they'd still be prisoners but less likely to offer resistance to us."

"In the battle, Kraloch called on the warriors of the past," said Urgon.

"Did it work?" asked Aubrey.

"For a time. It released some of the spirits from their domination, allowing them to fight for us. Unfortunately, Kraloch is but one shaman. Had we others at our disposal, the outcome might have been far different."

Beverly turned to Aubrey. "Could you learn such a spell?"

"Absolutely," said the Life Mage, "as long as someone was willing to teach it to me."

"Andurak could do that," said Urgon, "or even my sister, Kurghal, once the armies unite."

"How long would that take?" asked Beverly.

"Not long," replied the chieftain. "Kraloch tells me Lady Aubrey is a gifted learner. Though I am curious to observe the effects, once cast."

"How so?"

"When a shaman casts the spell, Orc hunters are called, but Lady Aubrey is a Human. Does that then mean Human warriors would be summoned from the Afterlife?"

"That's an interesting thought," said Aubrey, "but let's not let it distract us from the task at hand." She turned to her cousin. "You said we were going to link up with your father?"

"Yes, that was the queen's idea. We'll march south, avoiding the vicinity of Anvil. The plan is to unite the armies at Hammersfield, where we'll make a stand. We fought there before, so we're familiar with the terrain."

"You speak of a strategy to use against the ghosts," said Kasri, "but what of the Elves?"

"We know little of them at the moment," said Beverly. "The truth is we don't even know how many of them there are."

Two men approached the fire. As they drew closer, the flames revealed Arnim Caster and Revi Bloom.

"Where have you two been?" asked Aubrey.

"Dame Beverly sent us on a little expedition," replied Arnim. "Revi here has been keeping an eye on the enemy."

"And?"

"They halted just shy of Anvil. I suspect they're trying to decide on their next move."

"Do they have scouts?" asked Beverly.

"They don't seem to," replied Revi. "Although we mustn't discount the possibility they might be using magical means to do so."

"You mean scrying?"

"I'm not an expert on Necromancy, by any means, but I believe they may have the ability to create creatures that can operate much like Shellbreaker. Such things are referred to as homunculi—creatures created by dark magic that mimic the characteristics of living animals."

"Meaning they're dead?" asked Beverly.

"Not exactly. According to scholars, homunculi were never alive to begin with. Imagine a small statue animated by magic, and you wouldn't be far off the truth."

"A frightening prospect," said Aubrey. "Would such creatures have the power of reason and intellect?"

"No, they would essentially be nothing more than an extension of the Necromancer's senses. Of course, Shellbreaker can do the same, but he can also think for himself, unlike these dark minions of which I speak."

"And could these things fly?"

"I can't say for sure, but it seems a reasonable assumption. Such creatures may not even be distinguishable from actual birds at a distance."

"You are connected to Shellbreaker as a familiar," said Beverly. "If I understand things correctly, his death would leave you seriously weakened."

"It would indeed."

"Would the same hold true of a homunculi?"

"Homunculus is the singular form," corrected Revi, "but yes, I believe so."

"So if we could find and eliminate these creatures, we'd not only be depriving them of their scouts but would be physically injuring their casters?"

"I never thought to look at it that way, but I suppose that would be true. Why, have you an idea?"

"Indeed I do," said Beverly.

THIRTY

Albreda

SUMMER 965 MC

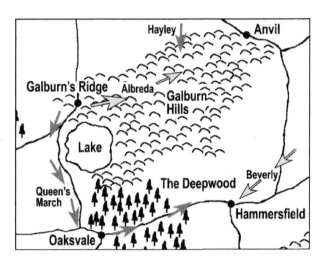

Albreda halted, standing atop the rise. Around her, the hills of Galburn's Ridge stretched on as far as the eye could see, giving her a majestic view. Herdwin arrived to stand beside her.

"Any sign of them?" he asked.

"Not from above," she said, glancing at a circling hawk, "but the wolves are picking up an unusual scent. I suspect that would be a three-horn."

"So we're close, then?"

"Only in the sense we're on the right track. The scent of an animal can carry for miles, and wolves can smell things that are undetectable to us. However, given the prevailing winds in this region, it's safe to assume they are northeast of us. We should adjust our direction accordingly." Her gaze shifted to the Dwarf. "How are the troops holding up?"

"You set a brisk pace, but they'll not tire."

"We shall soon be nearing the northern edge of the hills," said Albreda. "Once that happens, we'll need your arbalesters ready at all times."

"You fear attack?"

"Not directly, but the enemy may have eyes in the area."

"Eyes, as in…?"

"We are dealing with practitioners of Death Magic," she replied, "and they have no respect for life. It wouldn't surprise me if they animated dead birds and used them to scout the area."

"So they are to let off a bolt at any birds they might see?"

"For Saxnor's sake, no, but any bird that acts strangely should be targeted."

"And what's your definition of strange behaviour?"

"When flying, a bird will often turn its head, examining the ground below. An animated corpse would never act in such a manner; it would instead be stiff and ungainly. The vision of such a creature is a product of magic, not the eyes, and thus the head would not move around. Explain that to your archers, and they should have no confusion over which birds to fire upon."

"If you say so," replied Herdwin. He stared down the hill, watching as a fox ran from cover, carrying a hare. "Is that one of yours?" he asked, pointing.

She smiled at the sight. "No. I have nothing against the fox, but it's the wolves who have become my family."

"But they're back in the Whitewood, are they not?"

"Naturally, but I have a knack for communicating with them."

"So you conjure them from thin air?"

She looked at him in surprise. "No, I'm a Druid, not an Enchanter. I can't create living beings. Rather, I summon them."

"Is there a difference?"

"There most definitely is. I can only summon creatures that live in the area. If there were no wolves to call, then none would answer the summons."

"And then you control them?"

"No, I talk to them." She paused a moment, thinking things over. "Perhaps talk is a bit misleading. It's more accurate to say I share emotions with them, but the effect is more or less the same. In my experience, wolves are generally friendly creatures, more than willing to help out in any way they can. Still, I do not control them any more than I control you."

Herdwin couldn't help but chuckle. "I don't believe I ever heard a wolf described as friendly, but then again, I'm not a Druid. Does Master Hearn have such powers?"

Albreda frowned. "He is more of an expert with plants, but he has been known to call on a pack from time to time, although why they would follow his instructions is beyond me."

"I'm surprised to hear you say that. I thought the two of you got along pretty well."

"Aldus Hearn is a dear friend and colleague, but he can be as thick as a tree when it comes to understanding the world of animals." She laughed. "I suppose that's a fitting analogy, considering his specialty."

"So it is."

"Tell me, Master Herdwin, do Dwarves keep wolves as pets? I know the Orcs do, although perhaps pet isn't exactly the word I'm looking for."

"Not in Stonecastle, as far as I'm aware, although the old king used to have a favourite cave bear, but that's a whole different story. Do you have bears in the Whitewood?"

"We do," she said, "but they are much smaller than those of the mountains."

"And does your pack get along with them?"

"They keep a respectful distance and honour their territory. I've met several over the years and found them easy to get along with, although a little simple-minded compared to the pack."

"You talk to them?" asked the stunned Dwarf.

"As I said on several occasions, I can communicate with any animal I choose, providing they are willing."

"Might I ask why the fascination for wolves in particular?"

"Snow and Ice were the first denizens of the woods I encountered. They took me in when I was lost and looked after me."

"Snow and Ice?"

"Yes," Albreda said, "they led the pack. My names for them, of course. You must realize I was fairly young when I first encountered them."

"You're quite an amazing individual, Albreda."

"As are you, Master Herdwin."

"Me? I'm a simple smith."

"Yet you told Aldwin how to make a forge capable of melting skymetal. Without you, there would be no Nature's Fury."

"Aye, I suppose that's true, but you were the one who enchanted it."

"Empowered it," corrected the Druid. "I am no Enchanter."

"Pardon me," said the Dwarf. "I stand corrected." He was about to say more, but Albreda held up a finger, indicating he should remain silent. Her eyes closed, and he watched as her head moved slightly as if looking through someone else's eyes.

"I think we located Hayley and the others," she said. "One moment." She waved her hands, causing the air to swirl around her. Dirt flew up from the ground, creating little eddies of dust, and then she spoke a word of command. Herdwin felt a slight breeze emanate from the mage, and then all was as it had been.

"What happened?" he asked.

"I sent a summoning."

"For what?"

"Gryph."

"You mean Hayley's wolf? You can do that?"

"Of course," said Albreda. "I just did."

"And what will that do, exactly?"

"Gryph should start heading towards us, leading Hayley in our general direction." She looked upward to see the sun high in the sky. "With any luck, we'll be amongst them before dark."

Hayley knelt, cupping her hands to scoop the water and pour it down her throat. Beside her, Gryph lapped at the stream, then raised his head, his ears twitching.

"What is it, boy?"

He looked at her once before he moved upstream. Concerned he'd detected something dangerous, she strung her bow and followed. The water came from the southwest, although whether a pond fed it or an underwater spring was anyone's guess. Gryph disappeared from sight, and she ran forward, only to see him waiting for her.

"Where are you going?" she asked, although he was clearly incapable of answering. The young wolf moved farther upstream, leaving the ranger to ponder the situation. "All right," she said aloud, "I'll follow, but not until I tell the others. We can't just go running off into the wild, now, can we?"

Hayley turned around, heading back to the temporary camp, Gryph following at her heels. She soon found Shadra skinning a hare.

"*I'm going upstream,*" said Hayley, speaking Orcish. "*Let the others rest awhile before following my trail. I'll be sure to mark it well.*"

"*Do you think it dangerous?*" asked the Orc.

"*No. Gryph seems to like the area. Maybe he only wants to make some new friends?*"

"*The presence of wolves would be seen as a good omen,*" said Shadra. "*It would mean the Ancestors are looking out for us.*"

"*I can't speak to that, but it's worth investigating. Who knows, maybe we'll find some shelter? A nice cave or two to hole up in overnight wouldn't go amiss.*"

"*Good hunting, and be careful.*"

"*I will. After all, I'm the High Ranger. It wouldn't look so good if I ended up getting myself killed out here, now, would it?*"

The Orc screwed up her face, clearly missing the humour.

Hayley looked at her wolf, switching to the common tongue. "Where's Gorath when I need him?"

"*Did you say something?*" asked Shadra.

"No," she responded in the Orcish tongue. "*I was just speaking to myself. Now, I must be off before I run out of daylight.*" She took a moment to orient herself, then made her way back to the stream.

With the sun low on the horizon, Herdwin looked for a place to set up camp. Off in the distance, a wolf howled, putting everyone on alert. Albreda rushed past him, moving towards the distant sound.

"Trouble?" asked the Dwarf.

"That," explained the Druid, "is the pack. They found Gryph."

"Are you sure?"

"Well, they found a young wolf, but who else could it be? And where goes Gryph, so, too, goes Hayley. Now hurry, or it will be too dark to see them."

Herdwin put all thoughts of camp from his mind, rushing after the mage. Albreda must have been well into her sixties by now, but so accustomed was she to living in the wild, she showed no signs of slowing. He did all he could to keep up, but he soon lost sight of her. He kept moving in the same general direction, eventually emerging upon a hilltop to spot Albreda pointing with a satisfied expression.

"There, you see?" she said. "What did I tell you?"

He followed her gaze to spot the High Ranger emerge from a small copse of trees. A moment later, she waved, and then a young wolf ran towards them.

"This must be Gryph," said the Dwarf. "Strange name for a wolf, isn't it?"

"Not if you know Hayley," said Albreda. She knelt, petting the animal between the ears.

"So that's what this is all about," called out the ranger. She made her way up the hill. "Good to see you, Albreda, and you, Master Herdwin. I've much to tell you."

"We heard everything," replied the Druid. "Kraloch was able to contact Aubrey."

"He's alive, then?"

"Yes, but he's a prisoner, along with Zhura and the marshal."

"Gerald's alive? That's good news, although I don't fancy his chances of staying so."

"That brings us to the reason we're here."

"So you're not here to save us?"

Albreda smiled. "We are, but not solely for that purpose. We need your help, Hayley, or to be more precise, I need your help."

"I'm not sure how I'm to help, but I'm willing to give it a try. What is it you need me for?"

"We're going to rescue Gerald and the others."

"And how do you expect to do that?"

"We brought friends," said Herdwin, "but I believe this is best discussed around a nice fire."

"I'd love to oblige," replied the ranger, "but I must take care of the rest of my people."

"Of course," said Albreda. "How can we help?"

The last to enter the camp had been the three-horns, led by Lily. Herdwin stared at them, impressed by their sheer size.

"Are they dangerous?" he asked.

"Not so much," replied Hayley. "They're pretty peaceful creatures. Mind you, they stampeded during the battle and did frightful damage to the enemy."

"How did that happen?"

"I don't know. Maybe the ghosts spooked them, but it undoubtedly saved us and allowed Sir Heward to escape."

"Sir Heward is alive?"

"He was last time I spoke with him. I saw him later, from the hills, but he was too far away to contact. He managed to rally what was left of the horsemen, although I can't speak to numbers."

"That is good news," said Albreda. "Hopefully, he will find his way to Beverly's army."

"Speaking of armies, you mentioned something about needing my help?"

"Yes," the Druid said. "I intend to take us all to the eastern edge of these hills."

"To what end?"

"The queen marches to Hammersfield, there to unite with Beverly's army. They mean to make a stand somewhere north of the town."

Hayley closed her eyes, picturing a map of the area. "If I remember correctly, the road out of Hammersfield turns north, running parallel to these hills."

"That's correct," said Albreda. "I'm hoping we can get into a concealed position to the enemy's rear and strike when they least expect it. You know about the Elves, of course?"

"Elves? What are you talking about?"

"Our people have been in contact with Kraloch. He reports an army of Elves is following in the spirits' wake."

"Oh, great! Just what we need. Do you think they can do anything else to make it worse?"

"At least Elves aren't ghosts," said Herdwin.

"It's the Elves who hold our friends," said Albreda. "If we wait until the enemy is engaged in battle, we could come out of the hills and take them from the rear."

"A fine idea," said Hayley, "but there's no guarantee we'd be able to reach the prisoners."

"That's where you and I come in."

"Go on."

"I shall use my flying friends to locate Gerald and the others. Then, when the enemy is distracted, you and I will make our way through their camp to affect the rescue."

"Just like that? What makes you believe we can wander right through an army of Elves?"

"Oh, we shan't be wandering; we'll be riding."

"Riding what? We have no horses."

In answer, Albreda pointed at the three-horns.

"You can't be serious? I can't ride one of those things. And in any case, they're docile creatures."

"Don't worry. I shall communicate with them ahead of time."

"But couldn't their archers take them down? I know their hides are thick, but an Elven bow will puncture anything."

"That's where I come in," added Herdwin. "My arbalesters will keep their archers busy, don't you worry."

"The plan," continued the Druid, "would be for the Dwarves to move out of the cover of the hills. Once we have Gerald and the others, we'll make directly for their formation."

"And you honestly believe that will work? I can't say I like the odds."

"I'm sorry to hear you say that."

"Oh, don't worry," said Hayley, "I'll still do it. I just don't fancy the chances of surviving."

"What if you took the Orcs?" asked Herdwin. "That would improve the odds considerably, wouldn't it?"

"It would," agreed Albreda. "And I can summon some animal friends to assist in a diversion."

"Well," said Hayley, "now you've got me convinced."

"Good," said Herdwin. "I've got close to two hundred Dwarves, half of them armed with arbalests. How many Orc hunters do you reckon you have?"

"About a hundred," said Hayley, "but I'm afraid they're low on arrows."

"That, we can handle," said Albreda. "Time is the one thing we can take advantage of."

"It is?" said the ranger. "I thought we were in a hurry to move east?"

"Not at all. The truth is, the queen's army has to march south to get around these very hills. It'll be some time before she can get on the road to Hammersfield. In the meantime, I shall send out a hawk to find some suitable trees. I assume your hunters can make their own arrows?"

"I would certainly hope so. They are hunters after all."

"Good. Now, what else am I missing?"

"Food?" said the Dwarf. "We brought stonecakes, but we haven't enough to feed everybody."

"Looks like we'll need to do some hunting," said Hayley. She turned to Albreda. "How much time you do reckon we have?"

"I imagine it will take at least a week for the queen's army to reach Hammersfield, but they set out three days ago."

"So, four days, five if we're lucky. That doesn't sound like enough time, to be honest. How far are we from the eastern end of these hills?"

"No more than a day and a half," replied the Druid, "but we shall make good time, guided as we are by my friends." She pointed upward to where a hawk circled.

"That gives us only a day to hunt," said Hayley, "and there are a lot of mouths to feed."

"When your hunters are ready, let me know, and I shall have the wolves drive the game towards us."

"Are you sure you want to do that? I thought you favoured the balance of nature?"

"I do, but this is the natural way of things. Humans are predators, much like wolves, and therefore it's only natural they hunt meat."

Herdwin rubbed his hands together. "A pragmatic approach, I like it. I can't wait to get my hands on some fresh food."

"Just out of curiosity," said Hayley, "what do the mountain folk normally eat?"

"Well, I suppose that depends on the individual. Meat is reasonably common, of course. We raise our own animals for that, but there are also lots of other things we like."

"Such as?"

"Mushrooms are popular and grow well in underground caves."

"You have caves solely for mushrooms?"

"They weren't dug for mushrooms, mind, but after we dig out an area, there's no sense in wasting the space."

"How many underground farms do you have?"

"Last time I was there, at least fifty, ranging in size from my smithy, all the way up to palace sized."

"That large?"

"Of course," said Herdwin. "Have you never seen a Dwarven mine at work?"

"I can't say I have. Why?"

"When we find a vein of ore, it's typically at the end of a long tunnel. We start by widening it on either side and upward, using scaffolding to get to the top of the deposit. Once that's in place, we begin picking away at it, working along the entire front. It's much safer that way."

"Based on what I saw at Redridge," said Hayley, "it appears we use a more open concept."

"Aye, pit mining. I'm well aware."

"You don't approve?"

"It works well enough, I suppose, but your workers are exposed to the elements."

"And that's a bad thing?"

"Of course," said Herdwin. "Most of a miner's tools are iron. One good rain, and everything gets rusty. Not to mention the problem of flooding."

"You've given this a lot of thought."

"I have, as a matter of fact. There is much Merceria could do to improve its mining operations."

"You should bring it to the attention of the queen."

"She's far too busy, what with this war going on. No, I'm better off keeping it to myself for now. Perhaps I'll mention it when the war is over?"

"I'm sure she'd be interested," said Hayley. "Queen Anna always has the best interests of the people uppermost in her mind."

"So I heard."

"Are you two done talking about mining?" asked Albreda. "I only ask because I recall a High Ranger somewhere complaining she didn't have much time to hunt."

"Sorry," said the ranger. "I suppose we did get a little carried away. I'll go talk to the Orcs, and we'll get things moving."

"Good idea," said Herdwin, "and I'll get some fires set up. After all, we can't roast meat on the rocks!"

THIRTY-ONE

The Long March

SUMMER 965 MC

The army stretched out along the road, with Alric leading them, accompanied by his personal cavalrymen. Sir Preston, as senior knight, deployed his own men to act as a screening force, but so far, there'd been little to observe. Next came the footmen, interspersed with companies of archers.

Even though it wasn't the largest army Merceria had ever fielded, it made up for numbers with experience, for each warrior was a veteran, survivors of near-constant warfare for the last few years.

Anna joined the column, looking over her shoulder to watch the men marching behind her. Upon seeing their queen, they let out a cheer, and she smiled.

"They love you," said Fitz. "You're a far cry from your predecessor."

"I must admit, I never really knew King Andred. You worked closely with him, didn't you?"

"Not as close as you might assume. I spent most of my time in Bodden. I was trained in Wincaster, of course, under the tutelage of Sir Harold. However, once my brother became the baron, visits to the capital were few and far between. Andred came to visit us once, though, and that was when Beverly earned her spurs."

"Yes, I heard the story," said the queen. "It's also where Gerald was wounded. Did you ever stop to wonder what might have happened had the king never visited?"

"I can't say I have."

"Well, I, for one, am glad he did, or I never would have met Gerald."

"There is that, now you mention it," said Fitz. "And if he hadn't, Beverly would have never become a knight."

"She would have found a way," insisted Anna. "It was her destiny."

"Destiny, is it? Well, that's quite the compliment. I'd better not tell her. I'd hate for her head to swell." He looked at the queen. "I'm teasing, of course. Beverly's never been one to boast."

"She has become an excellent military commander."

"That she has. Who would have thought it? I can still remember her as a little girl, sitting in the map room in Bodden, staring at all the maps."

"Is that where she first decided she wanted to be a knight?"

"Yes. There were these wooden blocks I used to represent the men under my command."

"Wooden blocks?" asked Anna.

"Well, more like crude carvings. Beverly was entranced by the one that represented the knights. I believe that was the start for her. I still have it, you know, sitting in a place of honour beneath the portrait of her mother."

"You have done much for this kingdom, Baron. Foremost amongst your accomplishments is the decision to train her."

"I didn't train her. Gerald did."

"Yes, but you permitted it. Few nobles would give their daughters the chance to learn such skills."

"It's an old custom, to be sure, but the results speak for themselves. I daresay she has become the noblest knight in all of Merceria."

"High praise, coming from you."

"Tell me," said Fitz, "all this talk of Beverly can't be coincidental?"

Anna smiled. "Correct. Aubrey has sent word Beverly has formulated a battle plan."

"Oh? Do we know the details?"

"Not yet. She'll fill us in when the armies rendezvous."

He stared at her a moment before a smile crept into place. "You mean to have Beverly lead the battle."

"I have said no such thing."

"Not in so many words, no, but your intent is clear."

"And if I was?"

"It's a marvellous idea," said the baron. "She's more than ready for it."

"I thought you might consider yourself more qualified."

He laughed. "Think you so little of me? You may rest assured, Your Majesty, I am content to serve in whatever capacity you desire. I have no ego to bruise, and I know Beverly has learned her lessons well under Gerald's tutelage."

"The same as Gerald learned from you?"

Fitz smiled. "I suppose that's true, isn't it? I never thought of it that way."

"Can I ask you a question?"

"Of course."

"What did you see in Gerald that made you take him on as your protégé?"

"I don't know if I can put it into words. He's told you about the assault on the keep? His first kill, I mean?"

"He has," said Anna, "though his version of it was less than heroic."

"He was quite young at the time, yet he fought back against that raider. I know he was terrified, but he overcame fear to take action. That, more than anything else, impressed me the most."

"Well, I'm glad you looked after him. I can't imagine my life without him in it, or you, for that matter."

"You humble me, Majesty."

"I speak only the truth."

They rode on in silence, but it was clear the queen was going over things in her mind. Lord Richard remained silent, biding his time until she was ready to talk. He watched as Sir Preston rode back towards the column, a dozen of his heavy cavalrymen accompanying him.

"Trouble?" called out the baron.

The knight slowed. "No, my lord. I am merely rotating my men to give them a break. It's fearfully hot today."

"So it is. Tell me, did you notice anything of interest?"

"Not as yet," said Sir Preston, "but we will soon enter the Deepwood."

"And you expect trouble?"

"It's possible some Norlanders might have found their way there. We smashed the Earl of Hammersfield early in the invasion, and his warriors scattered. If any deserters are found, we shall tell them the earls are defeated."

"Good idea," said the baron, "and tell them to go home to their families. After all, it's not as if they deserted us." He noted the knight's distraction before he realized the fellow was staring at Sophie. "I should let you go," he added. "I shouldn't like to keep you from your duties."

"Yes, my lord," said the knight, continuing on his way.

Fitz chuckled. "Ah, young love. Is there anything like it?"

The queen returned her attention to him. "What did you say?"

"I was merely commenting on the object of Sir Preston's infatuation, Your Majesty."

"Oh, you mean Sophie. Those two have had a thing for each other for some time." She lowered her voice. "Just between you and me, I believe if it hadn't been for this war, they'd be married by now."

"And does this please you?"

"Of course. Why wouldn't it?"

"Well," said Fitz, "you would lose her as a companion, would you not?"

"Why would you assume that?"

"It's the usual way of things amongst the nobility. Granted, you are a queen, and that complicates matters, but you can't expect a married woman to give up her husband for you."

"I expect no such thing. That doesn't mean Sophie and I can't still be friends."

"But she looks after you, doesn't she? I'm taken to understand she does your hair, helps you dress, that sort of thing."

"She does, but others could do all that if need be. It's her companionship I value the most."

"Ah, well, there you are, problem solved. If you don't mind my asking, does Sir Preston have any property?"

"I don't know about land, but they are wealthy. His family oversees several wainwrights."

"Are you saying they're merchants? And here I thought him a noble."

"He is a noble," said Anna. "The business is how they supplement their income."

"I suppose that makes him quite a catch for Sophie, then," mused the baron.

"So it would seem."

"And has there been any further discussion on the matter?"

"Not at present," said the queen, "but we are in the middle of a fight for our very lives. Let's hope things will proceed more smoothly once we return to some semblance of normalcy. While we're on that topic, have you any idea whether or not Aubrey has shown any interest in anyone?"

"I can't say as I have. She might be my niece, but I've seen little enough of her during this campaign. Maybe I should have a chat with her? After all, she's the baroness now. It's only fitting she should settle down and produce an heir or two."

"I doubt that will happen," called out Sophie.

The queen turned in the saddle. "Why would you say that?"

"Aubrey's far too immersed in her magic to find any time for a husband. In that, she's not unlike Albreda."

The baron blushed. "Who told you that?"

"No one," replied the maid. "It's simply an observation. I meant no offence, my lord."

"Fear not," said Fitz. "I took none. I was merely… surprised by your remarks."

Anna laughed. "It seems we are all guilty of making rash conclusions. Perhaps we should be content to concern ourselves with our own relationships."

"Well put, Majesty."

"Yes, of course," added Sophie. "Though I do wonder where Sir Preston has gone. He's barely said anything to me since we set out from Galburn's Ridge."

"That's my fault," explained the baron. "I kept him busy with matters pertaining to the march. I shall endeavour to make him more available for you."

Sophie blushed.

The queen looked at Lord Richard. "You're enjoying this far too much."

"Can you blame me? For too long I sat back, insisting my daughter be a proper young lady when it came to affairs of the heart. It took news of her death to bring me to my senses. I shan't make that mistake again." He spotted Prince Alric riding towards them. "Here comes the father of your child. I'll give you some privacy." He turned his horse around and trotted off towards the rear of the column.

The prince fell into place beside Anna, noting the smile that spread across her lips. "Someone's in a good mood."

"And why wouldn't I be?" she asked. "Especially when a handsome young prince comes to pay court."

"Young? After all we've been through?"

"You're only a few years older than me," Anna reminded him, "but I must admit we've been a busy couple. It feels like we've constantly been at war since I became queen."

"That's to be expected," said Alric. "Your traditional enemies seek to take advantage of your perceived inexperience. The Clans do the same thing with Weldwyn whenever we get a new king."

"That bodes ill for Alstan," stated Anna.

"Yes, and that's what worries me. It's not that he can't command an army, but who's he to lead?"

"He'll call up the militia, won't he?"

"Naturally," said the prince, "but they are poorly equipped."

"Did your father not leave any troops behind?"

"Of course he did, but once you garrison the cities, there's not much left to repel invaders."

"There you have it, then," said Anna. "He can use the militia to man the city walls, freeing up the rest to march."

"You make it all sound so easy. We don't have the fighting heritage that you Mercerians do."

"I might remind you you're a Mercerian now."

"Yes, but it doesn't change the facts. Weldwyn's militia is woefully under-trained and lacks decent armour."

"At least you have a militia. In Merceria, there's a standing army, but in times of war, the Crown can order men into service. That's what happened when they passed through Uxley during the civil war."

"But those men were not trained," said Alric. "Of what use would they be?"

"Even a farmer can man a wall. Of course, it proved their undoing in the end."

"Then why not compel the general populous to take up arms now?"

"An interesting idea," said Anna, "but who would command and train such a force? Everyone is up here with us."

"I hadn't thought of that." He glanced back at the soldiers following in their wake. "I wish we didn't leave the Dwarves behind in Galburn's Ridge. We could have used the numbers."

"We'll have them when the time comes, but we must be patient."

"Easier said than done," said Alric. "The enemy could be upon us at any moment, and we need every sword at our disposal if we are to stand a chance of defeating them."

"Between Shellbreaker and Kiren-Jool's scrying, there's little chance of us being taken unawares. The real question is whether we can rendezvous with Beverly's forces before the enemy makes their move."

"I must confess, I'm a little nervous. After all, this enemy defeated my father's army, and that was no small feat."

"King Leofric was a good leader," said Anna, "but his tactics were some-what... archaic."

"What's that supposed to mean?"

"Look around you, Alric. Our army is comprised of all sorts of people, each with something unique to offer. The army of Merceria takes advantage of those gifts. Under Gerald's influence, we broke away from traditional battlefield tactics, and we've been very successful by doing so."

"Until the Minglewood," he reminded her.

"That happens in war, but we can learn from that lesson and apply it to our future endeavours. War evolves over time; you need only to look at your own men to see it. Your cavalry might be men of Weldwyn, but they're trained in the Mercerian way. You saw to that yourself, placing them under Beverly's tutelage."

"That's true, I did," Alric admitted. "I suppose I just got so used to being here, with the army, that I didn't recognize the changes until now."

"That's often the way of things, isn't it? A myriad of minor changes adds up to a greater transformation."

"Still, we could have at least brought some of the Dwarves." Alric looked at Anna, seeing a smile trying to escape. "There's something you're not telling me."

"I'm the queen," she replied. "I can't tell you everything."

"No, I mean about the Dwarves. You have something in mind for them, don't you?"

Anna cast her eyes around, looking to see who was close by, but only Sophie was within earshot. "Yes, they went through the hills with Albreda."

"But what about Galburn's Ridge?"

"They left a company behind to give the impression it's garrisoned."

"Who else knows?"

"Just you, me, and Sophie"—she paused—"oh, and the baron, of course."

"Then I shall be sure to keep it to myself, although I am curious as to why? Surely you don't believe anyone in our army would reveal our plans to the enemy?"

"I do not. It's merely an overabundance of caution."

"I suppose it makes sense," said the prince. "After all, we have the ability to scry out the enemy now. Who's to say they don't have something similar?"

"Exactly," said Anna. "I hope you're not upset?"

"No, of course not, though I do wonder how you managed to convince everyone that all the Dwarves were still at Galburn's Ridge? Wouldn't they have been seen marching out?"

"Not at all. They used the tunnels, the exact same ones Sir Preston used to enter during the assault. We also let it be known in the town that the fortress would be locked up tight under the Dwarves."

"Where did you ever come up with such an idea?"

"Books," said Anna. "In particular, an old story about King Aeldred."

"Who's he?"

"A leader back in the old Continent who fought off an ancient civilization known as Thalemia, despite the fact it was many times the size of his own realm. Of course, this was well before our ancestors came to this land."

"Wherever did you find such a book?" asked Alric.

"In the king's library at Uxley."

"I never knew King Andred was a scholar."

"I doubt he was," said Anna. "The truth is he never visited it in all the time I was there. I suspect it was put there long before his reign."

"So, is your love of reading inherited from your mother, then?"

"No, not in the least. I was a very lonely child; books were my only companion, that is until Gerald came along."

A bark caught her attention. "Well, Tempus was there too, but he's a little quiet when it comes to conversation."

Sir Preston reappeared, galloping up to them. "May I join you, Majesty?" he asked.

"Join me," she replied, "or Sophie?"

The knight blushed.

"You may fall in behind us."

"You're incorrigible," said Alric. "It's one of the things I love about you."

"Having said that, did you have a chance to give any more thought to names?"

"I have, in truth, though I've yet to make a decision as to which I like best. How about you?"

"Oh, no you don't. I asked first. Come on, out with it. What names do you like?"

"How about Arthur?"

She wrinkled her nose.

"All right," said Alric, "so Arthur is out. How about Harold? I understand it's a Mercerian name."

"It is. It means leader of armies. Fitting when you consider our history. In fact, a knight named Harold taught the baron everything he knows about chivalry."

"So it's decided, then?"

"No, not yet, but it's worth considering. What did you have in mind for a girl?"

"Now," admitted Alric, "that's a bit more difficult, especially since you changed the laws of succession."

"Why would that make it more difficult?"

"Well, she would rule, much as you do. We can't have a Queen of Merceria with a dainty name now, can we?" He gave his voice a nasal pitch. "Queen Primrose begs the ambassador to take his leave."

Anna laughed. "I see your point. What have you got to offer instead?"

"Anna has a nice ring to it."

"No, it would lead to confusion, and I've seen too many rulers with similar names."

"How about Ailith? I understand it means warrior."

"I suppose Queen Ailith has a nice sound to it, but once again, I'll need to give it some thought."

"All right," said Alric. "Now it's your turn."

"Oh, I'm far too busy for that right now." She looked behind her. "Sir Preston, I wonder if I might have a word?"

"Certainly, Your Majesty." He urged his horse forward, falling in beside her. "What can I do for you, my queen?"

"I know you were disappointed you weren't allowed to lead the rescue operation."

"Naturally, although I understand why Albreda was better suited for the duty."

"The truth is, I may have need of your valour in the coming battle."

"I am ever ready to serve," said the knight.

"As I knew you would be. I'm not yet familiar with Beverly's plan, but with her stepping into the role of general, we need someone to command the horse. I should like that someone to be you."

"Wouldn't Sir Heward be more qualified?"

"Possibly, but we are unaware of his location at the moment. He was last seen in battle, and for all we know, he now lies amongst the dead. There's the very real possibility he could show up as a ghost, fighting alongside the forces of our enemy."

"Saxnor protect us," said Sir Preston. "A chilling thought."

"Would you be able to fight him if it came down to it?"

"I would certainly give it my all, Majesty."

"There must be no doubt, for such things could mean the ruin of us all."

"I understand."

"Good," said the queen. "Then I shall inform Beverly of my decision. Now, you should return to your paramour and see she is well taken care of."

The knight blushed profusely before nodding, then he slowed, allowing himself to retake his place beside Sophie.

"What did I say?" said Alric. "Incorrigible!"

THIRTY-TWO

Hammersfield

SUMMER 965 MC

B everly pulled back on the reins, and Lightning slowed. Before her lay the town of Hammersfield, its streets bustling with activity, while over it flew the red-and-green flag of Merceria, billowing out in the gusty afternoon wind.

"There it is," she mused. "The army of Merceria, or what's left of it."

"Come now," called out Aubrey. "It can't be all that bad?" The Life Mage slowed as she drew closer, allowing her horse to match the pace of the Mercerian Charger.

"Somehow, I expected more," Beverly explained, "but it can't be helped, I suppose."

"You shouldn't be surprised. After all, they're missing the entire Dwarven brigade."

"Yes, that's true. It's only that it looks so small."

"Less than a thousand by my reckoning," said Aubrey. "In years past, we would consider that a decent size."

Beverly turned to her cousin. "You have a good point. I should be thankful for what we have, not worrying about what we don't."

"Race you to town?"

"You can't be serious. You know Lightning is faster."

"So say you!" called out Aubrey, nudging her horse into a full gallop.

Beverly watched her tear across the field, then patted her mount on the neck. "Well, Lightning. It appears we must teach her a lesson."

. . .

In the end, Aubrey was the one who entered the town first, surprising her cousin. She slowed as she passed the first building, allowing Lightning to catch up.

"How did you manage that?" asked Beverly.

"My horse isn't carrying a fully armoured warrior," the mage replied.

A company of archers made their way past them, their captain bowing his head as his eyes met those of the red-haired knight.

"We look to have a lot of bowmen," noted Aubrey. "I'd say almost all the warriors here are carrying bows."

"Yes, and over half of ours are as well. There should be plenty of arrows flying once we meet the enemy. Let's hope they can do some serious damage. In the meantime, let's find the queen. She'll be eager to know we arrived. Arnim will bring in the rest of our men, and I'll make the introductions to King Thalgrun when they arrive later this evening."

"Then what are you waiting for?"

Beverly laughed. "I don't know where she's set up her command."

"Someone around here must know." Aubrey called out to a passing horseman, "You, there. Where is the queen?"

The warrior paused for a moment before he removed his helmet, surprising her with the face that lay beneath.

"Oh, Sir Preston. I didn't realize it was you."

He bowed his head. "My lady, we didn't know you'd arrived. Shall I take you to her?"

"If you would be so kind?"

He nodded, then set off at a slow trot. Beverly urged Lightning forward.

"How fares the cavalry?" she asked.

"They are doing well, Dame Beverly."

"We're both knights, Preston. You just call me Beverly."

He half smiled, his discomfort clear. "If you say so. How were things in the north?"

"You haven't heard?"

"No, the queen's been careful not to speak of such things."

"Well, let's see," said Beverly. "Where to begin? Oh yes, I know—Revi and Arnim made some new friends."

"Meaning?"

"We have allies—the Dwarves of Ironcliff."

"And do these allies have warriors?"

"They do," replied the red-headed knight. "They'll be arriving tonight if you'd like to meet them. They're an impressive sight."

"I've seen Dwarves before."

"Not like these you haven't."

Sir Preston looked at her, trying to tell if she was teasing him. "What makes these ones so special?"

"Their armour," replied Aubrey.

"What about their armour?"

"They're completely encased in steel. They call it plate armour."

"How in Saxnor's name do they manage that?"

"Beats me," said Beverly, "but I'm sure Aldwin would love to get his hands on some."

"We shall have to arrange something once this war is over."

"That would be nice, but I can't see it. Once we deal with this lot, we may need to march clear across to Weldwyn."

"What makes you say that?" asked Sir Preston.

"If I know the Clans, they'll want to take advantage of Leofric's death."

"To be honest, I can't imagine us having many warriors to spare."

"There is little choice," said Beverly. "We're allies now, and that means we stand together. Leofric gave his life for us; the least we can do is send warriors to Weldwyn's defence."

"Let's not rush this," suggested Aubrey. "Perhaps things will calm down by the time we're finished here."

"We can hope, but I wouldn't count on it."

They turned up a side street, and the queen's pennant came into sight, flying atop a large tavern. "I wonder if they're still serving drinks?" Beverly asked.

They came to a halt, and servants emerged to take their horses. Once inside, they noticed the queen had arranged for all the tables in the place to be moved, forming them into a 'U' shape. She was in the midst of discussing arrangements with Sophie but looked up as the door opened.

"Your Majesty," said Beverly.

"You're here?" said Anna. "I wasn't expecting you till this afternoon."

"It is the afternoon," said Aubrey.

"Is it?" The queen looked out the window. "I suppose it is. I didn't realize how late it was getting." She said something to Sophie in a low voice, and the maid quickly ran off.

"Come, sit down. You must tell me all about these new allies."

"Arnim and Revi found them," said Beverly. They both sat, taking a cue from the queen.

"Yes, so your message indicated. I understand their armour is exceptional, but I'm more interested in your personal opinion of them."

Sophie reappeared with a tray of mugs frothing over with ale. "Her Majesty thought you might be thirsty after such a long ride."

Beverly took one, setting it down before her. "Arnim and Revi saw them in action. They're impressive, to say the least. By all accounts, they waded into the enemy and were almost impervious in their armour."

"And their king?"

"Thalgrun? He's not so different from other Dwarves we've met, but his daughter is something else. Her name's Kasri Ironheart, and from what I heard, she's their foremost warrior."

"I would agree," said Aubrey. "She commands their most elite company, a group called the Hearth Guard. In a lot of ways, she's their equivalent of Beverly."

The knight looked at her in surprise. "Why would you say that?"

"She's their finest warrior: commands an elite company. Sound familiar?"

Anna laughed. "I think we'll award that one to Aubrey."

Beverly shook her head. "In any case, she appears to have a level head on her shoulders and, from what I can tell, has a good understanding of tactics and strategy. Her father, King Thalgrun, is firm in his resolve to help. He's worried he'll need our help down the road."

"Yes, you mentioned something to that effect in your report. Can you be more specific?"

"As you know, Ironcliff lies within an area known as the Gap, which is a valley between two mountain ranges. Norland sits at its western end, but the east is another matter. I'm sure Revi can fill you with more details once he arrives. He spoke extensively with Lord Agramath."

"Ah, yes, the Dwarven Earth Mage."

"A master of rock and stone, to be precise. I rather gather he doesn't employ spells quite like Albreda's, or Master Hearn's, for that matter."

"Have you seen him cast, Aubrey?"

"I'm afraid not. They didn't use him at all during the battle with Lord Calder."

"Why is that?"

"They didn't need to," said the Life Mage. "After we neutralized the enemy cavalry, they advanced to melee and cut them to ribbons."

"And the Dwarven losses?"

"That's just it. There weren't any at all. Oh, a few minor wounds, but nothing that would make someone incapable of fighting."

"That," suggested Beverly, "may have something to do with the Norlanders themselves. They were mostly armed with swords, a poor choice against such armour. If they were equipped with axes, or better yet, hammers, they would have at least stood a ghost of a chance."

"I would agree," noted Aubrey. "As it was, their morale broke quickly. I think the shock of it was too much for them."

"Well," noted the queen, "I doubt spirits will be so afflicted."

"Actually," said Beverly. "I hoped to use King Thalgrun's forces against the Elves."

"Is that something they're likely to consider? After all, the Dwarves and Elves have always gotten along with each other."

"I'll broach the subject with Kasri first. She has a good idea of what her father will agree to. I'll include details of the discussion once I write up my official report."

Aubrey looked at her cousin in surprise. "I didn't realize you did so much writing."

"Oh yes. Gerald insists on it. It's a trait he inherited from my father."

"The baron likes to keep records," explained the queen, "and I must say it helps tremendously. Being able to look back over things with a critical eye can help us adapt our tactics in the future. Perhaps you should consider something similar for your casting of magic?"

"I already do," said Aubrey. "Ever since I found my great-grandmother's writings, I keep a diary. Well, maybe diary isn't quite the right word, more of a journal of magic, I suppose."

"Will you one day use it to instruct your children?"

"I imagine my studies will keep me far too busy for that. I'll leave it to Beverly to continue on the family name."

"But I'm a Fitzwilliam," noted the knight, "not a Brandon."

"True, but we're still related, and that's good enough for me. I'm going to be much too involved with helping Revi set up his Academy of Magical Arts."

The queen chuckled. "Somehow, I think it's you who's going to end up running it, not Master Bloom. He's far too concerned with making monumental discoveries."

Kasri Ironheart stared at the flames. As usual, she was amongst the Hearth Guard, sharing their hardships, foregoing the opulence of her father's lodgings in town. Her warriors respected her, and that, in her mind, was far greater praise than the plaudits of court. She heard the challenge as someone approached, and then Dame Beverly appeared.

"May I sit?" the knight asked.

"By all means," Kasri replied. "Can I offer you something to drink? We have some nice mead?"

"Thank you. That would be nice."

One of the Dwarves handed over a tankard, and Beverly took a swig. "This is quite good."

"It's the very lifeblood of the Hearth Guard," replied the Dwarven commander. "But you didn't come here to talk of mead."

"No, I didn't. I came to talk strategy."

"Go on," urged Kasri.

"We'll soon be meeting the enemy, and when that time comes, we must be prepared. I came up with a way to deal with the spirit army, but the Elves are another issue."

"I'm afraid I have little first-hand experience of that particular woodland race."

"Are there not Elves near you?"

"Yes, but they are Wood Elves, distant cousins to the ones who march here."

"What's the difference?" asked the knight.

"Well, they're smaller, lithe creatures who live a much more rustic lifestyle."

"Rustic? Are you saying they're country folk?"

"I would say they are more akin to the Orcs than the High Elves."

"And by High Elves," said Beverly, "you mean the taller ones?"

"Yes, the term High Elves refers to their civilization. Centuries ago, they were the dominant power in the region, with towering cities made of white stone, or so we're led to believe. Personally, I believe it a bit of an exaggeration, no doubt inspired by the Elves themselves. You see, when the old race, the Saurians, were destroyed, the Elves took over their trade routes, dominating all commerce. They spread their tales by this method, convincing everyone of their power and majesty, although we only had their word for it."

"Are you suggesting they lied?"

"Not necessarily," Kasri said, "but perhaps enhanced is a better word. To my knowledge, no Dwarf ever set foot in an Elven city, yet High Elves frequently visited the Dwarven realms."

"You seem to know a lot about them."

"It couldn't be helped. As the daughter of a king, I was expected to learn everything I could from our scholars. I hated it at the time, but with age, I came to appreciate the advantage it's given me. What of yourself? Were you forced to read books?"

"I'm well educated, if that's what you're asking, but I spent more time practicing with weapons and riding horses than reading books."

"Yet you still read?"

Beverly laughed. "Yes, I did. My father would allow me extra practice time if I read, so I learned to do so as quickly as possible, although I doubt I'm as well-read as you. Now, my cousin Aubrey is an entirely different matter. She could probably give you some competition in terms of reading."

"Interesting," noted Kasri. "I was always under the impression reading amongst Humans was looked down upon."

"Maybe it is in Norland, but our queen is a voracious reader, a trait which has rubbed off on most of the court. Have you poets amongst your people?"

"We do, as a matter of fact. We even have dramatic readings, where our bards will act out the great heroic tales."

"You must come to visit us in Wincaster and see our plays," said Beverly. "I believe you'd like them."

"I should very much like that. Hopefully, when the fighting is over, I shall do so."

"Now, where was I? Oh yes, I was talking about the Elves. I thought we might employ your father's forces against them. Do you suppose he would have any objections to being so employed?"

"My father can be a bit set in his ways at times," noted Kasri, "but I think he can be convinced, provided he thinks it his idea."

"Any idea how that might be accomplished?"

"Yes, but it'll take the two of us to do it, maybe even more."

"In that case," said the knight, "I shall fetch Revi Bloom. He's seen the enemy from on high and can at least give a better account of what we're up against."

"We'll do it right after dinner. My father's always more amenable once he's eaten."

"He wants what?" asked Revi

"A description of the Elven army," said Beverly. "You saw it through Shellbreaker's eyes; who better to give an account of them?"

"I suppose there is that."

"Come now. Have you something better to occupy your mind?"

The Royal Life Mage sighed, rising to his feet. "No, not really. With Hayley off in the hills, there is little for me to do."

"Then let's not keep the king waiting." She led him through the camp before passing by the Dwarven pickets. Kasri soon joined them, a look of mischief in her eyes.

"Ready for this?" asked the Dwarf.

"As ready as we can be," noted the knight.

"Good. Just follow my lead, and we'll have my father volunteering in short order."

They passed through the guarded doors unhindered, accompanied as they were by Kasri, to find King Thalgrun standing at a small table, examining a crude map.

"What have you there?" asked Kasri.

King Thalgrun looked up. "Oh, hello. This is a map Queen Anna sent over for my perusal. It purports to show the region hereabouts, although I can make neither head nor tail of it."

"A Human drew it," she replied. "Thus, the top of the map represents north."

"Why in the name of the Gods would they do that?"

Kasri turned to her companions. "By tradition, our people use east as the top of the map."

The king rotated the paper. "Ah, yes, that makes a lot more sense now." He noted the presence of Beverly and Revi. "I see you brought company."

"I did, Father. They seek your counsel."

"Certainly, but first, I have some questions. Dame Beverly, you participated in the initial attack into Norland, did you not?"

"Yes, Your Majesty."

"Can you show me, on the map here, where you marched?"

The knight moved closer, looking down at the drawing. "We crossed in two columns, one here at Wickfield, the other at Mattingly."

"And that's to our south?"

"It is."

"And what's this over here?" He stabbed down a finger.

"That's meant to represent hills."

"Hills? That's a strange symbol to use for hills. It makes them look like bumps."

"How else would you draw them, Majesty?"

He looked up at her, trying to formulate a response. "You'll need to come and visit the archives back in Ironcliff if you want to see a real map. This thing"—he waved at the map—"is a travesty."

"It was drawn in haste," said Beverly, "and meant as a rough guide only."

"Well, you succeeded on that point!"

"Father!" shouted Kasri. "These are our allies. You must treat them accordingly."

"Yes, of course," said the king. "I apologize if I gave offence. You said they came seeking my counsel?"

"Yes, there's a battle coming, Father. They seek guidance on the best way to deploy our army."

King Thalgrun turned to Beverly. "Tell me what you know of the enemy."

"They consist of two separate groups," began the knight. "The first, the ghost army, is composed of spirits summoned from the Afterlife and bound to this mortal realm through the use of dark magic. The greater threat, though, is the one that follows, for it consists of what you would refer to as High Elves."

"Is it, now? And can you show me their last reported position on this map?"

Revi stepped forward. "I can do better than that, Majesty. I observed them this very day using my magic. I can show you their precise location." He stared downward, looking at the indicated page. "Well, as precise as I can be with such a map."

"Go on, then," urged Thalgrun.

Revi's eyes roamed the landmarks until he finally pointed at a location roughly halfway between Hammersfield and Anvil. "Right there," he announced. "The Elves are trailing the spirit army by a few miles."

"Why wouldn't they march together?" asked the king.

"Elves like to keep to themselves," offered Beverly. "Even amongst the many races of the Mercerian army, the Elves were solitary."

"There are Elves in your army?"

"Not anymore," she explained. "The last of them left after the death of Telethial, the daughter of Lord Arandil."

"I've heard that name before," said the king. "He's the ruler of the Darkwood, is he not?"

"He is," said Revi. "I'm surprised you've heard of him."

"According to our archives, he was a rebel."

"A rebel?" said Beverly. "How so?"

"He fought against his own people." The king held up his hands to forestall any argument. "Not actual combat, mind you, but politically. There's some speculation he was against the war that destroyed the Orcs —said it would spell doom for his people. The sad thing is, in the end, he was right. The losses from that war are still being felt by his people today."

"I met Lord Greycloak previously," said the knight. "Even fought beside him on multiple occasions, yet that's a side of him I never saw."

"Not surprising. Like you said earlier, Elves are notorious for keeping to themselves. I'm surprised he let his daughter serve with you if I'm being completely honest. Of course, I don't know him personally, but history paints him as reclusive."

"Elf shall not kill Elf," said Beverly.

"What's that?"

"Something Lord Arandil once told our queen. We thought he was talking about our enemy. Now I wonder if he was referring to the people he led into seclusion?"

"Are you suggesting he was a pacifist?" asked Revi.

"No," said the knight, "definitely not. He came to our aid during the first rebellion and had no qualms about it, but perhaps he had a notion this Elven army was out here, somewhere, and didn't want to face it?"

"That would seem to fit his character," said the king, "but we're getting off topic. Tell me more about this Elven army."

"They appear to be armed primarily with spears or bows, and I saw no sign of cavalry."

"That's good. It makes my job easier."

"Your job?" said Kasri, the hint of a smile gracing her lips.

"Well, of course. Who else do you have who could take on an army like this?" He looked around at the group. "You lot are going to be far too busy looking after the ghost army. I'd much rather have a crack at something of flesh and blood."

"Then I shall inform Queen Anna of your decision," said Beverly.

THIRTY-THREE

To Battle

SUMMER 965 MC

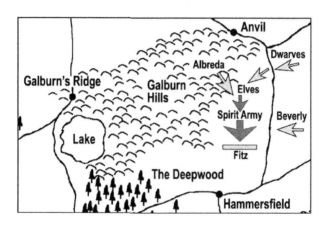

K asri leaned forward, looking at Revi with great interest, for the mage had closed his eyes and now moved his head from side to side while facing the ground.

"What is he doing?" she asked.

Arnim answered her question. "He's looking through Shellbreaker's eyes, much as he did when we marched here."

"I can hear you," said Revi. "It's only my eyes that are elsewhere."

"Can you see the enemy?" asked the Dwarf.

"Yes. They're heading south, on the road to Hammersfield."

"Is it time to move yet?"

"Not quite," said the mage. "I'd like to see them another few miles down the road before we march westward. I shouldn't like for them to note our dust trail."

"Dwarves don't leave dust trails," stated King Thalgrun.

"I meant no disrespect, Your Majesty, merely that we need our presence to go unnoticed. It is, I believe, important we come across the Elves with surprise."

Kasri chuckled. "He has you there, Father."

It had been two days since the plan had been finalized, two days during which there had been little to do but take up their position and worry.

"All of this inaction is driving me mad," said the king. "I want to get in close to this lot and have done with it."

"You'll get your chance soon enough," replied Kasri. "Now remember, once we do start moving, we head directly west."

"I know," he grumbled. "West to the road, then south, into the waiting arms of the Elves. I'm not a complete idiot, you know." Everyone looked at him in shock.

"Sorry," he mumbled. "All this enforced idleness weighs heavily on my nerves."

"Tell me," said Arnim, "is this the largest army Ironcliff has ever fielded?"

"This is only a portion of our entire army," said the king. "We can't very well march off and leave our home unprotected now, can we?"

"But your kingdom is only one city, isn't it?"

"Aye, that's right."

"Yet you managed to equip an army of over four hundred warriors. An impressive feat."

"Could you not raise that many troops in that capital of yours? What did you call it?"

"Wincaster," said Arnim.

"Aye, that's the place."

"I suppose we could, but we'd need to leave a large garrison to guard it."

"That's where we have the advantage," explained the king. "Ironcliff is, from the sounds of it, just as large as Wincaster. The big difference is almost our entire city lies within the mountain. Much easier to defend than a walled city."

"Yes," added Kasri, "and our engineers are masters of traps. Should an enemy ever appear at our doorstep, they would be hard-pressed to get in through the front door. It's never been tested, of course, but we Dwarves are firm believers in being well-prepared."

"And a good thing too," noted the king. "What with all the problems in the east. Mark my words, there's a shadow growing over there, one that threatens to make this war look like a childhood spat. Should they come in full strength, we will be forced to close our doors and disappear into the depths."

"That bad?" said Arnim. "And here I thought we only needed to worry about the Elves."

"I've seen a lot of armies come and go over the years," said the king. "You don't live to be as old as me and not notice such things, but this is different."

"Different, how?"

"Their leaders demand total obedience."

"Don't all military commanders?"

"I don't mean from their warriors—I mean everyone. We pride ourselves on following the rule of law, but even Dwarves can disagree from time to time. From what we learned of our neighbours, that sort of thing is not only frowned upon, it's against their laws."

"It's a difference of ideology," suggested Revi.

"I have no clue what that means," noted King Thalgrun, "but it's far more dangerous than a mere army. It's almost a religion onto itself."

"They don't worship the Gods?"

"Not according to what our scouts learned."

"What about the Saints?" asked Arnim. "The Kurathians worship them."

"No Saints either. As far as I can tell, they worship their emperor. That's it. In effect, he's their god."

"But he's only a man, surely?"

"I'm only repeating what I heard," said the king. "I'd like to know more, but there's only so much a Human is willing to tell a Dwarf. Do you think your people might be able to get more information out of them?"

"It's possible," noted Revi, "though not practical at this point, what with the war and everything." He paused a moment. "Ah, there's the tail end of the Elven army. I believe it's time we started making a move, Your Majesty."

Richard Fitzwilliam, Baron of Bodden, sat atop his horse, surveying the warriors lined up before him. They were nervous, which was to be expected, for everyone knew the enemy had done the unthinkable by beating their marshal in battle. Now they must face that same army, and many wondered if they would suffer a similar fate.

Sir Preston rode across their front, extolling them with words of valour, but it had little effect. Morale was low, dangerously so, and for the first time in years, the baron began to doubt their chances of victory.

The arrival of Alric and his men at least stirred them up. As they rode past, the men cheered, although whether it was pleasure at his appearance or simply the desire not to seem weak in front of the men of Weldwyn was anyone's guess.

Fitz was well thought of amongst the Mercerians, but even he had to admit he lacked the passion of Gerald. These warriors loved their marshal, would face insurmountable odds for him. Now that he was gone, they felt his loss all the more keenly.

A horse rode up beside Fitz, and he turned to see the queen.

"Your Majesty," he said. "You honour us."

Her gaze swept over the warriors.

"They're uneasy," said the baron.

"As are we all," she replied. "We're taking a terrible risk here. If even one of our groups fails to make contact, it could well spell disaster."

"You must have faith in your commanders," said Fitz. "They will see us through to victory."

"I would feel better with our marshal by my side." She turned to him with a look of remorse. "I'm sorry, Lord Richard. I didn't mean to imply you weren't up to the task."

"I understand, Majesty. If the truth be told, I was just thinking the same thing. These men... our men, feel the loss of their marshal greatly. Maybe a few words of encouragement from you might set them to rights?"

She paused, and Fitz saw her struggling with a response. Losing her oldest friend had hit her hard, and for the first time, he saw doubt on the face of his sovereign.

"Perhaps you would prefer me to address them?" he suggested.

A look of relief flooded her face. "By all means, General."

The baron urged his horse forward, taking his time to help him think over his words. Inspiring warriors was no small feat, but he knew it was needed. Better to hear it from him than a disheartened queen.

He halted, letting his eyes roam over the waiting soldiers lined up along the slight rise, not quite steep enough to give them an advantage in battle, but at least they could survey the approaching enemy. The footmen were formed up in four ranks, while behind them massed the archers of the Mercerian army. On either flank, Orc hunters were deployed where they could use their skills to the greatest advantage as skirmishers. Alric's cavalry would form a reserve, able to ride quickly to trouble spots should the need arise. It was not, perhaps, the most original disposition of troops, but given their numbers, it was the best option.

"Men of Merceria," he began, talking slowly to allow his voice to carry to everyone. "We stand here today to hold back the army that threatens our homes, but we do not stand alone. Even as we speak, two other armies are moving into position, ready to crush the enemy."

He saw the looks of hope. The plans had been kept secret for far too long. There had been rumours, of course, especially when his daughter led the cavalry eastward, but until now, these stalwart warriors had heard little of what was to befall them.

"You all know me," the baron continued, "and you know my son-in-law, Aldwin, the smith. Just as he uses the hammer and anvil to beat metal into submission, so, too, will we beat the enemy. We are the anvil, my friends, and the hammer…" he chuckled. "Well, everyone knows it's Dame Beverly's favourite weapon."

There it was—laughter! Amusement amongst the troops was a good sign. "Today, your duty is to hold your ground. Do that, and victory shall be ours!"

The men cheered, and although it wasn't with the customary bravado he'd come to expect, it would have to do. He turned, riding back to the queen.

"Will that suffice, do you think?" he asked her.

Anna smiled. "It must. Now come. Standing in front of the men is not the wisest of moves when an enemy approaches."

Beverly slowed, using her hand to indicate to her troops to do likewise.

"This looks as good a place as any," she said. "Any sign of the enemy?"

"Not at present," noted Aubrey, "or at least if there has been, they haven't seen fit to inform me as such. How long do you imagine they'll keep us waiting?"

"Not long, I should think. I might remind you we still need to ride all the way back to fight."

Tog bellowed out an order, his voice easily carrying across the entire brigade. As one, everyone came to a halt.

"Rangers out on picket," he called. "The rest, water your horses and get some rest." The massive Troll watched them spread out, then, satisfied they knew their business, he wandered over to Beverly and Aubrey.

"They are eager to fight," he noted.

"Good," replied Beverly. "Let's hope they're still as eager when we catch sight of our foe."

"I shall check in with Andurak," noted Aubrey. She cast her spell and was soon speaking in Orcish.

"Do the Trolls have shamans?" asked Beverly.

"It is said we did long ago," said Tog, "but there are no living Trolls who witnessed it first-hand. Perhaps, when this war is over, Aubrey might use her magic to determine if such a thing is possible. She has spoken of the ability to detect magical potential, has she not?"

"She's mentioned it in passing. I assume she and Kraloch discussed it at length, but it's not my area of expertise." Beverly looked down at the massive club Tog carried. "I see you added a steel cap to your club. Do you find it easier to use?"

"It is more or less the same."

"Then why cap it?"

"It prevents the end of the club from splitting. We Trolls use a great amount of force when striking with such a weapon. I had already gone through three in this campaign when I settled on this solution."

Beverly was about to say more, but at that precise moment, Aubrey dismissed her spell.

"Well?" said Beverly.

"Andurak reports Kiren-Jool has the enemy in sight."

"How long until they contact the main army?"

"They expect to be fighting by mid-afternoon, which leaves us plenty of time to get into position."

Beverly looked around the makeshift rest area. "We'll let the horses finish watering, then start heading back. In the meantime, I suggest you see if you can contact Kraloch. He's going to need warning of what's coming."

∼

Albreda snapped her eyes open. "It's time," she announced, turning to Hayley and Herdwin. "How would you recommend we proceed?"

"I'll take the Orcs first," said the ranger. "They can scout out the area and report back once they have visual contact. Herdwin, you'll likely want your arbalesters in front, with Dwarven axes to the sides to protect them. The job of the archers will be to clear a path for Albreda to make her move." She turned to the Druid. "Are you sure you don't want three-horns? I thought they were going to help?"

"They fear the enemy too much," she replied, "and I can't say I blame them. In any event, I can move faster if I'm unencumbered by others. I spoke with Lily, and she'll bring the three-horns in if things go badly, but the hope is we can leave them out of it. The main problem is they're not predators and more likely to panic than fight. If that happens, they could be as dangerous to us as our foes."

"Will the Elves recognize them?" asked the Dwarf.

"They might. After all, they did fight the Saurians long ago. Mind you, that was likely over two thousand years ago, and we don't know if they saw any three-horns at the time, so who knows? In any event, we're trying to sow as much confusion as possible."

"And did you spot our friends?" asked Hayley.

"I did." She pointed to a nearby rise. "They lie right over that ridge. Once your archers top it, they should have a clear view to pick their targets. Now remember, every arrow must find its mark. We won't be relying on volleys here but precise use of the bow."

"I'll have the Orcs call out their targets so we don't waste arrows."

"A good idea, as we don't have an unlimited supply. It took us days just to replenish what you lost at the Minglewood."

"My Dwarves have enough to get the job done," noted Herdwin. "And once the bolts run out, they're more than capable of using their axes."

"Good. Let's get moving, shall we? We want to be in position before the fighting starts."

"Just one question," said Hayley. "How do we know when we can start?"

"When you hear a wolf howl. Until then, you must be careful to remain out of sight."

$\sim$

Kraloch felt the familiar tingle, and then he allowed the ghostly image of Aubrey to appear before him.

"Things are moving quickly," she said. "Are you under direct observation?"

The Orc nodded, his eyes darting left and right as he sat on the dirt.

"The attack will commence shortly. We're going to be coming in with three different armies. During the battle, a fourth group will approach from the west, seeking to rescue you. Remain alert but don't try anything rash. I can see you're not bound. Are the others tied up?"

He shook his head.

"Good. Help will be there soon. I promise."

She broke the connection, fading from sight. One of the Elven guards, noting his movement, stepped closer.

"What are you doing?" she demanded.

"I have no idea what you are talking about," replied the shaman.

"You were moving your head around. Who were you talking to?"

"Myself. It is a habit I picked up from my chieftain, Urgon."

The Elf came closer, kneeling to look the Orc in the eyes.

"We shall soon destroy your so-called allies, greenskin. Once we do, we will return to end your miserable existence."

"You cannot defeat the Mercerians," said Kraloch.

"What's this, now? An Orc bragging about the invincibility of Humans? Have you no faith in your own race?"

Kraloch resisted the urge to reply, for it would do little good. Instead, he contented himself to simply stare back at his captor. The Elf, put off by the tactic, turned her attention to her Human prisoner, moving to tower over Gerald.

"You are old and weak," she taunted. "Yours is a pitiful race."

"Yet we are the ones who denied you your place in history. Why else would your queen go to such lengths to defeat us?"

"You know nothing of which you speak."

"Don't I? Correct me if I'm wrong, but Queen Kythelia attempted to overthrow Merceria twice, didn't she? Not to mention trying to orchestrate the invasion of Weldwyn. All of those failed. You might want to reconsider your opinions of Humans."

The Elf responded with a swift kick, taking Gerald in the ribs. The old man bent over double, clutching his chest.

"Keep your mouth shut," said the guard before wandering back to her post.

"You angered her," said Zhura.

"And here I was thinking I was making friends."

"Why do you choose to further antagonize her?"

"Her anger will be focused on me now, rather than wondering what Kraloch was up to." He shifted his gaze to the shaman, keeping his voice low while switching to Orc. "*I assume Aubrey contacted you?*"

"*She did,*" said Kraloch. "*The battle is about to commence. She was short on details, but the attack will be from multiple sides. There was also some mention of a rescue from the west.*"

"*Any indication of what something like that might look like?*"

"*No, but we must bide our time and try to stay out of trouble.*"

Gerald grimaced. "*Too late for that, I'm afraid.*"

⌒

Ilarian pushed past his Elven archers, gazing at the spirits that preceded them. The Volgath was easy to spot, mounted on his undead beast like some denizen of the Underworld.

He smiled, knowing the need for such a creature was soon coming to an end. Just as Leofric's defeat paved the way for the invasion of Weldwyn, so, too, would the Mercerian loss destroy any chance of repelling the Elven host.

Two thousand years ago, Kythelia destroyed the last of the Orc cities. Now she was set to do the same to those of the Humans, cleansing the land of the blight that had so infested it.

Inside, he raged. The time of Elves should have come almost a thousand years ago, but the arrival of the Human mercenaries had ruined everything. Kythelia had tried to resist, but their losses in the Orc war had been horrendous, diminishing much of the Elven power. All they could do at the time was sit back and watch as humanity spread across the land, but this time it would be different. The Humans would be defeated once and for all, their population executed or enslaved by the Elven mages, who would use their blood magic to gain new heights of power, allowing them to continue their war of vengeance, pushing on to rejoin their brothers and sisters on the Continent.

He saw a great Elven empire stretching from sea to sea, their enemies all defeated. They would find the glory that had been so long denied them and become the dominant power in the entire land of Eiddenwerthe.

A warrior pushed his way towards him. "My lord, we sighted the enemy."

"How many?"

"Seven hundred, consisting mostly of footmen and archers. Shall we send Leofric forward to deal with them?"

Ilarian smiled at the poetic justice. "By all means. Let's have the dead Weldwyn king defeat his ally. It somehow feels... fitting, don't you agree?"

"I do," the messenger replied.

"Good. Then send the army of spirits forward, and let's put an end to this. After that, it should only be a matter of marching before we are within the very halls of Wincaster itself."

"What of Weldwyn, Lord?"

"That is a foregone conclusion," replied Ilarian, "for even as we speak, Queen Kythelia herself is leading an attack on their capital. By the time the sun sets, we shall have defeated not one kingdom but two."

THIRTY-FOUR

Clash of Arms

SUMMER 965 MC

S ir Preston had taken up a position amongst the footmen, the better to steady the line. From the north came the enemy, marching in one solid mass. They looked like typical warriors, but their true nature became apparent as they drew closer, revealing their ghostly complexions.

The knight considered himself a brave man, and yet the sight of such spirits made the hair on his neck stand on end. He clamped down on his emotions.

"They try to scare us, but it's all an illusion," he called out. "They can be killed as easily as any man. Stand your ground, and let them feel the vengeance of Mercerian steel!"

A cloud of arrows sailed overhead. Sir Preston watched them rush like a flock of birds towards the enemy before they descended in a sudden cloud-burst, raining down death and destruction.

If their opponent had been Human, the results would have been more pronounced; bodies still fell, but with no cries of anguish or sounds of alarm, it all looked like some strange mirage. Arrows continued to fly in a steady stream, followed by more and more.

The knight took a step forward, looking at the Orcs on his flanks, who added to the barrage. His own men were solid enough, gripping their shields and weapons in anticipation of the coming melee, so he moved back into position, drawing his own sword.

Nervousness built within him. As a knight, he was used to being mounted; he felt vulnerable on foot. He looked at his forearm, seeing the kerchief tied there as a reminder of Sophie. Would he live to see her again?

He was struggling to put such thoughts from his mind and focus instead on the coming conflict when a terrible stench drifted towards him. He heard several men lose the contents of their stomachs.

"Hold fast!" he shouted, his voice harsh and bitter. He let the anger build, knowing it would keep his mind from dwelling on death. The last dozen paces felt like they took forever before the enemy was finally within striking distance.

Sir Preston sliced downward, feeling his blade meet a slight resistance before it tore a shoulder from his foe. He could have sworn his ears popped right before the body disintegrated into a light mist that drifted over him. Panic rose as it touched him, but then he realized it was only dust. Again his sword struck out, this time connecting with an ancient shield, and he recognized the symbol on it—the mark of Weldwyn. It was then that he understood this had been the army of Leofric.

The heavy cavalry drew closer before spreading out into a single line, with the lighter Kurathians behind them ready to exploit any gaps that might be created, while the Trolls and rangers would follow in their wake, picking off pockets of resistance.

Beverly drew her hammer and held it on high; the sunlight reflected off it. "For the queen!" she called out before sweeping it down. The horses increased their gait, soon thundering towards their tightly packed foe.

The moment of impact came quickly, and then they were in amongst the enemy. Nature's Fury struck a head, smashing it to pieces, turning its owner to mist. Lightning barrelled into another, the opposition melting away in the afternoon sun.

All around her, the horsemen of the heavy cavalry struck out, ploughing through the army of spirits. It was an odd sensation, for instead of littering the ground with bodies, they waded through an ever-growing cloud of mist.

The enemy didn't flinch, didn't even appear to care. They struck back with weapons in precise, practiced motions, but against mounted opposition, they could do little damage.

Beverly slowed to get her bearings, noticing dark shapes approaching through the mist. As they drew closer, she recognized the fallen horsemen of Weldwyn, shadowy ghosts riding beasts that were a mockery of horses. Moments later, the smell of death and putrefying flesh almost overwhelmed her.

She sensed Lightning's fear even as she felt her own skin crawling. Onward she urged her trusty charger as she started to swing the hammer. A spear lanced out, scraping along her vambrace, numbing her arm with its icy touch. She felt the air turn cold and then brought Nature's Fury down onto the head of the enemy's mount, striking true. It ploughed right through as if she were hitting a corpse, bits of putrid flesh exploding, splattering her, and then the thing went down, taking its rider with it.

~

King Thalgrun's Dwarves kept up a steady pace, slowly approaching the rear of the Elven forces, but there was no sign their advance had even been noticed. Instead, they saw only the backs of their enemy, standing ready to move south.

The king gave the command, and the arbalests loosed their missiles at the Elven archers who'd taken up positions on the flanks. The first volley was devastating, but the Elves soon turned, loosing arrows of their own.

Several Dwarves took hits, but by and large, their thick plate armour protected them. They drew closer, the poleaxes of the guards ready to bring death and destruction to their foes.

Sitting on his horse, Revi had a clear view of the enemy, which easily numbered over a thousand. Against this came the four hundred Dwarves of Ironcliff, their advance unwavering. The Mage tried to think of some way to use his magic, but aside from healing, he could do little against such odds. Desperate to learn how his comrades fared, he closed his eyes, calling on his inner magic to see through Shellbreaker's eyes.

It was always a little disorienting, switching to the coaster's eyes. Still, years of practice had honed his skills, and Revi settled into his new environment quickly. He kept Shellbreaker high, lessening the danger of an errant arrow severing his bond with his familiar.

Off to the south, he could make out the spirits pushing up against the Mercerian army. They'd evidently been fighting for some time, for the entire front line was enveloped in a fine mist, but his friends were still holding on.

He flew east to see horsemen hitting the flank of the spirit army. Clearly, Beverly had picked her moment to perfection as they cleaved through the enemy, drawing them closer to King Leofric. No, he thought, that's not Leofric, but a semblance of the once-mighty Weldwyn king, twisted to do the bidding of Queen Kythelia.

With any luck, the Mercerian cavalry would cut down the Volgath, disrupting the Necromancers' control over the spirits of the dead.

Of greater concern to the mage were the Elves, for they could think for themselves, unlike their ghostly companions. Armed with spears, their tightly packed ranks of seasoned warriors would have no trouble keeping the cavalry at bay, thereby neutralizing the Mercerians' greatest advantage.

A movement off to the west caught his attention, and he flew Shell-breaker to the area. The hills here overlooked the battlefield, but he could still make out Albreda's contingent even amongst the rough terrain. The Orc archers led, spread out before them in a thin line. Next came Dwarven arbalesters, their mighty weapons loosing bolt after bolt as the range closed. To their north lumbered the bulky three-horns, and even from this range, Revi was in awe of their quiet majesty.

~

"Send in Alric's horse," ordered the queen, pointing. "We need them there, on the left flank."

"Yes, Majesty," said Fitz. He rattled off orders, and his aide dipped a blue pennant. Moments later, the horsemen of the prince's personal guard, the pride of Weldwyn, moved to their left.

"Move up the right flank," Anna ordered. "We shall crush the enemy between our force and Beverly's."

The baron cast a quick glance to the east where the Kurathians, following in the wake of the heavy cavalry, had spread out, effectively surrounding the enemy's entire eastern flank. With Sir Preston pushing forward, it cut off any possibility of manoeuvring, forcing the Volgath to concentrate its efforts there if it were to have any chance of holding back the Mercerians.

Lord Richard gave the command, and another pennant was hoisted. Evidently, the order was expected, for Sir Preston's footmen surged forward almost immediately, pushing deep into the enemy forces.

"We are making headway, Majesty, but we are still vastly outnumbered."

"We must hold, Baron. The very survival of Merceria depends upon it!"

~

Albreda watched as the Elves took note of their presence. Between the Orc hunters and the Dwarven arbalesters, there were more than sufficient archers to neutralize the enemy's bowmen. She moved downhill, passing by the Orcs and onto the flat plain below. Under bombardment by close to two hundred bows, the Elves ignored the single individual, concentrating their volleys instead on trying to take out the approaching Dwarves.

The Druid halted some fifty paces from the enemy to study their forma-tion for a moment before she raised her hands, calling on the ancient power of the earth. The energy built within her, then she struck the ground with her staff, and a brown mist appeared, coalescing into the shape of an enormous bear. She simply pointed, and the creature lumbered off, rushing towards the waiting enemy.

The nearest Elves, panicking at the sight, redirected their energies towards taking down this new threat. Albreda followed up with another spell, sending small white lights that sank into the ground in amongst the enemy archers. Vines suddenly sprang up, grasping legs and crushing feet.

The panic grew, fed by the Orc arrows and Dwarven bolts that continued to dig into their ranks. The Druid risked a quick look over her shoulder to where Lily had summoned the mist. The three-horns soon exited the cover, revealing themselves for the first time. The Elven archers, now little more than a terrified mob, fled, many dropping their bows as they ran.

～

Aubrey realized the attack was stalling. Beverly had pushed far into the eastern flank of Leofric's forces, but now the tide threatened to turn against them.

The Life Mage knew what she must do. Indeed, she had carefully prepared for it. She closed her eyes, calling to mind the incantation Andurak had taught her. Then the power surged through her as she directed her spell towards Beverly's opponents.

Aubrey had never cast the spell before, for although she'd learned it over the last few days, there'd been no spirits to call. However, faced as they were with hundreds of them, it couldn't help but succeed.

She let the spell release, watching as the very air shimmered right before a large group of spirit warriors turned on their master. She was astounded to see the undead mounts rupture into piles of rotting flesh and broken bones, to be replaced by ghostly horses. These past warriors of Weldwyn now turned aside, allowing Beverly through before following in her wake.

～

Tog looked north. He'd followed behind the cavalry, but now, outpaced, he saw a greater threat—Elves to the north. He looked at the rangers to see Gorath staring back. All it took was for him to point, the Orc understanding completely.

The Trolls turned north, heading towards the Elven archers who anchored the eastern end of the enemy line. In response, a hail of arrows came their way. A number managed to puncture the tough hide of the Trolls before the rangers let loose with their longbows.

There now developed a duel of sorts, with the tightly packed Elves trying to wipe out the Mercerians, but the rangers, as was their custom, approached in a dispersed manner, making such targeting difficult.

Agramath waited until the Dwarves of Ironcliff were within twenty paces of the Elves, then let loose with a spell, kneeling to touch the ground. He sent a tremor towards the enemy, shaking the ground and heaving it upwards. The dirt only rose to ankle height, but the effect was quite remarkable. It served to break up the enemy's line of battle just as the Dwarven warriors struck.

Poleaxes jabbed out, smashing through the Elven armour with ease. The enemy tried to strike back, but their spears did little against the thick metal plates protecting the Dwarves.

The fighting intensified, and Agramath cast another spell. This time, he simply pointed at the ground. A small fissure appeared, little more than cracks to begin with, but they soon grew wider until a rocklike hand reached out from beneath the ground. Moments later, a head appeared, a massive block of grey stone, with glowing eyes like emeralds. A second arm emerged, and then the thing pulled itself free of the ground's embrace, towering over the Dwarves, easily twice the size of a Troll. But whereas the swamp folk had tough skin, this thing had no skin at all. Instead, its entire composition was that of stone.

The Dwarves stepped aside, clearly used to its presence when it lumbered forward and waded into the Elven warriors, brushing them aside as if they were no more than stalks of wheat. Some tried fighting back, but their spears proved no match for the creature's rough exterior.

Arnim watched in fascination. "What is that?" he asked.

"A creature of the deep," replied Agramath, "summoned by the power of my magic."

"I've never heard of anything like that."

"Nor would I expect you to. They live far beneath the surface of Eiddenwerthe, where air is almost non-existent and the pressure so great, mere mortals cannot withstand it. Our forefathers found them long ago and learned to live amongst them in peace."

"Are you saying those things are living creatures?" asked an astonished Arnim.

"In a sense, yes," said the Dwarven mage. "They can think and reason, certainly, but are not of flesh and blood like those of us who dwell on the surface."

"Can they be killed?"

"Yes, although destroyed might be a more fitting description. They do not breathe in the traditional sense, and we know not whether they reproduce. However, one thing is for certain—they are comprised of the very same rock that pervades the area in which they live."

"And you control this elemental creature?"

"Not at all," said the mage. "I merely call him. It is his decision whether or not to fight."

"Him?"

"I only use that term because it lets me see him as a living being. They have no defining physical features to identify gender."

"Do they talk?"

"I have no idea. I can conjure them, the spell serving to deliver my wishes, but as to speech, there is none I have ever heard. Now, come. We must hurry if we are to break through the enemy army."

"How do we do that?"

"Simple," said Agramath. "We follow my conjured friend."

Gerald looked at the guards who'd been watching the prisoners closely. The sounds of battle drew closer, and a deep-throated roar sounded off to the west, causing the marshal to smile knowingly.

An Elf moved to loom over him. "What are you smiling at?" she demanded.

"That noise. You have no idea what it is, do you?"

"One more word out of you, and I'll silence your tongue forever."

"Make up your mind. You were the one asking what I was smiling at."

A large shape advanced, towering over the Elven warriors. Two guards turned to face this new threat, but then the ground exploded beneath them, vines spewing forth to crawl up their legs, trapping them.

Kraloch brought up his hands, words of power flowing from his lips. The guard, who only moments ago threatened Gerald, suddenly yawned. The marshal used the opportunity to leap to his feet and run towards the nearest Elf, grasping her spear. There was a brief struggle for the weapon, and then the vines twisted tight, crushing the guard's legs.

Zhura launched herself at the remaining guard, driving her to the ground. They struggled for the sword, rolling around on the dirt, and then the Elf, blood on her blade, stood over the now injured ghostwalker.

Gerald heaved the spear with all the strength he could muster, striking the guard in the centre of the back. She staggered forward, nearly tripping over the still form of Zhura.

Kraloch rushed forward, seeking to help his fellow tribemate while Gerald leaped onto the Elf, knocking the wind from her as they fell to the ground. He rose up, grasping the haft of the spear protruding from her back, and pushing it in with all the strength he could muster. The guard twitched and then lay still.

Kraloch, meanwhile, cast, calling on arcane forces to heal Zhura's wounds. Around them all was chaos; Elves streamed past, ignoring them in their quest to escape what was coming.

Gerald noted a half a dozen Elven warriors forming a crude line, their backs to the prisoners, and then the massive form of a three-horn barrelled into them, knocking them aside as if they were nothing more than a pile of loose leaves.

Moments later, Albreda strode forth. She glanced at the trio, absently pointing her arm to the side and letting loose with a spell. A bunch of fire-flies flew from her hand to sink into the ground as yet more vines erupted forth. However, this time, they twined around themselves, forming into a thick hedge from which sprang thorns.

"Come," she said. "We haven't much time."

Gerald stood, pulling the spear from the Elf's back. Kraloch, having completed his spell, watched as Zhura's eyes opened. He helped her to her feet, then guided her towards Albreda.

"Hold on," said Albreda, "and stand close."

Ilarian rushed towards them, dozens of Elven warriors following along in his wake. "Kill them," he screamed. "Kill them all!"

Albreda started casting a spell, and the air began to buzz while dirt swirled around them. Gerald knew what was about to happen, for he'd travelled using the recall spell before. He also knew, however, this ritual took some time to cast. He stepped forward, placing himself between Ilarian and the others.

"You and me," he taunted. "Let's finish this."

"You are a fool," replied the Elf. "I have been a warrior for more than two millennia!"

"That may well be, but how many fights have YOU actually fought?"

The Elf slowed, then used his hands to indicate his warriors should halt. His helmet covered most of his head, but the lower portion of his face was exposed, revealing his grim smile.

"Killing you will be an absolute pleasure," the Elf announced.

Gerald stomped forward, using the tip of the spear to test Ilarian's defence. The Elf quickly parried the move before circling to his left. Gerald struck again, and the Elf took a step back, easily avoiding the hit, or so he thought. In response, the old Mercerian warrior brought the butt end of the spear up, using it as a staff to smack his foe on the chin.

The ancient Elven Necromancer staggered back, caught off guard by the blow, and then Gerald attacked again. However, this time he held the spear at either end, using its shaft to strike out at the Elf's neck, but Ilarian managed to twist his head, and the weapon struck the edge of his metal collar.

Elves are, on average, taller than men, while Humans are typically heavier of frame. Gerald now used his weight to force his opponent back before he kicked out, catching the Elf's thigh to knock Ilarian's leg out from under him. The Elf fell to the ground, and Gerald quickly reversed the spear, driving the tip into an arm. He met resistance as the metal rings tried to hold back the attack, but then he leaned in, and the mail parted.

A scream erupted from the Elf's mouth, and then the air whipped up a dust cloud, blinding them both. Moments later, he felt his ears pop, and he was in a woodland setting, Ilarian still at his feet.

"Where are we?" he asked.

"The Whitewood," replied Albreda. "I'm afraid it was the best I could do on short notice."

THIRTY-FIVE

Victory

SUMMER 965 MC

Lightning pushed forward, using his bulk to shove past an undead mount while Nature's Fury struck out, taking the rider in the chest, sending the thing back to the spirit world.

Beverly searched for another target, but there was a sudden lull in the fighting. Then she saw it, the Volgath, its eyes locked on her. A sense of panic threatened to overwhelm her. She gripped the magic weapon tightly, fighting to keep the feeling at bay.

Beverly recognized the face of King Leofric. In life, he'd been a mighty king, yet now he was but a twisted parody of himself, half his face missing, revealing the skull beneath.

It was almost as if she were frozen in place before she fought down the fear, tearing her gaze from her foe. Her eyes drifting down to her magic hammer. There, she saw the rose Aldwin had so lovingly engraved upon the handle, and a feeling of peace washed over her before she swivelled to Leofric once more. This time, she saw only a mockery of life, a blight on the land that must be sent back whence it came.

She calmed Lightning before urging him forward at a slow walk. The Volgath watched her from pitch-black eyes while it drew the sword of the Royal House of Weldwyn.

They met in a sudden clash of steel as Leofric reached out with blinding speed. Beverly used her shield to block before swinging out with Nature's Fury but missed the mark, striking the creature's saddle instead. If the Volgath's mount felt any pain, it didn't show any signs of it.

Leofric attacked again, his sword slashing out violently. The back of

Beverly's gauntlet deflected the blow, but she felt the iron strength behind it. Lightning twisted as the strange undead mount tried to tear out flesh.

Beverly shifted her focus, looking instead to take out what passed for Leofric's horse. She anticipated the next blow, twisting in the saddle to receive the full force of it on her shield. An ear-splitting noise echoed across the battlefield as the sword tore into the metal defence, nearly cleaving it in twain. The blade then scraped along her vambrace, leaving a dent as it bruised the skin beneath.

In answer, she lifted the hammer on high, bringing it crashing down onto the undead horse's head, the skull shattering, sending pus and rotting flesh flying. The Volgath leaped from the saddle, avoiding the crush of horseflesh as he struck out, slicing into Lightning's fetlock.

Beverly heard bone breaking just before Lightning went down with a terrible scream. She pulled herself from the stirrups as they fell, somehow managing to land on her feet. Moments later, she discarded her shield, now battered beyond use.

All around them, the battle came to a halt as the Volgath concentrated solely on this one battle.

~

Something's happening," said the baron. "The spirits—they stopped fighting."

"It's Beverly," declared the queen. "She's distracted Leofric. Order a general advance."

"Are you sure? We're still badly outnumbered."

"We must act quickly or lose the advantage."

The order was given, and then the entire line of Mercerian troops advanced, turning the spirits in front of them to mist. Even the archers joined in, drawing swords and axes to charge their foes.

Fitz watched in fascination. He had a clear view of Prince Alric and his men, mowing down the enemy in huge numbers. He surveyed the battle, trying to spot where Beverly fought, but the press of men was too much, their bodies obstructing his view while the mist settled in a thick blanket, the still air refusing to clear the obstruction.

He glimpsed Sir Preston, his armour distinctive amongst the footmen. Fitz turned to Sophie. "It appears your favourite knight has done his work so well, he has nothing left to fight." A look of relief settled on her features.

The baron shifted his attention to the queen. "By the love of Saxnor, I've never seen such a thing!"

Anna smiled. "They are not so mighty when their leader is kept busy, but it's not over yet. Beverly has still to defeat him in combat."

~

Tog swung his club, smashing it into the side of an Elf's head, failing to penetrate the helmet, but it didn't need to. The sound of a breaking neck was enough to tell the Troll his opponent was dead. He stepped forward, feeling his club strike targets left and right. Spears stabbed out at him, some even drawing blood, but even the luckiest hits did little other than surface damage.

He reached down with his left hand, grabbing a squirming Elf where he lay. Lifting him by the arm, he tossed him into a line of Elven warriors, sending them tumbling to the ground. Tog stepped into the Gap, sweeping his club two-handed to take out three more warriors with a single blow.

Another strike, and then a different foe appeared, one much shorter than he'd expected. He was about to continue his attack when he realized it was a Dwarf. Tog diverted the strike, letting the head of his weapon sink into the dirt.

"Gundar's beard, but you're massive," called out Kasri. She leaned to her left, looking past him to the remaining Elves. "I tell you what. You break the line, and I'll send in the Hearth Guard, agreed?"

Tog nodded, dropping his club and lifting another corpse, holding it over his head and then tossing it, sending it crashing into the enemy.

"Hold on," insisted the Dwarf. "You need to give us time to get there first!"

~

Hayley saw the dirt swirling in the air, instantly recognizing the effect. "That's it," she called out. "Albreda's got them."

She dug through her quiver, extracting a thin blue ribbon. This she tied to the neck of an arrow before aiming it skyward, searching for Shell-breaker.

"Come on, Revi," she said. "Turn this way."

The black coaster circled the battlefield, plainly watching the progress of the fight. She noted the pattern, waiting until it brought him into viewing range before letting loose the arrow. Upwards it flew, trailing the ribbon behind. She saw Shellbreaker wiggle its wings, and then she lowered her bow, content word had been passed on.

Hayley looked at Herdwin's Dwarves. They'd rolled up the western end of the Elven line, following in the wake of the three-horns. Having done their part to break up the enemy formation, the massive creatures now meandered around, picking away at tufts of grass.

Herdwin's heavier warriors were in close now, their axes doing frightful damage against the Elves. One group, in particular, looked like it would resist the attack, but then a massive being of rock and stone broke through them, flailing around with arms that crushed its enemies at will.

∼

Revi saw the signal and wiggled his arms. In response, Shellbreaker repeated the motion and then turned south, heading towards the queen's location.

Over the heads of the spirit army he flew, noting the lack of resistance. He caught sight of Beverly facing off against the Volgath. For a moment, he considered remaining in the area to witness the conflict, but then reason took hold, and he had his familiar continue on to the queen.

Shellbreaker alighted on the queen's saddle, letting out a squawk. Anna, at first caught off guard, soon calmed.

"Jamie," she said. "Does this mean Gerald is safe?"

Revi nodded, his familiar repeating the action.

∼

"Something wrong?" asked King Thalgrun.

The mage snapped back to his actual location. "No. Why do you ask?"

"You're grimacing. I thought your familiar might be injured."

"No, Majesty. It is merely a look of annoyance."

"Annoyance?"

"Yes. Queen Anna insists on calling Shellbreaker Jamie."

"Why in the Gods name would she do that?"

Revi groaned. "It's a long story."

∼

Beverly backed up, catching her breath. They'd traded blow for blow, none getting the advantage of the other, but now she could feel fatigue setting in, while her enemy showed no signs of tiring.

She heard chanting and spared a quick glance to see Aubrey casting a spell of healing on Lightning. The charger stood on three legs, favouring the wounded foot. The distraction cost her dearly as her foe charged forward, striking fast, glancing off the side of the helmet, but so hard was the blow that it rang in Beverly's ears.

She backed up, trying to make room to manoeuvre, but the Volgath pressed the attack, striking out yet again. Nature's Fury came up just in time, the sword scraping along the handle. She felt the air come alive as if two colossal forces fought for dominance. She swung back, the attack weak, but she'd taken the Volgath by surprise, scraping the head of her hammer across its chest.

Beverly next employed a two-handed attack to put more power behind the next blow. Although her foe blocked, the force of the hit drove the Volgath backwards, so she pressed her advantage. Again and again, she attacked, not letting up for fear Leofric's spirit would regain the initiative. Her arms ached now, her entire body wracked with fatigue, her energy almost completely drained from her near-constant exertions.

The air buzzed with energy as a black mist descended upon them, swirling around the melee, trying to pull the last ounce of strength from her. In desperation, she drove the warhammer down in a two-handed strike that shook the very ground. Vines erupted from the point of impact, rushing towards the Volgath to entwine its legs. Now trapped, it diverted its attention to releasing itself.

The black mist began to slowly dissipate, blown away by a refreshing wind. She backed up, gulping in the fresh air, desperate to rid herself of the foulness that permeated her lungs.

Her opponent thrashed around with its sword, severing the binds that prevented him from moving. It stood there a moment as if gauging her abilities before launching itself at her, the sword swinging out in a blur.

Nature's Fury came up, once more saving her as the blade scraped off its head, sending sparks flying before it jabbed out, catching the gauntlet of her left hand, puncturing the steel. She felt the tip sink into her flesh, and then a burning sensation shot up her arm.

Beverly attempted to back up, but the Volgath was tireless. All she could do now was to try to keep the blows from striking home. Slash after slash came at her until the sword was nothing but a blur. She tried to mount an attack, but so desperate was her defence, there was scant time to do much of anything save for attempting to parry.

Her heel caught on something, and she lost her balance, tumbling to the ground. The Volgath pressed the attack, striking out in quick succession. Once more, darkness intruded as she looked up into the face of death. The sky darkened, her throat constricted, and even the act of breathing became a chore.

Above her stood a nightmare, ready to dispatch her to the Underworld.

The Volgath raised the sword on high for the killing blow, and Beverly knew she lacked the strength to resist it. In that moment of final acceptance, Lightning appeared out of the darkness, crashing into the Volgath, sending it sprawling.

Beverly felt a surge of power and looked down to see Nature's Fury glowing with a white light. She got to her feet, clutching the weapon in both hands, feeling the power of nature surge through her, giving her much-needed strength.

Leofric's spirit tried to rise, but the knight turned to tower over her foe, lifting her hammer on high to bring it crashing down onto the Volgath's head.

A wail split the air as a dark shadow flew forth, rising high into the air. It exploded, sending out a shock wave that distorted the air as it spread across the battlefield. The spirit of the former Weldwyn king was all that remained. No longer possessed by dark magic, he slowly faded away, a look of peace on his face.

With the destruction of the Volgath, the Necromancers' hold on the spirits was strained beyond their limit. With no army left to protect them, they were cut down by the advancing Mercerians. Some tried fleeing north, but the Dwarves were waiting for them.

Beverly, her energy spent, could do little but watch the slaughter begin. Aubrey appeared at her side.

"Why don't they surrender?" she asked.

"They're worshippers of death," the knight replied. "We should expect no less."

Aubrey nodded northward. "It looks like the Elven army has had enough."

"It seems the Elves weren't so threatening after all."

She turned to her cousin, but the Life Mage had closed her eyes. "It's Kraloch," she explained. "He's trying to reach me."

Beverly returned her attention to what remained of the battle. Mercerians flooded past her, heading north to gather prisoners.

Sir Preston came into view. "Dame Beverly," he said. "You killed the Volgath!"

"I couldn't have done it without Lightning." As if in response, the mighty Mercerian Charger nuzzled up against her. She reached up to rub him between the ears.

Sir Preston surveyed the area, noting the rotting flesh that now sat, where moments before had stood strange, undead horses.

"What do you make of those?" he asked, wrinkling his nose.

"I'm not sure," she replied, "but one thing is clear, those were no ordinary beasts."

Aubrey snapped out of the spell, a smile on her lips. "Kraloch reports that he, Zhura, and Gerald are safe in the Whitewood."

"Why would they go there?" asked Sir Preston.

"Likely, Albreda was in a hurry. Recalling is only possible when the caster knows the destination, and the Whitewood is her home. What better place to go?"

"But that's more than a hundred miles away, isn't it?"

"Closer to two, I should think," offered Beverly. "But I'm sure they'll go to Wickfield once they have a chance to rest."

"And then what? We can hardly stay out here in the middle of nowhere."

"That's not so hard to guess. We'll send an army back to Galburn's Ridge. The earls who sided with us will be eager to put an end to this war, and there's still the matter of who will become King of Norland."

"What of Bronwyn?" ask Sir Preston.

"We've seen nothing of her since the defeat at the Minglewood, nor Heward, for that matter. I'm afraid we must face the very real possibility that they're both dead."

"I'm sorry to hear that. Sir Heward was an honourable man."

"We don't know he's dead," said Aubrey, "and now that the enemy has been dealt with, we can spare the resources to seek him out."

"And Bronwyn?"

"I couldn't care less about her," replied the mage. "She betrayed us at a critical time. That's not easily forgotten. Still, I suppose it would be nice to locate her if only to see her face a trial for her treachery."

"Well," said Beverly, "in that case, we'd best put Revi to work; if anyone can find them, it's Shellbreaker. Between him and our light horsemen, it shouldn't be too hard to locate the two of them."

"It is a glorious victory, Your Majesty," said the baron.

"So it is," the queen replied. "Hopefully, we can put this war behind us and seek common ground with the Norlanders." Her eyes drifted westward to where Alric's horsemen wandered around the field.

"It's a new day," Anna continued, "and it promises a bright future. The land shall be at peace once more. Now we can concentrate on strengthening our bonds with both Weldwyn and Norland."

"Speaking of Weldwyn, Majesty, we need to send them aid. Losing

Leofric's army will be a huge problem for them. It's only a matter of time before the Clans try to take advantage of the situation."

"We shall send an expedition to their aid as soon as we can, but first, we must see to our wounded and dead."

"And the prisoners?" asked Fitz.

The queen gazed north, to where the surviving Elves were being rounded up. "That's an excellent question, one I hadn't considered. What would you recommend?"

"We should march them back to Merceria. The real question is what we do with them once we arrive. We could send them to the mines?"

"No. That would only serve to make them slaves. We need to win them over to our way of thinking. Only then will true peace be achieved."

"So we just keep them locked up?"

"There's little choice at this point," she said. "How many do you figure we have?"

"Somewhere between two and three hundred, I would expect. Why?"

"Do you think some would take service in the army of Merceria? It wouldn't be the first time we hired on outsiders."

"It's worth a try," said the baron, "but what about those who refuse?"

"I'll send word to Lord Arandil; he might be willing to take the rest into his lands. In the meantime, I believe we'd best keep them under close watch. There's also the matter of where they came from."

"I'm not sure I follow, Majesty?"

"There's another Elven realm out there somewhere that we have yet to identify. Where else would all these people come from?"

"True, but don't they fall under the rule of Queen Kythelia?"

"Do they?" Anna asked. "I might remind you when we knew her as Penelope, she'd spent years in Wincaster. Does that sound like a ruler of an Elven land to you?"

"Yet they called her Queen Kythelia," Fitz reminded her.

"There could be a reason for that," suggested Sophie.

"Go on," the queen urged her maid.

"We know she was a queen long ago. The Orcs of Ravensguard told us as much, but what if the person we knew as Penelope is not the same Kythelia who destroyed their city?"

"I suppose that's possible," noted the baron. "After all, I'm not the only Fitzwilliam to bear the name Richard nor was King Andred the first king to be named so."

"There's another option," said Anna. "What if she was the queen, long ago, but then was forced to relinquish it for some reason? We're assuming these Elves are from the same kingdom as she is, but in truth, we know so little of the woodland race outside of the Darkwood. There could be dozens of Elven kingdoms spread all over the place, hidden away in the deep woods of the world."

"The prisoners might be more forthcoming in that regard," noted Fitz. "Unfortunately, without Kythelia in our hands, we have no way of knowing for sure."

"We'll get her eventually," noted the queen, "we have no choice. Her influence is what started this conflict, but Merceria and its allies are the ones responsible for ending this war of the crown."

Epilogue

SUMMER 965 MC

E dwina looked up from her books, distracted as a distant sound echoed in the courtyard. She rose, going to the window to peer outside. It was early morning on a late summer's day, the sun bright with a light breeze, and yet a distant rumble drifted to her ears.

"How is that thunder?" she muttered, more to herself than anyone else.

Tyrell Caracticus, her tutor this day, moved to stand beside her. "That's not thunder," he said, "but the heavy tread of feet. I fear an army approaches the capital."

"My brother will defeat them, surely?"

"We shall soon see," the mage replied. "Look, see how even now he prepares to fight."

Prince Alstan appeared in the courtyard, girded for battle, his armour polished, his blue surcoat bright in the morning sun. Around him rode a dozen men, each bearing the Royal Coat of Arms upon their shields.

"I hope he's in no danger," said Edwina as she watched her brother ride off, the horseshoes clattering on the cobblestones.

"I believe it best we get back to your studies, Princess, don't you?"

"Of course." Edwina returned to her seat. "Now, where were we?"

"We were talking of the magical alphabet, Your Highness."

They returned to their lessons, the day wearing on while the sun climbed ever higher. Luncheon came and went, barely interrupting their studies.

By late afternoon, the princess's attention started to lag. Even the mage found his mind wandering, seeking some respite from the endless repetition.

The clatter of horseshoes once more drew his attention to the court-yard. Below, he saw a group of horsemen arrive, Prince Alstan riding behind another, and it soon became apparent why.

"Oh no!" said Edwina. "He's injured!"

The men dismounted, lifting their prince from the saddle before carrying him inside.

"I must go see him," she said.

"I don't think that's wise," said the mage. "And in any case, there's little you could do to help. They will have sent for the Life Mage by now."

"Our Life Mage is dead, isn't she?"

"Lady Roxanne is, but her apprentice, Ekthyn Ramark, is more than capable of taking her place."

A sound to the west caught the mage's attention, and he fell silent, straining to listen, going so far as to lean out the window. There it was again, the distinctive sound of a mob.

"Malin's tears," he said. "Somehow, the Clans got into the city. We must leave this place, Highness. It's no longer safe here."

"Don't be silly," said Edwina. "We're in the Palace. What safer place could there possibly be?"

Tyrell was torn: on the one hand, he was sworn to serve the ruler of Weldwyn, and right now, that was Prince Alstan. On the other hand, he had a sacred duty to look after his student. He now found himself with a tough choice.

"Come," he said, finally making a decision. "We shall see if there's anything we can do for your brother." He led her through the halls of the Palace to see warriors rushing to man the doors. Was the enemy so close?

The mage slowed to a stop before turning into one of the rooms that faced the streets of Summersgate to the south. He'd intended to continue on, but the lure of the window was too much to resist. Advancing cautiously, he drew back the curtains only to view armed men threatening the very gates of the Palace.

He would have continued on, even then, but the crowd all looked skyward as a huge shape flew overhead, casting a long shadow over the gathering. Many of the warriors recoiled in terror before Tyrell pressed his face to the glass, desperate to see what had flown over them, but all was in vain. Whatever it was, had circled around to the back of the Palace.

The mage felt a sudden chill—he knew something ominous was coming. He looked at the princess, but all she could do was stare down at the enemy warriors.

"Come here," he snapped. "We must leave this place at once."

"We can't," she replied. "Alstan is injured, and even if he wasn't, where would we go?"

"To the Dome—it's the only safe place. Now stand close and don't move. I shall need all the concentration I can muster." He closed his eyes as he started the chant that would invoke his magic. Tyrell had been a mage for decades, spells coming to him easily, yet the spell of recall was a difficult task to complete. As a ritual, it was already a time-consuming process, but now, with the threat of destruction at hand, it was almost impossible.

The air around them started to mist, and then water vapour rose from the floor in a cylinder, blocking their view of the room before the lighting changed. Now, he and Edwina both stood in the magic circle beneath the Dome.

He grabbed the princess by the hand, rushing from the room, seeking a window. He threw open the shutters only to see his greatest fear realized— circling over the Palace was the largest creature ever to grace the land. It flew above the courtyard, then its long neck snaked back, the jaws opened, and liquid flame shot forth, disappearing behind the halls of the Palace. Moments later, flames shot up, illuminating the beast like a creature from the Underworld. A dragon had come to Summersgate!

The great wyrm circled once more, then flapped its wings and set itself down on the Palace rooftop, crushing stone and collapsing walls. An immense cloud of dust rose into the sky as the dragon lifted its head. It opened its mouth to let out a roar that shook the very walls of the Dome.

The mage's eyes went wild. He watched in horror as the remains of the Palace collapsed beneath the weight of the monstrosity, burying all those within.

<<<<>>>>

READ TRIUMPH OF THE CROWN

If you liked *War of the Crown*, then *Ashes*, the first book in the Internationally Best Selling *Frozen Flame* series awaits your undivided attention.
START READING ASHES TODAY

Cast of Characters, Places & Things

- **Hampton** - Heavy cavalryman under Sir Preston's command, sergeant
- **Harold** (Deceased) - Knight of Stilldale
- **Harold Wainwright** - Captain of the Wincaster bowmen 'The Greens'
- **Hayley Chambers** - Baroness of Queenston, High Ranger
- **Hector** - Knight of the Sword from Kingsford, Assigned as guard to Princess Bronwyn
- **Henry** (Deceased) - First son of Andred IV, previous King of Merceria
- **Heward** 'The Axe' - Knight of the Hound, Northern Commander
- **Hill** - Gerald's aide
- **Hugh Gardner** - Sergeant, Wincaster Light Horse
- **Ice** (Deceased) - Wolf friend to Albreda, mate of Snow
- **Jaran** - Leader of the Kurathian archers, Captain
- **Kiren-Jool** - Kurathian Enchanter
- **Lanaka** - Kurathian Commander of Light Horse
- **Lightning** - Beverly's Mercerian Charger
- **Lily** - Saurian, friend of Princess Anna
- **Linette** - Servant at Wincaster Palace
- **Lucas** - Baron Fitzwilliam's head servant in Wincaster
- **Mathers** - Ranger
- **Nikki** (Nicole Arandale) - Married to Arnim Caster
- **Preston** - Knight of the Hound, likes Sophie, maid to Queen Anna
- **Ragar** - Kurathian cavalryman under the command of Captain Caluman
- **Revi Bloom** - Royal Life Mage, Enchanter
- **Richard Fitzwilliam** 'Fitz' - Baron of Bodden, father of Beverly, mentor of Gerald
- **Ruzak** - Kurathian cavalry commander
- **Samantha** 'Sam' - Former archer of Bodden, Queen's Ranger
- **Shellbreaker** (Jamie) - Revi Bloom's avian familiar
- **Snarl** - Albreda's present wolf friend
- **Snow** (Deceased) - Wolf friend to Albreda, mate of Ice
- **Sommersby** - Ranger
- **Sophie** - Queen Anna's maid
- **Telethial** - Daughter of Lord Arandil, Elf
- **Tempus** - Kurathian Mastiff, the queen's pet
- **Tog** - Leader of the Trolls
- **Turnbull** - Mercerian cavalryman, member of the Guard Cavalry

- **Wilkins** - Member of the Wincaster Light Horse

THE ORCS:

- **Orcs of the Black Arrow** - Located in Artisan Hills
- **Orcs of the Black Raven** - Located in Ravensguard
- **Orcs of the Wolf Clan** 'Netherwood Tribe' - Located in the Netherwood
- **Andurak** - Shaman, Netherwood Tribe, also known as the Wolf Clan
- **Arshug** (Deceased) - Bowyer, Black Arrow Clan
- **Bagrat** - Hunter, Black Arrow Clan
- **Ghodrug** - Chieftain, Black Raven Tribe
- **Gorath** - Aide to the High Ranger, Black Arrow Clan
- **Gozar** (Deceased) - Ancient Orc ruler of Gar-Rugal
- **Kharzug** - Master of Earth, Black Raven Tribe
- **Kraloch** - Shaman, Black Arrow Clan
- **Kurghal** - Shamaness, Black Arrow Clan, older sister of Urgon
- **Mazog** - Chieftain, Netherwood Tribe, also known as the Wolf Clan
- **Morgash** - Cavalry commander, Black Arrow Clan
- **Ragash** - Master of Wolves in Urgon's absence, Black Arrow Clan
- **Shadra** - Hunter, Black Raven Tribe
- **Shular** (Deceased) - Shamaness who trained Kraloch, Mother of Urgon and Kurghal
- **Tarluk** - Hunter, Black Arrow Clan
- **Urgon** - Chieftain Black Arrow Clan
- **Urzath** - Ranger, Black Arrow Clan
- **Zhura** - Ghostwalker, Black Arrow Clan

THE DWARVES:

- **Agramath** - Earth Mage of Ironcliff, Master of Rock and Stone
- **Bremel** (Deceased) - Great uncle of Herdwin, died in the mines of Stonecastle
- **Brogar Hammerhand** - Warrior of Mirstone, guard to Princess Althea
- **Golmar Hengesplitter** - Engineer from Stonecastle
- **Grimdal** (Deceased) - Previous king of Ironcliff
- **Haldrim** - Captain of a company of arbalesters, from Mirstone

- **Herdwin Steelarm** - Smith, spent years in Wincaster, friend of Queen Anna
- **Kasri Ironheart** - Daughter of the king of Ironcliff
- **King Khazad** - Lord of the Stone, King of the Dwarven realm of Stonecastle
- **Thalgrun Stormhammer** - King of Ironcliff

OF WELDWYN:

- **Aegryth Malthunen** - Earth Mage
- **Alric** - Prince of Weldwyn, husband of Queen Anna of Merceria
- **Alstan** - Crown Prince, older brother of Alric
- **Althea** - Eldest daughter of King Leofric and Queen Igraine
- **Edwin Eldridge** (Deceased) - Earl of Farnham
- **Edwina** - Youngest daughter of King Leofric and Queen Igraine
- **Ekthyn Ramark** - Mage apprentice of the Dome
- **Godfrey Hammond** - Noble
- **Gretchen Harwell** - Enchanter
- **Igraine** - Queen of Weldwyn, widow of Leofric
- **Jack Marlowe** - Cavalier, friend and protector of Prince Alric
- **James Goodwin** - Noble of Weldwyn
- **Jane Goodwin** - Mother of James Goodwin
- **Leofric** (Deceased) - Past King of Weldwyn
- **Lindsey Martindale** - Viscountess Talburn
- **Osbourne Megantis** - Fire Mage
- **Parvan** - Baron of Tivilton, an Elf
- **Roxanne Fortuna** - Life Mage
- **Sherwyn Fletcher** - Lord of Walverton
- **Tulfar Axehand** - Baron of Mirstone, a Dwarf
- **Tyrell Caracticus** - Water Mage, Grand Mage

OF THE TWELVE CLANS:

- **Brida** - Daughter of High King Dathen
- **Calindre** - Clan Chief of Windbourne
- **Camrath** - Scholar of Glanfraydon
- **Dathen** - High King of the Twelve Clans, prisoner of Weldwyn, Clan Chief of Dungannon
- **Erlach** - Clan Chief of Glanfraydon
- **Lochlan** - Younger brother of Brida, son of King Dathen
- **Rurik** - Clan Chieftain of Halsworth

- **Warnoch** - Clan Chief of Drakewell

OF NORLAND:

- **Calder** - Earl of Greendale
- **Creighton** - Earl of Riverhurst
- **Halfan** (Deceased) - Past King of Norland, Grandfather of Bronwyn
- **Harriet** (Deceased) - Girlfriend of Marik in his youth
- **Hollis** - Earl of Beaconsgate
- **Marik** - Champion of Lord Hollis, Earl of Beaconsgate
- **Marley** - Earl of Walthorne
- **Princess Bronwyn** - Granddaughter of King Halfan, Leader of the Norland rebel army
- **Rupert** - Lord from Chilmsford, member of the Norland delegation
- **Rutherford** - Earl of Hammersfield
- **Thurlowe** - Earl of Ravensguard
- **Waverly** - Earl of Marston

THE ELVES (OF ESTLANETH)

- **Ilarian** - Masquerading as a human sorcerer named Jendrick, Necromancer
- **Kalaxial** - Masquerading as Lord Hollis
- **Kythelia** (Dark Queen) - Masquerading as Lady Penelope, responsible for the sacking of Gar-Rugal
- **Lysandil** - Emissary to the court of the Twelve Clans
- **Nerenya** - Necromancer
- **Sildan** - In the service of Kythelia

THE OTHERS:

- **Aeldred** - First King of Therengia
- **Malin** - God of Wisdom, revered by the people of Weldwyn
- **Margaret** - Older sister of Queen Anna, Necromancer
- **Prince Tarak** - Kurathian Prince of Kouras
- **Princess Olani** - Wife of Prince Tarak
- **Saxnor** - God of Strength, revered by the Mercerians

PLACES

MERCERIA: KINGDOM BETWEEN NORLAND AND WELDWYN

- **Artisan Hills** - Hills east of Eastwood
- **Bodden** - Barony in northern Merceria
- **Darkwood** - Forest east of Wincaster, home to Lord Arandil
- **Eastwood** - Earldom in the east of Merceria
- **Erssa-Saka'am** - City in the great swamp, home to the Saurians
- **Great Swamp** - The southern edge of Merceria
- **Haverston** - Viscountcy in Middle of Merceria
- **Library of Kendros** - Greatest repository of knowledge in the kingdom
- **Ord-Dugath** - Home village of Urgon, Kraloch, and Zhura
- **Redridge** - Town, known for iron mine
- **Rugar Plains** - Orc name for the area south of Eastwood
- **Shrewesdale** - City in the south
- **Trollden** - Town of trolls in the Great Swamp
- **Whitewood** - Forest north of Bodden
- **Wickfield** - Town on Northern Border

NORLAND: KINGDOM NORTH OF MERCERIA

- **Anvil** - Town
- **Brookesholde** - Village, across the border from Wickfield
- **Chandley** - Town
- **Chilmsford** - Town, where Bronwyn was raised
- **Easterly** - Town
- **Edgeholde** - Village, across the border from Mattingly
- **Galburn's Ridge** - Capital of Norland
- **Hakenell** - Town
- **Hammersfield** - Earldom
- **Holdcross** - Town near the Gap
- **Netherwood** (The Great wood) - **Forest**
- **Oaksvale** - Town
- **Ravensguard** - Earldom
- **Stratwick** - Town
- **The Deepwood** - Forest between Oaksvale and Hammersfield
- **The Gap** - Place between two mountains east of Holdcross
- **The Minglewood** - Forest south of Holdcross
- **Windstorm Depths** - Lake north of Galburn's Ridge

THE TWELVE CLANS: KINGDOM WEST OF WELDWYN

- **Banburn** - Town
- **Drakewell** - Town
- **Dungannon** - Town, home to Dathen, Brida and Lochlan
- **Galchrest** - Town
- **Glanfraydon** - Town
- **Halsworth** - Town
- **Hillsfar** - Town
- **Klinridge** - Town
- **Lanton** - Town
- **Meadmont** - Town
- **Strathlade** - Town
- **Windbourne** - Port Town

WELDWYN 'WESTLAND' - KINGDOM TO THE EAST OF MERCERIA

- **Abermore** - Town
- **Draenor Wood** - Large woods
- **Grand Edifice of the Arcane Wizards Council** 'The Dome' - Home to the mages of Weldwyn
- **Hollow Woods** - Wood west of Abermore
- **Loran River** - River on the western border
- **Loranguard** - City on western border
- **Mirstone** - Town near Obsidian Hills, baron is a Dwarf
- **Obsidian Hills** - Mines near Mirstone, full of iron
- **Riversend** - Large port city
- **Sea of Storms** - Sea to the south of Weldwyn
- **Southport** - Large port city
- **Summersgate**- Capital of Weldwyn
- **The Crow** - Tavern in Summersgate
- **Tivilton** - Western city, baron is an Elf
- **Walverton** - Western town

OTHER LOCATIONS

- **Eiddenwerthe** - The name of the world
- **Estlaneth** (Kingdom of Moonlight) - The realm of Elves, ruled over by Queen Kythelia
- **Four Kingdoms** - The kingdoms of Merceria, Weldwyn, The Clans, and Norland
- **Gar-Rugal** - Ancient Orc city, the ruins of which lie beneath Ravensguard

- **Halvaria** - Large empire to the east
- **Ironcliff** - Dwarven stronghold, northeast of Norland
- **Kouras** - Kurathian principality, where Prince Tarak lives
- **Kurathia** - Group of Island principalities, known for their mercenaries
- **Nan-Dural** - Ancient Dwarven city, located somewhere near Ravensguard
- **Petty Kingdoms** - Collection of kingdoms on the Continent
- **Thalemia** (Extinct) - Ancient kingdom on the shores of the Shimmering Sea
- **Therengia** - Ancient kingdom, pre-cursor to the Petty Kingdoms
- **Wayward Wood** - Home of the Wood Elves, south of Ironcliff

OTHER THINGS

- **Battle of Redridge** (962MC) - Where the Mercerians fought the blights
- **Battle of Riversend** (961 MC) - Repulse of Kurathian seaborne invasion**Battle of the Oak** (961 MC) - Gerald's victory against the Clans in Weldwyn
- **Battle of the Three Kings** (961 MC) - Final defeat of King Dathen in Weldwyn
- **Battle of Uxley** (964 MC) - Defeat of the Norland invasion
- **Homunculus/homunculi** - Artificial creature created by Death Mages
- **Nargun's thumb** (Moistroot) - Plant that retains a lot of water
- **The Hearth Guard** - Elite Dwarven company
- **Three-Horns** - Large herbivore with tough skin, controlled by Saurians
- **Vard** - Dwarven term for a king or queen that roughly translates as 'ruler'
- **Volgath** - Creature of the spirit realm called to the physical realm to command an army of enslaved spirits
- **Wood Elves** - Cousins to High Elves, smaller stature

A Few Words from Paul

War of the Crown is, as the name suggests, primarily about the war between Merceria and Norland, yet this conflict does not exist in a vacuum. Like many wars in the real world, some people are willing to take advantage of the conflict to further their own aims and nowhere is this more evident than in the Twelve Clans.

I conceived this storyline some years ago, though, of course, the details changed as the story developed. The real trick in writing this was showing the growing threat in the Clanholdings while centring most of the tale on the conflict in the north.

At its heart, though, it's about the individuals who, through their perseverance and bravery, overcome tremendous odds to see through to victory.

The Mercerians finally defeated the enemy in the north. Now, with their numbers greatly reduced, they must turn their attention westward once more to rescue the lost kingdom of Weldwyn. This time, however, they must face an enemy armed with dragons!

Gerald, Anna, Beverly, and all the others will return to face their greatest challenge in Triumph of the Crown.

War of the Crown could not have been completed without the valuable assistance of my wife, Carol, who has acted as editor, promotional expert, and inspiration for all my books. Because of her encouragement and support, I feel able to bring these tales to the world.

In addition, I should like to thank Amanda Bennett, Christie Bennett, and Stephanie Sandrock for their support and enthusiasm, along with Brad Aitken, Stephen Brown and the late Jeffrey Parker for their interesting and slightly quirky character inspirations.

Valuable feedback was also provided by my BETA team, so I would like to give them a shout of recognition for their continued efforts. Thanks to: Charles Mohapel,Will Groberg, Joanna Smith, Susan Young, Anna Ostberg, Debbie Reeves, James McGinnis, Don Hinckley, Michael Rhew, Jim Burk, Rachel Deibler, Phyllis Hinkley, and Lisa Hanika.

Thanks also go to you, my readers, who have followed along as I tell the story of these Mercerian misfits. Your encouragement and feedback has been most rewarding, and I look forward to hearing more from you in the future.

About the Author

Paul J Bennett (b. 1961) emigrated from England to Canada in 1967. His father served in the British Royal Navy, and his mother worked for the BBC in London. As a young man, Paul followed in his father's footsteps, joining the Canadian Armed Forces in 1983. He is married to Carol Bennett and has three daughters who are all creative in their own right.

Paul's interest in writing started in his teen years when he discovered the roleplaying game, Dungeons & Dragons (D & D). What attracted him to this new hobby was the creativity it required; the need to create realms, worlds and adventures that pulled the gamers into his stories.

In his 30's, Paul started to dabble in designing his own roleplaying system, using the Peninsular War in Portugal as his backdrop. His regular gaming group were willing victims, er, participants in helping to playtest this new system. A few years later, he added additional settings to his game, including Science Fiction, Post-Apocalyptic, World War II, and the all-important Fantasy Realm where his stories take place.

The beginnings of his first book 'Servant to the Crown' originated over five years ago when he began a new fantasy campaign. For the world that the Kingdom of Merceria is in, he ran his adventures like a TV show, with seasons that each had twelve episodes, and an overarching plot. When the campaign ended, he knew all the characters, what they had to accomplish, what needed to happen to move the plot along, and it was this that inspired to sit down to write his first novel.

Paul now has four series based in Eiddenwerthe, his fantasy realm and is looking forward to sharing many more books with his readers over the coming years.

Printed in Great Britain
by Amazon

22862149R00199